THE MOMENT OF TRUTH

The moment the door closed, he placed his hands on his hips. "Come here."

Fear streaked through her for the first time. He was too calm, too controlled. "What is your pleasure?"

"I said, come here." His voice was quiet and his expression did not change.

She stepped closer. He would not, could not, hurt her. A shiver climbed up her spine at the intensity of his gaze. Danger and desire flashed in his eyes, and excitement and alarm raced through her.

He brushed her hair away from her cheek and cradled her face in his hands. "Convince me that you did not betray me," he whispered as his lips descended on hers. Slowly, softly, his tongue stroked her lips as though tasting them for the first time.

She tried to move her lips from his, needing to know if he believed in her, but his fingers held her chin, refusing to let her end the kiss, until all thought disappeared beneath the seductive mastery of his touch. . . .

BOOK YOUR PLACE ON OUR WEBSITE AND MAKE THE READING CONNECTION!

We've created a customized website just for our very special readers, where you can get the inside scoop on everything that's going on with Zebra, Pinnacle and Kensington books.

When you come online, you'll have the exciting opportunity to:

- View covers of upcoming books
- Read sample chapters
- Learn about our future publishing schedule (listed by publication month *and author*)
- Find out when your favorite authors will be visiting a city near you
- Search for and order backlist books from our online catalog
- Check out author bios and background information
- Send e-mail to your favorite authors
- Meet the Kensington staff online
- Join us in weekly chats with authors, readers and other guests
- Get writing guidelines
- AND MUCH MORE!

**Visit our website at
http://www.zebrabooks.com**

HEAVEN
SENT

Marian Edwards

Zebra Books
Kensington Publishing Corp.

http://www.zebrabooks.com

To Jason, my independent free spirit.
To my real-life hero, Ed, who always rescues the day.
To my mom, for everything.

ZEBRA BOOKS are published by

Kensington Publishing Corp.
850 Third Avenue
New York, NY 10022

First Printing: December, 1998
10 9 8 7 6 5 4 3 2 1

Printed in the United States of America

Prologue

Wales. March 20, 1067.

Bronwyn took the vial of poison and clutched the container tight in her fist. Her heart pounded as she met her younger brother's gaze. "Caradoc, do not worry. I will slip this into the warlord's drink."

He nodded, his wild blond mane a tangle of thin braids and loose flowing hair that rippled like molten gold as he bent to kiss her cheeks. When he pulled away, the firelight danced across his angular features, revealing a rare smile. "Come, Fiona, give us the necklace."

Their sister's bright blue eyes were wide with fear. "This charade will never work."

He crossed his arms and his gaze narrowed. "He has never seen you. The only way he has to identify you is this." He removed the topaz necklace, Fiona's betrothal gift, and passed it to Bronwyn. "Fiona, this Norman the king has betrothed you to is a barbarian who murders whole villages for the slightest infraction. You would not make it through the ceremony without swooning, much less put the poison in his drink."

Fiona gasped at her brother's harsh words and backed away,

shaking her head. Tears shimmered in her eyes as she looked at Bronwyn. "Do not do this, sister. I fear for you."

Caradoc snorted with disgust. "There is no danger. Here is the antidote." He handed another vial to Bronwyn. "In case you are forced to taste his drink. Our healer will pronounce the warlord's death as one of excess. No one will doubt that the groom overindulged during his wedding celebration. It has happened before."

Fiona flinched from the harsh words and Bronwyn put her arm around her sister's shoulders. "You must go to the convent. You will be safe there. We will send for you after the ceremony."

Though Fiona wrung her hands, she kissed her sister and left to join her escorting guard.

Caradoc shook his head. "She may be the eldest, but her timidness makes me wonder if our father was cuckolded."

He chuckled, then grasping Bronwyn's hands in his, his voice turned serious. "You are a true daughter of Wales."

"The warlord has arrived," the serf's cry echoed throughout the vast hall. Silence descended on the waiting crowd; their torchlit faces, shadowed, solemn, turned toward the portal.

The friar gave her an encouraging smile, but Bronwyn closed her eyes and begged God for courage.

When the doors crashed against the walls, her eyes snapped open. A dark stranger with a huge, hairy beast at his side stood in the doorway, only their silhouettes visible. Her heart skipped a beat at the imposing sight. Like an avenging deity his huge shadowed form filled the enclosure.

"Where is my bride?" His booming voice reverberated off the walls as he folded his arms across his chest.

Bronwyn swallowed her fear, wishing as she stepped to the center of the hall she had chosen her mother's ornate wedding gown, instead of the simple white tunic trimmed in soft gold thread. The fire roaring in the hearth clearly revealed her features to him, but more importantly illuminated his betrothal gift, the amber-colored gems and gold chain glowing brightly in the warm firelight.

His hard, calculating gaze swept over her with an excruciating thoroughness that mentally stripped the clothes from her body. "At least you are passable."

The remark stung, but she kept her head held high.

Christophe Montgomery marched into the hall with the beast, a shaggy wolf following in his tracks. Beneath the Norman warlord's shorn ebony locks, dark eyes piercingly surveyed the assembly. The only relief to his jet-black attire was an embroidered collar of bright gold that did little to relieve the dark image. He reminded her of the devil. His stride was brisk as he backhanded a young serving girl who bowed before him. "Out of my way, wench."

The poor maid tumbled backward, the animal snarled, keeping others away as the Norman continued toward her. His gaze locked with Bronwyn's and never wavered as he approached. His men, dressed in full battle armor, filed in behind him, fanning out from either side of the door to line the walls. Wearing masks of cold disdain, they watched the Welsh within the circle.

One guard separated from the others and approached. "I will search the castle and secure it, my lord." He bowed and took his leave.

Montgomery grasped Bronwyn's wrist and yanked her forward with such brutal force that he nearly dislocated her arm from its socket. Humiliation burned her cheeks and tears stung her eyes. She could see her people's outraged expressions at the Norman's arrogance, but 'twas clear no one would interfere. Though they disliked the Norman's manners, they feared him more. Even her brother remained tight-lipped.

She took a deep breath and took her place beside him, in front of the friar.

Montgomery stood as rigidly as a seasoned warrior ready for battle. When he turned his cold black gaze on her, a chill crept up her spine and she trembled.

Beneath his heartless stare, a smug smile slashed his harsh features.

Her pride refused to submit to this sadistic monster. Holding his gaze, she squared her shoulders and tilted her chin.

His eyes widened, then contempt filled his gaze.

"Do you Christophe Montgomery take Fiona Llangandfan as your wife?" the friar asked.

"I do," he snapped, producing a huge golden topaz ring from his tunic. The rich jewel shone with an extraordinary light as though a flame burned within. There could be little doubt that this lovely stone matched the betrothal set, but without any regard for the rare jewelry or his bride, he jammed the band onto her finger.

She lowered her gaze, refusing to acknowledge the pain he had caused.

When the cleric turned to her, Bronwyn repeated her vows with dignity and grace.

The moment the ceremony ended, Christophe pulled her into his arms and crushed her against his chest. His mouth descended, grinding her lips into her teeth in a brutal and possessive kiss that tasted of anger and her own blood. She could hear gasps of outrage as he crudely ran his hands up and down her curves. She was light-headed from the loss of air when he finally ended the kiss. Before she could catch her breath, he pulled her after him toward the steps leading up to the master bedchamber. Her brother stepped in his path.

"My lord, the festivities."

The wolf growled, baring his fangs. The warlord motioned for silence, and the animal immediately crouched down.

"The only festivities that interest me are those of the bedding," he snapped. "Pray her meager talents satisfy my desires." He pushed Caradoc out of the way and yanked Bronwyn with such force that she tripped and fell. He dragged her across the floor, through the rushes, and only at the stairs did she regain her feet. He hauled her along behind him as if she were a hound that refused to heel, treating her worse than his animal, who followed and nipped at her ankles.

The thought of killing him was becoming easier by the moment.

The din of the celebration from the hall below mocked her

despair. He flung her inside the master chamber and slammed the door shut behind the wolf, who scooted in to lie by the fire. She stumbled once, before catching her balance. The sound of the wooden crossbar dropping into place echoed in the still room, and her heart pounded at the thought of being imprisoned with Satan. She drew a deep breath and forced herself to meet his pitiless black eyes. His dark gaze touched every inch of her, from the tip of her toes to the top of her head. Fists clenched, she endured his crude inspection. *Remember your duty,* a silent voice sounded in her mind.

"Some refreshment, my lord?" she said softly, pointing to the table which was set with an abundance of breads and meat, and a flask of wine.

"Non." He pointed to her. "Remove your clothes."

Her heart skipped a beat. "But my lord, 'tis our way for the bride and groom to toast each other's good health. 'Twould be a bad omen not to observe this custom."

He raised an eyebrow. "A tradition?"

"Aye." Unable to hold his gaze, her eyelashes slid downward, leaving only a tiny slit open. " 'Tis apt to make the night pass more . . . pleasurably."

At that, he nodded sharply, and she went to the flagon. With her back to him she filled two cups with the dark red brew, then poured the poison into his chalice. Taking a deep breath, her cup in one hand, she turned and offered him the wine laced with poison.

He accepted his wine, but before he took a sip, a sudden light appeared in his eyes. He abruptly knocked her chalice from her hand, spilling the contents over her gown and staining it a bright, blood red. "We will share my cup."

Terror washed over her, but she forced a smile. She had to drink his wine. If she refused he would know something was amiss and kill her anyway.

He placed the cup to her lips. Though a lifetime of memories sailed through her mind on a current of fear, she sipped the drink slowly. He tipped the chalice higher, making her swallow half the brew before he withdrew the cup and gulped down the remainder.

She felt the effect of the potent brew as he picked her up and carried her to the bed.

She wanted to scream. She wanted to stop him, but could not. She heard her clothes tear and felt the sudden chill. She looked up at him as he stood by the bed. His expression frightened her. He was unaware of the vial exposed in the pocket of her tattered clothes, lying in a heap beside her. Her fingers closed over the tiny bottle, hiding the medicine in her fist.

"For a peasant you are an uncommonly lovely woman."

"Peasant?" she said haughtily. "I am descended from royal blood."

His bark of laughter filled the air. "Then, my royal wife, delight me." His hand caressed her breast and waist, and a shiver of revulsion raced through her.

"You have a body made for love, and a face that would drive a man wild. William has done me a favor," he said, standing to shed his garments before falling upon her.

His lips descended on hers, cruel and hard, and she again tasted her blood. His breath was hot and fouled by the bitter poison as he savaged her tender mouth. If she could not drink her medicine, they would both be dead by morning.

He took her brutally, as she had expected. When he entered her, a look of surprise crossed his features. "A virgin? Who would have thought there was one left in this pathetic, pagan country."

To be ravaged by an insensitive beast was cruel enough, but that it would be her last memory on earth was too much to bear. When he at last rolled off her, she groaned with relief. Perhaps, he would now sleep, and she could seek the cure. But, alas, the poison was making her so warm, her limbs felt weighted, and useless. She could not move.

He flung his arm over his eyes and groaned. "What did you put in the drink?"

She managed only to turn her head. "Poison, my husband."

He tried to sit up but only managed to rise halfway before falling back. "Then you have destroyed your people."

"Nay, the king will think your death an accident."

"Foolish bitch," he spat. "William knows the difference

between accident and murder. Every last man, woman, and child will be drawn and quartered in retaliation for my death.''

"Slaughtered?'' Dear God.

"Oui. William will wipe this village off the face of the earth as an example to other rebels.''

"Nay,'' she cried.

'' 'Tis too late for regret. 'Tis too late for anything.''

"Nay!'' Though it took all her strength, Bronwyn lifted her arm and tipped half the vial into his mouth, then she swallowed the remainder and collapsed.

Chapter One

Detroit, Michigan. March 20, 1998.

In the crowded terminal the airline official waved a clipboard in the air and motioned to Regan. "This way, Miss Carmichael. Your charter flight is at gate eight."

Regan Carmichael took a deep breath and shifted her weight, leaning heavily on her silver-handled cane. She boarded the plane, indifferent to the glances her pronounced limp garnered.

"We're so proud to be sponsoring the first live telethon from the air," he said, leading the way down the narrow aisle and nodding to the camera crew already aboard.

"Let's hope it will be a great success," she said, wondering how in God's name she'd put up with Drew Daniels for three hours.

"Why wouldn't it?" he asked, pointing to her seat. "You're the David and Goliath candidates. After last night's fiery debate, who wouldn't donate money to keep you two handcuffed together?"

"You're right," she agreed. This was going to be a long day. The flight would only contain ten people, but already she felt crowded. Automatically she stored her cane against the bulkhead before slipping into the seat closest to the window.

"Can I get you anything before I return to the terminal to wait for Mr. Daniels?"

"No, thank you," she said, knowing she was early. She needed the time, especially after last night's public confrontation, to compose herself before mister *self-made man* appeared.

Drew straightened his shoulders, then weaved his way through the mass of humanity. Packed bodies always reminded him of his childhood. Though he had clawed his way to the top, the stench from the projects had never left him. At fifty-five he was single, powerful, wealthy, and unencumbered. He had only one regret. But his drive and ambition would have probably made a disaster of any marriage. No, he had done the right thing. He stuffed his ticket back into his pocket and boarded the plane, trying hard to ignore the shivers crowds gave him. He had left everything behind, everything but this fear. Reinventing oneself had its advantages; too bad he couldn't reinvent his memories.

Regan heard Drew Daniels's overbearing voice and gripped the armrest. Her antique amber ring dug painfully into her finger before she relaxed.

"Well, this is going to be the closest thing to hell known to man." He leaned forward and extended his hand. "If this wasn't for charity—"

"Neither of us would be here," she finished for him, accepting his greeting.

His mouth creased into a smile. "Regan, come work for me." He slid into the seat beside her.

"I only work for those interested in saving the planet. Not raping it."

"As always you get to the heart of the matter. Still, I admire you, even if we hold different opinions."

"Really?" She raised an eyebrow. "I hope that sentiment still holds when I beat you."

He roared. "When it comes to politics, honey, you're way out of your league."

The charity official cleared his throat and held up the handcuffs. "I have the iron bracelets. Are you two ready?"

Drew smiled as the reporters crowded in. Several cameras flashed before the bright lights of the camcorders flooded the area, and Jason Adams, the well-known television host, moved forward. "Wait, turn the lights off, we need the kid in this."

Little Lisa Smith, escorted by her mother and the representative of the Make-A-Wish Foundation, weaved her way through the crowd and stood where she was directed. Regan smiled at the seven-year-old and reassuringly touched her hand before the glaring lights of cameras were turned back on.

Adams cupped his hand to his ear transmitter and nodded in response. "That's right. Every year the Make-A-Wish Foundation, in conjunction with our station, grants the wish of a sick child." He held his hand out to Lisa, who joined him. "If you've just tuned in, we're about to wing our way to Disney World to fulfill the wish of seven-year-old Lisa Smith. . . ." On and on, he droned.

". . . And to watch our own battling candidates band together to raise money for this worthy cause." Adams turned toward them, and with a devilish grin, snapped the handcuffs on with a theatrical flair that wasn't lost on the fish eye of the lens.

Drew flashed a sympathetic smile and held his hand up higher, making Regan stretch. "If you want to see politicians suffer, make your pledge now. The number to beat is on your screen."

Regan leaned closer to the camera, pulling his arm with hers. "Our handcuffs symbolize that there are children who are trapped in wheelchairs and braces, prisoners of their diseases. As you sit back in your recliner and watch the telethon, remember that your dollars fund the research that will be the key to unlocking the cure for their ailments. Please, give generously."

The cameras turned to Jason Adams, who introduced the station and Make-A-Wish representatives. After a brief presentation he made another plea. "Let's keep our two political opponents cuffed for the whole trip." He smiled. "Back to you, George." The lights died. "Great, people. Now, Lisa, I would like to get you and your mom on tape. Let's step over here."

After the crowd moved away and took their seats, the plane taxied down the runway to prepare for takeoff. The handcuffs were more confining than Regan thought they'd be, especially when they each tried to snap their seat belts. It was impossible to buckle her belt with her right hand cuffed to his left. Though she was a southpaw, she needed both hands to accomplish the task.

With a loud sigh he turned to her. "Look, for this to work we both have to cooperate."

"I doubt you know the meaning of the word."

"You have me all wrong," he said, allowing her to buckle her belt first. She had not expected the rush of heat to color her cheeks when his hand innocently brushed her lap as she fastened the safety clasp.

He refrained from comment as he then snapped his belt closed, forcing her hand in the same compromised position as his had been.

This was not going to be an easy trip.

Once airborne the schedule was set. Every forty-five minutes the TV crew would do a five-minute spot for the local telethon. The reporters periodically came through the cabin to snap pictures and ask questions, but for the most part, the Fourth Estate just enjoyed the ride, looking forward to a little vacation in sunny Florida before the trip back. After two hours in the air, the ride had grown bumpy. Regan glanced across the aisle at Lisa and smiled seeing the child sound asleep next to her mother.

When she turned she found Drew staring at her. "I may have to spend time with you, Drew, but let's lay our cards on the table. The charm that you project so perfectly for the camera doesn't fool me one bit. You neither like nor respect me."

"You're wrong. I happen to hold you in high regard. I just feel, and rightly so, that you're way out of your element. Your area of expertise is rehabilitation. How in God's name did that wily old pol, Macafferty, talk you into this race?''

''He wanted to stop you.''

''He must have been furious when you wouldn't trade on your handicap for sympathy.''

''How do you know I still won't?''

He chuckled. His sun-weathered face crinkled into a mass of attractive laugh lines. When he again met her gaze, his smile was genuine, not the artificial expression he normally flashed. ''That's not your style. It's one of the reasons I admire you. But it's also one of the reasons you'll lose.''

''The polls show that I'm in the lead.''

''Your platform's unrealistic. I know it, and the voters know it. You're an idealistic dreamer. I deal in facts and figures. I can get the job done.''

''At what expense, Drew? Cutting the programs needed to save the city's poor?''

''I'll save the city.''

Regan shook her head. She had no doubt that he would, but in the process he would sacrifice the people.

''What good is your city without its occupants?''

''Your bleeding heart won't put meat on their tables. A thriving economy will.''

''The trickle-down method doesn't work, and you know it.''

''We'll see, won't we.''

She tried to shift in her seat and her hand slipped pulling his wrist. ''Sorry,'' she snapped, growing irritable at the confinement with him. The problem was, she understood his reasoning. If only he would just temper his attitude with a bit of humanity then it would meet both their objectives.

Drew's self-confidence bothered her, always had. She decided to rest rather than engage in any more fights. Exhausted, she closed her eyes and slipped into a light sleep. But no sooner had she started to doze then it seemed she was shaken awake. During her sleep she had unknowingly leaned against Drew. Embarrassed to find her head pillowed by his shoulder, she immediately sat up. Her stomach felt queasy and she became aware of the tumultuous motion. They were in a savage storm surrounded by dark clouds, arcs of blue-white light, and crashing thunder. The plane rocked about like a bobbing cork on the high seas.

She glanced out the window and saw only her frightened expression as the turbulence increased. A sudden air pocket sucked the plane violently downward, leaving the curious sensation that her stomach was somewhere above her. Buffeted about in the gale, a lightning bolt hit one engine. The rain extinguished the fire, but the plane continued to lose altitude.

The captain's voice was grave as he advised the passengers that as a precaution, emergency procedures were being implemented for landing.

The lights flickered as, the sound of frightened whispers and soft prayers filled the air.

Suddenly, there was another deafening crack of thunder. An explosion of blinding light filled the cabin, followed by total darkness.

The cold, black fear of night surrounded them, their cries and prayers sounded more frightening in the dark. The glow of the lightning outside flashed eerily through the windows, momentarily lighting the expression of fear on each and every face. The plane dove, the force pushing them back in their seats.

Dear God, they were going to crash! Regan couldn't see anyone, but she could feel Drew next to her.

His hand forced her head down.

When she leaned forward in her seat, shivering with fear, his hand held and squeezed hers. People cried out as the craft shuddered in the severe dive. Her hand trembled beneath his but somehow she managed not to cry as the plane descended.

Then miraculously the plane seemed to level off, and she breathed a sigh of relief. But a moment later they touched down, the wheels slamming into the runway. The tires exploded upon impact and sent the plane skidding across the ground on its belly. The ear-piercing screech of metal against concrete resounded, and for an instant the screams of passengers and tearing metal merged, creating a thunderous din of disaster. Then a quick wrenching jerk buckled the large fuselage in half as the craft stopped. At once a blinding black smoke filled the damaged cabin, burning the throat and eyes. Though no heat or light penetrated the black pitch, somewhere behind them a blaze had started. The muted sound of crackling fire and hissing flames could be heard.

"Help me," a child screamed. It was Lisa.

Regan quickly undid her seat belt and bolted toward the child's voice, stumbling over Drew, only to come up short, held fast by the damn handcuffs.

"Wait, I'm coming," Drew said.

"Hurry, she's over here." Regan quickly found her and unfastened her seat belt.

"Mama?" the child whispered, sobs shaking her tiny shoulders.

Regan called out to Drew. "Can you locate her?"

Even as she asked she knew it was a foolish request. Bound to her, how could he look? But the child reached across the seat. "Come on, Mama."

Drew reached over and shook the woman, who was suffering from shock. The moment Drew touched her she seemed to come to life.

Gripping her daughter, both mother and child jumped into the aisle and stumbled forward. Regan glanced back and her heart stopped. Through the billowing black smoke an orange fireball glowed. The fire was racing from the back to the front of the cabin. There were only seconds left. They all rushed toward a window exit. The mother climbed out first, joining the passengers who had already managed to get out. Regan and Drew lifted the child up, passing her out onto the wing and into her mother's waiting arms. Just as Regan started to climb out she felt a terrible blow, followed by burning pain. A piece of metal dropped onto her weak leg and she couldn't budge.

"What is it?" Drew asked when she stiffened and stopped.

"I'm trapped," she gasped.

The man on the wing peered in through the window. "Get out," he screamed.

"We can't," Drew yelled. "She's trapped."

The passenger frantically yelled to the men below, then left. After frenzied seconds he returned with the key to the handcuffs and tossed it inside. "Get free." He looked into the cabin, and his face paled.

"Leave me," Regan screamed to Drew, seeing the wave of fire closing in on them.

"Help me," Drew called out to the man on the wing as he tugged and pulled on the metal. But the fearful passenger was already gone.

Red lights flashed in the distance as emergency sirens wailed the rescuers' approach.

Drew unlocked his handcuffs and stared at the window exit for a second, contemplating his escape, then turned back to her. "There's still time, Regan."

Tears smarted her eyes. "No, there isn't."

The fire trucks screeched to a halt, and a large stream of water washed over the hull of the plane.

Though they still fought to be free, she was firmly trapped. The fire almost on them, the flames fairly scorching their skin. She grabbed his arm and squeezed. "You must leave now. Save yourself."

He shook his head. Although the safety of the water-drenched exit was only an arm's length away, he wrapped her trembling body in his embrace. "Don't be afraid, I won't leave you."

In the space of a heartbeat a flood of memories washed over him, and without stirring an ounce of sorrow, his last reflection was a silent goodbye. The flames engulfed them and still he held her tight. Her screams mingled with his, the pain unbearable, and then—

Sound ceased. Pain ceased. Only peace remained. Though their bodies were gone, their spirits had touched and linked.

Together they floated high above the wreckage. Cool clouds engulfed and cocooned them in a soft haze as they rose upward on a warm current of welcoming light.

* * *

*"It's a mistake. You're not suppose*d *to be here."* A voice spoke through the white cloud. *"A woman and her child are expected."*

Drew turned full circle but could see nothing through the fog but the bright light. The ray was too powerful to look at, and he turned away, letting the soft white clouds drift over him. Cool and misty, the fog created a peace Drew had never known. Suddenly he became aware of Regan's spirit joined to him. He knew they were dead, but he sensed her confusion, too.

So this was heaven.

The authoritative voice sounded again in his mind. *"No, it's not heaven."*

Though he hadn't spoken, his thoughts were heard.

"Through your selfless act you changed fate. You're going back to live out your life."

"Why?"

"Because your time has not yet arrived."

"But we are dead."

"Your body is gone, but your spirit lives. I will find a way to return you to earth. It may not be what you are used to, but it will be a full life."

Suddenly Drew was filled with an overwhelming sadness and knew it was Regan's feelings he sensed. She mourned her life.

Drew could understand her grief. She was too young to have her life cut short.

"She is all right. But I'm afraid her adjustment will take longer."

Who was this guy?

A deep chuckle sounded. *"Ever hear of angels? When I get my job right, it will be time for my reward."*

"What about my reward? I worked hard," Drew protested.

"Yes. But you worked only for money. You are getting another chance at life. Consider that your reward."

Drew again felt Regan's sorrow. He could hear her thoughts in his mind. "I'm not dead! This is a dream," she sobbed.

"Please, don't be frightened, Regan. Unfortunately, you must leave your life behind. I know you miss your family, and the children you worked with at the hospital. But your loved ones will be happy and your patients will be taken care of. You did a fine and exceptional job. You should be proud. Do not fear. Think of this as the next step to heaven. Ah! We have new bodies for you. It is time to start anew."

Chapter Two

It looked, Drew thought, like a scene from a Viking movie. A fire burned low in the hearth and candles in the wall holders sputtered and swayed in the draft. The walls and floor were dark. It was hard to tell where one stopped and the other began, for both were made of rough-hewn wood planks. A man and woman lay asleep beneath fur covers. There was a large wolf resting on an animal skin spread before the huge stone fireplace.

The wolf began to whine, as though sensing his presence.

He moved closer to the sleeping couple. In the warm firelight their skin glowed a pale peach against the dark animal pelts. The woman nearly took his breath away. Her golden hair framed her angelic features and fanned out about her in a long wave of spun gold that surrounded her like a cloud. The man slept with his arm thrown over his eyes, his body bulging with rippling muscles. He was a strong, young bull, and Drew envied his virility.

Suddenly he was drawn closer to the bed. Though he fought against the force dragging him forward, he could not resist. He felt himself hovering over the man's form, and then abruptly he was pulled into the body.

Light exploded in a brilliant blinding flash, and like being struck by a bolt of pure energy, he absorbed a life force—an essence. So this was a quickening, he thought. The spasm lasted only a heartbeat as Drew felt a soul pass through him, leaving the body he had entered. In the blink of an eye Drew knew everything about the man, a warlord sent by King William to quell a rebellion in Wales, married last night to a woman who had just poisoned him. Drew was engulfed by the warlord's last thoughts; white-hot rage at such a betrayal, an overwhelming need to punish.

As he inhaled his first deep lungful of air, the sense of smell returned. Though the room was dark, he recognized the season. The crisp clear scent of spring permeated the air as did the aroma of the woman and the lingering fragrance of their lovemaking.

He inhaled again and felt his body awaken. He was a warlord! The vitality of this body! The strength! He wanted to throw back his head and roar. By God, he did. The animal's ears pricked and he trotted to the bed.

It was incredible! Due to some clerical error in the cosmos, he was young again. Unbelievable! Dawn was just coloring the sky a silvery pink as he turned to gaze at the beautiful blonde lying next to him. His wife. He shook his head. Beautiful but deadly.

The wolf sniffed his hand cautiously, baring teeth that could rip out his throat. His yellow eyes shone warily. Fang—for Drew knew that was his name—was confused. He allowed the pet to nuzzle his hand, then slipped his fingers slowly into the animal's thick silver fur to scratch behind its ear. The wolf licked his hand. After several affectionate pats, he ordered Fang to lie down, and though the wolf sensed a change, he obeyed.

Drew closed his eyes and forced himself to think of his situation. He had left nothing behind that he would miss. He had been given a second chance and he would make the most of it. From now on, he vowed, he *was* Christophe Montgomery, the best damn warrior in King William's army. This was the most exciting moment of his life, and the most dangerous.

The woman turned her head, sliding deeper into the pillow. She stretched, smothering a yawn, then slowly her eyelashes fanned open. She blinked once, her mouth agape, staring at him as though she couldn't believe her eyes. "Dear God! Am I losing my mind? Am I dreaming?"

" 'Tis no dream, 'tis a nightmare," he said, surprised by the accent and dialect that flowed from his lips. He reached out and drew her closer, his breath mingling with hers. "Your plan failed. Next time, use more poison."

Her gasp was silenced as his lips descended on hers. She tried to push him away, but her struggles merely managed to excite and entice him. The sensuous feel of her naked body writhing beneath his awoke sensations too long at rest. God, he wanted her.

She turned her head, tearing her lips from his. "What do you think you are doing?" she breathed, her eyes narrowing and chest heaving.

He chuckled, enjoying his new power and vitality, and amazed at how naturally he had assumed the warlord's personality. "So much outrage. My dear, you tried to kill me last night. I would say I am entitled to a little compensation. After all, you are my wife."

Her gaze widened. "There has been a mistake."

"Indeed. If you ever try to poison me again I will hang you from the castle battlements as an example to your people."

She drew her hand back to strike him.

He easily caught the wrist and smiled. "You are a spoiled child. However, best you learn now that I am the master of this house, this land, and you."

She blanched. "You would rape me?"

"Rape?" he laughed. "What a strange creature you are. You are my wife."

"Please, listen to me. This is terribly wrong."

"I agree, but I am stuck with you until death do us part, which you tried to hasten along last night."

"I am not your wife."

"Enough!" he snapped, shocked that he had raised his voice. The idioms of this strange speech felt right, but Christophe's temper would have to be controlled. "Last night you became my wife in word and deed. I do not remember any protest."

Tears filled her eyes. "Have you no compassion?"

He stroked her hair, then his hand slipped down to caress her cheek. "As much for you as you had for me."

The words were ominous. "Please," she begged.

His lips descended on hers without mercy.

New and powerful sensations hit Regan, confusing her, robbing her of her wits. She needed time to think. She remembered the horrendous plane crash, but not much else. It was all a blurry haze. Perhaps she was injured and given anesthesia for surgery. Yes. That made sense. She was in a dream and couldn't wake up, so it must be narcotically induced. Why, she had even dreamed she was dead; she remembered the voice of an angel. There was no sense fighting, she must be asleep. Why else would she be kissing a warrior and talking to angels? Besides, this dream was surprisingly not all that unpleasant. The kiss had changed the moment her resistance ebbed. Now his lips moved over hers with a sensuous softness that sent shivers through her.

Pathetic little mouse, she thought, enjoying the vicarious thrill of a dream lover. Still, he did seem real. What harm was there in indulging her imagination? This was heaven and he made her feel wonderful. Why not lie back and enjoy? Hell no! She wasn't going to lie back, she was going to participate. After all, this was her fantasy. She could do whatever she wanted.

With a delicious sigh she ran her hands over him, caressing the bulging muscles of his shoulders and forearms. Her dream man must be a bodybuilder. And why shouldn't she have conjured up the very best specimen? His massive chest and broad shoulders, layered with thick hard muscles and corded sinews, tapering to a flat stomach, would make Mr. Universe appear small. His skin was so warm, smooth, and solid, yet quivered beneath her touch.

He kissed her neck, and goose bumps traveled from her shoulder to the ends of her fingertips. He chuckled at her little shiver, and she liked the deep husky sound. In fact, except for his manner, there was very little she would change about the man. In truth, he would be perfect if he just didn't speak.

Suddenly all thoughts fled as his lips fastened on her breast. He was good. Yes . . . he was . . . very good.

She quivered beneath his tantalizing lips. Her breath came in short gasps. She cried out, ''Please.''

''Say my name,'' he whispered huskily.

His name? What was his name? No sooner had the question formed in her mind then she knew. ''Christophe.''

His lips hovered over hers. ''I like to hear you say my name.'' Then his mouth covered hers in another scorching kiss. She felt hot all over. This figment of her imagination knew exactly where to touch her. Wrapping her arms around his neck, she met his kiss and matched his ardor. A fire consumed her, stealing her thoughts and soul.

She arched her back, heedless of anything but finding pleasure and reveling in the way he explored her body. She had never known such luxuriant freedom. It was so . . . so . . . she gasped when his fingers slipped between her legs and dipped deep inside her. Fire streaked through her. He started a rhythm, and with each thrust, molten desire—hot, wet, and wild— filled her being. Her hands grasped his shoulders, bunching his muscles beneath her grip. She didn't know if she wanted to urge him on or to stop him. Sensation after sensation overwhelmed her senses and she feared she would cease breathing for the sheer joy. Then his mouth replaced his hand, and his tongue drove her over the edge. She cried out, thrashing like a wanton as a million stars burst in her mind and body. Spasm after spasm of sheer pleasure coursed through her, building in intensity until she climaxed in a flash of utter bliss and slowly floated upward toward a soft downy cloud.

The moment the sensuous wave subsided, he spread her legs and entered her. Immediately the erotic waves of pleasure returned as he thrust deep inside her. His movements excited her beyond anything she had known. Never had she felt this exhilaration, this liquid fire that soared through her veins. Again his lips fastened on hers, swallowing her breathy cry of release as his body shuddered once, twice, before he collapsed on top of her.

Slowly the sounds, smells, and sensations returned.

His body's warmth surrounded her and she could feel his heart beat. Her hands slid across the width of his broad shoulders, hungrily caressing the smooth expanse of his skin, ridged with thick muscles.

Slowly she drifted to sleep while stroking the warm flesh of the man who moments before had driven her to staggering heights she had only dreamed existed.

Regan awoke hours later. Like a drowning victim surfacing and gasping for air, her eyes flew open, slowly, carefully, drinking in the view.

The bright light in the room distorted the image. Wooden walls, like that of an ancient fort, surrounded her. Where was she? Still asleep, apparently. The strangest images flashed through her memory. Bits and pieces of a woman's life— another woman's life—lingered in her mind. The sensation was strong that it was not a dream. She moved the covers and felt the sensuous slide of soft fur against her bare skin. Naked! She was naked. It was then that she felt the body heat and realized she was not alone.

Cautiously she turned over and came face-to-face with the most fierce-looking man she had ever seen. A scream rose in her throat, but she swallowed it, recognizing the sleeping figure. But he had been an illusion, a dream she'd had earlier. She covered her mouth, remembering her uninhibited responses to this lover. Her heart raced and she closed her eyes, praying that when she opened them his image would disappear. Silently she counted to ten, and opened her lids, but he remained. Good God!

What the hell was going on?

She turned over carefully, lying still so as not to disturb Christophe. Her heart raced. She had to think.

A few minutes later she felt the bed dip as he rose, and she closed her eyes, feigning sleep. She couldn't face him until she had time to compose herself. Terror shot through her. What had happened? Where was she? Flashes of the horrible plane crash, the screams, Drew's heroism, the unbearable pain, then her death streaked through her mind. Fragmented shards of the past crystallized; the dream of an angel was suddenly as real as the man who had made love to her.

She understood.

A knot of pain rose in her throat and she gripped the fur covers to her lips to stifle a cry. Her existence, her life had been taken away. Regret filled her for all she had left behind. Her family and friends wouldn't exist for centuries. But, why was she here? Why now? She wanted to scream.

Waiting for Christophe to leave unnerved her. The hardest thing to do was to lie still when she wanted to leap into action. Hurry up and go, she silently begged. As she anticipated his departure, the sounds of his dressing filled her mind with sudden images. She could picture his bronzed skin and thick muscled chest and thighs. Her face flushed at the memories that flooded her.

An animal growled menacingly, and she inwardly cringed.

"Come here, Fang," he ordered.

The beast whined but obeyed.

She heard him strap on his sword, then his heavy footfalls sounded on the wooden planks as he crossed the room. Her heart raced, but she waited a full minute after he had flung the door wide, then slammed it, before opening her eyes to cautiously survey the room. A pent-up sigh slipped past her lips as she found herself alone. Alone with the memories of a woman named Bronwyn.

She threw back the covers and stood—and stopped to stare in wonder at her right leg, which was now solid and strong. Tears pricked her eyes. A leg that was complete, not weakened or deformed. How could that be? But, then, how could any of this be? She took an experimental step and marveled at the strength of her new limb. A smile lit her face. It was a prayer answered.

She twirled around, reveling in the unencumbered action. Blond hair flew over her shoulder and she stopped. She was a blonde? Curious, she spied the polished metal and glanced at her image. Completely nude except for the amber necklace that circled her neck, she stared at her reflection. Dear mercy, she was beautiful. Not pretty, but *unbelievably gorgeous.* Long golden hair, thick and luxurious, like a lion's mane, adorned her head. She lifted the rich mass of curls and marveled at its vibrant color. She was no longer a little brown mouse, she thought with amazement as the golden tresses slipped through her fingers. Lord, but Bronwyn possessed uncommon features. Large amber eyes, long golden lashes, a turned-up nose, and lush full lips. The image staring back at her looked awed.

Reaching up to touch her face, she noticed an amber topaz ring on her third finger. It was the same as her own! Only it was new and shiny, instead of worn and aged. Bronwyn must have been her ancestor. She sat down cradling the ring. Her ancestor. How utterly amazing.

Reverently she touched the bright gold ring with the brilliant amber-colored stone, and her first instinct was to tell the truth, to tell who she really was. But who could she tell? Her family would not exist for another nine hundred years. Besides, history had taught that superstitious people considered anyone different a danger. No, she was on her own, and could never let anyone know the truth. " 'Tis an impossible task,'' she whispered, awed by the huskiness of her new voice. Her fingers touched her lips at the words she uttered. " 'Tis,'' she repeated, while thinking the words *it is.* She concentrated, squeezing her eyes shut and fisting her hands. "It is.'' She sighed. At least she hadn't lost her identity. But she had absorbed the speech patterns and idioms of this time, along with the history. Although it would be difficult to fool those who had known her all her life, it had to be done. She had no choice.

Slowly she gathered Bronwyn's clothes—her clothes, she amended—and dressed. How alien the long, flowing white tunics trimmed in gold and silver threads seemed after a lifetime of obscuring pantsuits. Yet, she knew exactly how they were worn and how to dress. The extent of her newfound knowledge staggered her imagination. She gazed down at the gown and had to admit that the apparel was indeed feminine. Both the under and over tunic possessed clean lines that hinted at her figure. After she finished putting on her girdle, she looked at her reflection, and a princess stared back.

A sudden flash of poison being poured into a cup streaked through her thoughts. Regan took a deep sobering breath. How, dear God, was she to live in this time and this body after Bronwyn had attempted murder?

She closed her eyes as Bronwyn's returning memories of the warlord washed over her. Her counterpart was terrified of Christophe Montgomery, and had acted to save her people. More memories assailed her along with a full range of emotions from anger to zeal, and she now remembered every intense detail of the woman's life.

Her eyes snapped open, her heart racing with pain, anger, and frustration as she recalled first the poison, then the brutal coupling. How would she face Christophe Montgomery, her husband? Then she remembered his passionate lovemaking this morning. Her emotions were in turmoil. His behavior didn't make sense. Disjointed images of a vengeful warlord and an ardent lover swirled through her mind.

Then she remembered the antidote. Unfortunately, the warlord was twice her size, so though they had each ingested the same amount of poison, Bronwyn had died. Though her reasoning made sense, she had a moment's pause. How would Lord Christophe Montgomery receive her?

Dressed in the simple white gown, hair combed and braided, she opened the door and stepped out onto the balcony that overlooked the great room.

She could see the warlord, his face like thunder as he stared at her father, Hayden. The room was overflowing with onlookers, both Welsh and Norman. It awed her that she had memories of half these people and knew them intimately.

She shied away from the fierce rage on her husband's features. All of a sudden his gaze shifted upward to her. Fury and anger sparkled in his storm-darkened black eyes. His damning glare shot her like a jolt of lightning. Could this be the man who had just made love to her so thoroughly?

She swallowed her fear and held his gaze.

"Come here." He pointed to the spot before him.

Regan drew a deep, calming breath, squared her shoulders and descended the stairs.

Every gaze followed her, but she kept her head high and walked through the crowd. Without looking at anyone but her husband, she stopped where he had indicated and held his gaze.

"Who are you?" he asked.

His question caught her unaware. Did he suspect she was not Bronwyn? But how?

Before she could answer, Bronwyn's father stepped beside her. "She is my younger daughter, Bronwyn."

Regan almost sagged in relief, until she noticed the open rage on her husband's face.

Hayden held out his hand. "If you will accept her as your wife, I will honor the agreement signed concerning her older sister."

Christophe's eyes narrowed. "Not the lady I was promised!" He grabbed hold of her arm and pulled her close. "Is there no end to your duplicity?"

Realizing her peril, she tried to jerk free, but his hold tightened, his fingers biting into her flesh.

"You cannot escape me," he warned, then stared at Hayden. "I will honor the marriage on one condition."

Hayden eyed him expectantly, as did every other member of the household.

"Your daughter, Bronwyn, must kneel before me and beg my pardon. She must also swear her allegiance."

A shuddered gasp reverberated through the crowd as her brother, Caradoc, shoved through the throng to reach them. "How dare you ask this of a lady and your wife?"

Christophe's wolf bared his fangs, but the warlord did not still his animal.

"That lady," he sneered, "tried to poison me."

"My sister is blameless."

Christophe arched his black brows. "Who, then, is the assassin?"

"Enough!" Regan cried, relieved that all the warlord wanted was an apology and a vow, instead of her life. Ignoring her countrymen's shocked expressions, she knelt before the warlord and bowed her head. The position put her throat precariously close to his animal's sharp white fangs. She tried to ignore the wolf, but she couldn't. His teeth seemed to grow larger as his lips curled up.

"I do humbly ask your mercy and solemnly promise my loyalty," she whispered quickly, glad to have the matter done.

"While you are on your knees you might remember who is your master." He turned to gaze at the crowd. "As should all of you. Norman rule is here to stay."

He walked toward the hearth, and thankfully his wolf followed, which left Caradoc to help her to her feet. "Damn the invader," he whispered under his breath. "Someday I will kill him for the humiliation he made you suffer."

She looked quickly at Christophe, but saw no sign that he had overheard her brother. "Please, Caradoc," she murmured. "You must not do anything."

Caradoc glared at the warlord's back, hatred etched upon his handsome young face. "I talked you into this, Bronwyn. Thus, I will find a way to rescue you."

Before she could respond, Christophe turned back and studied them through narrowed eyes. "I have always found that a coward never acts alone." Then his stare fell directly on Caradoc.

She felt her brother tense under the weight of the insult. She gripped his arm, a silent warning not to take the bait. His body fairly trembled beneath her fingers, but he restrained his anger.

She released her breath when Christophe scanned the crowd. "We will build a stone castle to protect William's holdings. Work will begin at once and will not stop until the project is finished."

Murmurs of dissension filled the hall, but the huge warlord silenced them with a steely look. "My brother, Nicolas, will hand out your assignments. There will be no exemptions. Everyone works, including," he turned his gaze on Bronwyn, "the women."

Rage filled the Welsh faces as they stared at their new taskmaster.

"You cannot ask this of our women," Regan gasped. "They

have neither the muscle nor strength to work on the construction of such a castle.''

He raised one eyebrow, his glare harsh as his wolf snarled and snapped. ''My *wife* will set the example.'' He took hold of her arm and dragged her over to Nicolas. ''Find a suitable job for this lazy creature.''

Her pride burned as she stared at a younger version of her husband. But unlike Christophe's stern features, Nicolas Montgomery had a pleasant mien.

''My lady, you will bring the men their daily rations.''

She nodded her head.

''Do not be too easy on her,'' Christophe mocked. ''I am sure she can do a little labor and still find time to attend her wifely duties.''

She turned and faced her husband. ''My lord, what attention I give you will be exactly what you deserve.''

Christophe watched her throw him a defiant look, then turned to the Welshmen. By not calling Bronwyn to task for her insolence he had shown her mercy. But though he had no desire to punish a woman, he could not forget her treachery.

He motioned for the villagers to gather closer. ''In addition to your work on the castle, you will spend one hour each day at military training.''

Michau, his trusted friend, now captain of the guards, removed his chain-mail hood and brushed back his thick iron-streaked hair. ''My lord, do you really wish to start today?''

''You would wait to train them until they have shown their loyalty, would you not? I have not that luxury. Their allegiance will come faster if they see the benefit of supporting us,'' Christophe said.

Michau smiled. ''I had not thought of that.''

Drew grinned back, thinking that his experience in mergers and acquisitions was certainly going to come in handy.

Chapter Three

Bronwyn glared at the warlord's back as he left the castle, but she tempered her ire, reminding herself that he had shown leniency. By the time she reached the kitchen to organize the cooking and feeding of all the people, her natural humor had returned.

Nesta, the cook, met her at the hearth. "My lady, what are we to do?"

"We will do as we are bid," she said. "And we will do it with such grace and proficiency that the Normans will realize we are neither lazy nor stupid."

Nesta's ample chest swelled. "We will not fail you, my lady."

Immediately, Bronwyn saw several areas that needed improvement. "I think the work will go much faster and smoother if we divide the tasks."

"How so, my lady?" Nesta asked.

"You should oversee the cooking. Let someone chop the vegetables, another the meat, and another prepare the seasonings," she said, thinking of the efficiency of a restaurant's kitchen.

Cordelia, Nesta's daughter, touched Bronwyn's arm. "But, my lady, we have never done that before."

" 'Tis necessary to try different ways."

Cordelia raised an eyebrow and glanced to the other women, who also seemed puzzled. "My lady, mayhap you have not fully recovered from the poisoning," Cordelia suggested.

Regan realized her behavior seemed queer, that they attributed it to the poisoning was a blessing in disguise. "All our lives have changed with the advent of the Normans. We must also be prepared to change our ways or perish," she said, thinking those words applied doubly for her.

Though they said nothing, they gave her a peculiar look. Nesta shooed her daughter to her task. "Do you doubt my lady's words?"

When the women returned to work, Nesta put her arm around Bronwyn. "Are you fit, my lady?"

The whispered concern brought a smile to Bronwyn's lips. "Aye, I am well."

"I have noticed you are limping. Did you injure your leg?"

She was startled to realize she was indeed favoring the leg. From years of being careful with her weak limb, she had acted out of habit. "Aye, I twisted it, but 'tis nothing," she responded, knowing she would have to make a conscious effort to walk with her weight displaced evenly over both limbs.

Several hours later, Bronwyn's hair hung limp from the steam in the kitchen, and her clothes clung to her damp skin as she toiled to make sure everything was not only done, but done with panache. After the women saw the advantages to her new procedures, it was easier to institute more change. Every member worked harder than ever before. To them it was a matter of honor. Lazy indeed!

Huge trestle tables were set up for the evening meal. Normans and Welsh sat side by side. A rare and unusual sight.

Refusing the privilege her rank accorded, Bronwyn insisted on serving the food along with the other women. She set the heavy trenchers and platters out, then refilled the cups when needed. The men fell upon the food, their hands and faces glistening from the grease. Bronwyn silently grimaced. The next things she would have to introduce were eating utensils. Knives, forks, spoons, and plates would be a definite benefit. She would see the farrier this very day, as only the blacksmith would be able to fashion cutlery.

As she waited on the first table, she noticed no room had been left for her to join her husband, who ignored her as he laughed and talked to his men. Though the slight was aimed at Bronwyn, Regan found it amusing. The pig, she thought. The arrogant pig.

Well, two could play his game. *You're playing with fire,* an inner voice warned. *I don't care,* she mentally argued, knowing she had to make it in this time on her own terms.

After she finished her service, she and the ladies set up a table in the middle of the room, then she bid all the women to sit down with her and enjoy their meal. When she noted the amused smile flickering on the warlord's face, she lifted her chin and looked the other way. She had experienced the same satisfaction whenever she had bested Drew. But her former life was over, and she had the present to handle.

Despite her small victory, she knew the battle was far from over. Several times during the meal, shivers ran up her arms as she felt his gaze upon her, but stubbornly she refused to acknowledge his interest. After the tables were cleaned up and the food stored, she was exhausted. Although the day had been long, she still had one chore left before she could relax. With a sigh she wrapped her mantle around her shoulders and slipped out the side door.

Bone weary, she returned from giving the farrier her sketches for the silverware and plates, and wanted nothing more than a long hot bath. Yet, the thought of such a project drew a groan from her.

Still, she could not stand the thought of retiring with the day's grime. Deep voices drifted in from the main room as she started the kettles to boiling in the now empty kitchen.

Suddenly she felt a prickling on the back of her neck. Instinctively she knew Christophe had entered the room and he was watching her. She pretended to be unaware of him as she brushed a strand of hair from her brow. As the seconds passed and he remained in the doorway, perspiration dotted her upper lip and she pressed a hand to the small of her back and stretched her sore muscles.

"Good, I am pleased to see you are preparing my bath," he finally said.

She whirled around and the room seemed suddenly small as he took a step into the kitchen, his pet by his side. " 'Tis *my* bath I am attending to."

He folded his muscular arms across his massive chest. "Have you forgotten? 'Tis *my* needs you see to before yours."

She silently counted to ten, then resignedly bent to lift the heavy kettle.

When he took the handle from her, relieving her of the heavy burden, a smile of gratitude rose to her lips. He did have his redeeming qualities.

But instead of pouring the water into the tub, he set the kettle down on the floor. "I will not bathe here, but in my chamber. I will be with you directly."

She stared first at the kettle on the floor, then at the two others that were heating over the fire. An image of hauling the heavy hot water up the stairs sprang in her mind. Kind thoughts be damned, she thought, clenching her jaw. "As you wish."

He chuckled softly. "Do not worry, wife. I will not take you to task for your show of temper." He drew his finger down her cheek and over her lips.

The sharp retort died in her throat as she saw the raw desire in his eyes. When his lips covered hers she felt her knees give way, but his arms wrapped around her, drawing her closer into his embrace. His kiss was hot, wet, and sensual, and during that brief instant she forgot her ire.

When he left she tried to compose herself. It took longer than she cared to admit, for the man turned her bones to jelly. Being very careful not to burn herself, she carried, dragged, and at times slid the heavy kettle along the uneven planked floor. Nicolas saw her plight and, ignoring her protests, carried the kettle up to the master room.

Forced to acknowledge his chivalry, she murmured her thanks.

"My brother has much on his mind. Know that he works harder than any of his men."

She nodded, aware of the castle construction before them. Though she objected, Nicolas carried up the remaining two kettles of water, then helped drag the huge tub from its place behind the screen before he left. Unlike his brother, Nicolas was kind. As she added the cold water to make the bathwater temperature more acceptable, she sighed. Oh, how she longed to sink into the warm depths and soak her aching muscles.

Lost in her own thoughts, she did not hear Christophe enter the room. When he dropped the bar into place she jumped up, feeling suddenly trapped. He leaned against the door and folded his arms across his chest as his wolf approached his position by the fire.

Her gaze followed the animal, wary of the predator's watchful eyes. It wasn't until he had curled up on the throw, ignoring her, that she looked at Christophe. "I must prepare my bath," she said, knowing she would have to leave, and the bar weighed as much as she.

"You can use mine."

She was stunned. "Yours?"

"Oui."

She shook her head. "Is there anything else, my lord?"

"You have the chore of bathing me to attend to first."

"Bathing you?"

He raised one brow. *"Oui."*

So, this was beck and call, she thought. Oh, well, she was alive and well. Far be it from her to complain over an overbearing male. She would just consider this a job.

"What are you waiting for?"

She looked up and saw that he expected her to help him undress.

These medieval men sure did have it made.

She walked over to him, thinking how very decadent this time was. What was all the nostalgia and hoopla about knights in shining armor? So far, she had seen little of chivalry. His armor was made of chain links, dirty gray in color and very heavy. She gasped as she caught the weight of his hauberk and set it aside.

When all that was left were his braies, she turned away to fold his clothes. The sound of him stripping just behind her made her heart flutter. She knew she had to carry off this ritual, but it was going to be difficult. "My, my l-l-lord," she stuttered as she turned and stared only at his face.

"What?" he asked, clearly amused by her obvious embarrassment.

"Do you need further help?" She pointed to the bath.

Her face flushed under his knowing look and she closed her eyes to his inspection.

"As you well know, 'tis the custom and a sign of respect."

Damn, he was right. And he was beautiful.

He chuckled, and her pride burned. She was a twentieth-century woman, not some repressed prude. Bathing a man should be nothing at all for her. She was a trained physical therapist, after all. However, this wasn't the impersonal contact of a professional, this was the interaction of a man and a woman, and it scared the hell out of her.

"Do not tell me you are blushing, Bronwyn."

Though Regan knew she was beet red, she brazenly met his gaze. Regan blushed; Bronwyn didn't. "Nay, I never blush." The moment the denial left her mouth, she realized Bronwyn's persona and her own had comfortably merged.

"Then you must be standing too close to the fire."

In more ways than one, she thought.

She lifted the wash linen and waited for Christophe to step into the tub. The very thought of touching him made her breath quicken and her fingers tingle. When he sat down, his sun-bronzed skin stretched taut over the corded, ropey muscles of his back, while his triceps and biceps bulged as he gripped the rim and slowly leaned back.

Abruptly he turned and his knowing grin made her face grow even hotter as he offered her the soap.

"If you are through feasting your eyes, you can get started," he murmured, his deep voice like velvet against her skin.

She slapped the washcloth into the water, creating a splash.

He wiped the droplets away without comment, held her gaze for a moment, then handed her the soap.

The chunk of coarse soap was rough in her palm, and her show of temper over, she extended her hand for the cloth. He shook his head and pointed to the soap, his meaning clear as he submerged the cloth beneath the water.

Her heart beat faster at the thought of lathering his body with her bare hands. How intimate this had suddenly become. Though she hated to admit it, Christophe excited her. He was her fantasy come to life. Handsome, strong, virile, and lord help her, a typical arrogant male, yet underneath a man of honor. He stole her very breath away. Rubbing the soap between her palms, her hand slid ever so slowly over his shoulders.

She shut her eyes as her hands roamed over his expansive back. His skin quivered at her slightest touch. Like the rhythmic waves against the shore, his muscles rippled beneath her fingertips.

Catering to his needs, she fulfilled her own. She caressed the thick ridges and deep valleys of his rib cage, and her heart pounded as she washed the wide expanse of his chest. The thick, curly black hairs sprang to life beneath the onslaught of her fingers.

He suddenly gripped her hand and held it still over his heart. "Do you not feel the beating?"

She nodded, unable to answer as she stared into his eyes.

"Every time you touch me, my heart races."

His husky voice made her shiver. "My lord." She tried to pull free. "Please, my lord, release me."

He drew her closer. "There is no need for you to heat another bath. Join me in mine."

She pulled away.

" 'Tis not a request, Bronwyn; 'tis an order," he said softly.

She reached for the towel, attempting to ignore him.

"Make no mistake, *mademoiselle,* you *will* join me either willingly or not."

She swallowed the lump in her throat. The tub was large enough to accommodate her, but suddenly nervous, she could not change her inhibition, and the intimacy it would induce.

"I cannot," she breathed nervously.

Christophe rose from the bath. Water sluiced off his body, emphasizing his bronzed skin as it glistened in the firelight.

Mesmerized, she stared at him. An exhilarating shock shivered over her nerves as he approached her, not in haste, but in a slow calculated tread.

He stopped in front of her. His fingers brushed her cheek before slipping down her neck into the top of her tunic. A quick twist of the neckline rent the material in half. She gasped, trying to catch the open edges of her robe as it slipped down her body to pool at her feet. Instantly he lifted her into his arms, and the contrast of her overheated body against his cool skin caused her to tremble. When he carried her to the bath, a tear drifted down her cheek.

"Tears?"

"It is just . . . I am shy."

"You?"

"I suppose it is beyond you to understand."

"You are right, 'tis beyond me. I remember a tigress in my arms, not a shy maiden."

His muscles rippled as he stepped over the rim of the tub and lowered them both into the steaming water. She clutched him tight about the neck.

"Do you fear drowning?"

She was fearful, all right, not of drowning, but of him. "Yes."

He chuckled, softly, seductively. "Then hold on tight, my lady."

The water lapped against the sides of the tub, spilling over the edges while they sat down in the luxuriant depths.

Waves lapped against her breast, and the sensuous water sluiced over her skin. She hid her face in the crook of his neck, unable to play the experienced lady. Though she considered herself a liberated woman, Christophe could make her feel utterly vulnerable.

His stark masculinity engulfed her. She could feel every breath he took, every beat of his heart. She waited, not moving as the moments stretched without a word or deed. After what seemed an eternity, she lifted her head.

A smile teased the corners of his lips. "You amaze me." His hand caressed her skin, sending shivers through her. "A lover's expertise that drives a man wild, yet you manage to display an innocence that engenders a man's natural inclination to protect. However, my dear, I know your shyness is but an act." His lips tasted hers. "If not for the wedding night, I could believe in the performance. There is a certain magic to your eyes, lips, and voice. And I am only a man."

Bronwyn couldn't believe what he was saying. Worse, she couldn't concentrate on her reply. His lips tormented and teased her wits beyond control. She was losing herself, and that frightened her more than she cared to admit. She tried to inch some space between them but he kept his body molded to hers. She could feel every sinew and hard muscle and knew his desire. His calloused hands slipped downward over her skin in a sensuous caress.

"Shall I bathe you, my lady?"

She shook her head, senses spinning. "Please," she murmured, trying to gain her freedom. She needed time to think.

"What is it you beg for, Wife?"

The sound of his voice, low and husky, caused her thoughts to scatter. The warm water lapped against them as his lips covered hers. His slow, provocative kiss slipped past her defenses. His lips sampled and savored, like satin against velvet, caressing, and creating a heat within her, while warm waves drifted over her in a rhythmic massage of incredible sensuality. When his hands slid over her ribs to her breast, she moaned. The sensations were too much. The heat of his kiss, the warmth of the water, and the fire of his touch ignited her desire.

Her hands slipped over his broad shoulders and around his neck. The moment she parted her lips to him, receiving his kiss, she knew she was lost.

"Love me," his deep voice rumbled.

When she kissed him again, she held nothing back, pouring out her desire, hope, and need. A deep curling sensation grew deep in the pit of her stomach. The heat grew with every caress, every kiss. Her hunger for him and her own release neared unbearable; then he suddenly rose, holding her in his embrace. Dripping wet, he held her against his chest as he stepped out of the tub and walked to the bed. His sun-seared body shone in the firelight as he slowly lowered her to the fur robes. She shivered from the loss of his touch, and watched the firelight dance across his rippling muscles. Like a bronzed statue come to life, his body was sheer perfection. Catching her regard, he grinned, then drew her close and banished the chills. The heat from his body and hands made the fire quickly return.

He kissed her with fierce intensity, the gentleness gone as pure primal need engulfed him. The sudden change excited rather than frightened her. Their bodies arched and moved as one. In a rhythm as old as time, yet new to her, she moved to the music of her heart. The sexual fulfillment was secondary to the need within her to be loved and to love. When he entered her, her movements became as frantic as his, her need as primal and strong. She scored his back with her nails, urging him on, crying out his name. He gave one final thrust and they climaxed together. Slowly she floated down from the plateau like a feather floating to earth.

Bronwyn sighed heavily. Never had she expected to know such sweet fulfilling sensuality with any man. In her former life she had believed that no one would ever have given a crippled brown mouse a first, let alone a second, glance. Suddenly she realized it was not her leg that had handicapped her, but her own fear. Thank you, Bronwyn, she mentally acknowledged, for the valuable lesson.

Her hand slipped down and caressed his furry chest. "Heaven," she breathed, speaking her thoughts aloud.

"I keep forgetting what a little performer you are." He captured her hand and held it over his heart.

His words crushed her spirit. She stared into his calculating eyes, not wanting to believe what she had heard.

She swallowed the lump in her throat as her perfect illusion shattered. She could not deny the truth. "People can change. And I did give you the antidote."

"Only because you thought to save your people," he scoffed.

Then he pulled her closer. "Being a warm bedmate is not enough to make me forget your treacherous heart."

She tried to pull away, feeling sick.

"There is no escape, Bronwyn."

"Someday, Christophe, you will eat your words and beg my forgiveness. I have accepted your authority. You have no more to fear from me."

His smile was cold. "That's right," he said, then his lips covered hers in a bruising kiss that tasted of domination and humiliation.

She struggled beneath him. When he raised his head, she glared at him. "I am your wife, not your whore."

"You are what I wish you to be."

Bronwyn's heart plummeted. "Very well, my lord. If that is all you want from this marriage, that is all you shall get."

He lifted her chin and forced her to look into his eyes. "Then, my little rebel, give me what I want." She was prepared to resist his kiss, but instead of brutality, there was an unexpected gentleness in his lips. His tenderness shattered her defenses instantly. She found herself responding to each caress, each kiss. Although she wished it otherwise, she was powerless to resist his allure.

She had been wrong. She had not died and gone to heaven. Oh, she had died all right, but this was not paradise. . . . This was purgatory.

Chapter Four

Bronwyn turned over on her side and opened her eyes to find herself alone. Soft light filtered in through the window, and she stretched. Chilled, she pulled the covers up and rolled into the slight depression left by Christophe. He must have arisen before dawn. The bed was as cold as her thoughts. He treated her with even less regard than a one-night stand. It hurt.

But Christophe's disregard paled in comparison to what she had faced in her prior life. The only way she had endured the surgeries and the pain was by pure will and steel determination. That same iron determination now surged through her. She hadn't always been respected in her last life, but she would be in this one.

She tossed back the covers and smiled. Their Norman warlord was about to face his greatest challenge—a modern woman, and he didn't even suspect it. She chuckled. The day suddenly loomed before her filled with great possibilities. She slipped on her kirtle and tunic, and again stared at her refection in the polished silver. The blond-haired creature staring back from the mirror still awed her. Yet, no matter what image presented itself, whether in her mind's eye as Regan, or in her mirror as Bronwyn, in her mind and heart she had changed. She would never again be a brown mouse. She stared down at her ring, wishing Regan had possessed Bronwyn's inner courage and poise. Strange, but far from unsettling, was the realization that she seemed to have inherited and retained the best traits from both women. An idea formed as a warm glow filled her. She would see the farrier and have him engrave three words inside the band to help Regan.

When a hand touched her arm she screamed.

"Bronwyn, hush," Caradoc warned. "Do you wish the guards to come?"

Her heart raced from the scare. "Do not sneak up on me ever again."

Caradoc grimaced. "Last night must have been terrible to leave you in this ill humor."

Guiltily she turned away.

"Bronwyn, just endure his touch for a little while longer. We have a plan."

'Twas not a hardship to bear his touch. In truth, the mere thought made her blush. "Caradoc, please. We can do no more. The Normans are here."

"What? Where is the Welshwoman who agreed to poison the hated invader?" He grabbed her chin between his fingers and inspected her face. "I see no bruises. Has the bedding changed you to a Norman bitch who heeds her master?"

She slapped his face, leaving a red imprint. "How dare you!"

From the doorway, Fiona gasped.

"Welcome back from the convent, dear sister. Enter." Caradoc waved Fiona in, then turned his back on her when she joined them. Disdain filled his eyes as his gaze traveled from the top of Bronwyn's head to her toes. "My sister would not have submitted to the enemy. Has a changeling appeared?"

The question was so close to the truth that her breath caught in her throat.

"Brother, for shame," Fiona said. " 'Tis blasphemy to speak such superstition."

Bless Fiona's sweet nature.

"Blasphemy or not, she has changed," Caradoc growled angrily.

"What ails you, Caradoc? Is it that your plan went awry? 'Tis not Bronwyn's fault, nor mine, that the Norman survived."

He glared at Fiona, his fists at his side.

"Father has given his word that we will obey the invaders. Would you have him punished?" Bronwyn asked.

"I will not surrender," he snapped, pointing at his sisters. "You will join me, or else." Then he stormed from the room, his shoulders rigid, his blond hair flying.

Fiona touched Bronwyn's arm. "Do not let him upset you. He is young and hotheaded. It is hard for him to accept the changes."

" 'Tis not easy for any of us," Bronwyn said, thinking Caradoc manipulated everyone to gain his purpose. She did not like his spoiled, selfish ways.

"Father will not let him act," Fiona said.

But what if he takes it upon himself, thought Bronwyn.

A mile from the wooden castle, on a site he had selected, Christophe possessed a "license to crenelate", royal permission to construct a fortress. He stood with his brother, Nicolas, on a small rise that overlooked the valley below. "Here is where I want the castle built."

" 'Tis a defensible position." Nicolas approved.

Christophe turned full circle surveying the outlying land from the high ground. The trees shedding their dark winter-color and starting to bud, offered a clear view of the forest circling the far end of the valley. "An approaching army will have to traverse the overgrown and uneven ground of the forest, then emerge into the vast open ground of the valley, before reaching our castle." He pointed, directing his brother's attention to the valley. "That tilled earth will not only provide us with the earth's bounty, but protect us from surprise attack. Also, the river that cuts through our land provides water and an added defense."

" 'Tis a bafflement that the Welsh did not build here."

Christophe nodded and motioned for his brother to follow him as Fang trotted behind. He walked to the outer perimeter of the area and began driving wood stakes into the ground, then stringing twine from each.

Soon, hundreds of artisans, carpenters, blacksmiths, plumbers, quarriers, mortar masons, thatchers, sawyers and masons would be dispatched from London to work on the Norman fortress. Building a castle was a tremendous undertaking.

Christophe assigned the Welsh to dig a wide ditch around the foundation. Once the carpenters arrived, they would erect a palisade, a tall wooden fence, along the inner edge of the moat that would serve as protection for those who toiled within until a stone wall could be raised. "This construction must be done before the foundation can be started."

" 'Tis a strange perimeter you have marked off," Nicolas said as he bent down to pet Fang.

"I want round towers instead of square ones."

Nicolas looked surprised. "Round? But why? What is wrong with square towers?"

Drew's knowledge of history and architecture was an asset. "Because cylindrical keeps will ensure no blind spots."

Nicolas stared at him in surprise, then nodded. "*Oui*, 'tis a good idea. 'Tis a wonder no one thought of it before. I will see to the work."

A rider galloped up, his salt-and-pepper-colored hair glinting in the sun, and Christophe recognized his captain of the guard long before the burly warrior reined in his horse and dismounted. "My lord," Michau said. "I have located a place where we can dig and cut the stones."

"Is it far?"

"*Non*. Only two leagues. When they arrive, I can assign the quarriers, freemasons, and roughmasons to cut and load the stones onto carts."

"See to it," Christophe said, relieved to know they had a ready supply of heavy stone.

Nicolas and Michau left as Lucien, his man-at-arms, approached. He was wearing his usual pinched expression as he stared down his thin nose at those around him.

Christophe stroked Fang's back and felt the animal's fur

stand on end. "Easy, boy," he soothed, knowing the wolf had always disliked Lucien.

"My lord," Lucien said as he eyed the wolf closely, "during the night there were several acts of retaliation, all minor, the spoiling of food and the theft of several tunics."

"Appoint some men to watch the villagers day and night."

Lucien's thin nostrils flared. "My lord, 'twill stretch our forces thin."

"Nevertheless, until we are sure of our position I want it done."

"The killing of one man would make an example they would not forget," Lucien said, pointing to the crowd of villagers, who kept their heads downcast.

The casual suggestion made it clear that this was the norm, not the exception. *"Non,"* Christophe said, still calmly stroking the tension from the wolf.

Lucien's narrow lips pursed. "My lord, are you sure?"

Christophe raised an eyebrow. "Are you challenging me?" He knew Lucien still felt rankled over William's choice of commanders.

"Non, my lord." Lucien could not hide his sneer as he bowed his head. "As you wish."

The wolf relaxed the moment the soldier turned and withdrew. Christophe continued to absently stroke the animal as he watched the stocky villagers work. They were strong of body, and from personal experience, he knew them to be strong of mind. Yet, living among the enemy had its trials. He trusted no one.

One Welshman, a scar-faced brute, looked up and met his gaze. Pure hatred shone in the man's stare, but worse, he didn't bother to hide his contempt.

Christophe mused that his counterpart had been a cruel brute and perhaps rightly hated. He did not want to act the same, but his men expected a certain harsh behavior from him. He could not afford to lose their loyalty or respect. Perhaps here and there he could show mercy without raising too many eyebrows.

"Nicolas," he called.

His brother left the serfs toiling to excavate the moat. Christophe pointed to the regiment William had assigned to him. "Why are those soldiers standing around?"

"There is nothing for them to do."

"Every able-bodied man, woman, and child will work on the castle until the foundation is complete and the exterior takes shape. No one will be truly safe until the construction is finished."

" 'Twill cause unrest to have William's soldiers do manual labor."

"No one is above William's command," Christophe said, his voice easily carrying to the lazy men. "This castle is his project. Let those soldiers return home and explain why they sat around and did nothing to help their king realize his dream."

The Norman soldiers scrambled to get shovels, then began to find and haul stumps from the ground. Nicolas grinned. "If you will excuse me, my lord, I will see to the added workforce."

In the distance Christophe saw someone, possibly a young woman, emerge from the old castle's wooden frame. He watched the feminine figure as she climbed the path that ran alongside of the fields until he recognized his wife. The wind whipped Bronwyn's tunic against her body, outlining her figure to his appreciation. Her hips possessed a gentle sway that taunted and tempted a man. The memory of last night materialized, and a smile teased his lips. But though he understood her allure, he did not confuse sex with love. She reminded him of a venomous spider, and although he intended to sample her charms whenever he pleased, he had no intention of getting caught in her dangerous web.

She walked up the last few feet of the path and stopped next to him. Perspiration dotted her upper lip and she folded her arms across her breast. "My lord, I beg a word."

He inclined his head as others listened closely from their place.

"I pray thee, my lord, you must allow us to plant the fields." She pointed to the workers. "Your castle will be useless if we all starve. Though Normans place great stock in their monuments, no one will be here next spring to pay homage unless the crop is brought in."

The Normans glared at her for her insolence, but the Welsh eyes shone with pride.

Nor did it escape Christophe's notice that all work had momentarily suspended.

His laughter rang out and hung in the air. "*Oui,* my lady, I grant your request, provided you, too, serve in the fields."

Annoyance momentarily flashed in her brown-gold eyes, but she bowed her head slightly.

"Agreed, sir."

The sound of picks and shovels could be heard as Lucien ran up, a fierce scowl upon his long face. "My lord, the castle must come first."

Fang instantly came to his feet, his lip curled back.

Displeased that Lucien had again dared to challenge his decision, Christophe folded his arms and glared at the soldier until he lowered his gaze. Though the soldier was ambitious, he was not a fool.

"Lucien, no one will survive the winter if the fields are left unharvested and the flock wanders off. I do this not for them, but for us."

Bronwyn's face blanched with hot outrage, but she held his regard.

"I beg your pardon, my lord." Lucien bowed. "I did not understand."

"On the morrow I will have Nicolas assign a group to plant the fields. We cannot afford to forget our own welfare."

When Lucien left, Fang relaxed his predatory stance. Christophe held the animal's collar, then turned his attention back to Bronwyn. "That is what you wanted, is it not, *cherie?*"

She nodded, then took a step to rejoin the ladies back at the fortress.

"One moment."

She stopped and slowly turned back. When her gaze met his, there was a wary look deep within her eyes.

"From now on, my lady wife," he said in a low deep voice that could not be overheard. "You will ask for boons in private. You will never again plead before your people or mine."

Although she paled, she raised her chin. "Then, may I speak with you in private now?"

"*Non.*"

Her sharp intake of breath was followed by an indignant expression.

"You are dismissed."

She whirled around, her hem whipping her legs as she stormed off. He grinned at her haughty exit. Though he wasn't about to forget her treachery, she was easy on the eyes.

After she disappeared, he turned and came face-to-face with Caradoc. Fang had adopted an attack stance, and Christophe softly signaled the animal to his side.

"My lord," Caradoc snapped, "I have prepared the list your man requested."

Christophe accepted the paper and scanned the names. He knew several had been omitted. There were more men working than showed on the tally sheet.

"Are you a poor cipherer?"

Caradoc's face turned red. "Nay."

"There must be a reason why this list is so short. Either you are a simpleton or you are a subversive. Think well before you try to deceive me again." He shoved the list back at the Welshman. "Do not return it until the number of men and names are the same."

Not a sound followed Christophe's edict. All the workers who had stopped to watch returned silently to their chores.

Christophe walked several paces away from the construction and turned to stare at the wooden fortress in the distance. The place would house them well enough until the stone castle's completion. But the Welsh castle was a warrior's nightmare.

"Lucien," he bellowed.

As his man returned, Christophe pointed to the wooden walls. "Have several women soak the logs. A fire would destroy the structure. We cannot afford to be vulnerable. Also, see that the water supply is adequate for a siege. And tell Nicolas I want every man, woman, and child accounted for from now on."

Lucien nodded.

Christophe shook his head at the wooden structure. Had the

Welsh built stone castles, their country would never have been invaded.

The Normans knew better and resorted to wooden structures only when immediately forced to war with an enemy. They carried a prefabricated fortress made up of tree trunks, which could be assembled and dismantled as needed. The temporary stronghold provided them with shelter during campaigns. Now, this temporary structure would serve as housing for the artisans who would need lodging.

The Welsh had erred, he would not. 'Twould take all his resources to hold this land and its people together. But he had always been very good at mergers, and at corporate takeovers, he excelled. He crossed his arms, excited about the prospects. Drew had wisdom and education, Christophe strength and power. The combination was exhilarating, and as far as he could see, unbeatable.

In a cloudless blue sky the sun shone directly overhead. Without the benefit of shade the fields, where the women toiled, were hot.

Bronwyn wiped her brow and looked at Fiona. "I wish Nesta would sound the meal call," she said, knowing they needed a rest. When her sister agreed, she looked up the path to the new construction. The men were already marching toward the castle.

"We will take a break in a minute," Bronwyn assured. Her back ached as she reached for another stone, which had worked its way to the surface, and tossed it out of the clumped dirt.

Fiona leaned close. "Caradoc is coming and he looks angry."

She heard the footsteps behind her but was unprepared when his fingers closed over her arm in a vise grip and she was pulled from the row of freshly turned earth.

"Stop it, Caradoc," she demanded. "You are hurting me." When she noticed the Norman soldiers were even with the fields, she lowered her voice. "Let me go."

Caradoc angrily flung her arm aside. "Did you see how he humiliated me in front of our people?"

"Nay."

"I will make him rue the day he ever insulted me."

" 'Twas your own fault," Fiona whispered, stopping beside him. "You tried to deceive him and he caught you."

A muscle in Caradoc's jaw twitched. "The Normans have taught you disrespect."

Bronwyn tried to step between them, but it was too late.

Caradoc slapped Fiona's face. The force sent her sprawling into the dirt.

"Caradoc, stop!" Bronwyn cried out and rushed to her sister's aid. Suddenly, Caradoc was hauled up in Nicolas's meaty fists.

"What knight strikes a lady? You cowardly cur," Nicolas angrily accused as a crowd gathered.

Caradoc struggled within his hold. "Stay out of this, Norman," he hissed. " 'Tis a family matter."

Bronwyn was relieved Nicolas had intervened and saved them from the brunt of Caradoc's temper, that is until she saw Christophe shouldering his way through the throng. She held her breath, knowing the warlord's presence would escalate tension.

"What happened?" Christophe demanded, his black gaze as hard as stone.

Welsh and Normans crowded closer, their voices a low buzz. Christophe ignored the crowd and watched Caradoc's face as he listened to Nicolas's explanation.

A large red bruise already covered Fiona's tender cheek. The warlord leaned over and grasped her chin to study the mark. "Does the maiden not have a protector?"

Caradoc glared at Christophe as Bronwyn helped Fiona to her feet. "Nay," Caradoc said. "Only my father and I."

Christophe's eyes narrowed, but he raised his hand. "Release him."

Nicolas shoved the younger man forward.

Caradoc stumbled, then caught his balance. He straightened his tunic and ran a hand through his tousled blond hair. "You understand, my lord, that what transpires between a brother and sister is not to be tread upon."

''I understand that you have a penchant for attacking those weaker than yourself.''

Their father ran up with a serf in tow. ''What has happened?'' he asked, seeing his son at the mercy of the guards.

Fiona's face wore Caradoc's handprint, and Hayden's eyes missed nothing. He listened to the Norman's account and turned to his son. ''These times are trying enough without taking your frustration out on Fiona. Give your sister her due.''

Caradoc turned. ''Forgive me, Fiona,'' he gritted out, his bluster losing force as his gaze scanned her face. Guilt colored his features. ''I truly am sorry.''

Satisfied, Christophe dismissed him, but Nicolas took Fiona's arm. ''I would be honored if you would allow me to escort you to your room, *mademoiselle.*''

Fiona's gaze darted to Bronwyn and her father. Only after receiving their subtle nod did she accept the Norman's gallant offer.

Caradoc's face blotched with color as Fiona left on the arm of the Norman, and hatred again shone in his eyes. ''By his wounds,'' he exclaimed, and heaped Welsh curses on the couple.

Bronwyn's heart sank. Though Christophe did not know their language, Caradoc's angry tone was unmistakable.

''My lord,'' she said to distract him. When his dark eyes settled on her, her stomach lurched. Heaven help her, she couldn't think of a thing to say.

''*Oui?*''

Perspiration dotted her upper lip as heat rose in her face. She lowered her eyes under his scrutiny. ''My lord, 'tis heartening to know Normans have a chivalrous nature toward the fairer sex.''

''My brother is kinder than I.''

Her gaze shot to his, which was dark without the hint of a smile lurking in their depths. She swallowed her trepidation. ''I am glad for Fiona's sake.''

Caradoc placed his arm over her shoulder, and she cringed from his support. ''What matter? A marriage between a barbarian and a princess is unnatural.''

Instead of anger, Christophe's eyes lit with amusement at

Caradoc's insult. "Forgive me, your royal highness." He bowed low, then straightened and pointed to the field. "And are these weeds your loyal subjects?"

Caradoc stiffened and took a threatening step toward Christophe.

Hayden grabbed his son, holding him back as Fang's teeth appeared. Bronwyn stepped between the men. "No matter the title, I believe we all have work to do."

"Hear, hear," Hayden said, pulling Caradoc after him.

Christophe touched her arm. "You cannot protect him forever, Wife. The time will come when you have to make a choice. When it does, I wonder where your loyalty will lie?"

His nearness disturbed her and she stepped away. "No one should ever be made to choose between family and spouse. 'Tis an impossible choice."

"Nonetheless, with Caradoc's ill temperament it is a decision you shall one day be forced to make," he said, then left to rejoin his men.

Her stomach roiled from the thought. Sick and frightened, she turned and walked away. The meal bell sounded, but the very thought of food made her nauseous. Bronwyn loved Caradoc, but she thought what he was doing was wrong. Not even Solomon could solve this dilemma.

After the meal the ladies returned to the fields, but Bronwyn noticed her sister was not among the workers. Worried, she stopped the cook's daughter, Cordelia. "Where is Fiona?"

"The Norman said she was to rest," Cordelia said.

"Really," she said, thinking that Nicolas was a considerate man. He had been most solicitous this afternoon.

"Aye, your husband surprised us all when he told Lady Fiona we could manage without her this afternoon."

Christophe? It was Christophe who had given her sister permission to rest. When she saw the avid curiosity in Cordelia's eyes, she softly smiled. "I am not surprised. A true knight would behave thusly," she said, then bent to her task, effectively stopping the woman from prying further.

The sun beat down on her, but the afternoon breeze lessened the effect. Her arms and shoulders ached from the toil. As Regan, she had never worked in a garden, much less a farm. Her handicap had prevented such tasks. It felt exceedingly good to ache from manual exertion.

After four hours in the fields Christophe came up behind her and pulled her to her feet. "Your sister needs you."

Bronwyn immediately dropped her shovel.

His strained expression did not bode well as he took hold of her hand. Running with him back to the castle, she was assaulted by a host of fears. "What happened?"

"She fell and severely injured her leg. The limb is lying in an unnatural way."

Bronwyn shuddered. A broken bone in Regan's time was nothing, but now it was a serious affair.

When she ran through the hall, she gasped at the sight that greeted her. Fiona lay at the bottom of the staircase, her gown pulled back to reveal her leg bent at midthigh like a twisted pretzel. Agony etched deep lines in her pale face, distorting her lovely features into an aged mask of pain. She clung to Nicolas, tears streaming down her cheeks as she whimpered.

"Bronwyn." Fiona stretched her hand out the instant she saw her.

"Shush." Bronwyn knelt beside her and brushed her tears away. "Everything will be well."

Fiona bit her lip and shook her head. "Nay . . . it will not."

"Of course it will."

"You do not understand," Fiona whispered. "Someone pushed me. I didn't see who it was."

Bronwyn's eyes widened, and she quickly looked to see if Nicolas had overheard. Thankfully, he had not.

Bronwyn squeezed her sister's hand. "We will find out who harmed you," she murmured before moving to gently examine the leg. Her simple touch caused Fiona to cry out. Bronwyn pulled back and took a deep breath. She was the skilled healer in the castle. Steeling herself against her sister's torturous pain, she started again. Her hands trembled as she pressed her fingers lightly on the leg, ignoring her sister's cries, until she felt the bone. The thighbone was cracked in half but not splintered. "Move your toes, Fiona."

"I—I cannot."

Bronwyn's heart clenched. Fiona had obviously injured a nerve. She would have to straighten the bone, then immobilize it. But unfortunately, she would have to keep Fiona awake during the process to relieve the pressure on the nerve.

She looked at her sister. The suffering in her lovely eyes was hard to bear. "I will help you, but 'twill be difficult for you. There will be much pain. And I cannot give you any sleeping potion."

A flask of wine was shoved into her hands. "Make her drink this." Christophe held Bronwyn's gaze. " 'Twill help ease her suffering."

She nodded, wishing she could give her something stronger to dull the pain, and frustrated because she couldn't.

Fiona pushed the wine away. "Nay, I want it not."

Nicolas reached over and took the flask. "You must take it, my lady. If you do not, you will cause yourself and your poor sister needless suffering."

Fiona pursed her lips tightly together, then looked into the Norman's eyes. Several moments passed before she allowed him to place the flask to her mouth.

Bronwyn drew a deep breath and smiled at the Norman. He had succeeded where she had failed. His psychology was brilliant.

When Fiona had finished the flask, and her glazed eyes were half closed, Bronwyn directed the men to carry her sister to a pallet by the fire. She kept Fiona's leg secured as the men carried the patient across the room. Fiona's moans and cries tore at Bronwyn's reserve as each step caused her sister agony. When her sister was arranged on the pallet, Bronwyn bent to her task. "Hold her still," she commanded and felt the leg to determine how to pull each bone into place.

The break was worse than she had thought. She looked up, and was surprised to see Caradoc, who ordinarily couldn't stand to be around the sick. She turned and bade the servants, "Find me two slats of wood and several long strips of linen."

Not a trace of emotion crossed Caradoc's features. His gaze harsh, he leaned forward. "What do you wish of me?"

"Hold her shoulders while I set the leg. Christophe and Nicolas must help me pull the bones into place and tie the slats firm. No one can move her once this leg is set."

They nodded, and with great trepidation Bronwyn began. Perspiration covered her body. She truly did not want to do this, but there was no one else who could. Bronwyn was the healer, but Regan knew how dangerous this procedure was.

Her fingers traced the leg again, every muscle, every tendon. If she did not do this right, Fiona would be maimed for life, or she could die from infection. She felt the break. Gritting her teeth, she placed Christophe's hands above the break, and Nicolas's below, then her fingers returned to the injured area. "When I am ready, I want you to pull on her limb. We must separate the halves and realign them." Saying a silent prayer, she nodded to the men. Ever so gently they exerted pressure, pulling the broken ends apart. Her sister's anguished screams tore at her heart as she tried to reset the bone. "Fiona, move your toes," she commanded.

No movement occurred, and Bronwyn swallowed her failure to try again. Without an X-ray machine she could rely only on her hands and on the results that were visible.

"Nay, no more, Sister," Fiona begged.

Bronwyn steeled herself against her sister's pain and concentrated on her task. She squeezed Fiona's muscles together, feeling for the difference in their density. It took over three hours and several painful tries before she was sure the bone was in place, and Fiona could wiggle her toes. Bronwyn positioned the slats on either side of the thigh, then quickly bound the linen around it to hold the leg firmly in place until it healed. When she finally finished, her back was stiff and her shoulders tight with tension.

"She will mend," Christophe said.

She looked into his eyes. "I know," she replied, her sight blurred with tears. "But if the leg is not set right she will be left with a limp."

His arm went around her shoulders, pulling her into his

embrace. His lips grazed her forehead. "You did the best you could."

A shiver coursed through Bronwyn. She wanted to tip her head back and taste his lips. A need grew within her to be comforted, but she remembered her vow. Though it would be so easy to nestle deep into her husband's arms drawing the solace he offered, she wanted more.

Chapter Five

After the eventide meal Caradoc carefully snuck away from the men taking their ease from the hard day. Torches burned low, throwing shadows on the narrow hallways, as he crept toward the rendezvous.

A sudden draft of night air rushed through the hall. The candle flame wavered wildly as someone grabbed his tunic and pulled him into a small alcove. "I have just received more weapons from another chieftain. Later tonight we will hide them in the secret room."

In the flickering light the jagged vermilion scar that covered half of Rhett's face resembled the torn flesh of an animal's rotting carcass. Caradoc pulled his tunic free. "Good, but after today I cannot hide you and your men among our villagers. The warlord questioned the tally and wants an accurate account."

"Then find another way to deceive the warlord. We need more weapons if we are to attack." He slapped Caradoc on the back. "Hiding the weapons right here under Christophe Montgomery's nose was brilliant. I am sure the Welsh soldier who showed such mettle at tweaking the enemy will not disappoint me now."

Caradoc momentarily basked under the praise, but shook his

head. "The Normans are watching every move I make. My sister's accident gave us an opportunity to hide the weapons from the last raid. It will not be as easy next time." Caradoc's gaze suddenly narrowed as a nasty thought occurred to him. "Did you have anything to do with Fiona's injury?"

"We needed a diversion. I had little choice. Besides, she does not know who pushed her."

Caradoc grabbed Rhett by the throat. "You will pay for hurting her."

Rhett thrust Caradoc's hands away. " 'Tis common knowledge you struck her this very day. Or would you prefer that I pushed Bronwyn?"

"If you had harmed Bronwyn, I would kill you. But do not mistake my feelings for Fiona. She may be weak, but she is also my sister."

"Aye, but she is no Bronwyn." Ugly laughter filled the air as Rhett mocked Caradoc's anger. "That one is a true warrior. Do not forget our bargain. I will have her for my wife."

"As soon as the Norman is dead."

Rhett's eyes narrowed to thin slits. "You promised she would only have to say her vows, not bed him."

Caradoc shrugged. "He survived the poison."

"Do not make me regret my trust in you."

Caradoc felt a twinge of unease. Under Rhett's penetrating stare he straightened his shoulders and puffed out his chest. "Nor mine for you," he snapped.

Fiona moaned in her sleep. Nodding awake, Bronwyn patted her sister's arm, offering a soothing word of comfort. She pulled the covers up and helped her drink some wine. When Fiona slipped back into a fitful sleep, Bronwyn rested her head against her arm. She smothered a yawn and glanced about. The fire had died. Only glowing coals remained in the hearth while the candles sputtered, their wicks low.

" 'Tis late, my lady." Nicolas bent down and touched her arm. She blinked, noticing Nicolas and Christophe, then looked around to see the great hall empty of the warriors who had taken their meal earlier.

"I cannot leave her," she protested sleepily.

Nicolas looked at Fiona, and his features softened. "I will stay by her side. If she awakens, I will send for you."

"Thank you." She rose to her feet, her legs wobbly from the long hours spent in the cramped position. Nicolas reached out, but it was Christophe's hand that steadied her.

He guided her up the stairs and into their bedchamber. She smothered another yawn as he closed the door and barred it. " 'Twill be best if we have an understanding." He folded his arms across his chest and leaned against the door.

Her head shot up at the harshness of his tone. She eyed him warily, noting his rigid stance.

"What understanding?" she asked, combing her fingers through her tangled hair.

"The acts of rebellion must cease, or the consequences will be dire."

She gulped. "You cannot possibly hold me accountable."

"Because you did not draw back the bowstring, does not mean you did not supply the arrows."

He was right. She knew this. "I have done nothing to enflame them against you."

His smile did not reach his eyes. "It is not so much what you have done, but what you have failed to do. You will at all times give me the respect due the lord and master of this castle."

Her gaze slanted to the floor. "I have not shown you disrespect."

He stepped forward and touched her chin, lifting her gaze to meet his. "You will never disagree with me again in public." He held up his hand to stop her interruption. "And Bronwyn, I will no longer tolerate your family's disrespect."

Ah, her family. Now she understood. "My brother is a proud soldier—"

"*Oui,* he is a soldier, and knows what happens when you don't obey your commander's orders. You are a woman and therefore ignorant of the consequences; that is why I bother to explain."

Her gasp filled the air, and she spun around to leave.

He caught her wrist and pulled her back, catching her hard against his chest. He held her close, his lips inches from hers. "Your brother knows I will have him flogged if he ever dares question an order. And that goes for anyone else. Do you understand?"

"So there is always to be mistrust between us."

He looked down at her, his gaze intense. "I cannot forget the past."

Her gaze locked with his, and her chest constricted at the cold finality of his words.

Late that night, while others slept, Hayden met with his son in private. "Rhett is dangerous. I want this alliance dissolved."

" 'Tis too late." Caradoc ran a hand through his long hair. "He plans to attack the Normans before the castle is built. We must join with him if we are ever to realize our dreams."

"Nay, we have lost. I did not think it possible, but after seeing the forces the king has sent, I now understand the futility of resistance."

"If you do not support me, you stand with the enemy."

Hayden sighed, realizing he had done his son a disservice by indulging his every whim. "Caradoc, it is time you think of our people."

Caradoc's eyes widened. "What has happened to my family? Are you all cowards?"

Hayden's fist sent his son crashing to the floor. Panting, he stood over him, his fists clenched, ready to strike again. "Coward, is it?" he hissed angrily. "It was not I who injured an innocent maid."

At Caradoc's surprised then shamed expression, Hayden grunted. "Aye, I knew."

"I swear to you, Father, I did not know he planned such a thing."

Hayden held up his hand. "Hear me well, Son. We have little choice but to change. It is that, or certain death. If we join the Normans now we may secure a position for ourselves.

Let other Welshmen waste their time fighting the inevitable, but I forbid you to continue supporting Rhett in this rash manner.''

"Father, you do not understand. I have no choice.'' With a vile oath Caradoc turned and stormed away.

Unable to sleep, Christophe rose in the middle of the night. All day long, a problem had chased through his thoughts, and now he found he could not rid himself of the riddle. He ran a hand through his thick hair. He knew the answer lay just outside his conscious thought. He dressed to leave the room, but Bronwyn caught his eye. Her hair spilled out over his pillow like ropes of spun gold. A deep, almost painful longing grew inside him to feel the soft tresses beneath his touch. Her very image beckoned him back to bed. He watched the soft rise and fall of her breasts, and his mouth went dry as her soft, red lips parted slightly in sleep. He turned from the tantalizing sight. The woman disturbed him far too much. He had to think this out. Fang rose to accompany him.

"Stay,'' he commanded.

In the predawn hours Christophe walked the battlements. At the far post he found Lucien asleep on duty. "God's teeth.'' He grabbed the soldier by his tunic and shook him. The noxious fumes of ale assailed him. Lucien could not be roused from his drunken state, so Christophe dragged him over to the closest guard. "Call the captain on watch and have him place this lazy sot in the dungeon for the night. When he awakes, strip him of his rank and give him the worst assignment for a fortnight. I will stand his post until a man is awakened and comes to relieve me.''

Once the replacement arrived, Christophe continued his walk. The rest of his men were alert and standing their watch. Though they probably found his stroll unusual, they said nothing.

He knew a plot when he saw one. Too many corporate takeovers had left him with a sixth sense in such matters. Who had the most to gain? Answer that question and you would know the players.

Hayden? No, he was too smart a man. He would see the futility of resistance.

Caradoc? Now, he was one to watch. Young. Impetuous. Bold. But who else aided him? Who indeed? Pray God, it was not his lovely wife.

Troubled thoughts accompanied him as he marched through the castle. Arriving in the great room, he shook his brother awake.

"Assign someone to watch Caradoc."

Nicolas rubbed his eyes. "Don't you ever sleep?" he asked, rising from his pallet next to the injured girl.

"This could not wait. I trust no one but you."

Nicolas nodded. "What is it you suspect?"

He glanced at the sleeping girl and lowered his tone. "Not until today when Fiona was injured did I see the depth of Caradoc's hatred. He is the one behind the attacks. I am sure of it. But he has help. Whoever it is, they must be stopped."

Nicolas sighed heavily. "The fool jeopardizes his family. Nothing but sorrow can come from this."

Suddenly a woman's terrified scream rent the air. Christophe and Nicolas charged up the staircase and down the hall.

He found his door slightly ajar and thrust it open as he rushed into the room. Bronwyn sat up in bed, her eyes wide with fright. She pointed to the hearth, trembling, her breath coming in short gasps. He rushed across the room, but saw nothing.

He turned to his wife. "Did you have a nightmare?"

She shook her head and kept pointing to the fireplace as huge tears streamed down her face.

He went to his wife and wrapped his arms around her. "Tell me what happened."

"I." She hiccuped back a sob. "I awoke with a strange sensation. I felt someone's gaze on me. At first I thought I had dreamt it. Then I saw him hiding in the shadows." She pointed again to the hearth.

"His face was horribly scarred." She grabbed hold of his tunic. "His eyes seemed to glow from the firelight. I'll never forget it. He vowed he would have me, that he would bed me soon."

" 'Twas a dream, or Fang would have warned you."

Nicolas approached the bed. "Christophe, where is Fang?"

Christophe immediately turned and surveyed the room, his gaze traveled to the fur rug, but Fang was not there.

Apparently, there had been an intruder, and Fang had chased him away. He turned back to his wife. "Where did this man go?" Christophe asked.

"He was here, and then he was suddenly gone."

Christophe covered her hands and pulled her close as he spoke to his brother. "Take a look over by the hearth. And tomorrow see about a guard for my door." He turned to his wife. "Who would wish you ill?"

"I know of no one."

"Well, there is someone. You Welsh aren't as close as you thought."

Christophe rose and started for the door when a slight movement in the corner of the room caught his attention. The corner was dark and he pulled his sword free as he advanced. He saw a bundle of fur rugs thrown in the heap. But the pile moved. He lifted the covers carefully. "Oh, no! Fang," he whispered as he knelt down.

Bronwyn rushed to his side as Nicolas brought a torch closer.

Fang had been stabbed. He whimpered as Christophe stroked his fur.

"Nicolas, alert the guard, then return," Christophe commanded.

Nicolas placed the torch in a wall holder and sped from the room.

"Poor beast," she whispered. She touched Christophe's arm, her eyes filled with tears. "If you hold him, I will treat his wound."

"Fang," he said softly, and taking hold of her arm, he rubbed her palm over the wolf's fur. "Friend," Christophe commanded.

Christophe's eyes met hers over the wounded animal. "He will let you treat him now."

She nodded, and the compassion and pain in her gaze reached out to him.

Nicolas returned, and Bronwyn moved away so he could kneel beside his brother.

Bronwyn gathered her tray and said, "Nicolas, would you have some hot water brought to me?"

"*Oui,* my lady."

"Christophe, I will try my best to save him, but he has lost so much blood."

"Is there anything I can do?"

"Aye, fetch several clean sheets."

"Anything else?"

She wanted to whisper, aye, courage, she needed more courage, for this beast would surely bite her hand off. But she shook her head and he left. Once alone, she mixed several potions together, grabbed the wineskin, and knelt before the panting wolf. Mustering her courage, she reached out to the animal, praying he would not smell her fear. She gently raised the wolf's head and he whimpered. Compassion filled her at the pitiful sound. "You must take this," she soothed.

As though he understood, the wolf lapped the milky-white mixture that would ease his pain. She stroked the fur, waiting for the potion to take effect.

By the time Nicolas and Christophe returned, the animal was thoroughly drugged. She added wine to the water, then began to bathe the blood from his fur. The wound looked deep and bled profusely. Silently she prayed no vital organ or artery was pierced, and hopefully, only several layers of skin would require her sewing. She drew the needle and thread into her hand and poured the harsh spirits over both the thread and the wound. "Christophe, you must tear the linen into long strips for bandages. Once the wound is sealed, I must bind it."

He nodded and rose to rip the cloth into strips.

As Bronwyn waited, her hands began to shake. She tried to calm herself and still the horrible shaking, but after the events of the prior day she could not stop her trembling.

Christophe knelt beside her and held the wine to her lips. "'Twill steady your nerves."

She nodded, grateful he was so observant, and fairly gulped the liquid.

"Too much will defeat the purpose," Christophe warned, pulling the wine away.

Though he was absolutely right, she would never admit it. With the needle raised, she separated the fur to see the wound. "Nicolas, hold the light closer," she insisted, then ordered, "Christophe, I can't see, please wipe the blood away."

By the time the wolf's wound was tightly stitched, she felt as though she would collapse. She rinsed her hands, then softly stroked the animal's fur. Christophe touched her shoulder, then pointed to the bed. "You need to sleep."

"Nay, I will rest here until you come to bed."

His gaze held hers for a long moment. He looked as though he wanted to say more. Instead, he nodded, then left the room with Nicolas in his wake.

At dawn a messenger arrived and was received in the great room. Christophe Montgomery read the missive, then looked up and said, "You have had a long journey. Seek your rest."

When the messenger left the room, Christophe handed the missive to his brother. Nicolas briefly scanned the paper. "The king is leaving England and returning to Normandy. Is there trouble at home?"

"Keep your voice down. If we need reinforcements William's emissary, Lord Odo, might be reluctant to send them, for fear he will need his own men if there is an uprising in England or Scotland. Then again, William might need soldiers sent to Normandy for support. Lord Odo is a prudent man and hesitates when he should act." Christophe took the note, crushed it in his fist, and tossed it into the fire. "We will have our hands full. Our position is precarious. No reinforcements, a castle to build, and a revolt to put under." He shook his head.

"How can we defend this pitiful wooden fortress if we are attacked?" Nicolas spat.

Christophe ran a hand through his hair. "We need to fortify this structure, at the same time as constructing the new castle and the temporary quarters that will house the artisans."

"Do you really want to drive the people that hard?" Nicolas asked.

"*Oui,* I do," he said, slapping his brother on the back. "In the end they will thank us. Otherwise if we come under attack by the rebels, none of them would escape without injury."

Christophe returned to his room to find Bronwyn asleep on the floor with her arm over Fang. He shook his head at the sight. The ferocious animal picked up his ears slightly, but when he saw his master he relaxed and remained cuddled next to Bronwyn.

He stripped to retire, but the sight of the lonely bed looked uninviting. He lifted a fur robe off the pallet and carried it over to where Bronwyn rested. Carefully he covered her before slipping beneath the blanket. Exhausted, he smothered a yawn, drew her into his embrace, and as naturally as if he had always done it, lightly kissed her forehead before closing his eyes.

In the morning he left orders that the mistress was not to be disturbed and started his day's work. He told himself he was not softening toward her, that she had earned a rest.

When he returned for the midday meal, he was surprised to find her still sleeping. After he had sated his hunger, he sat down on the floor next to her. He ran his hand over her back. Her eyes blinked open several times before she awakened. "What time is it?"

"Midday."

"Oh, you should not have let me sleep." She leaned over the wolf, stroking his fur softly and whispering soothing words. Then she looked up. "Did you catch who did this?"

"*Non,* but once Fang is well, that will not be a problem."

She nodded, her golden hair rippling down her back as her amber eyes met his.

"Yesterday was extremely trying." He ran a hand through his hair. "But I promise you, *mademoiselle,* I will find and punish the attacker."

When she remained quiet, he wondered what was going through her mind. He hadn't figured her out, but he would.

"I would hazard to guess it will take several weeks before your charges are well enough to be left alone. You are free of your duties in the field until then. In the meantime you will care for your sister and Fang, and perhaps oversee the domestic problems here."

He moved closer to her, knowing he was lightening her load because she had earned it, not because he was showing her preference. "Can I count on you to do that?"

Her eyes widened. "Aye." Her lips parted slightly as she moistened them. "Thank you, my lord, for showing me such kindness."

He swallowed. He had momentarily lost his train of thought staring at her lips. Christophe Montgomery was a war-hardened soldier, not a besotted lover. Angry at himself for how easily she could distract him, he summoned the memory of the poison.

" 'Tis not kindness to change the duties of a servant."

Bristling, she raised her chin. "Has the master spoken?"

"He has." He rose and walked to the door.

She closed her eyes to calm herself as he left the room. He kept her at arm's length. She knew the exact moment he had seen her as a woman, and she knew the exact moment he had pulled back. How would she ever break down his barriers?

" 'Twould not be difficult," she murmured, stroking the wolf to ease her tension. " 'Twould be impossible."

Chapter Six

The plants were ankle high in the first month of summer. 'Twas a good sign. The spring weather had been mild, with enough rain and sunshine to make a farmer smile. Her sister's recovery was progressing, though she was still confined to her pallet. But Bronwyn's other patient had more difficulty. Twice she almost lost the wolf, but he had stubbornly managed to pull through. Over the past week he had recovered enough to accompany her on her walks. In fact, he had become her constant shadow. Thankfully, Christophe did not seem to resent the wolf's sudden defection.

Bronwyn wrapped up the last of the food in a linen cover. She had instituted many sanitary practices.

"Why is the master doing this, my lady?" Nesta asked, handing her a basket of bread while warily eyeing the wolf.

Bronwyn shrugged as she stowed the parcel, then reached down to run her hand over the animal's thick fur. " 'Tis the way he wished his food prepared."

"Not that, my lady. I don't mind a little soap and water before I cook. I wish to know why he works our men so hard."

Bronwyn sighed. She had no idea why Christophe behaved the way he did. "I am not privy to his thoughts."

The older woman looked her in the eye. "But you share his bed."

Her face flushed hot. "I am his wife, but also a Welshwoman. Do you really think he shares his plans with me?"

"I am sorry, my lady. But 'tis hard being treated as a child. My Wilford has his pride," Nesta said.

Bronwyn patted the cook's hand. "I will try to find out more."

"Bless you, my lady."

Bronwyn, Nesta, and Cordelia each carried a pailful of food out to the cart. Three more trips saw the food transferred from the kitchen to their travel conveyance. After sneaking Fang a juicy tidbit, Bronwyn looked around and frowned. Where was Caradoc? His job was to drive the cart to the workers.

"Cordelia, run to Caradoc's quarters and see what delays him."

After several minutes Cordelia returned. "My lady, he says he is too ill to drive the cart."

"Ill?" She shook her head. "I will have to drive the cart." With more bravado than sense, she climbed up onto the cart and looked down on Nesta as the wolf scrambled into the back. "Will you please see to Fiona, then look in on Caradoc? He might truly be ill."

"More likely he is up to no good," Nesta scoffed.

Cordelia stepped forward. "My lady, please do not do this. You have never driven the cart."

"I will be fine," she assured, waiting until the women entered the castle before muttering to Fang, "You might be safer if you stayed behind."

The wolf just nuzzled closer to her and closed his eyes, totally unconcerned.

"Then, we are both fools," she whispered, and gently snapped the reins. Fortunately, the well-trained horse knew what to do, which enabled her to drive the cart out of the courtyard.

"How am I to convince Christophe that Caradoc is sick

when I do not believe it myself?'' she mumbled to Fang, her brow furrowed. ''No wonder my husband doesn't have faith in me.'' Her emotions in turmoil, she considered her problem. ''I'm no closer to making him trust me than I was when I first awoke in his bed. Ha! What I need is to get beneath his skin like he does mine.''

The wolf whimpered at her increased agitation, cocking his head at her as though she made no sense. Then, as though giving up, he rested his head on his paws.

She smiled at his human reaction, then quietly contemplated her thoughts. Maybe being a modern woman put her at a disadvantage. Instead of being civilized, perhaps she needed to act more primitive.

The cart bumped along the deeply rutted road, and before long she turned into the field. Only two months had passed and already the foundation and part of the walls were done. She looked at the structure and felt awed. It truly was a backbreaking chore. But since Christophe's arrival they had managed both to fortify the old wood castle and start this one of stone.

Her calloused hands showed the effects. Though she had not built any of the castle, she had seen to the preparation and distribution of the daily meals. With the arrival of the three hundred Saxon artisans, every hand was needed to feed the additional work crew. In addition, for the last two weeks, she had ignored Christophe's order to remain in the castle and secretly labored in the fields. The women needed her help. Even now they were busy preserving the ripe spring berries so the winter months were not too lean.

''My lady,'' Sumner said, helping her down, then moving quickly to unload the barrels and baskets of food. As she reached for a basket, she noticed Nicolas running toward her.

''Good day, my lady.'' He took the basket from her, and stopped her from reaching for another bundle. ''How is your sister today?''

''Fiona is fine,'' she said, looking about somewhat hesitantly for her husband, but she did not see him. Ironically, this was one time she was thankful that his days were extremely busy.

Anxious to finish her chore before someone thought to question where her brother was, she pitched in and carried the heavy baskets along with the men. After the cart was unloaded, she hurried back to the Welsh fortress.

Not until she was safely inside the stable and the horse unhitched did relief wash through her. Thank God, she had managed to cover her brother's absence. She patted Fang. Her luck had held, and Christophe would never know about Caradoc.

"Wife?"

She whirled around. Her heart raced as she stared into Christophe's dark eyes and saw the storm brewing.

"What is this?" He pointed to the cart, his features harsh, his voice cold.

She hesitated, unwilling to lie, but afraid to speak her fears. "Caradoc is ill."

"I see." He folded his arms across his chest and raised an eyebrow as disbelief shadowed his stern expression. He continued to stare at her and she felt her courage fail under his emotionless regard.

Though uncertainty about Caradoc wound itself around her heart, there were others to consider. She took a deep breath and plunged forward. "I vow to you that I was told Caradoc is truly sick."

"If you swear he is sick, then I have no reason to doubt your word. Do I?" He turned to leave.

But he did, she could see it. Still, she would let the subject drop.

"My lord," she called out, running after him. "Might I have a word with you about another matter?"

He sighed and stopped to face her. "My lady, I pray you let this concern rest until tonight. I yet have much work to do."

She nodded, unused to the exhaustion in his voice. "Aye, my lord, it can wait." On impulse she reached up and brushed an errant lock of hair back from his brow.

He captured her hand and brought her palm to his lips. "My lady, I truly wish I had more time to devote only to you."

Her insides fluttered from the intimate contact. She drew a

shuddering breath as her body trembled. Then he turned on his heel and left.

She stared after the tall, thick-muscled warrior as he strode out of the stable doors and across the courtyard. Lord, but the man could drive all rational thought from her head. Once he was out of sight, she spared her constant shadow, Fang, a glance. "You could have warned me."

The wolf ignored her reprimand and sidled up next to her for a pat.

"Just like your master," she whispered, and ran her hand through the thick fur, wishing it was the crisp short hair on Christophe's chest beneath her fingers. A memory suddenly sprang to life—his powerful body, naked in the firelight, the solid, flat plane of his stomach and bulging muscles of his arms and legs like a bronzed statue come to life. His blatant masculinity touched a chord within her.

She shook her head to dispel the sensuous picture. Fanning herself to cool down, she admitted Christophe played far too much on her mind for her own good.

On her way from the stable, Braden, the castle's farrier, stopped her. "My lady, wait." He ran up to her with two bundles tucked under his thickset arms. "Are these to your liking?" The blacksmith withdrew the lovely set of utensils she had commissioned.

"Oh, they are beautiful." The flatware was remarkably simple, but the plain forks, knives, and spoons delighted her. Granted, they were crude, but she would have rejoiced over chopsticks.

"And these, my lady?" Braden produced another bundle, and she gasped at the sight of such precision. After having to make do with those damn bread trenchers, it would be heaven to eat off a plate.

"My lady, please do not cry. I will do it again if you are not pleased."

"Oh, Braden, I am happy, not sad." She hadn't realized how homesick she was until she saw the simple convenience.

A relieved smile brightened his weathered face. " 'Tis hard

to tell if one is happy these days. I am glad I could bring you some joy."

"You must take pride in your accomplishments. They are truly works of art."

He scratched his head. "I am sorry, my lady, but I cannot see the warriors using such items."

She chuckled at his doubtful expression. "Do not worry, Braden. I promise you, 'twill be more popular than falconing."

His widened eyes revealed his opinion.

"Never mind," she smiled. "Time will prove my words true."

"I hope so, my lady. Though I fear the master may find these not to his liking." After handing her the bundles, he tipped his hat and departed.

"Wait, Braden." She had almost forgotten her ring and the engraving she wished to have done.

"My lady?"

She removed her ring. "I wish you to etch three words into the band. Can you do it?"

He studied the band for several seconds. "What are the words you wish?"

She was about to tell him when she realized he probably couldn't read or write. "I will show you," she offered, following him to the blacksmith's building. There she drew the words on a board with a piece of charcoal: Believe in love.

He scratched his head. "Are these like the utensils?"

She laughed and shook her head. "Nay, this is something I wish to pass down to future generations until the one person who needs the message reads the words."

"My lady, my dear wife feels the same about her tunics."

Bronwyn smiled. Picking up her bundles, she left the farrier, and her thoughts quickly returned to Christophe. After the blacksmith's disparaging words, she thought Christophe might not like her innovations. She shrugged and lifted the bundles, shifting their weight as she walked back across the courtyard. " 'Tis time to tame the beast," she mumbled, then chuckled out loud as she recalled her earlier thoughts. "Just call me *Wild*

Thing," she said, laughing and humming the song as she walked toward the kitchen.

Within the dim confines of the kitchen she unrolled the bundles on a clean worktable and offered the newly made utensils to Nesta.

A perplexed expression crossed the cook's features as her gaze traveled over the strange-looking gift before her. She raised her flour-covered hands from the bread dough and wiped them on a linen cloth as she approached the table to study the new marvels. "These are for me, my lady?"

"Aye, they will help in the preparation of the food. And these . . ." She held up a knife, a fork, and a spoon. ". . . are so the people you cook for can enjoy your efforts without using their fingers."

Nesta's brown eyes narrowed. "And what be wrong with their fingers?"

She sighed. "Nothing, Nesta, but if their hands are dirty and sweaty, how can they appreciate the delicate spices and delicious herbs you use to season their meats?"

As though the idea suddenly had merit, Nesta turned to her kitchen maids. "Gwen and Cordelia, be quick about helping me unpack these. Only the finest cooks use . . ." She turned to her mistress for assistance.

"Cutlery," Bronwyn supplied.

Upon seeing the joy on Nesta's face, Bronwyn leaned forward and whispered. "I have a special recipe that will save you time now that we have the plates and utensils. 'Tis called a casserole, and this is how you make it." After disclosing her casserole recipe, Bronwyn stepped back to see the woman's reaction.

Nesta walked around tapping her finger to her chin. "I've never known you to cook, my lady."

For a minute she held her breath, then smiled. "As of late I have been giving it a lot of thought."

Nesta winked knowingly. " 'Tis time that you did."

Now she understood how con men worked. People wanted to believe the best. Out of necessity, she was getting very adept at lying.

After checking on Fiona and talking with her father, she hurried to see how Caradoc fared. When she rapped on his door and failed to gain a response, unease swept through her. With a sinking dread she pushed the door open and entered his room.

The bed was empty. She turned full circle, dismayed by his deception. He was gone. She stormed down the steps, an unladylike two at a time, and rushed into the great room. "Have you seen Caradoc?" she asked her father and sister.

Hayden shook his head, but Fiona looked at her and sadly nodded. "He said he was meeting his destiny."

"Dear God," Hayden whispered.

"When did he leave?" Bronwyn asked. Every fiber in her heart knew that her brother's treachery would cost them all dearly.

"Midday."

Hayden's eyes clouded over. "I told him to stop this foolishness."

Fiona leaned forward on her pallet and reached for Hayden's hand. "Father, do not worry so. You will make yourself sick."

Hayden looked past Bronwyn and his face suddenly paled.

A shiver of apprehension coursed through her. Please don't let it be Christophe, she thought, and turned to find her husband but a few feet away. How long had he been there? What had he overheard? "I did not know," she whispered.

He shook his head as he covered his sword with his hand. "More of our weapons and armor are missing." His icy gaze chilled her. "You cannot protect him."

Dread traveled through her at his harsh words. "What are you going to do?"

Christophe's level gaze never wavered. "I am going to find him, try him, and punish him."

"Nay," she begged, cringing at Bronwyn's memory of a man being whipped. She grabbed his tunic in her fists and pounded his chest. "You cannot."

"Did I not warn you what would happen?" He removed her hands.

"But he does not deserve to be flogged," she whispered.

"My lady, he has earned his punishment. Not only are the weapons missing, but he also injured a guard." He grabbed her wrist. "Come, the man needs your attention."

As he dragged her away, she turned to see tears in her father's eyes.

"My lord, please, I beg you, do not punish him. I fear my father cannot stand to see his son so disgraced."

"He has left me no choice."

"Everyone has a choice," she argued as he pulled her to the armory. "You choose to do this."

He rounded on her so fast she lost her footing and stumbled backward. *"Non,* woman, I *must* do this. I *have* to."

Hot tears rose into her eyes. "If you flog him I will never forgive you."

"I will live with that. The law must apply to all, or it will fail."

"But surely there can be mercy, too."

"I am showing mercy. I could have him executed."

The moment they entered the room and she saw the bloody gash on the back of the soldier's head, a glimmer of hope burned in her breast.

She turned to Christophe. "Your man was struck from behind and could not have seen the face of his attacker."

Christophe's face tightened and he pointed to the polished shield on the wall. "Michau saw Caradoc's reflection just before the blow."

Her stomach churned beneath Christophe's condemning glare. She knelt beside the warrior and examined the cut. "I will need to stitch it." To calm her nerves, she inhaled deeply. She had sutured a wolf, but this was a man, and the magnitude terrified her.

Her hands shook as she sent a servant for her healing tray, then rose to put the kettle into the fire.

The endless fighting would have to stop. She had thought her brother knew that. Her father had assured her that Caradoc would honor the truce.

Michau was a good man. He had never caused her or the others any trouble. In fact, except for Lucien, all of Christophe's men were chivalrous to a fault. She had never expected the conquering army to be this way.

"Please." She looked to the servant holding the candle. "If you would hold the light closer, I will make short work of this job."

She touched the wounded soldier's shoulder. "I do not wish to hurt you, but it cannot be helped. Please forgive me."

"My lady, I have been stitched before. Do not distress yourself," Michau said.

She smiled at his brave response. "Thank you."

Michau took a long pull on his ale, then signaled her to begin. She threaded the needle, but before starting, she took the strong brew from his hand.

"I will return it in a minute," she answered his protest. She poured a small amount over her needle, then her hands, and finally a liberal amount on his wound.

At his hiss of indrawn breath, she leaned over and handed him the ale, whispering in his ear, "I know it was painful, but it will aid in the healing."

She did not think of what she was doing. She had to focus on the cut and the crude sutures that must join the jagged edges together.

Though it only took a few minutes, she felt each pierce of the needle, and the job seemed to last forever. When she tied off the last stitch, her hands were covered in blood. She washed several times, nearly scrubbing her skin off to rid her hands of the red stain before drying them on a linen towel. She turned to bandage the wound and felt the room sway. The sight of blood had always disturbed her. Steadying herself, she took a deep gulp of air and quickly reached for her patient's ale. After swallowing the potent brew she handed the ale back to the dumbstruck soldier, then reached for the linen strips. When she finished, she sank down, physically and emotionally exhausted. Without a word Michau offered her more of his ale. Smiling weakly, she accepted another sip.

A soldier entered and bowed before Christophe. "My lord, we can find no trace of the Welshman, Caradoc. No one has seen him since early today."

Christophe nodded and dismissed the man.

Secretly pleased, she mentally toasted her brother's escape by swallowing another gulp of Michau's numbing brew. Hayden would not suffer the agony of seeing his son punished; and she, thankfully, would not be caught between her husband's wishes and her brother's.

Christophe took the ale from her grasp, handing it to Michau. "My lady, thank you for caring for my man." His voice was impersonal as he extended his hand.

She tried to focus on his face, but it was so fuzzy.

Michau reached over and patted her hand. "You have a very gentle touch, my lady, as well as a mighty thirst." He grinned, tipping the empty tankard over.

Again she tried to focus and blinked rapidly, but that only made Christophe's image blur even more.

Christophe leaned forward to help her up, and she placed a trembling hand in his. "I might add, Wife, that if your stomach is so weak, perhaps you should train another healer."

What was Christophe talking about? It was her brother that was causing her distress. The dizziness persisted, and she knew it was not from nerves, but the Norman ale. Oh, no! She was drunk.

"My lord, could we discuss this later? I fear I am to be sick."

After helping her to their quarters, he placed her gently on the bed. Fang wasted no time in jumping up to lie beside her. "Do not worry, the effects will wear off in a few hours."

"I am sorry, Christophe. I did not know your ale was so strong." She yawned.

"I think my men will be injuring themselves just to have a delightful drinking partner," he said drolly.

"I'm so glad I provided you with entertainment," she said glumly.

He softly chuckled. Covering her with the blanket, he brushed a kiss on her forehead. "Sleep, Bronwyn. By supper you will be feeling better."

She *must* be drunk! Christophe was actually being nice to her.

* * *

The men sat looking perplexed. Several lifted their plates, looking under them for their bread trenchers, while others held up the knives. " 'Tis a very small dagger," one Norman whispered.

"Perhaps my lady's bout with our ale has addled her wits," Michau said, eliciting guffaws from his comrades, who had all heard the story.

Bronwyn continued to set the table, assuming a blasé air she was far from feeling. Her head ached from the Norman ale, and troubled thoughts drifted in and out of her muddled mind. Worse yet, Christophe's watchful gaze unnerved her. She felt like a bug under a microscope.

"My lady, exactly what is this?" Nicolas asked, holding up a fork and staring at it as though it came from hell.

"For pricking a slow servant," a soldier answered before Bronwyn could.

She turned to Nicolas and came face-to-face with Christophe's curious scrutiny. "They are eating utensils."

"Our fingers are not good enough?" Lucien challenged, his expression hostile.

Fang stood at her side and his lip curled in a silent snarl.

Apprehension spiraled inside her. "Nay, but you work so hard. Some of you have not even had time to wash before sitting down to eat." She walked over and turned Lucien's hand palm up, revealing the grime. "I thought these utensils would enhance the meal by keeping your food free of the dirt that still resides on your skin."

Lucien's face tightened angrily as his fellow Normans chuckled at the barb. He ripped his hand from her hold. "Are you insinuating that Norman manners are inferior to Welsh?"

Though her stomach twisted into knots, her answer was smooth. "Not at all, kind sir. Whether or not you use these is up to you."

Silence descended on the hall as Lucien glared at her. Disgust shone in his beady dark eyes, but she held his gaze and raised her chin.

Christophe said nothing, but he picked up the knife and fork. He began eating as though he had always used them, without error or awkwardness. She marveled that he could do so without being shown, but then he constantly surprised her. He had so many talents. She sighed, thankful for his silent support.

The other soldiers immediately followed his example. Though their efforts were not as smooth as their master's, they were quick to learn.

"My lady, this is truly remarkable," one soldier called out, pleased by the innovation.

"Daughter, this is a wonder," Hayden said, holding up the meat he had cut and speared with his fork.

When Christophe called her to his side, she eagerly turned from Lucien's contempt.

"Where on earth did you come up with this idea?"

"My . . . my grandmother talked about this, but never had the chance to do it. I decided to follow through on her idea, but added a few improvements of my own."

As though testing the truth of her words, his brow furrowed. He studied her for a moment, before his features softened. "Wife, the next time you wish to improve our lot, I suggest you ask me first."

"But, my lord, is not the care and comfort of the castle my domain?"

He inclined his head. "Indeed it is. However, as a courtesy, I ask you to consult me first."

"Then as a courtesy I shall." She leaned down and whispered in his ear. "Thank you."

His lips brushed across her cheek before she could pull away. "You are most welcome."

Bronwyn's heartbeat raced at his touch. When she looked back, his features were solemn. She could almost believe she had imagined his kiss.

She had just begun to relax at her meal when a sudden commotion at the door gained her attention. "Dear Lord," she gasped as two guards hauled her brother through the hall, not stopping until they stood before the warlord.

In the descending silence, scuffling footsteps echoed in the room, and all eyes centered on the prisoner.

"Release me," Caradoc shouted, viciously fighting the soldiers as they tried to hold him still.

Her heart clenched as Christophe rose from his supper and walked around the table to stand in front of Caradoc. She glanced at Hayden. Expecting his usual stoic expression, she felt her throat constrict at her father's naked pain. Moisture rimmed his eyes as he gazed at his beloved son.

Chairs tipped over as Welshmen gathered together, softly voicing their fears as they watched their former master held captive by the Norman soldiers.

"Caradoc Llangandfan, I charge you with the theft of our weapons and the attack on Michau. What say you?"

Still struggling, Caradoc's gaze was belligerent. "I am innocent."

"You pleaded sick, yet your pallet was unused."

"When I felt better I decided to get a breath of fresh air."

Christophe folded his arms across his chest and stood legs apart, braced for battle. "I say you lie."

Caradoc's expression turned wary. "If I am guilty of anything, 'tis laziness, not lying."

Normans yelled out their scorn for his excuses.

After Bronwyn patted her father's arm, she stepped into the center of the room beside her husband.

"My lord, would you allow me to plead on his behalf?"

Christophe looked at her and frowned. "You have that right."

"My brother is willful and used to having his own way. He expected to inherit this land. The loss of our home and customs does not come easy to any of us, but to him, it is especially hard. I ask for your mercy, sir. He is young and needs time to learn the wisdom of peace."

"Hear! Hear! Well said, Daughter," Hayden called out, lifting his chalice. The rest of the Welsh raised their mugs and voices, but the Normans did not.

"Although I understand your argument, my lady, the law must stand. I do not doubt that this is hard on Caradoc, but it is hard on everyone. Yet, Caradoc is the only one who rebels. He will be taken out to yon courtyard at daybreak and flogged."

Her heart plummeted to her stomach. "Nay! That is barbaric! You cannot whip him like a beast of burden."

He rounded on her, his stance towering and his expression hard. "Do you question my decision?"

She drew a deep breath and raised her chin. "Indeed I do. Justice will not be served by a public whipping."

"Would you ask another to take his place?"

At once her father stepped forward. "Nay, Father, you cannot!"

Hayden ignored her as he marched into the center of the room. His complexion was gray, and his eyes seemed to belong to an older man. He opened his mouth to speak, then suddenly he grabbed his chest. He tried to talk, reaching out to his son, then collapsed.

"Father," Fiona cried out as Bronwyn rushed to Hayden's side. He was breathing shallowly. Pressing her ear to his chest, she listened to the irregular beat of his heart. She suspected angina. The extent and severity was impossible to know. She loosened his tunic and adjusted his clothes. When his color did not worsen, and the panic lessened in his eyes, she said to the soldiers, "Please carry him to his chambers." Shooting Christophe a damning glare, she quickly sent for her tray of medicines, then stood and accompanied the litter to the stairs.

Her father held her hand as they climbed the narrow staircase. "Bronwyn, you must help your brother."

"Shush," she soothed as they entered his chamber and the soldiers placed him in bed.

He gripped her hand so hard the bones ached. "Bronwyn," he begged in a hoarse whisper, "help Caradoc. Your husband will listen to your plea."

"I will go and see what can be done, if you drink this medicine," she said while mixing a strong sleeping potion. The medicine had helped him in the past, and she prayed it would ease his pain now. She lifted his shoulders so he could swallow the dark liquid with more ease.

When the last drop was gone he pushed the cup away. "Go! Do not fret over an old man. 'Tis just a spell that I have had before. I shall be fine by tomorrow."

Though she wanted to stay, she held her tongue. He was too ill to argue. She left after bidding the servants to watch over him, and ran down the stairs.

Caradoc was still being held in the great room when she returned. Not a soul had left since her departure. Her husband raised an eyebrow at her hasty entrance. "Father is very ill, but he would not rest until I gave my vow to help Caradoc."

"I need no help from a woman," Caradoc snapped, his handsome face contorted with rage.

Christophe was upon her in an instant. He grabbed her arm and she tried to pull away, but his painful grip only increased. "Do you dare defy me?"

Silence descended on the hall, and Caradoc looked incensed.

Tears sprang into her eyes as she swallowed her fear. Her father was too frail to protect his only son. She looked at her brother. His arrogant features had crumbled into a mask of belligerence.

She shivered and glanced back at the lord and master. "My brother swears his innocence."

Grumbles filled the hall. Christophe studied the men before turning back to her, his face harsh, his eyes like cold chips of steel.

Fear sliced through her, but she met and held his gaze.

"Take him to the irons and see no one gives him aid," Christophe barked, his eyes filled with fury.

Her mouth went dry.

"And take the lady to the dungeon, as well!"

Her gasp was hardly audible, but the wolf's snarl held the soldiers at bay, which angered Christophe further. "Come," he commanded the animal, pointing to the floor at his side.

For a brief moment it seemed Fang would disobey him, then reluctantly, with head lowered, the wolf did as he was ordered.

As two soldiers took hold of Bronwyn's arms, Christophe

leaned close to her. "You thought I would treat you differently.
You were wrong."

Her throat tightened. "Indeed I was." She refused to
acknowledge the ache within her chest and held her head up
high. "Indeed I was."

"I am not a man to be manipulated. You should have learned
that by now."

"You are half right, my lord. You are not a man." The
momentary flare of rage in his eyes gave her a small measure
of comfort as they led her to the dungeon.

Torches burned low as she descended the steps in silence.
The flicker of light barely cast shadows against the wall as her
footsteps echoed in the cavernous depths. An ominous shiver
passed through her as her foot hit the ground, and she crossed
the dirt foundation that smelled of musty fungus and decay to
enter a small cell.

All the while Michau was shackling her wrist to the wall,
he avoided her eyes. When he was finished, he whispered,
"Courage, my lady." Then he turned and left. The cell door
closed with a sharp finality. She heard the guard's footsteps
recede as they left the dungeon.

"Bronwyn," Caradoc's deep voice interrupted her thoughts.

"Where were you?" she asked, straining against her bonds.

"I had an errand to run."

"Did you steal the weapons and hurt the guard?" she asked,
praying he would deny it, that it was all a terrible mistake.

"What difference does it make?"

Her heart sank. "Father gave his word. We must honor it."

"Father is wrong," he spat.

"Nay, you are, but even so, Father was willing to take your
whipping."

"He is too old. I would not have allowed it."

"I spoke out on your behalf because that old man bade me
to." She moved slightly, trying to find a position that would
lessen the pull of the irons and discovered the rough wooden
timbers of the dungeon scratched her back.

"Bronwyn," he warned.

"If you do not stop your scheming, you will kill him."

"Leave be, Sister. If I wish to hear a sermon I will attend church."

She shook her head at his selfishness and closed her eyes.

She had a long night to pass—a long frightening night. Every time she thought of her husband, a painful ache filled her. How could he do this to her? No. She could not allow herself to dwell on his actions. Her only hope was to remain strong.

But Christophe had opened a wound in her heart, and she feared she would never heal from his cruel treatment. So absorbed was she in her own misery that she was startled by the sound of a door creaking open. "Caradoc?" she called out softly, her heart pounding with trepidation.

Hushed voices sounded, the whispered conversation too muffled to understand.

"Caradoc, is that you?"

Finally his face appeared in the door's small opening.

"Bronwyn, I am sorry. I must leave. I wish I could take you with me."

"You are leaving?" She could not believe it. Did he not understand the consequences of his actions? Dear God!

"I cannot take you with me. Please try to understand."

Again she heard the fierce whispers in the background. Her brother frowned and nodded, then he was gone.

Bronwyn gave way to tears. What was she doing here? Why had God sent her to this barbaric time, to suffer this fate? Worse, what would Christophe do tomorrow when he found he had only her to punish?

Chapter Seven

Caradoc's escape left Bronwyn truly alone. The torches had burned out, and the dank smell of earth and mold seemed to grow stronger with each passing minute, until every breath she drew nearly gagged her. Though she had been handicapped in her past life, she had never felt vulnerable. Now, shackled to the wall, her hands drawn above her head, she was completely helpless. She fought against her bonds, and the manacles rubbed her wrists raw, while the rough texture of the wall dug into her back. Exhausted, she dozed off several times. But each time, her knees buckled beneath her, causing agonizing pain to shoot through her arms and shoulders and awaken her. Forced to stand up and still, her muscles ached. What seemed like hours could have been only minutes; she had no way to gauge the passage of time. She tried not to think about what kind of animal was scurrying around and making those hideous scratching sounds. When something brushed against her foot, she screamed and kicked the vermin away. It let out a shrill, high-pitched squeal, confirming her suspicions. A quiver of revulsion overtook her. She stayed awake, for fear the rat would return to gnaw on her foot. Perspiration dotted her upper lip and forehead as she fought against her fears.

To dispel her mounting panic, she tried to focus on pleasant memories from her past life. Unbidden, Drew's face appeared in her mind's eye. His arrogant manner reminded her of Christophe. It was uncanny how much he had in common with her medieval husband. She chuckled out loud. He would be appalled to hear her think him primitive. Thinking admiringly of his determination and strength, she actually missed Drew, and prayed he was happy wherever he was. Despite their differences, their debates had made her feel intelligent and alive.

But she was alone now, and the only one who challenged her was Christophe. It seemed unlikely they would ever reach any kind of common ground.

The hours passed slowly. Even though she was terrified of this black pit, she dreaded dawn, knowing they would then discover her brother's escape, leaving her to be his scapegoat.

Almost as though her thoughts had been put into action, she heard the stairway door swing open and bang against the wall. The sound echoed in the dungeon, and a glimmer of light shone through the slits in her door. Several footsteps sounded on the wood steps as two guards descended the staircase.

Her breath caught in her throat as she listened to them open Caradoc's cell. Within seconds bedlam broke loose as the guards sounded the alarm. At once, more men raced down the steps, and before long, her door crashed open, letting in a harsh, blinding light.

"Where is your brother?"

Blinking against the painful glare, she glimpsed a silhouette of a man and an animal outlined by brilliant light. Even if she hadn't recognized Christophe's voice, the image was too reminiscent of her wedding day.

"Caradoc is gone?" she innocently asked.

"You do not claim this is a surprise?"

As she adjusted to the light, she was able to look him in the eye. "Nay." She shook her head, there was no use pretending. "But I do not know where he went."

"Pity," he said, but his voice held none. It was as cold and unfeeling as his expression.

"Why?" She held her breath as fear again shot through her.

His gaze traveled over her in a slow appraisal, lingering on her breasts and hips. Her heart beat so madly she was sure he could see her pulse flutter in her neck. When his dark eyes met hers, all the moisture in her mouth dried. She licked her lips and lowered her gaze from his. He moved closer to her, his hand covering her shackled ones. Fang whimpered, but was silenced by his harsh command. She felt the intimate press of his body as he pinned her to the wall. "Someone must take his punishment. As of last night, you were his only champion."

Her throat ached from the lump that formed. "You would truly expect that of me?"

" 'Twas not I but you who wished to spare your brother pain."

She closed her eyes. Her counterpart had been terrified of Christophe Montgomery. She had thought him to be a sadistic brute. A shiver coursed over her skin. It would appear that the original Bronwyn had seen his character far better than she.

His breath fanned her face, and her eyes flew open. "I missed you last night," he whispered. "Do you really wish to feel the whip rather than my caress?"

His lips covered hers, and with her hands shackled beneath his, she could not move. Her body instinctively strained against his, meeting his silent demand with her own. When she ended the kiss, she was amazed to find her hands free to hold him. "Well, my lady?" he said, drawing her into his arms.

"I no more wish to feel the whip than you would. But you, Husband, not I, must make the decision."

"You cannot be permitted to challenge me in front of my men. Therefore, you must beg for mercy before everyone."

She lowered her gaze.

He led her out of the dungeon and through the great room. Her sister's face was filled with terror.

"Bronwyn!" Fiona cried, and Hayden rose slowly from his seat beside her pallet.

Christophe sighed, and stopped. Bronwyn's heart broke at the sight of her family's pain. Hayden's color seemed dangerously pale; he should not be out of bed.

"My lord," Hayden staggered forward. "Take me instead."

"Bronwyn has made her decision."

She touched her father's arm. "I will be fine, rest now."

Hayden could stand no longer, and Christophe helped him back to his chair. Hayden clung to the warlord's arm. "I beg of you, do not harm my child."

Christophe whispered in the old man's ear, and Hayden's hands fell away as he sank back into the chair.

Christophe straightened and returned to her, his face a hardened mask as he silently escorted her to the courtyard, where her people lined the inner yard. The Normans stood behind the villagers, swords drawn.

All eyes fell on her, but hers were fixed on the pole in the middle of the square. The very sight of the barbaric whipping post struck terror into her heart. Her time had never prepared her for this type of justice.

Christophe left her alone by the pole. She met his gaze and knew what must be said. Her pride be damned. "My lord, I humbly beg your mercy."

Sweat trickled down her skin as she waited for him to grant his pardon. Suddenly it occurred to her that he might whip her anyway to set an example. He had not promised her anything. The moments stretched into eternity, and with them, her nerves. When at last he spoke, she had convinced herself that he would make an example of her.

"I want it understood that no one is above the law, not even my wife."

A gasp went through the crowd, and she closed her eyes, unable to bear any more. His words washed over her, but she heard nothing. In her mind she could see the whip flaying skin, hear the sound of her flesh being torn and her own agonizing screams. This could not be happening to her. But it was, and when a hand touched her arm, her knees buckled and she fainted.

Christophe quickly caught her in his arms and shook his head. He had watched the terror cross her features and knew she had not heard his reprieve. He carried her through the courtyard to the castle and up toward the master chamber with

Fang at his heels. She stirred in his arms, and her eyelashes fluttered open.

"My lord?" She placed her palm on his chest as she tried to sit up in his embrace and look around.

"You fainted."

"Are you going to carry out the whipping?"

Her eyes were woefully large, two huge amber pools of doubt. He hugged her close as he climbed the stairs and entered their room, to lay her tenderly on their bed. *"Non,* if you had not fainted you would have heard that I do not hold you accountable for your brother's actions."

She sat up onto her elbows, her bewilderment evident. Fang joined her, snuggling close.

He nodded to the courtyard below. "Like you, they would not believe in Norman justice until they witnessed it."

"You have strange ways. I thought Normans do not spare their conquered."

He ran a hand over the back of his neck. "If this land is to heal, and all the people survive, we must work together."

She stared at him. "You believe this?"

"Oui, I do."

She touched his face tentatively, as though she were seeing him for the first time. "What do you suggest?"

He took a deep sigh. Though his logic warned against it, he had decided to give her a chance. "Perhaps it is time that we start anew. I tell you, *cherie,* if you work with me, together we can build an empire."

Caradoc looked at Rhett over the campfire. "How did you get into the dungeon?" He had thought the man would be miles away after the diversion, instead of only several leagues from the castle, hidden safely in a coastal cave.

Rhett's laughter filled the cavern. "I would not leave you to rot, my friend. But you should have let me take your sister, too."

Caradoc surveyed the cold damp lair with distaste. The sea foam crashed outside, the spray dotting the floor with small puddles; while further back, stores of meager supplies lined the moss-covered walls. "Nay, this is too hard a life for a woman. We will rescue her when our forces grow stronger."

"Remember, she is mine. How magnificent she was standing up to the Norman and offering her tender back to the whip to save her brother. She is a woman worthy of a king."

Caradoc nodded, though for the first time since joining forces with this clansman, doubts began to plague him. His father's words came back to haunt him, and he suddenly wondered if he had indeed made a grave mistake.

In an inebriated stupor Lucien swilled his ale as he loudly lamented the fact that their leaders had all gone soft. "Useless cowards every last one of them."

"Be quiet, you braggart," Michau ordered. He looked to the other men who were slowly rising from the table. Only a fool would remain in the company of a man who spoke such treasonous thoughts out loud.

Lucien lifted his head. He looked at them through red-rimmed eyes and swallowed his tankard. "There was a time when Christophe Montgomery would have executed anyone, man or woman, for the slightest infraction. That Welsh whore has bewitched him."

With a grunt he dropped his head on the table, content with his own misery and thoughts.

Michau shook his head in disgust and left.

Nicolas's lips thinned as he stood unobserved in the opposite doorway. The departing soldiers had proven their loyalty, but Nicolas did not like what was happening. After several questions to the Normans on watch he found his brother in the armory.

He quickly explained what he had chanced to overhear. "He is bitter about the demotion."

"He has only himself to blame for being drunk while on duty."

Nicolas nodded. "I know. But he blames you."

"I am aware of the man's poor attitude. But as long as he does not defy me openly, I can do nothing."

Nicolas was puzzled at his brother's mild response. The old Christophe would have moved swiftly to eliminate the threat. "When he learns that William has left for Normandy, he may challenge you," he said worriedly.

"Mayhap, though I think he is more wind than substance," Christophe replied. "But I promise you, I will be prepared."

In the fortnight since her brother's departure, the castle had fallen into an almost peaceful and comfortable routine.

For the first time since her miraculous appearance here, Bronwyn felt satisfaction from the orderly unfolding of her days. Christophe deserved the lion's share of the credit. Under his rule the land and the people both prospered, and the animosity seemed to be lessening. She smiled as she looked around at the women and children in the field. It was a beautiful day and all seemed right with the world. Fang whimpered and whined, and she looked about to see the reason for the wolf's distress. Nothing seemed wrong and she reached down to pat the animal. To her surprise his body trembled. "What is it, boy? What's wrong?"

Suddenly a deep rumble reverberated beneath her feet, and thunder sounded, though the sky was clear. Bronwyn thought she was seeing things as trees wavered and the massive wooden citadel swayed. Another tremor shook and sent her staggering as the ground shuddered and quivered. A sharp crash resounded and she gasped as she watched the Welsh castle crack in half, the bulky supports giving way under the pressure of the shaking earth.

A waking nightmare unfolded before her eyes. "Fiona," she moaned, knowing her sister along with other servants and guards were trapped in the crumbled structure. Unable to comprehend the devastation, she stood mesmerized, shaking her head in denial even as the chaos continued.

Timbers, the full width of a huge tree, snapped like small twigs, and the sound of destruction filled the air. Frightened peasants screamed and began to run, frantic to go home. Village huts collapsed, but thankfully, most occupants were in the fields preparing the land for the harvest or at the construction site.

Although the Normans' solid stone foundation had withstood the earthquake, it had creaked and swayed, shaking the frightened workers until they had toppled over like drunken sots.

Terrified mothers cried and clasped their wailing children close in their arms. Bronwyn herded the women and children into the open, far away from the wavering trees. Christophe ordered his men to remain on the solid foundation, but away from the walls.

When the ground stilled and the dust finally settled, Bronwyn looked up to find the great wooden castle had completely collapsed. Oh, my God! She started running toward her home, Fang howling at her side.

Christophe rushed toward her, intercepting her halfway to her destination. "Help the villagers," he shouted.

"Nay," she screamed, tears in her eyes. "My sister is in there." She broke free of his hold and ran ahead.

Hayden, puffing and gasping for air, was already trying to help the men to move the timbers and unearth those buried inside. Tears streamed down Bronwyn's face as she clawed at the earth and wood until Christophe's strong hands clasped her arms and pulled her from the rubble. "Do not worry, Lady Wife, we will rescue those inside."

He held her close, but she fought him. "Please let me go, I must find her. She is helpless—they all are!"

He shook her gently. "I promise you, we will find those trapped, but you are in our way."

She wrapped her arms around him, needing his strength, and silently begging God's mercy.

He tilted her chin up and brushed her lips with his. "Take your father. Go help the women and children. They need you now, too."

She stared at him, then nodded.

He was right. Her arms slipped from his side and she took two steps away before turning back. "Please, the moment you have any news, send for me."

"Oui, I will.''

Taking her father firmly by the arm, she walked back to the terrified villagers. Their faces were masks of fear and dread.

Nesta's daughter voiced what many were feeling. "Why are we being punished, my lady?"

" 'Tis not God's punishment, Cordelia, only nature. Like a storm or a flood. God would not do this. He is merciful and kind.''

A glimmer of hope chased the fear from their eyes. Clinging to one another for comfort, they nodded, wanting to believe what she said.

She walked among them, touching a mother's shoulder to offer support or soothing a child's cries. As they waited, all eyes remained trained on the castle ruins.

She closed her eyes, praying that those inside were alive, but as the day progressed, her fears increased. The waiting was hard on everyone, she realized, and it would help to keep busy. To that end she started the women preparing a meal for the workers. Though she had no appetite, the men would have to be fed.

Finally in the late afternoon shouts were heard, and Bronwyn ran with the others to the ruins.

Christophe's men were carrying a woman on a litter. Cordelia screamed at the sight of her mother's crumpled body. Wilford stood to the side, with eyes tear laden and hands folded in prayer.

Bronwyn pushed her way through the crowd and quickly examined the rotund cook. She ran her hands over every thickset limb. No bones appeared broken and her abrasions were minor. She was shaken but unharmed. After Bronwyn treated her injuries, she moved back, allowing the men to carry Nesta over to the fire. Cordelia followed, hovering over her mother like a mother hen herself. Wilford held his wife's hand and whispered her name as he softly placed a kiss on her forehead.

Christophe came up behind Bronwyn and wrapped his arms around her. "We will find her," he whispered.

She sighed and leaned back, wanting to believe, and taking solace in his arms until he left to order a rest period.

The women fed the dirty and tired men who came from their duties in shifts. Everyone worked together, Norman and Welsh alike, resting only long enough to finish their meals before returning to the heap of broken timbers and crushed tiles.

Exhausted but unable to rest, for fear her thoughts would overwhelm her, Bronwyn worked to clean up the remains of the dinner, then helped the women find shelter for the night. Hastily constructed pallets were made by campfires to wait out the vigil.

Her gaze strayed to her father, whose face suddenly appeared very old and fragile. "Father," she cried, afraid he was having a relapse.

He held out his arms and she ran into them.

"I must go and see how the men are doing." When she began to object, he raised his hand. "I promise, Daughter, I will only watch."

She wished he would sit and rest, but knew his need to be there was too great. With a sad smile she watched him move off with the other men as they returned to the castle. Covered in grime, the soldiers labored, straining muscle and bone to move the crushed timbers and find those trapped within.

Soon after nightfall a Norman guard was recovered. Bronwyn knelt over him and felt for broken bones. She thought several ribs were broken. She bound them tight, praying a lung had not been punctured. He moaned, and her concern increased. Soldiers did not cry out in front of the women. She made an herb brew that would ease his suffering and stayed by him to monitor his breathing.

The Norman guards who were taking their break sat by their fallen comrade and offered words of support.

One heavyset guard patted her hand. "Do not fret so, my lady. Sumner will be fine. He is hardy and will recover. And with God's help we will find your missing kinsmen along with Michau."

The words stunned her. Raising her head, she stared at the concern in the Norman's eyes and realized that these men actually cared for the Welsh. She swallowed and nodded.

Christophe came to the fire and filled his cup with hot cider.

His brow was lined and his features creased with worry. As he sipped his brew, she went to him. His arms opened to accept her and without words they clung to each other, neither speaking.

Tucked beneath his arm, she felt his heartbeat drumming against her ear. Though his embrace was light, with his arms draped loosely over her, she stood within his hold and shamelessly drew comfort from his masculine warmth.

"We will find the rest of them," he assured her again.

Tears filled her eyes and she could not meet his gaze. The longer the rescue took, the more she believed that the others were dead.

He smoothed the side of her cheek. "Keep hope alive."

A flutter of faith stirred within her. She wanted to, she truly did. But—then he kissed her lips and she tasted the savage determination in his embrace. The fierce contact took her breath and fears away. She felt his mouth move insistently over hers, and she opened to his demand. He wouldn't give up and neither would she. Returning his kiss with her own resolve, she gave herself over to him and accepted his strength. They shared each other's courage, drawing and giving hope and faith. Slowly he ended the kiss, then rested his forehead against hers. "Believe," he said. He curved his arm around her shoulder and walked her back to the site. At the ruins he tipped her chin up and whispered, "Believe," sealing the word on her lips with a kiss. She felt a warmth flow through her that chased the cold dread away, and when he left, she did believe.

As Bronwyn watched her husband work, she knew he was tired. Even so, he drove himself harder than the others. He labored relentlessly, his muscles straining as he moved heavy beams and debris. Every now and then she would catch his tired expression when he wiped the perspiration from his brow. Yet, he refused the rest periods the others seized. When they took breaks, he would remain. Gratitude filled her heart. If this man did nothing else for her in his entire life, she would admire him for his sacrifice now.

Her father slipped his arm around her. "He is a good man."

"I know," she whispered.

* * *

All night Christophe dug in the rubble and crawled in the narrow tunnels along with his men. They had approximated where Fiona had been and worked steadily toward her. The tunnels had to be shorn up, or another cave-in could occur, and there was always the chance of an aftershock.

He looked over at his brother, whose eyes and teeth shone within a black mask of dirt and sweat. Nicolas was a man possessed. "You should rest, and join us again after you have eaten."

"*Non.*" Nicolas continued to dig, his expression grim as he continued to work without a break.

Christophe touched his arm. "If you do not rest, you will collapse."

"She is alone in there, waiting for a miracle. I intend to make that miracle happen."

Christophe shook his head and let his brother go. Covered in dirt, scratched by the sharp timbers that had torn holes in his tunic and scraped his hands raw, Nicolas threw debris aside and pushed forward.

Christophe joined in, and shoulder to shoulder they worked. Spying an edge of clothing among the dirt, they dug out another servant. The poor soul was dead. Solemnly they carried the man out, and a woman wailed at their find.

Bronwyn helped the family prepare the body for its resting place, and Christophe sent two men to dig a grave. At sunrise they stopped work and paid their respects to the servant.

Only three people remained missing in the rubble. After a quick breakfast they immediately started the rescue attempt again. This time Bronwyn joined them, and Christophe did not forbid her. Though she looked haggard, she worked alongside the men, digging in the tunnel as Fang whimpered and whined beside her.

Christophe stayed close to her side, torn between offering his brother comfort and insuring her safety.

Suddenly a shout was heard in the far tunnel. His brother

emerged, staggering slightly, a small form in his arms. 'Twas Fiona, covered in dirt, but clearly alive.

Bronwyn let out a cry and rushed to her sister's side.

"Let me examine you," Bronwyn said, trying to pull Fiona's hands free of the Norman's tunic.

Her sister burrowed deeper into Nicolas's embrace.

"She is fine, just frightened," Nicolas said. "I will hold her until the fear passes."

She nodded and rejoined Christophe just as the captain of the guard was pulled from the debris.

Terror seized her heart as she bent over Michau and could barely feel a puff of breath. Without thinking she covered his mouth with hers and gave him her breath. Soldiers gasped, but she continued to give him mouth-to-mouth until the man could breathe on his own.

Michau gasped and coughed as his eyes blinked open and he focused on her. He tried to reach out for her but his hand barely grazed her arm. "My lady?"

She placed her hand over his. "You are all right now." She started to rise but Michau stopped her.

"My lady, my life and my sword are at your disposal."

Tears filled her eyes at his high tribute and she patted his shoulder. "Michau, you are making a terrible habit of needing my services." The men cheered as she stood up, then crowded in to help their companion stand.

"Where did you learn that?" Christophe asked.

Bronwyn felt a trickle of apprehension. She could be condemned as a witch. " 'Tis an ancient remedy handed down from healer to healer."

Christophe seemed to accept this, as did the men. Many secrets were kept by the healers, to be revealed only to their apprentices.

Soon after, the last man was pulled from the rubble and laid to rest. A timber had impaled him on impact.

With the day barely begun, and two funeral services held, Bronwyn felt exhausted. Now that her sister was safe, she stared at the rubble and realized that everything she owned in the world was buried beneath timber and dirt. Compared to the lives lost, the possessions were nothing, yet the loss of security hit her. She was homeless. A deep sense of futility descended on her with crushing weight. She wanted nothing more than to curl up and go to sleep. But the warlord roused everyone. "We have no shelter. It is imperative that we concentrate on building new lodgings or we will be prey to the weather, as well as our enemies."

Every man, woman, and child pitched in. Welsh and Norman were united in one goal. Survival transcended all other considerations.

The castle's inner bailey was under construction. The villagers would have to sleep in the open until the structure was complete. Now, no sabotage could be tolerated, for it would jeopardize everyone's life.

In the aftermath of the quake, the women dug through the debris to recover what they could. Fortunately, most of the preserved food was retrieved.

"Look, my lady." Nesta held up the beautiful plates and eating utensils.

"Be careful," Bronwyn called out as the collapsed structure shifted slightly. Christophe's orders had been clear, they were to recover only the necessities. "Nesta, we can live without the utensils."

Nesta bristled. "I know we can live without them, but how will the men appreciate the food with dirt in it?"

Bronwyn chuckled as her own words came floating back to her. "What was I thinking? Even so, I do not want you risking your safety."

"Do not worry, my lady. I will be very careful."

Bronwyn worked from sunup to sundown, mostly tending the sick, including Fiona, who had reinjured her leg and suffered several bruises and a sprained wrist in the quake. When time allowed, Bronwyn helped the women with their chores, and even sometimes with the construction of the castle.

She also made sure to set the example for cleanliness. Every night without fail she would wash in the river. Though the water was extremely cold, they needed to institute good hygiene. With their crowed living conditions, it was important that the women haul water from upstream for drinking and washing to insure a clean supply of water.

After an exceptionally hard day of digging among the debris, her hair limp and clinging to her sweaty, gritty skin, Bronwyn headed for the river.

"Where are you going, Wife?" Christophe asked, suddenly appearing on the path behind her.

"Christophe, you scared me," she gasped, whirling around to face him.

He grinned. "Where are you going?"

"Down to the river." She held up her linen and soap. "I cannot bear to sleep without a good wash."

"Good, I will join you."

Her cheeks warmed.

"Do you have a linen?"

"I will use yours."

"Verily, my lord, you will catch a chill. 'Tis best if you have a wrap for yourself."

Christophe smiled and produced a fur robe he held behind his back. "I do not think either of us will catch cold, Wife."

"I really mean to take a bath, Christophe." The very thought of making love while she was so filthy was abhorrent to her.

"So do I."

"Good, then you may accompany me."

He bowed low before her. "My lady is too kind."

She ignored his sarcasm to signal Fang, and continued to walk to the river's edge. At the bank she looked first one way, then the other.

"What are you doing?" he asked as he sat down and pulled off his boots.

"Making sure no one is around. Even though Fang is here, and would warn me of an intruder, I still like to check for myself. I do not want to be the object of your soldiers' scrutiny."

He chuckled.

"What, may I ask, is so funny?"

"I will tell you after your bath."

"Tell me now."

He shook his head, wearing that inflexible look that drove

her patience to the limit. She sighed in frustration. "Christophe, sometimes I think you would make a saint swear."

He began to remove his tunic and she turned away, realizing that he was deliberately ignoring her. "Stay," she commanded Fang so he would not follow her into the water.

Awkward about stripping as Christophe watched, she removed her clothes quickly and edged her way into the water. Suddenly her husband ran by her to dive into the chilly water. The big splash he produced covered and chilled her. The cold water had an awful bite and it took her several minutes to ease into waist-high water. He swam around while she tried to step into deeper water.

"If you dive under, you will not feel the cold so badly."

Her shivers raised goose bumps on her skin. "I am not cold," she lied through chattering teeth.

While she washed her hair, Christophe lathered the soap across his chest, shoulders, and arms. The white foam glistened on his sun-bronzed skin. Bronwyn sighed, for the image conjured up pleasurable memories. She knew those muscles intimately, and thoughts of stroking his powerful body made her suddenly warm. Sighing, she leaned back to swiftly rinse her hair.

Christophe dove under the water as she lathered the soap and started to wash her upper body. Suddenly something grabbed her leg and tipped her off balance. With an outraged cry she fell backward into the frigid water and went under, then surfaced, sputtering and fighting mad.

Christophe's deep laughter echoed across the water. Funny, was it? Well, two could play at this game. Placing the soap on a low hanging branch, Bronwyn gasped and pretended to slip. "Help me," she screamed, and gave a good imitation of falling. Once beneath the water, she headed in his direction. When his leg came into view, she grabbed hold and lifted. Unfortunately, her big husband was not as easy to tip as she had been. She surfaced quickly, gasping for air as she jumped up and tried to push his shoulders down. It was useless. He was too big and too strong to dunk. And the moment her hands touched his muscular shoulders, she was too aware of him.

He chuckled. "What are you trying to do?"

"Give you a taste of your own medicine," she breathed hoarsely.

"As you wish." He let her push his shoulders under, but as he went down, he wrapped his arms around her and pulled her with him.

Beneath the water his lips covered hers as he crushed her to his chest. His hands caressed her back, shoulders, and buttocks, leaving a trail of heat immediately cooled by the surrounding water. The two extremes created a new sensual experience. He teased and tantalized her lips, not stopping until they broke the surface. Pushing the water from her eyes, she gasped, "I wish once, just once, to best you."

"You just did, *cherie*," he murmured, his gaze dark and hot.

A warmth curled in the pit of her stomach when she realized she was affecting him as strongly as he was affecting her. She trembled at the raw desire flaring in his eyes. Of their own volition, their bodies pressed together, and the water's temperature had ceased to matter. She floated in his arms, light and free, exhilarated. His hands stroked her flesh, roaming over her with an expertise that took her breath away.

She explored the width of his shoulders, running her hands over his brawny muscles and up to caress the nape of his neck. Beneath her fingers the thick corded muscles tensed and she thrilled that he could no longer ignore her.

Slowly he eased her onto his shaft. Her first instinct was to pull away. "Here?"

He rained kisses along her neck to the sensitive area at the nape. "I cannot wait to make the bank," he breathed. "You have driven me mad."

Mad was good. She could accept that. A cry of joy escaped her as she kissed him with an ardor that surprised and delighted them both. Her tongue slipped into his mouth, then her teeth grazed his lips before her mouth traveled to his ear and nipped.

"Woman, slow down," he whispered, his breathing labored.

Breathless, she cupped his face. "I cannot, Christophe. Oh, I cannot."

He growled and covered her mouth as his rhythm increased. Nothing about their joining was gentle. Wave after wave of desire washed over her. A deep moan escaped her as she scored his back with her nails. His demanding, passionate kisses ground her teeth against her lips, but she did not care. Higher and higher they climbed toward a teetering plateau, relentless in their quest as they pushed with raw need and desire, giving themselves over to reckless abandonment. Then in one glorious moment Bronwyn found her release and cried out, feeling reborn. His cry followed hers, and he clung to her. And when they finally came down to earth, the river flowing around them was the only sound as he carried her to the fur robe and covered them in the warmth of the lining.

He pulled her close, wrapping his legs and arms around her.

She snuggled into his body's warmth and suddenly remembered his promise. "Christophe?"

He kissed the top of her head. "Hmmm?"

"What were you going to tell me after my bath?"

He drew back and smiled. "Only that, my sweet little wife, you have never bathed alone. I have kept watch each time."

She looked at him, realizing Fang would not have growled at Christophe. "Why did you not tell me?"

"Two reasons. First, I did not want to rob you of the joy of your solitude. But whether you realize it or not, it is not safe to be out here alone." When she started to object, he held up his hand to forestall her. "Fang has been wounded once in an attack and could not defeat a rebel bent on harm."

"And the second reason?" He grinned. "I did not want to be deprived of the delightful show."

Chapter Eight

Dawn had barely broke the next day before Nicolas shook Christophe awake. "Christophe, wake up, there has been another incident." Nicolas looked uncomfortable as he met his brother's eyes.

"What do you mean?" Christophe asked, rubbing the sleep from his eyes.

"Someone poisoned the horses' feed during the night."

He bolted to his feet. *"Mon Dieu!* Are they all right?"

Nicolas's expression was grave. "Most of them will survive, but one has died."

Even before Nicolas led the way to the stall, Christophe's gut told him it was his own mighty steed. At the sight of the black horse lying motionless in the straw, a bloody foam covering the animal's lips, his stomach heaved. His horse had clearly died in agony. He turned away, furious.

"Post a guard. No one gets near our horses again but us."

He looked back at the dead animal; the lifeless image burned into his brain. He left the stable without another word.

* * *

Insects covered the animal's carcass, and Bronwyn closed her eyes, sickened by the horrid sight. She drew a deep breath and turned to face her husband. "I had nothing to do with this."

His harsh features chilled her as never before. The doubt had returned, and her insides roiled as she followed her husband from the stable into the sunshine. "Do you believe me?" she asked, needing to know.

"You have used poison in the past."

She cringed at the reminder.

Drawing a deep breath, she raised her chin. "How could any Welshman approach them and not be noticed?"

He rounded on her so fast she jumped back and stumbled over Fang. "Do you accuse a Norman?"

Righting herself, she swallowed and nodded.

He shook his head as his brother joined them. "My wife thinks a Norman poisoned our stock."

Nicolas looked stunned. " 'Tis treason to suggest such a thing."

Christophe held up his hand when she tried to defend herself. "That's enough."

Her throat ached with the effort to bite back her frustration. At his inflexible expression, she turned and stormed off.

Though he had not openly accused her, the doubt was back. Of course it was possible it was a Welshman, but she could not believe it. The only one who would dare was Caradoc, and he was gone.

Still, she feared for her troublesome brother. If he was responsible, there would be no stopping the warlord's wrath.

In the weeks that followed, the men pushed harder than before to complete the necessary construction. With the horses now recovered from their sickness, the stones were moved from the quarry, and the work progressed fairly smoothly.

One afternoon as Bronwyn carried the rescued vats of brine and meat to the temporary shelter, her father approached her. "I overheard a conversation today that greatly upset me. Tell me, Daughter, does Lord Christophe still believe it was you who poisoned the horses?"

"Aye," she said, wishing her father would not listen to the Norman soldiers.

She was about to change the subject when Nicolas ran up to them. "Hayden, I wish a word with you. I have just left the Lady Fiona and she bade me to seek you out. With your permission, I wish to wed your daughter."

Bronwyn stood stock still, praying her father would agree. His answer was a hearty yes. Both she and Nicolas smiled in relief.

Christophe walked over and joined them. "What makes you so cheerful today, Brother?"

"I am going to join you in the state of matrimony. Wish me well."

"Who is the lady?"

Bronwyn held her breath.

"Fiona." Nicolas smiled.

"*Non.*" Christophe shook his head. "If you make such a match, your fate will be sealed. She brings to your bed no money, land, or connections."

"God's teeth, I care not for all that."

Christophe studied his brother for several long moments. Finally, he slapped his brother on the back and extended his hand. "Then with my blessing, be content."

His answer so shocked Bronwyn that her mouth fell open.

He turned to his wife, his smile fading. "I can, when the mood strikes, be charitable, Wife. You act as though you have never seen this."

"In truth, my lord, the occurrence is rare," she said solemnly. "But, nonetheless, welcome."

He shook his head at her. "I could take that as an insult, but instead I choose to look at it as a witticism."

A group of soldiers had been close enough to overhear. "A Welsh wife?" Lucien sneered. "Bed her, but do not wed her. That is all she is good for."

Nicolas's fist crashed into the man's face, forcing Lucien to his backside. He cursed loudly as he gained his feet, but found little support among his comrades.

"Good fortune, my lord," Michau said, extending his hand to Nicolas.

"*Oui*, Lady Fiona is a lovely one indeed," another man declared, and one by one, the other soldiers offered their support.

Lucien wiped the blood from his mouth and turned around, ignoring those who chose to celebrate.

"Why is he so bitter?" Bronwyn asked Christophe.

"He is just lonely for his homeland."

"My lord, he is angry and resentful, not lonely."

"Leave the men to me, Wife. Concern yourself with woman's things."

She raised an eyebrow. "As you wish, my lord. I have a wedding to plan."

"Pray my brother does not have the wedding night that I did."

"Will you never let that be?" she asked, a familiar pain slicing to her heart. When he said nothing, she shook her head. "I vow you have a memory longer than the winter."

" 'Tis good for me that I do."

"Christophe, if I wanted to kill you, I would have done so by now. Will you never come to trust me?"

When he reached out and grabbed her, she gasped. His eyes darkened as he pulled her close. His head bent to capture her lips in a kiss that burned of sensuality, but lacked warmth. "Never," he whispered.

Then he strode away, leaving her in a daze.

"Daughter, you love him," Hayden said, his tone soft, yet surprised.

She glanced at Hayden and murmured, "Aye, Father, I do." Absently she stroked the wolf at her side as she watched her handsome husband walk away from her. Studying his broad shoulders and his sure steps, she sighed. "But I am afraid he is not so pleased with me."

" 'Tis only a matter of time. What man could resist such loveliness?"

"Christophe can. What he feels for me is not love."

Hayden draped his arm over her shoulder and turned her in the direction of the half-erected castle keep. "Cease fretting and go to your sister. She needs you."

"What of you, Father?"

"I am going to send a message to your brother."

She touched his arm. "I beg you, do not try to contact him. He is in trouble, and if he returns now, Christophe would surely see him flogged, or worse."

He patted her hand. "Do not worry. I shall only warn him away."

He pushed her in the direction of the temporary encampment, which was little more than a dirt mound surrounded by a wooden wall. She looked over her shoulder, noting the tired lines in his face. Concern filled her. He was not well.

Lady Fiona rested on her pallet in the middle of the open-air enclosure, smiling from ear to ear. The way she blushed and her eyes sparkled, no one would guess that she was recovering from severe injuries. "Can you believe it, Sister? He wants the wedding as soon as I am well enough to stand."

Bronwyn grasped Fiona's delicate hands. "I am so happy for you."

"I never dreamed I could feel this way about a man, especially a Norman. It is heavenly."

Bronwyn chuckled at that. Her sister's happiness was contagious.

"Why did you not tell me, Bronwyn? If you had, I would never have considered joining the church!"

"Because I did not know myself. Besides, there is more to living as a wife than these glorious feelings. Although these feelings help when your husband vexes you so."

Fiona chuckled. "I do not fear. Nicolas loves me."

Oh, it was hard not to envy her sister. As much as Christophe wanted her, she knew he did not love her. With a sigh she put her fears aside. This was Fiona's time. She would not spoil it.

"What do you wish to wear?"

"Mother's gown, of course."

"Of course." Bronwyn agreed, at the same time wondering

if the gown could be found in the rubble—and if it was still in one piece.

"Can I ask a favor of you, Bronwyn?"

"Aye, ask away."

"Will you sing at my wedding?"

Bronwyn paled. Though blessed with a nightingale's voice, she was somewhat apprehensive about drawing attention to herself. But the anticipation in her sister's eyes could not be ignored.

" 'Tis your wedding day. If you want me to sing, then I will sing!"

The cave's dampness permeated his bones, and Caradoc sneezed as he poured himself a hot mug of mead. Already miserable, his mood only worsened at Rhett's news. "Fiona is going to marry the warlord's brother?" He wiped his nose. "You must be mistaken."

Rhett smirked. "Nay, she is going to bed the enemy."

Caradoc wrapped the thin blanket around his shoulders and huddled by the fire. "How did you learn this?"

"The same way I learned that someone poisoned the horses."

"Poisoned the horses? Who would do that? We need those horses."

"Aye, we do. But there is someone who does not care about what we need, nor the Normans."

Caradoc scratched his beard. "Who in God's name would be so witless as to harm good horses? 'Tis a heinous act!" He looked up. Rhett's sly smile made him feel like a mouse facing a hungry cat.

"Not all the horses died, just one: the warlord's beast. We must find out who this man is who hates the warlord. He could be very useful."

Christophe watched the work progress with a critical eye. Every day he supervised and worked alongside the men. The dire consequences of being caught without shelter, either by the winter or by the rebels, spurred him on at a neck-breaking pace. He ordered the women to bring the noon meal out to the work site. The less time spent journeying to and from the temporary shelter meant increased production. He also instituted four breaks during the long day and staggered them—with a relief crew taking over, so production never stopped, yet the men were rested.

Hayden huffed and puffed as he joined the Norman at the construction site. "We will have the castle shell completed by the end of the year."

"Aye, but we will be defenseless until the walls and battlements are erected."

"It could not be helped." Hayden's attention strayed to the ruins.

"An act of God," Christophe said, following the old man's gaze.

Hayden sighed. "Perhaps, my lord, a blessing in disguise. Though you are vulnerable to attack, this crisis has united *our* people."

Christophe smiled. He agreed, and now his brother's forthcoming marriage would help solidify his position. However, the rebels were still out there just waiting for their chance.

"At least, we will be warm when the attack comes."

"You are sure that we will be attacked."

Christophe looked at Hayden. "Your son will not rest until he tries to wrest control from me."

"How do you know that?"

"Because if I had lost everything I had known, I would not stop until I had regained it."

"But Caradoc is not like you."

"Nor is he a man of peace, like you. He will, at least, try to regain his former life. Most men would."

Hayden shook his head. "I have seen the devastation of war, and experience told me that we could not win this battle. I would not put my people through a conflict to salvage my pride."

"You are a wise ruler, your son is not."

He did not dispute the words, instead he asked, "What will you do?"

"I will defend what is mine."

Hayden sighed. "Even if it means killing Bronwyn's brother?"

"I would defend what was mine, even if it meant killing my own brother."

Bronwyn poured her sister a cup of mead at the temporary shelter, and tried to calm down. Christophe had denied her simple request to ride out through their land, then smiled benignly at her and gave her a mock bow before he left. She gripped the cup tightly, to stop herself from flinging it at his smug back, and moved toward Fiona. Her sister's approaching marriage made her wish again that he had wanted her for his wife, instead of being forced to take her as part of a political alliance.

"What troubles you, Sister?" Fiona said, taking the offered mead.

"Nothing, Fiona, just thoughts of the castle, and hopes for the future."

Fiona eyed her sister sharply. "You are a poor liar."

"Aye, I am," Bronwyn conceded. "But let me have these private thoughts. There are some things one cannot share."

Fiona nodded, her expression one of gentle understanding. "What do you think?" She held up her wedding dress for Bronwyn's inspection.

The embroidered gown brought a lump to Bronwyn's throat. She reached out and softly traced the delicate stitches sewn with such love. " 'Tis beautiful. Your husband will be pleased."

"All my life I have hoped to find someone who would understand me and cherish the things I do."

Bronwyn marveled how her sister was blossoming right before her very eyes. It was a rare and lovely transformation. "You seem different to me."

"I feel different," she said, placing the gown aside. Her eyes met Bronwyn's. "I wish Caradoc could be here."

"He was not always kind to you," Bronwyn said, fluffing the covers around her sister.

"He is still my brother."

Bronwyn drew a deep breath. "He has chosen his path. Mayhap someday he will see the folly of his decision." She helped Fiona get comfortable, and thought it best to change the subject. "Your leg should be completely mended in another few months." She adjusted the elevation of Fiona's leg, placing several linens carefully beneath the injured limb. She straightened and looked her sister in the eye. "Then you will have to work very hard."

"I cannot wait," she said, ignoring the warning. "This board you have me laced to itches and is most uncomfortable."

Bronwyn chuckled at her sister's enthusiasm, knowing that the hard work began with rehabilitation. "You will thank me when you walk with a straight gait."

Fiona caught her sister's hand, her features suddenly serious. "Did you fear your wedding night? Oh! I know it was awful, but . . . was the bedding . . . ?"

Bronwyn smiled sympathetically. "I think any maiden is apprehensive. But 'tis nothing to fear. You will find that there is much to look forward to in the marriage bed."

Fiona stared at her for a long time, and Bronwyn suddenly felt uncomfortable. Hoping her sister would not ask for further specifics, she began to tuck in the coverings.

"Why have you not told your husband you love him?"

Bronwyn looked up from her task, surprised and unsettled by her sister's intuitiveness. "He would not believe me. Our life together did not start out as yours will."

"Still, he seems a fair man. Why would you not seek your happiness?"

"I have tried," she said, sitting down. "He believes the worst of me and is content with his thoughts."

"But you have changed. Everyone can see the difference. Besides, you did not want to poison Christophe in the first place."

"Still, he suspects me of being behind every trouble. Whether he says so, or not, the distrust lurks in his eyes."

"If you wish I will talk to him," Fiona bravely offered.

Horrified, Bronwyn shook her head. "He must come to trust me on his own. Nothing else will bring us together."

Fiona reached over and clasped her sister's hand. "You must have faith."

"Oh, I do." She forced a bright smile. "Enough about me. Your wedding approaches. We will talk of nothing else but your happiness." Though she wore a happy face, her thoughts were deeply troubled. Christophe would never forgive her, and fool that she was, she wanted his forgiveness and his love, more than life itself. She loved him, and it mattered not that he did not return her affection. She could not choose who she loved. All she could do was choose how she loved. And for Bronwyn, it was all or nothing. She had given her heart to him, and now he possessed the ultimate power to hurt or heal their relationship.

Christophe looked out over the courtyard, or what would soon be his newly improved courtyard. And try as he might, he could not concentrate on what he was doing. His mind kept going back to his wife. His beautiful, sensual, complex wife. How could a woman of these times be so unique, so fascinating? She seemed every bit as intelligent as he, sometimes more so. Memories of their lovemaking at the river flashed in his mind. He could never recall feeling this way in his past life. Oh, he had lusted after women, but not this way. Never this way. Was he a fool? She had once wanted to kill him. Did she still?

"Christophe?" Bronwyn's voice drifted to him from behind.

He turned to watch her approach, Fang glued to her side. Though he understood why the wolf was unsure of him, it amazed him to see the animal's transfer of loyalty. Did Fang sense something he did not? He shook his head to clear his troubling thoughts, and just stared at her breathtaking beauty.

The sunlight glinted off her hair, which hung like a curtain of gold to her tiny waist. He would never tire of looking at her, or wanting her. His loins tightened. God, how he wanted her. If he were the real Christophe, he'd take her here and now, and privacy be damned.

She stopped before him and cocked her head to one side. "Christophe, are you all right?"

He blinked. "I am fine," he said, his tone gruff. "What brings you out here? I thought you were busy helping to plan a wedding."

"I am," she conceded. "But you have been working so hard. I have seen you so little."

He raised a brow at what she left unsaid. "Are you saying you miss me?"

Her amber gaze met his, bold and unwavering. "I am."

Her response made him happy, yet uncomfortable, too. This was leading to a place he did not want to go. He had to tread carefully.

"That is good."

"Good?" A soft, seductive smile made her even lovelier.

"Oui!" he said, keeping his response cool. "A wife should miss her husband."

"And should a husband not miss his wife?"

He looked her in the eye. *"Non."*

"Non?" Her smile began to fade.

He held her gaze. "That is what I said."

The pain that slashed across her face caused guilt to stab his gut.

"What is it you expect of me?" he snapped, unnecessarily angry. "A declaration of love? It will not happen, Bronwyn. It cannot. I thought you understood that."

"I do not want anything from you," she snapped back. Tears glittered in her amber eyes as her wolf protectively crowded in.

Christophe's intent had not been to hurt her, for he did enjoy her. That was the problem, he enjoyed her too much. But her pain was so obvious that he felt like the lowest of knaves. "Bronwyn . . ."

"Nay," she interrupted, holding up her hand. "Say no more. I now know how you think and feel. You have made yourself painfully clear."

Turning on her heel, she half-ran, half-stumbled back toward the castle; Fang running in her wake.

"Bloody fool," he cursed himself, while fighting the urge to go after her, take her in his arms, and kiss away her tears.

Chapter Nine

Red and gold fingers of light streaked across the morning sky, coloring the castle's dun-colored stones a golden bronze. Like a giant's toy building blocks, huge cubes of granite were erected in various stages of construction. Christophe stared at the structure as he walked, trying to pace off his problems. If they continued their current pace, the shell would not be done before the snow fell. He sighed. Somehow, they would have to increase production. His gaze fell on the battlement wall as he ran a hand through his hair. He could only tackle one problem at a time. Once the shell was constructed, he would instruct his men to start on the defenses.

A movement caught his eye and he turned. A man weaved his way through the fields, his gait unsteady. Whoever he was, the man was drunk to the bone.

"God's teeth," he swore as the figure came closer and he recognized Lucien. The fool could barely stand, stumbling over the level ground. Christophe marched over to him and was about to reprimand him, but the drunk interrupted him. Clearly the knave was so far into his cups he didn't realize who stood before him.

"Fools . . . fools. The Montgomerys will rue the day they

crossed my path.'' Lucien brushed by Christophe and started toward the castle, but lost his footing.

Christophe hauled Lucien's limp arm over his shoulder, a sick feeling forming in the pit of his stomach as he steadied him. ''Why do you say that?''

Lucien went on without appearing to have heard. ''If he is not strong enough to hold this land, another will take it away from him. It's only right. You know this should have been my demesne.'' He blinked rapidly and tried to focus on his companion.

Christophe ignored the man's foul words and breath. *''Oui,* but William has made his choice,'' he replied calmly.

''If I impress the king, he will change his mind. This,'' he continued, flinging his hand wide, ''should all have been mine. All of it. Every acre, every tree, everything, including that bitch.'' He stepped from Christophe's hold, and staggered once, then fell facedown in the dirt.

Christophe's anger rose at the thought of this wretch touching Bronwyn. He half-dragged, half-carried the sotted soldier to his pallet. When he had deposited the drunk onto his narrow bed, he stared at him for a long time. As he did, Bronwyn's voice sounded in his mind about the poisoned horses. ''How could any Welshman approach them and not be noticed.'' God, had he misjudged her? Turning, he alerted the watch to Lucien's condition, then walked back toward the palisades, and his brother's pallet. After shaking his brother awake, he motioned for Nicolas to follow him.

''What troubles your sleep now, brother?'' Nicolas asked. ''Mayhap your wife can fix a sleeping potion for you so that others might rest,'' he mumbled while following Christophe through the sleeping pallets to the field outside.

Ignoring his brother's sarcasm, Christophe pointed to the construction. ''I have decided the keep must be finished first, before the battlements.''

Nicolas sighed and knuckled the sleep from his eyes. ''Christophe, it takes six years to complete a castle.''

''I have some thoughts on how to improve production.''

Nicolas turned to face him. ''We will have to suspend work

when the snow falls. It will be too cold. The stones and mortar cannot be laid. The artisans return to their families in the winter months."

"I am going to institute some changes that can see the castle raised in half that time."

"Three years? You're daft, Brother, it cannot be done."

"*Oui,* it can, and this is how."

Christophe explained his plan to start an assembly line to minimize expenditure and maximize efficiency. "It will cut the time in half."

Nicolas stared at him, his mouth agape. Several moments went by as he digested the idea, then his interest piqued. "What about the winter months?"

"The exterior walls will be constructed now. The interior will be finished in the winter months."

Nicolas thought on it. "I suppose it could be done, but it would mean working the men to their limit."

"Which brings me to my other suggestion. We will institute shifts."

"Shifts?" Nicolas asked.

"*Oui,* think of it as the three guard watches. We can have the workforce split into thirds, working three shifts of eight hours each. It will triple production and reduce the construction time to one year."

"But how will they see at night?"

"Torches, man. The light will be adequate enough to lay the mortar and brick," Christophe explained. "Nicolas, we must have the castle keep finished by winter. If we are to survive an attack, we also have to have the battlement walls partially up."

Nicolas grumbled something unintelligible as he yawned.

"What was that?"

"I think you spend too many of your sleeping hours thinking up work for me."

Grinning, Christophe clasped his brother on the shoulder. "Indeed, I do."

Nicolas shook his head. "I hope when I take on the responsibilities of a demesne I do not become so worried that I age before my time.''

Christophe started to walk away.

''Where are you going?'' Nicolas asked.

Christophe turned around. ''To check the armory, then the condition of the half-formed battlements. We need to be prepared for war.''

Nicolas quickly joined him. ''You think the rebels will attack?''

''*Oui*, as soon as we are at our weakest,'' Christophe said, nodding to the guard as they entered the temporary armory.

Nicolas's eyebrow raised. ''But, that is now.''

''*Non*,'' Christophe said, checking the swords and replacing a shield, ''that will be when we are cold, hungry, and without shelter. They want us vulnerable and beaten before they ever raise their arms. Right now we are still too strong.''

''What do you plan on doing?'' Nicolas said as they walked out of the armory and over to the half-constructed wall.

''I have been considering a trap,'' Christophe said.

''How?''

A slow smile spread across his lips. ''Let them think we are worse off than we are.''

''So when they are assured we are weak, they will attack,'' Nicolas spoke his thoughts aloud.

''Any ideas?''

''If it were me, I would probably attack when we least suspected it.''

''Exactly,'' Christophe said. ''Your wedding celebration would be the perfect time.''

Nicolas nodded, his features suddenly drawn. ''We have four months to prepare.''

Christophe drew a deep breath and slowly exhaled. ''We also have the problem of a traitor in our midst.''

''Who?''

''It is just a gut suspicion, but I think Lucien is responsible for the horses.''

''He would not betray his own people,'' Nicolas scoffed.

''No, he would not,'' Christophe agreed. ''But notice that

only my horse died. And both you and I know how resentful he was when William passed him over for this estate. If he could make me look bad in William's eyes, then he might not consider it treachery so much as advantageous to his rightful cause. He has taken every opportunity to challenge me, and since his drinking has increased, he has grown more bold in his attacks.''

Nicolas's features were cast in dark lines of outrage. ''He should be in irons!''

Christophe shook his head. ''I have other plans for him. Find a chore to take him from the fortress, guard duty on the hill or hunting excursions. I do not want him to know we are fortifying the castle. What information he ferrets out will be the information I wish him to know. If he is innocent, then no harm will have been done.''

Nicolas leaned against the stone wall and shielded his eyes against the sunlight. ''I can send him to the end of Wales to report on the rebels.''

''Excellent.'' Christophe grinned. ''That will have him out of our midst for the greater part of the preparations.''

''Do not worry about the men, Christophe,'' Nicolas said. ''Lucien has very few friends among them. His drunkenness has driven most of those around him away.''

''I truly hope I am wrong, but I cannot see anyone else.''

''You do not suspect your wife?''

''Not of this.'' He sighed. ''Now that Caradoc is no longer influencing her, she seems to be changing her ways.''

''I am glad you have begun to accept her. Fiona confessed that Bronwyn did not want to harm you. She was caught in a tangle of family, love, and honor.'' Nicolas looped his arm over Christophe's shoulders as they turned toward the quarry. ''Time will give you your answer. Be patient. You have changed since coming to this strange land. I cannot remember such tolerance and forbearance. During a conquest you showed no mercy.''

''This is not a conquest,'' Christophe said, walking from the battlements and out of the castle. ''We must live and work among these people. The only way to survive is to win their acceptance.''

''William knew what he was doing by choosing you for his emissary.''

''I could not have made it without you.''

Nicolas pushed his brother on the path toward the early workers. ''We will always stand together. I have been fortunate that my best friend happens to be my brother.''

Christophe felt a new awakening in his heart. He smiled as he walked to the stone quarry with his brother to see the day's work done. Never in his previous life had he experienced a man's friendship. Such loyalty humbled him.

After leaving orders with Michau at the quarry, they looked back at the castle, staring at the mammoth structure taking shape.

Nicolas nodded. ''With your changes implemented, how much do you think will be completed by my wedding?''

''I am hoping a six-foot wall will surround the castle. It would give us the advantage we sorely need.''

''Will it be enough?''

''Hopefully,'' Christophe said. ''But if not, I also have a few ideas on how to deter the enemy.''

''What are they?''

''Some things I have read about, but do not know if I can implement here.''

''Will it truly make a difference?''

''*Oui.* It will turn the tide in our favor.''

''Then get to it, Brother, while I set up the rotation schedule for the workers that you wanted.''

Nicolas's forthcoming marriage reminded Christophe of his own. He had mistakenly condemned Bronwyn. She had weathered his ire and suspicion with a dignity that he had once thought an act. He was a big enough man to admit when he was wrong, but didn't know the first thing about apologizing. He ran a hand through his hair. He had forgiven her; that would have to be enough.

An inner voice warned that it was insane to want a woman who had once tried to poison him. He silenced the voice, for he wanted Bronwyn with a passion that consumed him. Where his wife was concerned, he was, he admitted, his worst enemy.

He thought briefly of his past life. Drew Daniels had been successful by many standards, but personal happiness had eluded him. Now he had a chance to better his life, and the lives of those around him, and he would not fail.

He would not rest until he was assured his men and his people were safe. Already he had seen a change in the Welsh attitude toward the Normans. If he could foster more of the same, then the rebels would not be such a threat. He needed to know that the Welsh would support him if their countrymen stormed the citadel.

"Father, you must rest," Bronwyn insisted, laying her hand on his shoulder to detain him after the morning meal.

The interior of the palisades was warm; she wiped his brow and worriedly searched his strained features.

"See to your sister," Hayden snapped.

"She is resting," Bronwyn said, noticing the sympathetic look Fiona gave before she leaned back into her pillow.

He scowled. "Do not treat me like an invalid." He tried to rise but had difficulty. "The men are already at work. Would you have them think I am lazy?"

She sighed. Moving Fang out of her way, she supported his arm, helping him rise. "Father, you have trouble breathing."

"Then make me that cursed potion and leave be." He fell back in the chair to catch his breath.

His face was chalk white, and his breathing slow and labored. "The medicine will not cure you, Father," she said. "You must rest to insure you recover fully from these spells."

"Daughter," he warned.

She looked up to see Christophe enter the palisades.

"Hayden, what vexes you?" Christophe asked.

Hayden drew a deep breath. "My daughter wishes to coddle me. When are you going to give her some babies so she stops mothering me?"

"Father!" Bronwyn gasped, her face bright red.

Christophe chuckled. "Indeed, I will, just to save us all from her constant nagging." He poured a cup of mead and moved behind Hayden.

Too startled to rise to the bait, Bronwyn turned toward Christophe, thinking she had imagined his good humor. He placed a finger to her lips while glancing at Hayden's downcast head.

"I come to you with a problem of my own. I have need of someone to oversee the Welsh workers." He laid his hand on Hayden's shoulder. "Can you take this on?"

When her father nodded, Bronwyn nearly collapsed in relief. Her father would have an easier job, yet his pride would be saved. "Thank you," she mouthed.

He leaned forward and stole a kiss, his playful mien surprising her anew. Then he softly whispered, "Do not thank me. Your father is well liked and respected. This is in my best interest."

Bronwyn had to blink back tears of gratitude.

Hayden rose and turned toward the warlord. His lined face relaxed into a grateful smile. "I will not fail your trust in me." He took two steps, then turned back to his daughter. "You really should have a family of your own to worry about."

Christophe raised his drink to her, and she smiled. Did she dare hope that at last he had put the past to rest?

Like England, Wales was a strange country, its people stubborn and determined. Stories of fairies and mythical creatures seemed to come alive in this realm, where giant stone monoliths and eerie structures abounded.

Christophe looked down on his demesne from the hill. He had called in favors from warlords all over England, and additional supplies and workers had streamed in. After two months of strenuous labor the castle exterior and part of the wall had been raised. An immense pride filled him at the structure's shape. By virtue of sheer will and determination, he had created this dream.

He surveyed the terrain, looking out over the lush valley

below with a calculating eye. "Come, rebels, for I will be ready," he whispered to his enemy.

Wales, its land, its people, and its myths, were now an integral part of him. The air filled his senses with a familiar taste, with long forgotten scents. He belonged here. This was home.

Bronwyn often fell onto her pallet so exhausted she never heard Christophe joining her when he retired, and only rarely did she hear him rising before dawn. The summer days were filled with so many chores that they merged into one another. Bronwyn lost track of the hours, let alone the date, as she toiled to finish an impossible workload.

Day in, day out, with only an eight-hour respite for sleep, all worked a grueling schedule. Unfortunate refugees, displaced from their homes by the earthquake, they lived closely together in the crowded confines of the palisades, where tempers often flared. It took all of Christophe's wisdom to hold the men in order.

Although June and July had had tolerable weather, August was miserable, hot and humid. The very air hung stifling and muggy as sweat-laden clothes clung to the body like second skins. The sweltering heat increased the irritability, and drained the workers.

Bronwyn wiped the perspiration from her brow and thought of air-conditioning with ardent longing. Now, one prayed for a nice breeze and a cloudy day.

"Bronwyn," Nesta called, running through the field toward her, "let someone else do this chore." She pulled the hoe from Bronwyn's hands.

"The crops have to be weeded; soon the harvest will be upon us." Bronwyn reached for the tool, but Nesta moved it from her grasp. "We need to gather and preserve this food."

"Aye, but you do not have to do it alone. There are many women who can help. You wear yourself out, working like this."

Bronwyn straightened. "I thank you for your concern, Nesta, but I need to keep busy." Every villager had been pressed into shifts two months earlier and worked without complaint. She dared not rest, for fear of setting a bad example.

"My lady, we will be worse off if our healer is ill."

"I am fine. Besides, in only another week or two we will harvest the vegetables."

"Aye, we will be ready for the long winter."

Bronwyn looked around at the rich rows of leafy produce and smiled. "We have much to be proud of and thankful for." Then she looked to the castle. The half-constructed battlements shone in the hot sun. "It still amazes me what that man has accomplished."

"Oh, my lady, that is why I was sent. The master wants us to start moving our things into the newly constructed castle."

"But the interior is not complete."

"It makes little sense to me, but those are his orders."

Even though she thought the work on the inner structure would be hampered by everyone living there, she looked to the palisades. "The artisans will have some room with us gone. And we will be able to breathe a little easier with the additional space."

"Aye, my lady, the master said you were to supervise the move. Only to supervise."

Bronwyn dusted off her hands, and sucked in a breath at the sudden pain. She looked at her blistered and calloused hands.

"You see, my lady, your husband is right."

Bronwyn looked back to the cook. "Do I really look that bad?"

"Not bad, my lady, just tired. You tend the sick, and then work beside the women in the field. There are dark circles under your eyes and you have lost weight."

Bronwyn drove herself because Christophe needed her help. She had not thought he noticed.

"All right, Nesta, I will just supervise."

Nesta grinned. "Come, my lady, the women await your orders."

* * *

"Where are you going?" Nicolas asked Bronwyn.

"I have brought these." She whirled around to uncover the basket brimming with biscuits and meat for the men's noon meal. As she did so, a wave of dizziness assailed her. She had helped the women move their belongings all morning, and though she had promised only to supervise, she had worked a bit. Bronwyn cried out as she tried to stem the light-headedness that the heat and overwork had caused.

"Christophe," Nicolas called as he reached out to steady her. "Do you think it seemly that a warlord's wife is about to drop in her tracks from exhaustion?"

Christophe walked over, and her heart did a somersault at his closeness. She wanted to reach out and brush the weary lines from his brow. "I can spare neither the time nor the patience to see to her well-being." He turned to Bronwyn. "My dear wife, see to your own care. And I beg you, please stay out of trouble."

She bristled at his words and shrugged free of Nicolas. "I have never put myself in harm's way, sir. For you to suggest such a thing is insulting."

"I mean it, Bronwyn, you are to rest. If you must have attention, do it another way."

"Attention," she exclaimed, shoving the basket into Nicolas's hands as she approached her husband. "Sir, as much attention as you pay me, if I were a flower I would wither and die. However, know this, I do not seek or want your favor."

Amusement sparkled in his dark eyes. "Now, now, a good wife always seeks her husband's favor," he said, pulling her into his arms.

"My lord, let me go," she demanded. "Others are watching."

He held her close, his heart beating beneath her ear. The masculine scent of hard work and raw power filled her senses. Though she wished for more willpower, she melted into his embrace. It had been so long, so very long since he had even touched her. How could she not respond?

"My lord, please," she begged, knowing that if he did not

release her, she would easily succumb to his charm, with God and everyone watching.

He shook his head. "If I were not so busy I would make you pay for your foolish words in a most delightful way." His gaze fairly scorched her as he lowered his head and kissed her. Her heart raced as his mouth devoured hers, and shafts of desire streaked through her. Her hands slipped up his chest and gripped the thick muscles of his shoulders, the nails biting into his flesh conveying her need.

A moan rumbled deep within his chest as he drew her closer, crushing her in his embrace. His lips moved over hers, fanning the fire he had started. Not until a moan escaped her, did he end the kiss. By the time he pulled away, she was breathless. But a warm satisfaction traveled through her when he seemed as shaken as she.

"When we are alone you can offer your apology. And beg my favor."

Unable to stop herself, she stroked his chest. "My lord, I was just jesting. And though you think me a poor wife, I will confess I want you as badly as you want me."

"I know," he rasped, his voice husky and raw with need. He leaned close and whispered, "Later."

She could scarcely breathe as she watched him walk away. Later, indeed.

Chapter Ten

September brought a respite from August's heat. Children were less cranky and their parents breathed a sigh of relief. Thankfully, the women no longer had to haul water into the fields to water the thirsty plants. With the moderate temperatures, the vegetables ripened and produced a bountiful yield. Every woman and child worked in the field, harvesting from sunup to late at night, for Bronwyn had followed her husband's lead and organized her workers into shifts. It still amazed her that Christophe's thinking was hundreds of years ahead of its time. He was indeed a rare genius. But even with the time-saving innovations, bringing in the crop was still backbreaking work.

Once the crops were harvested, the work did not diminish. For two weeks the women cleaned, cut, boiled, blanched, or dried the vegetables for preserving. Heat radiated from the kitchen. A thick cloud of steam hung in the air from the three huge cauldrons boiling over the fires. In the field large lines were strung, where herbs, peppers, beans, and carrots were hung to dry in the sun. After the produce was salted, pickled, or dried, it had to be stored in a cool dry place. All the arduous work was made even harder by the chaos of the construction, but through it all, Nesta smiled, going calmly about her job and keeping her kitchen help in good humor. No grumbles were heard; perhaps they were too tired to complain. Whatever the reason, the women put up the stores of food in a fortnight.

It often seemed the days would never end. Then suddenly a month had elapsed since the crops were harvested and preserved. The cold winds chilled the fields, stripping the trees of leaves, blowing the seeds far away, as a lonely melody played in the treetops. The castle's exterior was completed, but the men still worked steadily on the walls. Every Welshman knew how hard the winter would be without protection, and no one slacked from their chores.

In the evening hours Bronwyn worked with Fiona on their mother's recovered wedding dress. The intricately embroidered tunic of white and blue had remarkably survived the earthquake with only minor damage. The sisters passed pleasant evenings mending and altering the treasured dress, and adjusting their ideas for the wedding celebration to fit the construction as best they could. Soon Bronwyn would start the rehabilitation of Fiona's leg, for after the jostling Fiona had received during the earthquake, there had been no question of removing the splints.

With the crops harvested and preserved, and the workload lightened, the days now had a different quality. Though the move from the open-air palisades offered them protection from the elements, Bronwyn was frustrated with the living conditions. The encampment had been bad enough, but the castle shell was worse. Now they were all enclosed in a smaller area. Sleeping pallets touched each other and completely covered the floor. Her husband seemed to understand her feelings, for though he often slept with his arms around her, he never tried to make love. His soldiers and the whole village slept in the great room. Until the rooms inside could be finished, and the village huts erected, there would be no privacy for anyone.

After an especially frustrating night pressed against Christophe's hard body, and knowing his desire matched hers, Bronwyn stormed into the kitchen, where several maids stepped aside to give her and her wolf shadow a wide berth. She went to the trestle table and began her early-morning chores, feeling a measure of composure settled over her by the time she kneaded the dough for the day's bread.

Nesta bustled into the room, her arms ladened with herbs, and dropped her leafy bundle onto the table. "I wish, my lady, the rooms of this castle were finished."

"Aye," Bronwyn agreed, "but until Christophe is satisfied with the defense, we will have to wait." Even as she said the words, an idea was forming in her mind. She had thought her preoccupation with privacy was her own twentieth-century quirk, but now she glanced around at the women in the kitchen and noticed they shared the cook's frustration. "Mayhap," she said, thinking Christophe would have to listen to her plea if others were involved. "I will speak to my husband."

"My lady, I do not want you to risk his displeasure on my account."

"It is for everyone," she lied, feeling only a slight tinge of guilt. "Besides, if someone is to approach him with an unpopular idea it should be his wife." Bronwyn dried her hands and reached down to scratch Fang's ear. "His opinion of me cannot sink any lower."

Nesta just shook her head, and Bronwyn patted her hand. "Listen to me. I sound like a spoiled child. All will be well." She left the kitchen and walked out into the great room, Fang following quietly behind her. Fiona lay on her pallet sound asleep, and the night workers were coming in to take their rest. Looking around the hall, she wondered how on earth she would ever convince her husband to suspend work on their defenses and start work on the interior.

She shook her head. He would never agree, and with good reason. Their defense had to come first. It would be midwinter before any work could be done on the interior.

"My lady, what has you so vexed?" a deep voice from above asked.

Startled, she looked up to the ceiling to see Nicolas hanging from a rafter on a rope ladder, and stringing several cords between the beams. "Nicolas. I did not see you there."

He climbed down and patted Fang. "I am taking measurements." Then he looked at her. "Why do you frown, my lady?"

"I wonder how to approach my husband for a boon."

Christophe's voice nearly shook the rafters. "You approach your husband, not his brother."

Startled, she whirled around. "Christophe!"

Several tired men turned over in their pallets, ready to take the man to task, but when they saw who disturbed their sleep they merely grumbled and pulled the covers over their head.

"Oui, your husband," he said, his voice quieter as he threaded his way through the pallets of his men. When he reached her, he took hold of her arm. "What is it you wish to ask and find so difficult that you must first tell my brother?"

"I . . ." Now that he was here, how did she ask for privacy? She glanced around at the men on their pallets, wishing she could have chosen another place for their talk. But one look at Christophe's tired features discouraged that idea. "I wish to speak to you of a very important matter."

"Then, speak of it," he said, giving her his undivided attention.

She hesitated, mindful of both Nicolas's curiosity and his men's awareness, then took a deep breath and plunged forward. "Ah, well, the villagers feel—along with myself—and everyone I have spoken to agrees . . ."

He raised an eyebrow. "Agrees on what, Wife?"

"Living together in this room is worse than the palisades. We are more crowded in here than we were outside. Sleeping side by side . . . has created hardships," she whispered, her insides churning as she tried to ignore the men whose shoulders were now shaking in silent laughter. Lifting her chin, she met Christophe's amused gaze, and swallowed her embarrassment. "There is a great need for privacy."

Christophe's knowing look made her cheeks blush.

"I am aware of the problem, *cherie,* as is every man who sleeps next to a woman," he said, his husky voice soft and seductive.

"Then, what do you plan to do about it?" Even though her face was flushed, she refused to back down.

"I am going to start the men working on the interior when the battlements are secure."

"But that could take all winter."

"*Non*, Wife, it will not." He touched her cheek. "I am glad to know you are hungry for me, but you did not have to tell the whole world."

Several guffaws sounded from the pallets, and her pride burned. She was mortified to have his men think she could not keep her hands off their precious leader, even if it was true. His gloating irritated her. She slapped his hand away. "You conceited, pompous, arrogant—"

"Man," he supplied.

"Pig," she yelled back childishly, then ran out of the room, needing desperately to have the last word for once.

His laughter followed her into the kitchen.

"I would say that went rather badly." Nesta hid a smile as the servants tried to smother their mirth.

After a moment Bronwyn, too, saw the humor in the situation and she burst into laughter.

"My lady," Cordelia said. "I would suggest that from now on when you want your husband's attention, you simply act rather then speak. Except, of course, to agree with him that he is the greatest lover of all time."

"Oh, he is that. But I want the rooms partitioned, not a quick toss in the hay."

"Are you sure, my lady?" Cordelia asked, patting her now pregnant stomach as Nesta chuckled, showing a mischievous smile.

Her face turned red and she laughed. "I guess I want everything. And why not, I am a princess, am I not?"

Nesta chuckled. "Indeed you are, my lady. But you want no more than any of us."

Bronwyn grinned. "Well, I am tired of waiting. After our chores we could start working on the interior."

"My lady," Nesta said, her humor replaced with concern, "I think you go too far. Your husband might consider that unfitting for a lady. And he would be well within his rights."

"I am not talking about true carpentry. Just a few temporary partitions that would afford us some privacy."

"My lady," Nesta's tone warned. "I know that look in your eye."

"Aye, I cannot fool you. I am talking about true carpentry."

Nesta's eyes rounded in surprise. "But the ladies know so little about construction."

"If we can cook the meals, clean the castle, plow the fields, and harvest them, then we can certainly figure out how to build some walls."

Cordelia waddled forward with her awkward gait and placed her hand on Bronwyn's arm. "But, my lady, we would need a knowledge of ciphering, scribing, and tallying to do that."

"I can assure you I have sufficient knowledge of each to see us through the task." Bronwyn crossed her fingers behind her back and prayed she would be forgiven this little lie.

Nesta folded her arms over her chest and shook her head sadly. "I do not remember you being that diligent with your tutor."

"I will surprise you," Bronwyn insisted. "Is it not worth a try?"

The ladies in the kitchen nodded hesitantly. "Aye," they chorused.

Excitement bubbling over within her, she walked around the room, gesturing here and there. "We could make our plans and build little sections here, then assemble them in the great room."

"Would it not be better to receive your husband's permission?" Cordelia asked cautiously.

Her note of reason dampened the women's elation as quickly as a wet blanket chills the flesh on a cold day.

"Very well, Cordelia," she agreed, looking at the solemn faces turned her way. "Do not trouble yourself overmuch. The warlord will grant the boon."

Though she doubted her own words, she smiled brightly to the women before she stomped off to find Christophe. On her way she racked her brain, trying to find a way to gain her husband's permission. The very thought of approaching him after the embarrassing episode put her teeth on edge.

She found him supervising the work on the battlements. She

drew a deep breath and stepped up to the brick and mortar wall. "My lord, I beg a word."

He spared her a glance before turning back to the work. "It will have to wait until tonight."

She gritted her teeth. "Pray, my lord, grant me a moment of your time."

He stared at her so long she thought he was going to deny her request again, then he took her arm and led her away. "What is it?"

"The great room is so austere, the women and I wish to add a woman's touch."

"You could not wait to ask me this?"

"I beg your pardon, my lord, but the men who sleep there during the day would have to move to the palisades." When he started to object, she quickly said, "It would only be for a day, and the women are so discouraged; this would help to cheer them up."

"Very well," he said, expelling a deep breath as he massaged his neck. "See to it, but do not bother me again."

"Certainly, my lord."

She had her permission, grudging though it was. Now all she needed to do was draw up the plans and organize the women. In a few days they could start. Why, she would even be saving Christophe time by building the partitions. She couldn't wait to see his face and hear his words of gratitude.

"Bronwyn, this hurts," Fiona cried. The newly discarded splints and bindings lay among the covers next to her as she tried to swing her leg over the pallet and stand up.

"I know, dear, but you must exercise," Bronwyn said, handing Fiona the crutches and helping her up. "The leg has been inactive for too long."

Fiona struggled on the supports, barely able to stand. She stood there, looking helpless as Bronwyn stepped back. Fiona wobbled in place, hopping on one leg as she favored her injured limb. Suddenly she lost her grip on the crutches and they clattered to the floor. "Help me."

Bronwyn hurried to place an arm around Fiona's waist to take most of her weight. "That is good, slowly ease your weight onto the weak limb."

Tears sparkled in Fiona's eyes, but she did as she was bade.

"It will take time, Sister, but you must do as I say." Bronwyn reached for the crutches and helped her sister balance with the supports.

"I trust you." Fiona leaned into the crutches and fairly dragged her leg in place. The sweat beaded on her upper lip, but her mouth set in a firm line as she struggled forward. " 'Tis very painful," she gasped.

"Aye, I know," Bronwyn soothed, hovering by her sister, ready to catch her, should she fall. But Fiona mastered the supports, even though she moved slowly. Bronwyn patted Fiona's back. "When these simple little tasks I have set out for you are accomplished without pain, you will know the leg has mended."

"I want to be well for my wedding." She gritted her teeth, and though perspiration broke out on her forehead, she took several more steps without a word of complaint.

"I am very proud of you, Fiona," Bronwyn encouraged, following her sister's progress until she was done. "That is enough for now. Tomorrow we will increase the distance. Rest now, tonight we will try a few more steps." Bronwyn eased her sister back down onto the pallet, then whirled around to resume her chores.

"Bronwyn, will you ask your husband if Caradoc could attend?"

She stopped in her tracks and looked back at her sister's hopeful face. Bronwyn drew a deep breath. "If that is your wish, I will ask Christophe. I promise." The moment she had given her vow, she wished she had not. Christophe would probably be enraged. But the custom of allowing a truce so members of feuding families could attend weddings had been observed for years in Wales, and the time-honored tradition would allow Christophe to agree without losing prestige. Bronwyn walked over and kissed her sister's cheek. "I will take care of it. Give me a little time."

Fiona held her hand when she would have pulled away. "You talk of my resting, but you are the one who is exhausted. Bronwyn, you must stop this frenzied pace. I fear you will become sick."

"Who is the healer here?"

"Please, Sister, heed me."

"I promise, as soon as your wedding is over, I will rest all winter." Bronwyn lied to ease her sister's distress. She was tired, but so much had to be done. Besides, her husband never seemed to rest and it had become a matter of pride to keep pace with him.

At midnight an eerie glow filled the sky. Christophe and Nicolas were summoned to the wall. To the east an orange-red cloud shone bright in a black sky. "Fire," Christophe said instantly.

Nicolas's troubled features shone in the torchlight. "A whole forest will be gone by morning. Do you think the rebels started it?"

Christophe pointed to the eastern sky. "What else? There is no storm, no lightning."

"Shall we ride out?"

"Non. In the darkness we would be easy prey for attackers. The fire is far enough off. It will not reach us."

"How could they set fire to this land?"

" 'Tis war." Christophe turned away from the bright sky.

"But it is their homeland they destroy. If they lay waste to the land, what will they win?"

Christophe looked at his brother. "They think only of their cause. They may win, only to find they have lost."

"By morning there will be nothing left of that forest but charred stumps and smoldering ash."

"And game will be harder to find," Christophe observed thoughtfully, turning back to stare at the ever increasing glow. God help them, it would be a lean winter.

Nicolas slung his arm over Christophe's shoulder and leaned

forward on the wall. "We will have the comfort of knowing that while we feast, our enemy does not."

"If the rebels do not take the bait at your wedding, we will have to meet them on their own ground, which would be a dangerous proposition."

"Another month, and the wall will be fortified," Nicolas offered.

Christophe steepled his fingers while he mentally calculated the days needed. "God willing, that will be enough time."

"For what?"

"I told you I have been working on some ways to repel an army."

"Are you finally going to tell me what you have in mind?"

Christophe grabbed a torch and motioned for Nicolas to do the same and follow him. He held his torch high to illuminate his path as he walked outside the gate. He pointed to the ground before them. "Besides the circular ditch around our wall, which will be filled with water, I intend to dig another circle farther out and fill it with spikes."

Nicolas walked with him as he paced off the area. Christophe picked up several small sticks. "Imagine these as sharpened tree limbs," he said and positioned the sticks in the ground to demonstrate. "They will have trouble gaining access to the wall, and with it under construction we have to use every strategy to our advantage. Also, the fire has given me an idea. Underneath the stakes in this ditch we will put leaves, dried twigs, and small branches. When the enemy attacks we can set fire to this moat with flaming arrows and trap the rebels between the two moats." Christophe grabbed his arm. "What do you think of my idea?"

Nicolas looked first at the ground that would contain the stakes and flammable material, then back to the first ditch. When he met his brother's gaze, he was grinning. "I think, Christophe, that the enemy will not stand a chance."

Christophe beamed, then pulled his brother with him toward the castle. "Also, I have talked with the bow maker. I have plans for another design, which I believe will be far superior to the bows we now use."

Nicolas shook his head. "Mayhap, Brother, you should let your wife poison you more often. Since your wedding night you have been filled with most inventive ideas."

"*Non,*" Christophe said quickly. "I have always had these ideas, yet until recently never had reason enough to put them into practice. Now that I am a lord and landowner, I must see to those under me."

"This will do it," Nicolas said, entering the castle. "They will not know how to breach our defenses."

Christophe smiled. "I have several other ideas, but I wish to put these into effect immediately."

Nicolas slapped his brother on the back. "I hate to admit it, but you truly are the wit of this family."

Christophe pushed him away. " 'Twill give you a mark to shoot for."

Nicolas's features sobered. "I have never looked to best you. I improve, but it is against my own standard, not yours."

Christophe felt as though he was seeing his brother in a new light. "Then, you are a happy man," he said thoughtfully. "It seems I can never rest until I have come out on top of the heap."

"Our differences make us strong." Nicolas's hand covered the hilt of his sword. "Know that I would die for you, but I have no desire to be you."

Though startled by Nicolas's admission, Christophe grinned and quipped, "I will remember your vow the next time a warrior disarms me and places a sword to my throat. I will ask him to wait while we switch places."

Nicolas chuckled as he waved good night to his brother.

Though he had jested, the magnitude of Nicolas's words hung in Christophe's mind long after his brother had gone to bed. In his former life he had known only the lip-service his money had purchased. He was damn lucky that fate had given him Nicolas as his brother. He was good-natured, unselfish, and totally committed. Christophe didn't deserve such loyalty, but he treasured it.

The sky was overcast and the bite of rain filled the air. Shivering, Bronwyn approached her husband. "My lord, a word, please."

He raised an eyebrow, but escorted her away from the battlements. They walked through the open field. "What is it, Wife?"

"I have a boon to ask, my lord."

"You always do."

She wanted to glare at him, but quickly reined in her temper and looked at the sky. It would not do to antagonize him when she wished a favor.

He chuckled. "Do not pretend to be humble, Wife, you do not have sufficient humility to carry it off."

Resolve forgotten, she placed her hands on her hips. "Very well, Christophe. It galls me to ask you for permission, but I must."

"Who is it this time that you beg a favor for? I know you would die rather than ask for yourself."

That he had noticed caused a warm feeling to grow and curl in her belly. The lout was full of surprises.

When he brushed a finger across her cheek, warmth traveled to her face. "Your pride is far too great to allow you to be beholden to me."

Instantly the kind feelings evaporated. Her eyes narrowed and she moved back, evading his touch. She mentally counted to ten. "Fiona wishes permission for Caradoc to attend her wedding."

He stared at her so long she thought he was going to deny her request, but then he smiled, a slow smile that made her heart flutter.

"I am not so mean-spirited that I would deny your sister her family on her wedding day. I will let the word be spread that a truce will hold that day."

Bronwyn had been expecting the worst, so several moments passed before she stammered, "Thank you."

His smile grew, full and warm, rich with male charm. "Thank me with a kiss."

She looked around and realized they had walked into a secluded part of the field. Standing within the shelter of a clump of trees, they were effectively hidden from view. Her hands slipped up his chest, and her fingers caressed the nape of his neck as she pulled his head down to receive her kiss.

The moment his lips touched hers, heat consumed her. It had been so long. Too long! His lips moved over hers with a hunger that excited and thrilled her.

He gathered her into his arms and crushed her to his chest. His tongue slipped past her lips to sensuously sweep the inside of her mouth, before darting in and out to tease and tantalize her. A deep moan sounded in her throat as she clasped her hands tighter around his neck and leaned into his heated embrace. His hands roamed down her back, caressing and massaging every inch of her until they clasped her buttocks, pulling her tight against his desire. She gasped against his lips as her fingers combed through his hair, then slipped down into the laces of his tunic, frantically trying to untie the knot. He groaned, his kiss turning fierce and carnal.

She melted into his embrace. Her hands eagerly roamed over the vast expanse of his muscular chest, sweeping his tunic open, then off his broad shoulders. She caressed every solid inch of his bare flesh, selfishly savoring every firm line and solid ridge of his chest, shoulders, and back. Unable to fill her need to touch him, she pulled and tugged at his remaining clothes. Her nails scored his chest, then her hands slipped beneath his braies, and she thrilled when his thick muscles rippled beneath her fingertips. Her fingers grazed his manhood, and he sucked in sharply as his body trembled with need. Suddenly he pulled her hands free and crushed her to him, kissing her with a possessive heat. When he lifted his head, she saw his raw desire. Her heart beat faster as he removed her gown, his fingers brushing her flesh with a featherlike touch. For just a moment he stepped back and devoured her with his hungry gaze. She shivered with anticipation as his sleepy-lidded gaze returned to hers. Slowly she knelt on the heaped pile of their clothes, pulling his braies down with her as she went. The sun broke through the clouds to outline naked perfection as he knelt over her, his body warm and wonderful.

She reached out to trace her finger over his heart, and his muscle jumped and flexed. She reveled in the quiver and continued to trace little swirls on his chest.

His mouth captured hers. Suddenly she felt his control snap and his urgency return. His kiss was hot, wet, and wild. She slipped her hands down his chest and latched onto his manhood. His groan drove her on, and she moved her hands over the rigid rod, her nails grazing the thick muscle ever so softly. He tore his lips from hers. "Witch," he groaned, "I am going to drive you as wild as you drive me."

"Christophe," she sighed as his lips covered her breast. When his tongue swirled around her nipple, liquid heat streaked to her core. She ached with need, and grabbed his hair. But he tantalized and teased her nipple until she cried out.

Slowly he lowered his lips to her stomach, and short stabs of electricity sizzled through her. She could hardly breathe. "Christophe, please," she begged.

His lips trailed a line of light kisses up her chest, his teeth grazing the side of her breast. She quivered as a tingle of sensual warmth rippled over her. When his lips at last closed over hers, she deepened the kiss.

"Love me," she whispered.

He entered her and she lost thought of everything: the day, the year, the millennium. She was experiencing wave after wave of pleasure. She held onto him, meeting and accepting every thrust. Pure sensations of ecstasy washed over her at a speed that both frightened and excited her. Her senses absorbed tastes, smells, his touch, then suddenly magnified them into bursting impressions of color, light, and sound. She climaxed, fast, swift, hard, crying out his name. Moments later he also reached fulfillment and collapsed, his body warm and covered in a soft sheen. She wrapped her arms and legs around him, and they clung together in a contented daze.

* * *

Bronwyn hammered her partition into place and stepped off the ladder to admire her handiwork. Hands on her hips, she cocked her head and smiled. "By heavens, we have done it. Wait until the men see this."

The room suddenly grew quiet. Turning to view what she was sure would be awe on the women's faces as they examined their work of art, she saw instead shock. The men were just beginning to enter.

"What brings you back so early?" Bronwyn cried.

Christophe raised an eyebrow at her greeting. He took two steps into the room, then stopped. "Good God, what have you gone and done now?"

"You told me I could make a few changes."

"To the decor, not the structure." He pushed on the supports the women had hammered, and the entire frame shifted. "God's teeth, woman! This is a death trap."

" 'Tis not! 'Tis a bedroom. One of many," Bronwyn snapped.

The men stood gaping, their eyes wide. The realization that the women had worked all day to build separate bedrooms to offer privacy could not elicit anger, but the job was so wholly inadequate that the men could not keep a straight face.

"Are you trying to put these poor husbands into an early grave? Look close. 'Tis more a coffin than a bedchamber."

Bronwyn crossed her arms over her chest. "How dare you! Everyone worked so hard. I tell you, it is not that bad." She leaned against it, and the wood groaned under her light weight. She quickly straightened. "It just needs a few minor supports."

Christophe did not respond, but his look said he knew that she knew it was not safe.

"We will take it down," she said sadly.

"*Non*. We will." Though bone weary, the men took down the structure and began to construct new, sturdier rooms.

By the time the women had put the evening meal on the tables, the men had roughed out partitions. Bronwyn turned full circle, delighted with the progress. "Oh, 'tis truly a marvel." She looked sheepishly at Christophe. "I should have asked your help earlier."

He chuckled. "You could not have done that for fear of my refusal."

"How did you know?"

"I guessed," he said wryly.

"No matter." She smiled, then pointed around. "Look how lovely. Why, in a few days the interior will be completed."

"Do not even think it. I will allow one more day spent on the interior. Whatever we can accomplish is what you must live with."

"How very kind you are, my lord." She nodded all the while thinking there were ways around such a pigheaded edict.

As the first rays of morning lit the sky, Christophe was awakened by the duty guard. "My lord, there is a messenger from London."

Groggy from little sleep, Christophe shook off the lingering remnants of exhaustion and quickly rose from his pallet. Hastily dressing, he walked over to his brother and summoned Nicolas. After several loud groans, Nicolas rose and fumbled with his clothes, then both men followed the soldier to the courtyard.

The messenger bowed and handed the lord his missive. Christophe read it and silently handed it to his brother. Then he turned to the king's man. "Rest and refresh yourself before your journey back."

"Thank you, my lord." The soldier followed the guard into the castle.

" 'Tis well, we are prepared," Nicolas remarked.

"Indeed," Christophe said. "But I am not surprised Lord Odo has deserted us. I always suspected that there would be no help forthcoming from London."

"God's teeth, Brother, you plan to stay?"

"*Oui.* If the rebels wish to drive me from my home, they must kill me." He looked solemnly at his brother. "But I want you to know you have a choice. You may leave."

Nicolas chuckled. "I would rather stand with you in the midst of chaos than lounge in the king's court during peace." He gripped Christophe's arm. "You are my brother, and if you make a stand here, then so will I."

Christophe shook his brother's arm. "Then we stand together."

Chapter Eleven

The wedding day dawned gray with rain and howling wind. In the partitioned suite, Cordelia frowned.

" 'Tis an ill omen. Mark my words, my lady, there will be days shadowed by sorrow."

Fang lifted his head at the servant's raised voice.

Bronwyn gave Cordelia a sharp glance. "Everyone knows sorrow. Stop trying to ruin Fiona's day. You are just out of sorts with your great bulk."

Fiona twirled about, her arms flung wide. "Do not worry about me, Bronwyn. Nothing can destroy my happiness."

"Be careful, Fiona. Your leg needs more gentle activity."

"Drivel." She lifted her skirts and extended her leg. "You see it is fully mended."

"But still not strong. Please, Sister, heed my words."

"Very well, if I must rest, then I do so . . . here." With a dramatic sigh Fiona collapsed into a gentle heap upon the floor.

"My lady!" Cordelia gasped while Nesta chuckled.

" 'Tis all right. I am but obeying Bronwyn."

Shaking her head, Nesta held up the soft undertunic. "Come and undress, my lady. Here is your smock."

Tears stung Bronwyn's eyes as she helped her sister dress

for the ceremony. Fiona turned this way and that, fussing and fidgeting until Bronwyn had to tell her sternly to hold still. "I will never be able to fix your hair if you do not stop your squirming."

"But I am so excited." She turned and grabbed hold of Bronwyn's hands. "I wish Mama could be here."

"So do I," Bronwyn whispered as a sudden pang of loneliness struck her. It was times like these that made her remember . . . remember and wish . . . Oh, how she missed her own family.

"But you and Papa are here." Fiona brightened.

"True, and Mother is here in spirit." Neither of them mentioned Caradoc.

Bronwyn finished the preparations, then turned her sister to face the polished metal.

An image of two beautiful women stared back, one with golden hair and amber eyes, dressed in a lovely gown of gold and brown. The other had light blond, almost silver, hair with pale-blue eyes, and wore the silver wedding tunic with a rich-blue underdress.

"Is that truly me?" Fiona breathed, staring in awe at her reflection. From her crown, her loose flowing hair fell like a soft cloud about her delicate shoulders, and Bronwyn's beautiful amber jewels, interwoven in a braid, formed a lovely headdress atop Fiona's head. "Why, I feel as pretty as you."

Bronwyn showed her surprise at her sister's remark, and Fiona clasped Bronwyn's hands. " 'Tis true. For years I have envied you. Forgive my vanity as I could not help it. Now, however, I am happy with myself."

Bronwyn hugged her sister, ashamed by her own twinge of envy over Fiona's relationship. Nicolas was marrying Fiona, not for king and country, but for love. "Happiness is what I wish for you," she whispered, then kissed her sister's cheek. When she pulled away, she smiled. "Let us hurry, you do not want to keep your handsome groom waiting."

"Nay, not after waiting all my life to find him," Fiona said, walking from the room, with confidence and poise.

When Fang stood to follow them, Bronwyn shook her head

and pointed to the floor. "Stay," she ordered, not wanting him to come, for fear he might disrupt the ceremony.

She followed her sister into the narrow hallway and out to the courtyard, where she noticed thankfully that the sun had emerged and a huge rainbow shone in the sky. This was a good sign that the marriage would be blessed by happiness.

A soft dry cushion was provided for Fiona, and she knelt beside Nicolas before the friar as Bronwyn joined her husband.

Tears misted Bronwyn's eyes when they spoke their vows. She rapidly blinked her eyes to clear the moisture, then drew a deep breath. She could not explain why the solemn vows had moved her to tears, except that lately her emotions seemed very close to the surface.

Her gaze drifted to her father, who wiped at his eyes and sniffed loudly. When he caught her glance, she saw regret in his eyes. Was it for this wedding, or the last?

When it was time Bronwyn stepped forward to sing the song she had promised, a ballad of Lady Guinevere and her love for King Arthur's knight, Lancelot. Her voice was clear, the notes true, every word filled with love and sadness for the doomed lovers. 'Twas the song Fiona had chosen, and a hush lay over the crowd when Bronwyn was done.

Nicolas placed an amber ring on Fiona's finger, then kissed her palm. Bronwyn glanced at her own wedding ring. Amber must be a family stone, she thought as she cradled the band in her hand. Tears again welled up in her eyes, and she could not explain why the similarity in bands should move her so. *Believe in love,* she reminded herself, and she smiled, drawing strength from the message. Soon the kiss of peace was given, the friar pronounced them man and wife, and a loud cheer went up from the assembly.

Men and women rushed forward to congratulate the happy couple, the musicians played their instruments, and the merriment began. Bronwyn quickly joined the bride and groom to offer her congratulations, then made way for other well-wishers.

Christophe pulled her aside. "Your song was lovely," he

said and kissed her palm. "And so are the decorations." He pointed to the evergreens and ribbons she had hung at the gate and the fresh flowers that draped over the wall.

Her fingers had ached with twisting the branches and tying them off, but this was the only place where the ceremony could be held and she had to see it beautiful for the occasion. "'Tis not I but the weather that deserves to be praised," she demurred.

He ignored her modesty. "The weather be damned. With all the hardships we have suffered, you still managed to do all this. You are a marvel."

A lump rose in her throat and she looked away.

"Here, what's this? Tears?" He tilted her chin up to gaze into her eyes.

Embarrassed, she tried to push his hand away.

"Is a compliment so foreign to your ears that it reduces you to tears?"

"Nay. 'Tis the wedding."

"Why tears?"

"Women always cry at weddings," she said. "Look around you."

He glanced about, and to his amazement every woman's eyes glistened with unshed tears.

"If I live to be a hundred I will never understand women."

His droll comment made her chuckle. "If you lived to be a thousand you would never understand us. But, then, men are still a mystery to me, as well. Thank goodness."

"You find that a comfort?"

"Aye, every day is an adventure. I am constantly surprised by you."

He raised an eyebrow. "Are you?"

She nodded and her smile broadened. "You are a soldier, yet you have an amazing talent for invention. You bear the reputation of a sadistic brute, yet you show kindness and charity. You are an enigma."

He wrapped his arm around her shoulders and pulled her close. "I do not know what to say."

She looked up and met his gaze, and her breath caught in

her throat. Pure desire burned in his eyes . . . and a glimmer of love. Did she only wish it, or was it there? Never mind, she needed to believe that somewhere in his heart he loved her. She leaned into him, drawn to the unspoken demand in his lovely, dark eyes.

His hands gripped her shoulders as he crushed her in his embrace. The warmth of his body and his subtle masculine scent surrounded her. She suddenly wished they were alone. But the sound of the merrymakers intruded on her thoughts, and she patted his chest. "My lord, you must congratulate the couple."

His scorching gaze fairly melted her heart. "I know," he sighed.

His obvious disappointment delighted her. "Come, Husband, duty calls."

Before he could follow her, a Norman guard approached and murmured in Christophe's ear. He nodded to the soldier, then joined her as she weaved a path through the crowd.

The gates suddenly opened, bringing in a gust of wind and leaves—and Caradoc. "I came to wish my sister well on her wedding day."

"Caradoc," Fiona cried happily, running to greet him, her arms flung wide.

At first he did not embrace her, waiting, as was custom for Nicolas's approval.

"If my wife welcomes you, then so do I," Nicolas said.

With a curt nod Caradoc hugged his sister, then turned to greet his father. "I could not stay away."

Hayden's pallor was ashen. "As long as you come in peace, all will be well."

Caradoc looked to Christophe and bowed his head. "Upon my word I vow to honor the terms of the truce."

Bronwyn's gaze darted between her brother and her husband. Even though Christophe had given his word, would he honor it?

"Then you are welcome," Christophe said, extending his hand.

Though Caradoc's eyes widened, he accepted the greeting

and clasped the warlord's hand, then turned to Bronwyn. "No greeting for me, Sister?"

Bronwyn looked once at Christophe, still amazed by his gracious manner, then she turned back to Caradoc. "If my manners seem lacking, then forgive me, Brother. I am surprised, but pleased. Pray, enjoy the day with your family."

He embraced her and kissed her cheek. "I hated to leave you," he whispered. "But I could not expect you to accompany me."

"I understand," she murmured.

"I feared your reaction most of all," he softly replied. "I am glad to see I have not severed all my ties."

Christophe put his arm around her and drew her back from her brother's arms, his subtle message clear. Although there was a temporary truce, the sides must still be separate.

Caradoc bowed to the warlord, understanding immediately. "May I ask your permission to dance with my sister?"

"*Oui*, but only one, for I am very possessive of my wife." He kissed her fingers and she felt tingles clear to her shoulder. Then his gaze locked with hers. 'Twas not desire she read there, but caution.

Bronwyn laughed, her fears forgotten, as she danced with Caradoc to a lively little tune. She had never been able to dance in her former life. Music and laughter accompanied her moves and she could not help showing off her ability. Her feet flew in intricate steps and she kicked up her skirts as she wheeled and twirled to the wonderful music. On one full turn her heart skipped a beat, for the gates opened again, and there in the portal stood a hideous-looking man and his servant. The very same man she had seen in her room.

She gasped, "It's him," and looked around for Christophe.

Caradoc's grip tightened, and he whispered urgently, "Do not give him away."

She pulled her hand from his. "But he is the man who stabbed Fang," she explained. "He threatened me."

"He has threatened to kill one of my family if he is betrayed. He caused Fiona's accident. Do you wish to be responsible for worse? If you expose him, he will kill her, or mayhap Father."

"Caradoc, what hold does he have over you?" she asked, unable to believe he was willingly involved with someone who would hurt his family. "Tell me." She clutched his tunic as the music stopped.

"Sister—"

"Caradoc, where is the lovely bride?" the intruder inquired in a booming voice. "Point her out so I can pay my respects."

Caradoc gave Bronwyn a warning glance.

Hayden approached, his eyes narrowed, his stance challenging. "Rhett, what business brings you here?" he demanded.

"As your son's chieftain I have come to honor his family."

"Chieftain?" Hayden turned toward his son, his face a mask of disbelief. "You are sworn to him?"

"Aye, Father. When I saw, there was nothing left for me here, I ventured out to make my own fortune. Much like these visitors." He pointed to the Normans.

Christophe smiled at the jab. "And have you been successful?" he asked, joining his wife.

"More successful than if I had remained at home."

Christophe raised an eyebrow as he took in the young man's tattered clothes and unkempt person. "Then, you are happy with your lot?"

Caradoc looked him in the eye. "Aye, very happy."

Hayden clapped his son on the back. "It is good to have you home. Perhaps during this time you will change your mind and decide to rejoin your family."

Caradoc looked ill at ease but he did not dispute his father's words.

As Rhett moved through the courtyard, accompanied by an aide, a hush fell upon the crowd. People made way for him, averting their eyes as he marched through the crowd. Bronwyn knew it was more than his disfigurement that made the assembly uncomfortable. Instinctively they knew evil had entered their midst, and fear pervaded every corner of the walled yard.

Rhett bowed before her. "My lady, 'tis a pleasure to see you again," he said boldly.

She glanced at Christophe, aware that he was wondering

where she had made this man's acquaintance, but she remained silent.

Christophe stepped between them, forcing the man to acknowledge him. "Although my wife is lovely, and many men are overcome by her beauty, 'tis customary to pay your respects to the lord before his lady."

"My lord," he said, and bowed low, but there was no semblance of respect in his gesture.

"We have met before," Christophe said.

Bronwyn closed her eyes, praying Christophe would not remember her description, and thankful she had left Fang in her room.

Rhett remained silent, ignoring the warlord to stare at Bronwyn.

She shuddered at the frank appraisal, and moved closer to her husband.

Christophe drew her hand through his arm, then stared at the stranger. "You have a face that is hard to forget. I will remember where it was that I saw you."

Rhett grinned, which forced his puckered lower lip into a hideous, crooked twist. "Perhaps you will."

"Never fear, Welshman, in time I will know exactly where it was that I first laid eyes on you." The quiet threat was more menacing than an angry retort.

Rhett walked away as though the warlord had simply said good day. His manner was arrogant, his expression unflinchingly cold as he and his aide joined the wedding party.

Bronwyn shivered. She wanted to tell her husband that Rhett was the man who had threatened her, but she could not. After what he had done to Fiona, she knew he was capable of anything.

Bronwyn felt her husband's gaze upon her and met it. He stared at her so intently that she felt he had divined her thoughts.

"Wife, the time has come to make a decision. You must choose your husband or your family."

"Christophe, please," she breathed, wringing her hands as she watched Rhett hover next to the wedding party.

"Bronwyn."

She tore her gaze from her sister, and looked up into those dark eyes. The stern inflexibility she saw there chilled her, and she could not hold his gaze.

"You are keeping something from me. I can see it in your eyes."

She drew a deep breath, trying not to ruin the evening for both herself and her sister. "Christophe, I cannot deny that, but neither can I tell you what it is. You must trust me."

He crossed his arms over his chest and stared down at her. "Who are you protecting?"

When she remained silent, his eyes narrowed. "Do you refuse to tell me?"

"Aye," she breathed.

"Then, you have made your choice." His features hardened as though turned to stone, and he turned away from her.

Her chest constricted, and at the same time her pride rebelled at such an arrogant decree. She reached out and touched his arm. "You ask much from me, but what are you willing to give?"

"Give? Woman, have you lost your mind?"

"Nay, Christophe, what price would you pay for my sake? Would you betray your family?"

" 'Tis not the same."

"If our places were reversed, would you want to have to prove yourself to your spouse?"

"What proof would you wish?"

"I would ask nothing of you."

"Then, you are a fool."

"I would wish for a spouse who is a partner, not a loyal servant," she responded, knowing all the while that she was indeed a fool, the biggest fool in the entire castle. She had fallen in love with her husband, a man who at the slightest provocation suspected her of the worst.

"You have duties to perform," he suddenly snapped. "And I must speak with those whom I trust."

The musicians began to play another lovely tune on the mandolin and lute. She tore her gaze from her husband's, and with a bright smile firmly in place she moved off to make sure that her sister's night was a glorious one. Not for all the world would she let her husband or anyone else know that he had just crushed her.

Christophe was absent most of the night. She did not notice where he had gone or when, but she did notice that no matter where she was, Rhett managed to be close by. Her skin crawled when she caught him leering at her. Even though she was upset with Christophe, she dearly wished he would return, and soon, for she did not like being the object of Rhett's attention.

She turned away to find her brother watching her. "What troubles you so?"

"I do not like your friend," she said bluntly.

He cupped her arm to lead her toward the dancing. "You did not like your first bridegroom, either?"

"Bridegroom!" She stopped and pulled her arm free of his grasp. "Caradoc, what have you done?"

"Lower your voice," he hissed, leading her away from the crowd. "I have promised him your hand when we defeat the Normans."

She gasped. "Are you lack-witted, or cruel?"

His face flushed. "Bronwyn, it was necessary to enlist his aid."

"Then, Caradoc, you marry him." She started to pace, trying to work off her anger.

"Bronwyn?"

"You tell him right now that I will never consider such a match."

"Nay," he cried, his face growing red. "I need his men to regain our land; then I will be your protector and you will have no choice but to honor my agreements."

"I am sorry for you." She pushed away, intending to confront the chieftain herself, but halfway across the courtyard, Hayden stopped her.

"What is wrong, Daughter?"

She clasped his hands, his concern a balm to her frazzled

nerves. "Caradoc has promised me to that chieftain as his wife. I am going to tell him our marriage is not acceptable."

Hayden's face tightened in anger. "Nay, Daughter, Rhett is the devil himself. Do not anger him." He escorted her away from the crowd. Once inside the castle she faced him.

"Father, I cannot let him think I would ever go through with it."

" 'Tis my responsibility to arrange my daughters' marriages. I will inform him."

She laid her hand on his arm. "Father, please, I do not want you to make an enemy."

He patted her hand. "See to your sister and her husband. I think they are ready to retire."

She nodded. Although she did not want Hayden confronting Rhett on her behalf, she could not refuse to see to her duties. Besides, as much as she relished delivering a set-down to that despicable man, she knew it would be ill-advised.

Not for the first time she wondered where her charming husband had gone. Once she helped to prepare her sister for the wedding night, she would find him.

In the gatehouse, Christophe leaned forward into the small group of soldiers. "You must appear to be drunk. I want no man to drink any brew but that served by Michau."

His men listened, then left the battlement and quickly spread the word. Michau moved among the wedding guests and filled the soldiers' chalices. If they had a moment he explained the reason, if not he remained silent.

"I will assign someone to keep an eye on the chieftain," Michau said, pouring a chalice of wine for Christophe.

"They will try to cause a diversion," Christophe said, sipping his wine slowly as he surveyed the wedding guests. His gaze settled on Rhett and his eyes narrowed as he set the wine down. "Keep alert. I will find Nicolas."

He passed his brother in the hallway and quickly pulled him into a shadowed alcove to apprise him of the situation.

Nicolas stared longingly down the hall at the wedding chamber, before he turned and said, "I will join you."

"*Non,* stay with your wife. If they think we suspect anything, they may not carry out their plan."

Nicolas nodded and proceeded down the castle hallway to his chamber room set aside from the revelers.

Bronwyn came out of the room, barely nodding as she passed Nicolas and went down the hallway. She walked slowly, obviously preoccupied.

Patches of torchlight washed over her, and Christophe observed her closely. He knew she was hiding something, something that troubled her. He had to talk to her, and now was the perfect opportunity. Just as Christophe was about to call out to her, a man stepped out of the shadows and stopped her, then led her down the corridor toward the side hallway.

Christophe followed, determined to have a word with her. He caught up with them just as the man was pulling her into an alcove.

She screamed for help, but the attacker covered her mouth, muffling her cry. She clawed and kicked, but was easily overpowered, and he quickly dragged her into the darkness.

Rage filled Christophe as he ran forward, recognizing the assailant as Rhett's aide. Christophe grabbed the attacker, throwing him to the ground. Over and over, he pounded the assailant, smashing his fist repeatedly to the face, until the man cried out, "I beg you to stop."

Christophe hauled him to his feet and shook him. "Mercy, my lord," the man whimpered.

Christophe dropped him and turned to Bronwyn.

Before he could reach her, she looked past him to scream.

Instinctively he wheeled about to fend off a knife thrust.

"Lord Rhett bade me bring this woman to him. Now, I have the added pleasure of gutting a Norman pig," the assailant laughed.

Christophe ignored the taunt to push the knife back and twist the man's arm. He screamed, but lunged away.

"It would appear you will have more trouble than you had anticipated."

The man's face turned bright red as he dove at Christophe and they crashed to the ground. Rolling back and forth, they fought for the knife as the blade hovered dangerously between them. "You will all die tonight!"

His back on the ground, Christophe slipped his leg around his opponent's and flipped him off. Once free, he quickly jumped to his feet and saw Bronwyn trying to swing a torch at the assailant. "Stay back," he ordered as he turned and grabbed hold of the knife. He twisted it and with a shove drove it into the man's gut.

The assailant looked stunned as he stumbled back and grabbed hold of the dagger. He staggered to his knees and fell face forward.

Bronwyn rushed into his arms. "Are you all right?"

Her hands touched his chest, his arms, his face. He took hold of her shoulders and held her away from him. "Bronwyn, what did he mean?"

She slumped against him. "Christophe, he was trying to abduct me." Of course. It was a perfect diversion. "Rhett's going to attack tonight."

"Shhh," he murmured to calm her.

"Christophe, listen to me," she said, pushing his arms away. "Rhett's men are on their way. He will meet them in the old castle, where their weapons are hidden. Before dawn they will retrieve their swords and bows and launch an attack."

"The old castle?"

"Aye." She grabbed his hand and pulled him down the corridor. "He bragged to me about it."

"This way," Christophe said, pulling her down the hall to the private area set aside for the wedding night. He called his brother's name softly. When silence met his summons he rapped on the door. After a muffled curse Nicolas appeared, bare chested and pulling his tunic back over his head. "God's teeth, Christophe. What has happened?"

Christophe ignored his brother's irritation and quickly explained.

Nicolas nodded in understanding. "I will stand with you."

Christophe turned to his wife. "Tell us about the weapons."

She drew a deep breath. "After the weapons were stolen, there was no way to take them from the fortress without being caught. So they were hidden in the castle in a secret room that Ca . . . someone had shown Lord Rhett."

"Is that what Rhett was doing in our chamber?"

Bronwyn gasped and turned to face her husband. "You knew?"

"Why did you keep it from me?"

She sighed, spreading out her hands in an imploring gesture. "I could not tell you. He would have harmed Fiona again."

"Again?" Nicolas asked, rounding on her.

She met her brother-in-law's gaze. "Aye, Fiona did not trip down the stairs, she was shoved. I found out tonight that Rhett was responsible for her injuries. I was told if I exposed him, he would do the same again—or worse."

Nicolas's features tightened into an angry mask. "By His wounds, I will kill him."

Christophe grabbed his brother's arm. "This is not the time to settle personal scores."

Nicolas took several deep breaths and nodded.

"Go on, Bronwyn. What else did he say?"

"They were still waiting for a chance to retrieve the weapons when the stronghold collapsed. Over the past months they have been tunneling to them."

"Where is the room?"

"There is a secret area, more an alcove than a room. It is located behind the master suite. I will show you. But we must hurry. Rhett's men are on their way. They plan to attack at daybreak, when the guards are still sotted."

Nicolas shook his head and stepped forward. "*Non*, it is too dangerous, Bronwyn."

"Nay, I must come." She turned to Christophe. Her eyes held an earnest plea. "You and I must end this distrust. If you let me come, then you will know once and for all if you should trust me."

He hated to admit it, but she was right. He had doubted her the moment Rhett had entered the courtyard and she had not told him who he was. Christophe looked at Nicolas. "If the plan is to work, she must come with us."

"See to alerting the men, while Bronwyn and I keep the guests occupied," Christophe said as he escorted Bronwyn back to the festivities.

He drew her closer. "Do you think you can act like a wife in love with her husband?"

She pulled out of his arms. " 'Twill not be hard, my lord," she murmured, her eyes shimmering.

He merely grunted and recaptured her hand. An uneasy feeling settled in the pit of his stomach when he considered his decision to drag her on the mission. He had never exposed a woman to peril before. An inner voice warned it could be a trap.

With Bronwyn on his arm, he walked among the wedding guests, covertly signaling out the men he wanted to accompany him. After they had circulated through the crowd, he continued to throw off suspicion by dancing with Bronwyn. He was amazed how light his wife was on her feet. As though the music traveled through her body, she moved to the rhythm like a cloud in the wind. And when he looked into her eyes, they sparkled. She loved dancing, and it showed in her smile, sounded in her laughter, and captivated all within her sphere. Many dancers stopped and watched them, and when the dance ended he clapped along with the guests at her grace and beauty. Her father moved to the center of the room, raising his hands for the crowd's attention. "Our bride has asked that her sister sing a special song tonight. The bride and groom are tucked away in their nest, and wish to be serenaded." He nodded to the musicians, then motioned to Bronwyn.

Her hand trembled in Christophe's and she looked at him. "This wasn't planned," she whispered.

"Apparently, Nicolas needs more time. You must provide it. Sing your heart out, Bronwyn. Sing as you have never sung before." He squeezed her hand, then shoved her gently forward.

She drew a deep breath, closed her eyes, and let all her tenderness and emotion echo throughout the hall. The purity of her voice and the honesty of the song reached out to everyone there. Even hardened soldiers stopped talking and stared awed by her melodious voice and the exceptional power of her song.

When the last word of the song lingered in the air, a round of deafening applause filled the courtyard. After the ovation Christophe smiled and carefully signaled the guards watching the two guests. The guards sauntered over to them, as though they were going to congratulate the lady on her performance. While they bowed and paid tribute to her, Christophe whispered, "Make sure Caradoc and Rhett enjoy the feast. Drug their wine. I want them watched at all times. And send someone to take care of the body." His orders given, he danced his lady around the courtyard and into the shadows, where they snuck out of the castle with a handful of men.

The old castle was a dangerous heap of broken timbers. Nicolas met them at the south end of the fallen keep. "The tunnel is in the north end. I will stay and stand guard," he offered.

Christophe led his men to the far side, where they discovered a tunnel had indeed been dug.

As they entered the narrow hole, Bronwyn gripped Christophe's hand tightly, then moved ahead of him. He realized the danger he was putting her in and felt a twinge of guilt. Still, if she were to betray them, too many would suffer.

Crawling on their hands and knees, they moved down the tunnel. The smell of wet earth and rotting timber filled the air. If this tight space made his skin crawl, he could imagine what it was doing to his wife. The resemblance to a grave was all too fitting. A cave-in would bury them alive. He cringed at the image. Sweat formed on his brow, and he put the thoughts from his mind.

At the end of the tunnel they found the room, containing all their missing weapons, as well as a host of others. Once they were collected, they were in and out of the tunnel within an hour. Christophe had his answer about Bronwyn, and a great weight was lifted from his shoulders.

Nicolas organized the men to carry the weapons back to the stone castle. They entered the castle as though they had returned from duty, with the additional weapons hidden beneath their tunics or cloaks. Once inside, they walked through the courtyard and into the temporary quarters of the great room right under the noses of their enemy.

When Christophe returned to the castle, his wife was by his side, her hair messed and her tunic covered in grime. "If Rhett could see you now, he might not want you," he teased. He brushed her hair from her face and was struck anew at the light shining in her eyes. "You enjoyed that, didn't you?"

She nodded, her windblown hair falling in gentle cascades down her back. " 'Twas a marvelous adventure."

"I have another warrior," he whispered as he pulled her into his arms. But he rather liked her like this, her hair mussed and her eyes shining with eagerness. It reminded him of how she looked when they made love.

"Am I forgiven for doubting you?" he asked, his voice husky.

"Aye," she breathed. "You cannot help your suspicious nature."

"If I were more trusting, Wife, I would not be alive today. That nature, as you put it, has kept me alive."

Her face sobered, and she reached out and touched his cheek. "Then I am very glad, my lord, for your mistrust. I would not want you in harm's way."

He stared at her, having trouble reconciling his first image of her with the woman before him now. "I swear, you confound me."

She smiled. "Good."

Nicolas approached them in the dimly lit great room, his features drawn. "Michau reports that Caradoc is still sleeping in the palisades, but Rhett has disappeared."

"How did he get away?" Christophe asked.

"The man guarding him was knocked senseless."

"Very well, call the men to arms. I think it is time to meet the enemy."

"Christophe, you are not going to attack?" Bronwyn asked.

"It is the only way to end this."

"But we are safe here," Bronwyn argued. "Without the weapons the rebels cannot attack."

"We will not be safe unless we eliminate the problem. We have an opportunity to defeat our aggressors before they can gain strength and bury us. We have no choice."

Bronwyn shook her head. "I think you enjoy war."

"*Non*, I seek peace. But peace has a price."

Chapter Twelve

"I want to come," Bronwyn insisted as her husband dressed for battle. "I promise to stay out of the way." As he crossed the floor to strap on his sword, she marched behind him.

He wheeled around so fast that she ran into his chest. With her dirty face and untamed curls, she looked so adorable that he had to steel himself against her appeal. "Is this your battle dress?" He reached out and touched her sheer gold tunic smudged with dirt.

"But how can you leave me behind? What if the minute you leave I run to my brother and tell him all your plans?"

"So you do believe your brother is involved?"

Her face paled. "Nay, but you do," she said, then swiftly lowered her eyes.

He lifted her chin with his finger. "You are right. I do believe your brother is involved, but fortunately for you, he is here."

She reached out and touched his arm, her face suddenly serious. "I fear for you. Please, Christophe, take me with you."

"*Non.* You must stay here, Wife." He leaned forward and kissed her. The kiss was fast and hard. There wasn't time for anything else, though his body ached for more. "I promise to be home soon."

She smiled. "Then you trust me?"

"Stay with your sister while I am away," he said, not answering her question. "Nicolas would feel better, and so would I. There was one attempt on your person, I do not want another. I will have a guard assigned to watch over you and your sister." He reached for the door, then stopped and leveled her with a look. "Bronwyn, do not make his job difficult."

She wrapped her arms around his neck, and lightly kissed his chin. "Husband, you do not know me, if you could think such a thing. Why, anyone will tell you that the only one whom I make things difficult for, is you."

Her eyes sparkled and she moistened her lips as a mischievous smile formed. He couldn't help himself as he lowered his head and muttered. "You certainly do make my life a trial." He kissed her and felt her body bend to his. Every soft muscle yielded to him as her lips caressed his and her tongue tantalized and teased his. Blood rushed to his head and his body pounded with need. God, he wanted her. Instead of growing tired of this maid, his longing grew with each and every contact.

She pressed against him, and his arms crushed her in his embrace. Her nails combed through his hair to slip slowly down his nape and caress his shoulders. He devoured her lips, needing, wanting more. Her soft moan nearly drove him insane. Her body molded to his, speaking the language of the senses. Though he wanted to do far more, he could not. He ended the kiss, his lips traveling to her ear. "You are a temptress. When I return we will continue this discussion."

Before he could pull away, she cradled his face, her expression intense. "Take care, warlord. I do not want to be put to the trouble of burying you in yon field."

Her eyes glimmered with unshed tears, and he covered her hands with his. "I would not be so ill-mannered."

"I love you, Christophe."

He turned and left, giving no indication he had heard her whispered confession.

Bronwyn watched him go, her heart aching. Every fiber of her body cried out to chase after him, to beg him to stay, but she knew she could not. The thought that he might not come back filled her with a pain far greater than any physical discomfort she had ever known. Choking back a sob, she ran to the door, throwing it open to watch Christophe's soldiers mount their horses in the courtyard. Her breath caught as he turned to catch a last glimpse of her. As the sun crested the horizon, the bright red and gold light washed over his face, softening his harsh features. Then he turned back, and the sight tore at her heart as he led his men into battle. She watched until he was out of sight, then ordered Fang to follow her as she ran to her sister's room.

Christophe sent sentries out to ride ahead and find the rebels, who must have fled when they discovered the weapons missing.

He rode with his brother at the front of the column of men. "How far do you think they managed to ride?" Nicolas asked.

"Not far. I expect we will find them before nightfall."

Nicolas pointed ahead to the north, then swung his arm to the west. "Do you think they will head for the sea or the mountains?"

"I expect to find them by the sea."

"Why?"

"Because the route is easier and they have been up all night."

The morning passed comfortably and Christophe was about to call a meal break when several riders approached.

The sentries galloped up to the column and reined in their horses. "My lord," Sumner said, "the rebels have made camp up ahead."

With a knowing grin Nicolas saluted his brother. "You were right."

Christophe turned to Sumner. "We will rest here. You and your men will make a full report."

After their meal Christophe bent over the ground and drew a map of the terrain. He pointed his sword to the area he wanted covered by Michau and then laid out his plan.

"Make sure you take care, my lord," Michau warned, rising to head for his men.

"Just make sure you cut off their retreat."

Michau shook Christophe's hand. "I will not let you down."
"I know."

Christophe walked among his troops, bolstering their courage, before he ordered them to break camp. Though his men were tired, none complained.

The sun was straight up when Christophe separated his forces. Half the command followed him and Nicolas, the other Michau. The Welsh rebels were camped in a clearing. Only a few guards were posted as the main body of men slept. Christophe let out a war cry and charged into the camp, as Michau did the same at the flank.

Panic and confusion reigned as the Welsh rebels awoke to the surprise attack. Some managed to run for their meager supply of swords and bows, while others grabbed whatever was at hand: hoes, axes, pitchforks, and poles. Though the rebels tried to defend their position, the fight was a pitiful display of untrained farmers fighting against a superior force of well-trained military men. Yet, though the Welsh were greatly overwhelmed, they rallied and fought as warriors.

Christophe's men on horseback drove them back toward Michau's force, which cut off the rebels' escape. An hour passed as men battled men, and screams rose from the battlefield. Swords and axes cut deep wounds as neither side gave ground. The ground ran red with blood as hacked and mutilated bodies littered the area.

There was no sign of Rhett, but Christophe fought and disarmed a man who seemed to be in charge. With his sword to the rebel's chest, Christophe called for surrender. The rebel nodded and called to his men to throw down their weapons. With more than half the enemy captured or dead, and their leader seized, the rebels surrendered.

Christophe surveyed the carnage and shook his head. Though his forces had suffered no losses, the enemy was not as fortunate. He ordered the burial of the slain men, and in lieu of clergy, offered up a prayer for the souls of the departed. Both Welsh and Normans bowed their heads and observed a moment of silence, before gathering the shovels and leaving the dead to their peace.

Past sunset Christophe's soldiers marched over two hundred captured men back into the courtyard. The air was tense. Under Norman rule captured soldiers did not fare well. Though thrilled Christophe was safe, Bronwyn rushed into the courtyard, ready to speak on the Welshmen's behalf. One look at her husband's dark, stern face silenced her. Instinctively she reached for Fang and nervously ran her fingers through his thick fur, making him sit. Fiona entered the courtyard moments later, her gait slower, followed by Hayden and Caradoc, who looked around with eyes vacant and devoid of hope.

The beaten rebels, a gaunt and half-starved lot, made a sorry picture as they were herded into the center of the courtyard and surrounded by Christophe's men. Nicolas walked around the group until all grumbling and shuffling stopped. When order was restored, Christophe moved in front of the assembly, drew out his sword, and raised it high. "I could have each and every one of you put to death. 'Tis my right."

Not one Welshman disputed the warlord, yet they held their heads high, waiting for death.

Bronwyn swallowed her fear as her father reached out and clasped her hand. Fiona softly cried out and huddled close to Caradoc.

A hush fell over the courtyard, and every pair of eyes focused on the warlord. The sharp lines and hollows of his face were shadowed by the flickering torchlight, so that his unyielding features appeared chiseled out of stone.

"I could be put to the time and trouble of dispensing with you, but . . ." He slipped his sword into its sheath. "I will give you a choice. I wish to bring peace to this land. If you swear fealty and work as my serfs you will be granted your life. If you decide you prefer death, my men will accommodate you."

Bronwyn nearly collapsed in relief. Christophe had shown both insight and mercy in offering the Welsh an honorable reprieve. She glanced around at the faces of the captured men. They stared at the warlord, a strange mixture of mistrust and hope in their eyes.

Hayden smiled, and nodded his head in approval.

"Thank God," Fiona said.

Bronwyn shook her head at her sister. "How could you have ever doubted Christophe?"

Caradoc watched, his mouth thinned, as every prisoner chose to kneel before the warlord to pledge his loyalty. He shook his head, as though unable to believe his eyes. Then, without a word, he suddenly turned and stormed away from the proceedings.

Bronwyn ignored her brother's ill humor, and smiled at Christophe. Not a drop of Welsh blood would be shed, and with these men they now had a virtual army to construct the castle.

Once the men were dismissed and taken to their quarters, she ran to her husband and hugged him tightly. "Christophe, you have the wisdom of Solomon."

"Do I?" He frowned, staring off at the departing men.

"What is wrong?" she asked, turning his face to her.

"They are alive now, but will they be next spring? How will I house and feed such a vast number?"

She had not thought of that. "We will find a way."

"We?" He raised an eyebrow. "Will you help me, Bronwyn?"

"Aye, I will."

He chuckled as Michau walked up to him and handed him a list. Bronwyn's face flushed as she pulled out of his arms.

Christophe looked over the list. "We will have to house them outside the castle in the temporary shelter. In their spare time they can build cottages. In fact, I think I will assign teams to build the crofts."

"Without a guard?" Michau questioned.

"They have sworn their allegiance, and I have accepted them. We must now depend on one another to survive."

When the answer did not seem to appease Michau, Christophe shook his head. "You may exercise caution and mix the captives with our castle crew. In fact, soon all the men will have to move out when the inner construction starts."

Michau smiled, then pointed to the list. "Some men should be assigned to hunt."

Christophe nodded. "With the fire, game will grow scarce

and the hunting parties will have to go farther into the woods. Select a detail to guard them.''

"*Oui*, my lord." He bowed and left.

Once he was gone, Christophe pulled her back into his embrace and whispered, "I suppose we can do anything if we put our heads together."

She smiled. "Aye, my lord." Her husband had the situation under control, yet it was still a serious problem. She decided to do all she could to help him. "Together we can move mountains."

When his lips descended on hers, she forgot all about the difficulty of feeding such a large number of men. He held her close, their hearts beating in unison, their breath mingling. She was home, safely enclosed in his arms. Content beyond anything she'd ever known.

He pulled away and Bronwyn moaned, not wanting to end their kiss, their closeness.

He rested his forehead against hers. "We no longer have a choice; we must band together, or die."

She shivered at the thought and he pulled her closer. "Cold?"

"Frightened," she corrected.

"As am I," he said. "But you must keep that a secret."

He had doubly surprised her, first by sharing his fear, then by making light of it. She hugged him tighter. "Whatever is ahead, Christophe, we will face it together."

Hayden followed Caradoc along the path that led to the old castle.

"Caradoc, you must leave Rhett," he pleaded.

Caradoc increased his gait. "It is too late for me. He will be furious about the weapons."

"The brute tried to kidnap your sister!"

Caradoc rounded on his father. "I did not know about that."

"But you know now," Hayden said. "Do the right and proper thing."

Caradoc turned away, muttering, "I wish I had never started this. I wish I had listened to you."

Hayden clasped Caradoc's shoulder and felt the tense muscles beneath his hand. "It is not too late."

"Aye, it is." He ran his hand through his hair.

"Why?" Hayden shouted. "What is it you are not telling me?"

"I owe my allegiance to another."

Hayden grabbed hold of his son. "Even I can see you regret joining Rhett. Why do you honor him?"

Caradoc turned away, unable to answer. "Forgive me, Father. I can not stay." He ran down the path ignoring his father's bid for him to return.

Rhett paced back and forth in his lair. The instant Caradoc entered, Rhett grabbed him by the tunic and smashed his fist into his face. "How did they know?" he shouted.

"Are you accusing me?" Caradoc's jaw clenched as he wiped the blood from his nose and rose to his feet. He met Rhett's gaze without flinching.

Unease wormed its way into Rhett's gut, but he decided he was mistaken. Fear had always worked to control Caradoc. "Who else could have told them where the weapons were hidden?"

Caradoc walked clear around Rhett, his eyes shining with a knowing gleam. "Perhaps it was the man you sent to kidnap my sister."

Rhett lost his bluster as he reconsidered Caradoc. "You knew about that?"

"Nay. I did not. I found out from my father. I thought we agreed that Bronwyn would become yours *after* her husband had been disposed of, not before."

Rhett chuckled, the sound an evil laugh. "You have a man's appetite. You should understand that I do not wish to wait for her."

"She is my sister. You will not dishonor her."

Rhett looked at Caradoc's determined features and knew this was not the time to balk. Changing tactics, he slapped his hand on the younger man's back. "Come, we will drink as warriors."

Caradoc shook his head. "Not until we reach an understanding."

Rhett narrowed his gaze at the stubborn set to Caradoc's jaw. He could not afford to alienate the Llangandfan. "I give you my word. I will wait until she is a widow to bed her." He shoved a mug of ale into Caradoc's hands. "Is that more to your liking?"

"One more thing: You will not harm any member of my family."

Rhett's blood boiled at the demand, but he held his temper and nodded. "Even though that was not part of the bargain, I will agree to it."

He watched Caradoc drink, and smiled. He knew another way to control the fool. "Ariana is here."

Caradoc spilled his drink. "Are you mad, bringing your daughter here?"

"Ariana," Rhett called. A lovely maiden walked from the back of the cave into the dim light. "Lord Caradoc," she said sweetly, and curtsied.

Caradoc bowed.

"I will leave you two while I check on my men. Remember, Caradoc, if I must honor your sister, you must honor my daughter."

The moment Rhett disappeared, Caradoc ran to her and engulfed her in his embrace. "Ariana, I love you."

"My beloved," she crooned. "Please, do not anger my stepfather. He talks of arranging a marriage to a northern chieftain to rally more men."

"Nay, you are mine," he said.

"Shhh, if he hears you, he will send me away."

He smothered her in his arms. "I would die before I allowed that." He kissed her with all his heart. She was why he had to honor his alliance with Rhett. At first, he had believed in Rhett's dreams, but no more.

She wound her hands around his shoulders. "Beloved, I am with child."

Caradoc felt his world rock. "Dear God."

She hung her head. "You are not pleased?"

Her forlorn voice stabbed his conscience. "Nay." He cradled her face in his palms, and kissed her lips. "I am pleased. But

I had hoped to take you away from your father. Now, how can I possibly ask you to live on the run with me?''

''If my stepfather finds out, he will kill you.''

Caradoc doubted that. Rhett needed him, he suddenly realized. His father had been right. '' 'Tis not I that he will harm, but you.''

She shivered in his arms.

''Don't worry. I will not allow him to hurt you.''

Rhett grinned smugly in the shadows. He had the fool back in the palm of his hand. With Caradoc Llangandfan at his side, he could raise another army. The Normans would pay, and pay dearly.

A fortnight saw the completion of the castle, stable, soldiers' quarters, and farrier's shop. With so much stonework done, the workers could concentrate on the battlements, whose walls were now twelve feet high, and on building village huts. As a town began to grow around the castle, word spread throughout the land of Lord Montgomery's fairness and of the prosperity brought by his rule.

Late one night Christophe was awakened by Michau. ''My lord, come quickly. Your brother has been injured.''

Christophe lit a candle, his features strained and drawn. ''Michau, fetch Lady Fiona.''

The minute the door shut, Bronwyn jumped out of bed and threw her clothes on. She grabbed her tray and followed her husband to the courtyard.

Bronwyn had to ease her sister aside to discover the extent of Nicolas's injuries. His lashes flickered open.

''I was pushed,'' he said, then groaned in pain.

''Oh, no, not again,'' Fiona cried.

Though Christophe's face tightened, he spoke softly to his brother. ''Rest, we will find out who did this.''

Bronwyn ignored Christophe to concentrate on Nicolas, she feared his back had been injured. ''Where do you have pain?''

"My back, and shoulder."

She continued her examination, touching his calves, thighs, and hips. When each proved to have feeling, she examined his chest, arms, and neck. "Do you feel my touch?"

"*Oui*. But why do you bother with my feet and hands, when it is my back that pains me?"

"I am the healer, Norman." She smiled, swamped by relief. "Do not question me."

Gently she lifted his arm. There was no restriction, and although he suffered discomfort, it appeared no bones were broken or separated. She prepared a potion and gave Nicolas the sleeping powder.

Michau joined them and whispered something to Christophe.

Christophe nodded solemnly, then turned to his brother. "Nicolas, I just found out that a rope was tied to the sentry tower. We did indeed have a visitor."

Nicolas nodded. "I wonder if it was the same man who pushed my wife."

Bronwyn looked at her husband, her insides roiling. In the past every incident had resurrected doubts. She waited for the recriminations.

His gaze locked with hers, and her heart soared as she saw the trust shining in his eyes. Standing up, she instructed Christophe's men to move Nicolas gently onto a litter and take him to his pallet.

Thankfully, nothing was broken. Oh, he would be sore. The area around his shoulder was swollen. But she suspected he had sustained nothing more than a bad bruise.

"You must stay in bed and rest for a week."

The soldiers guffawed at the cure prescribed for the new bridegroom.

Bronwyn followed the litter beside her sister. "Do not worry, Fiona, he will be fine. But I do want him to rest. You must make sure he does nothing to tax his strength."

Fiona nodded. "He will lay abed and do as he is told. I promise."

Bronwyn nearly chuckled at the serious expression on her sister's pale face.

Christophe pulled his wife to the side. "And, Lady Fiona, you must stay by his side for your sister will be extremely busy."

"Busy?" Bronwyn asked, turning to her husband.

"*Oui*, I have a chore for you that will take all your time."

"Verily?" She wondered what menial task he had devised.

"I want to assign a crew to work on the interior. Michau will be placed at your disposal."

At first she stared at him, too shocked to speak.

"Wife? Are you not up to the task?"

"Aye." Her face beamed. "You are going to trust me to command a Norman detail."

"If you wish to have cooperation, I would not use the word command."

Giggling, she threw her hands up in the air and danced around the courtyard.

He chuckled, enjoying his wife's antics. It occurred to him that no other woman had made him laugh.

After a minute she returned to him and took his hands to pull him into her dance. "When can I get started? I have ideas to set a room aside for tending the sick, and one for—"

"Is tomorrow soon enough?"

She stopped dancing and leapt into his arms. "Oh, Christophe," she whispered, then kissed him.

He kissed her back, and all thoughts of how amusing she was disappeared. She had bewitched him and he was lost to her magic. His last sane thought was a warning. Was she bewitching him—or bedeviling him?

Chapter Thirteen

Although Bronwyn had asked and received his permission for the celebration, Christophe looked startled as he entered the great hall and saw the preparations. "What is it we're doing exactly?" he asked.

"It's Samhain, the last night of October. There are games planned, and stories to be told."

"More pagan customs, my dear?"

She chuckled, unafraid of his reaction, because he had proven his heart fair and open. "Aye, my lord, our ancestors believed the supernatural world and ours come very close on Samhain and the dead could come back. So to protect ourselves, we put out food for the souls who roam the earth and tell stories of their lives."

He reached over and picked a piece of straw from her tunic. "Is this to scare away the ghost?"

"Aye." She grabbed his hand and led him over to a pile of rags and straw. "You must also observe our traditions."

He picked up some straw and raised a brow.

Bronwyn held her breath; if he did not join in, neither would his men.

"For you," he whispered, and stuffed a handful of straw in

his tunic. The Norman soldiers followed his lead, and all was ready for the festivities.

Her squeal of delight blended with the music. A pungent aroma filled the air as Nesta poured hot cider into earthen jugs, and Cordelia, barely able to walk with her advanced pregnancy, placed another tray of baked goods on the table. Fiona rapped Nicolas's hand when he tried to steal a biscuit. "Those are for later. Leave be," she admonished.

Nicolas sucked on his finger and gave her a boyish pout that had her instantly contrite, and giving him not just one treat but two.

He walked by Bronwyn and winked as he ate both treats without a trace of remorse. Shameless, she thought; Nicolas had fully recovered from his injuries, and still he played on his wife's sympathy. She turned to her husband. "You Montgomerys have a way about you."

"*Oui*, we do," Christophe agreed. " 'Tis lucky for you Llangandfan women that we happened to come to Wales."

"Oh, aye," she said, wryly. She started to mentally tick off his accomplishments, so she could find fault and call him to task. The people were cozy, warm, and well fed at Castle Montgomery, because of his ingenuity. No, she couldn't berate him for that. Due to his generosity and wisdom, the men captured from Rhett's aborted attack had been reunited with their families and were now living peacefully in their own huts. No, he would be commended for that. The walls of the battlements were finished, which made them safe from attack. Aha, she thought. The interior construction of the castle needed to be completed, but he had left that important job under her careful management. She felt small and petty. Instead of teasing him, she looked into his eyes, and said humbly, "We are indeed lucky. Thank you, my lord."

He wrapped his arms around her and kissed the top of her head. "I have decided that life is good."

She relished the feel of his powerful arms around her and nestled closer. "You have done a phenomenal job. William should surely be pleased."

Fiona ran by. " 'Tis time to meet the traveling wicca, who

has agreed to read your fortune," she squealed, and grabbed Bronwyn's hand to drag her away from her husband.

"Must I?" Bronwyn protested, not at all eager to have a druid priestess read her future. She looked longingly back at Christophe.

"You must have your fortune told," Fiona said. "It is expected."

"Very well," Bronwyn acceded, but though this was an old tradition, she found herself feeling afraid.

In the kitchen Bronwyn's apprehension increased at the wicca's strange appearance. White tufts of hair escaped a dull-brown head covering to stand out like a spiked crown. A network of lines cut through the sunken hollows of her cheeks and over the loose folds on her neck. Her dark robes were as somber as her manner. She held a chicken and nodded for Bronwyn to take a seat, then she ordered everyone else out.

The old woman killed the chicken, then drew a stick through the entrails and peered closely at the mess. Her face grew very strained.

"What is it?" Bronwyn asked, unable to stop herself.

Instead of answering her, the wicca grabbed Bronwyn's hand, staring intently into the palm.

Bronwyn's heart began to pound. "What do you see?"

The old woman looked up, her beady eyes glowing. "You do not belong here."

The words drained the blood from Bronwyn's face. "What do you mean?"

"You are a changeling, you do not belong here."

"Enough!" Bronwyn rose to her feet, knowing that such an accusation could see her burned at the stake. Memories surfaced of just such an event in another shire. Though there had been a lengthy trial, and Hayden had spoken on the condemned's behalf, hysteria had won out and both the victim and her family had been put to death. Though she did not know if she could face down the woman, she had to try. "You will not repeat this to anyone," Bronwyn warned, her hand covering her dagger. "If you do, I will see you put in the dungeon and condemned to death."

"You could not kill me," the wicca spat.

From the side of the kitchen hearth, Fang growled, his teeth bared and hair raised. His yellow eyes glowed from the firelight as he snarled at the disturbance from his sleep.

"I might not be able to, but my pet could," Bronwyn said as relief washed over her.

The old woman slowly nodded her head, her gaze never leaving the wolf's as she bowed her head. "I mean you no harm, my lady. The truth is between us, and shall remain so." She spread her hand over the table's contents. "Do you not want to know the future?"

"Nay." Bronwyn leapt back from the table, and Fang came to her side. There was a cunning light in the old woman's eyes that terrified her. Bronwyn dug into her tunic to produce a coin, and she flipped it to the old woman. "Leave here. Begone, and do not return," she said, opening the door to the courtyard.

The old woman cackled softly as she took her time putting her things into a pouch.

Goose bumps rose on Bronwyn's arms at the hideous sound. She watched the wicca stand up from the table, and knew something evil had touched her.

"Sending me away, my lady, will not change what I said."

Bronwyn ignored the jibe and watched until the woman was out of the kitchen and through the gates. Her hand trailed over Fang's back. "I am so glad you were asleep by the fire," she whispered.

Bronwyn almost collapsed with relief when the wicca disappeared into the night. "Get hold of yourself," she admonished. "You're letting all the superstition of Halloween get to you." Though she told herself it was only her overactive imagination that had unnerved her, she could not shake the terror that had possessed her. She fixed Fang a treat, and softly combed her fingers through his fur.

Once her emotions were under control, she reentered the party. Fiona rushed up to her.

"What did she tell you?"

"Nothing I did not already know. I am sorry, Fiona, but this wicca is not as good as last year's."

"Oh, I was hoping you had something wonderful to report for our people."

"I think our future is not yet written. Best consider the riches we have today and be thankful for their bounty. Tomorrow will take care of itself, Sister."

Fiona smiled. "I know she told you something that you are refusing to share."

Bronwyn shook her head at her sister's persistence. "Let it be. Oh, look," she said to change the subject, "here come our husbands."

When they had joined them, Christophe studied her for a minute, then whispered, "Are you well, Wife?"

His observant gaze missed nothing; she was still shaken from the wicca's words. "I am fine, just a little tired," she lied.

Nicolas smiled and leaned forward to Bronwyn. "I was just telling my ornery brother that he has changed, and it is due to his sweet wife."

"Is that the same sweet wife who slipped her groom a deadly drink?" Christophe teased.

"Aye, it is." She forced a smile, thankful that the subject had changed.

He raised an eyebrow at her failure to take the bait, then pulled her to his side. "My lady, your party is rather subdued."

She looked around and saw that the people were milling around the food, but no one was dancing. They were waiting for her to make an announcement about her spiritual reading, and then to tell the stories that always kept the children up. Neither one appealed to her at this moment.

"Might I make a suggestion that will allow you to rest for a spell? I know you are supposed to begin the storytelling, but I would like to make an announcement, and I think it will liven your party."

She nodded, wondering what he would say.

He stepped to the middle of the floor and held up his hands. The music stopped and all faces turned toward him.

Christophe signaled his man, and the guard opened the door, ushering in all the sentries who had guard duty on the battlement. The hall now contained every man, woman, and child of the demesne. "Since all have labored to fulfill this dream, all will share in it. Not just Norman, but Welsh, and not just the men but the women, as well." Not a sound could be heard as the crowd took in this unprecedented announcement.

"Hear me well! I will assign land to every man here. The parcel will be twice that offered by the king for service rendered. If the owner dies, the land will stay with his family. No longer will a widow be put off her land. After the castle is completed, I will require only four hours' service from each adult for repayment. In addition, a scribe will keep the ledger, and every man will receive a fair share of their bounty."

Never had any lord, Norman or Welsh, been so generous to his people. This meant that the Welsh would not lose their land. In fact, they would fare better under Norman rule.

"From now on, we are united. It will take all our efforts to make this venture a success. There will be no more division of our peoples. We must take the best from both and merge them together. This will give us strength against our enemies. You have seen what your countrymen have done. Already the forest has been burned, and in the spring I expect we will be under attack.

"If we wish to prosper we cannot be at war. To withstand a siege and overcome those who would plunge us into petty conflicts, we must defeat our enemies. To do so, we have to stand together.

"Should I fall in battle, my brother, Nicolas, will keep my promises. And if we should both die, your lady Bronwyn will treat you fairly. But she cannot do that if Rhett or some other warlord takes control. You have seen how little he cares for the people. He would sacrifice any of you in his greedy quest for power."

Heads nodded as the men agreed. The Norman leader they had been sent was truly just. They had seen first-hand how Rhett had sacrificed them.

"We are with you, as always, my lord." Michau marched to the middle of the room and stood behind his lord, followed by every Norman.

"My lord, I will follow you," Wilford said, and he stepped forward and stood alone for several seconds.

Then the farrier, Braden, moved beside Wilford, and they were quickly joined by their countrymen. Only the captured Welsh remained on the outskirts.

"Aye, I have served Lord Rhett, and he is no leader. I will follow you and I will honor you." A captured Welshman joined the circle and suddenly, as though a dam had burst, the other men poured forth and joined the ranks. Not one man abstained. "Aye." A unison of strong, vibrant voices filled the room.

Tears misted Bronwyn's eyes. The house of Montgomery was truly united.

Christophe gestured for his wife to come to his side. "My lady, would you offer these good and gentle folk your solemn vow to see my promises fulfilled?"

"Aye," she said, while pride for her husband filled her soul.

The men cheered, and suddenly they were in the midst of a grand celebration, of song and dance. Bronwyn turned to her husband, her heart full of love. "You truly are a wonder."

He pulled her into his arms. "What did you expect? That I was an ogre?"

"It would seem we both misjudged the other. Can we start fresh? Can we not pretend that we are just meeting at this moment?"

He smiled. "How do you do, my lady?"

Tears suddenly spilled from her eyes, wetting her cheeks.

"Here, what is this?" he murmured gently, wiping them away.

"I am most happy," she half-cried, half-sobbed.

"You are the strangest woman." His voice was a soft caress.

"I am just so touched by your generosity and your goodness." She brushed a stray lock from his forehead, and her breath caught in her throat as she looked into his eyes and saw what she had only hoped for. Could it be, did she dare believe? Was he really looking at her with his heart?

"And I by your spirit of commitment to your people. If you would promise to give me that devotion, I would promise never to question your loyalty again."

"Done," she breathed, then launched into his arms, and laughed out loud with sheer joy.

Nicolas and Fiona danced by and teased the lord and lady for indulging in an embrace. Nesta and Wilford merely chuckled as they twirled around the master and his lady. Bronwyn's face flushed as she smiled in return. Christophe held her close and whirled her around. "Shall we show these poor dancers how it is done? Remember, we have to set an example. Besides," he whispered, "I am with the prettiest woman in the room, and the most graceful."

Breathless with happiness, she readily agreed. Being in Christophe's arms was exactly where she wanted to be. This was their new beginning, and she would let nothing mar its beauty.

As they danced, they laughed and teased each other like lovers in the first blush of their romance. The night floated by, harmonious and magical, and soon they were alone in their new bedchamber. The bar dropped into place and locked out the noise and chatter of the others below. The fire burned, and the room held a soft glow.

He drew her into his arms, and danced her around the room before stopping at the hearth. "Tonight will be our first night together," he said, his voice hoarse with passion.

"I hope I am not too bold for a proper wife."

"Heaven forbid! I like your boldness. In truth, I love being seduced by such a hot temptress."

A smile curved Bronwyn's lips and she fluttered her eyelashes coquettishly. "Whatever do you mean?"

He laughed at her playful antics, and she walked around him, trailing her fingers across his broad chest. "But, my lord, is it seemly for me to know your body with such familiarity? After all, we are to start over."

Tracing a calloused finger down her arm, he said, "I give you permission to explore to your heart's content."

When her gaze met his, hot desire glowed in her golden eyes, and her open passion excited him. He felt himself grow hard as she seductively reached up and slipped her hands beneath his tunic. He sucked in his breath as her nails scraped over his chest and teased his nipples. Her touch was heavenly torture. Her fingers slid across his chest and up to his shoulders, slipping his tunic off, then trailed down to his waist and slipped beneath his braies. Her fingertips grazed his manhood, then fastened on with a greedy hold. Blood pounded in his ears and he could stand the teasing no longer, pulling her tight against his chest, his lips devouring hers.

She met and matched his ardor with a hunger that drove him nearly out of his mind. He knew he had to slow down, but she kissed him with an urgency that pushed sane thought from his mind. His lips traveled to her ear. "Bronwyn," he gasped.

"Love me," she breathed.

He groaned, knowing he could take her fast and furious, but he wanted this moment to last, to be more than a physical mating. He pulled back and looked at her rapturous face. He steeled himself against the desire building within him, and lowered his lips to hers. Slowly, he thought; make love to her with a thoroughness that will drive all ghosts from her mind, and his.

She moaned when his hand brushed across her breast. He rubbed the nub until it was hard and she leaned into him.

Sweat broke out on his forehead as he peeled the tunic from her body and beheld her beauty. "God, you are perfection," he murmured. Then his lips traveled to her breast, his teeth grazing the edge of her breast before covering the nub. Her hands raked through his hair as she moaned in delight.

He lifted her in his arms, carrying her to the bed. Her arms wrapped around his neck and she placed hungry kisses on his chest. Going slow was going to be impossible, he thought as he laid her on the bed and quickly peeled off his remaining clothes.

He stared at her soft, curvaceous body, so pale against the dark fur covers, and his heartbeat raced. Her hair spilled out behind her in a golden cloud that begged to be crushed by his hands. When his gaze traveled to her face, his chest tightened with need as her amber eyes glowed bright with passion and desire, and her lips parted slightly. Her arms stretched out to him, beckoning him to her. He reached out and was lost to her touch. A spell of love and passion surrounded him.

Her kiss was not soft or innocent, but hot and bold. Her body molded beneath his, her hands frantically exploring his chest, her nails raking down his back and buttocks.

Desire sung in his veins and he tried once more to slow the pace, but when her tongue slipped over his flesh, and her hands reached his manhood, he groaned.

He held her still. "Bronwyn," he whispered, his voice hoarse with need. He kissed her, then crushed her to him. While his tongue darted in and out of her soft mouth, he poised at the gates of her womanhood. She was wet, hot, and ready. His elbows braced, he entered her, feeling her warmth wrap around him like a tight sheath.

Her tiny moans drove him on as he started the rhythm, trying to bring her to fulfillment. He tried, God how he tried to keep his desire reined in, but she met his movements with a need that pushed him to a frantic pace.

Her hands roamed over his back, pulling him closer. He felt her shudder as she found her release, and suddenly he joined her in an explosion of light and sensation. He soared higher, faster, and farther than he ever had. He cried out her name, clutching her to him as he drifted slowly back to earth.

Pure ecstasy engulfed him. He could barely breathe as he cradled his wife in his arms and contemplated the solemn rapture of their lovemaking.

The missive arrived at dawn.

Nicolas's features tightened, showing both disbelief and anger. "Lord Odo has recalled the regiment?"

Christophe nodded, his heart heavy. "*Oui,* to put down a rebellion in Scotland."

"By His wounds," Nicolas cursed, slamming his fist onto the table. "Lord Odo is leaving us defenseless. There will only be you and me and our eight personal guards."

Christophe understood his brother's frustration; he felt it, as well. He sat down and poured two chalices of ale. After he handed Nicolas his drink, Christophe sipped his slowly and considered his options.

"Christophe, do you think the people will stand with or against us?"

Christophe set his chalice down and looked his brother straight in the eye. "It matters not. Our die is cast. We will stay."

Nicolas grinned and took a seat beside Christophe. "This is your land and my home." He raised his chalice in a salute. "To family," he said, clinking his cup to Christophe's, and drinking all the brew before throwing the chalice into the fire. Then he leaned forward. "I would never desert you, Brother."

"I will order the men to return to London at the end of the month," Christophe said. "That is when the artisans are returning to their homes and the regiment's withdrawal will be a little less noticeable. Lord Odo's orders say at my earliest convenience, and the extra four weeks will also give us some time to prepare in case our Welsh have to fight."

"Quit frowning, Christophe. At least, no one else knows about this."

Rhett sat down to eat and drink with the hated Norman. But not just any Norman. His men had heard that this particular one boasted of his hatred of the Montgomery brothers to anyone who would listen.

"To your health," Rhett said, raising his drink in a salute.

Lucien squinted his bloodshot eyes. "You look familiar. Though I swear, with a face like yours, I'd rather forget it than remember it."

Rhett's rage boiled to the surface, but he forced the anger down, and let the rude comment pass, for he needed the man's help. However, after he proved useful he would kill him for the slight.

"I am told you have been demoted, sent riding all over the countryside on a fool's errand. Apparently, there are those who would rather forget *you* exist."

Lucien grabbed the man's tunic in his fist and lifted the

Welshman clear off of his seat. "I am Lucien Darcy of Normandy. Do not anger me or you will wish our paths had never crossed."

Rhett felt the power in the sotted man's limb, but showed neither fear nor respect. "If you be a great warrior, then why are you out here?"

"A soldier does not question orders."

"Aye, that is true," Rhett said as the tall Norman unsteadily lowered him to the ground.

"There are leaders," Lucien snarled, "and then again, there are leaders."

Rhett knew the man's hatred was close to the surface, and he had to pander to the Norman's pride. He watched the Norman down the second drink. "Verily, I know there are commanders who should not be put in charge of livestock, let alone men. But it happens."

"Oui," Lucien agreed morosely.

"I have found in my own country it is usually those who have ties to the king, rather than those who have earned their place."

Lucien nodded, readily agreeing. "My family is one of the most prestigious in all of Normandy. But every time I tried to distinguish myself, that damn Christophe or his brother bested me before the king. I swear there is a conspiracy."

"Then distinguish yourself now." Rhett slammed his tankard down on the table.

" 'Tis easier said than done," Lucien whined, then guzzled his drink, the brew spilling from his mouth and drizzling down his chin into his beard.

Rhett threw his arm over Lucien's shoulders and leaned close. "You could put down the revolt," he whispered. "You would be hailed as the hero of Wales. But unfortunately, you must first dispose of the Montgomery brothers."

Lucien spewed his ale out. "Dispose of them? How?"

Rhett wiped the ale from his sleeve. "I wish to rule Wales— as a loyal subject of William, of course. If you and I work together, we could rule jointly. However, you must first eliminate your competition, as I must mine.''

''You have the means?'' Lucien asked, his interest piqued.

''I already have the support of both the north and south chieftains. They do not realize once I am in power I will be rid of them, too.''

Lucien stroked his bearded chin. ''All I would have to do is get rid of the Montgomerys?''

''Aye. One brother had already suffered from a fall.'' Rhett smirked, remembering pushing the man he thought was Christophe.

Suddenly the warrior turned on Rhett, his eyes unusually clear.

''Why would you need me?''

''Because I do not want William storming my land. If we ruled together, we would not be bothered by anyone.''

When Rhett called for another ale, the men were deep in talk.

Wilford led Bronwyn through the newly constructed village huts toward his daughter's croft. The chilly morning air swept under her hem and she shivered, wrapping the mantle tighter around her as she hurried along. Cordelia's husband, Edwin, paced outside his home, and when he saw her, his face brightened. He opened the door to usher her in, while he remained outside with Wilford.

She entered Cordelia's warm hut to find the woman in extreme distress. Her face was beaded with sweat and her features lined with pain. Nesta sat by her side, offering soothing words.

Both women looked relieved when Bronwyn opened her sack. ''How fast are the pains coming?''

''One right after the other,'' Nesta said anxiously, and as if to punctuate the words, Cordelia moaned with the next spasm.

Bronwyn went to her side and laid a hand on the woman's distended abdomen.

The contraction was hard and lasted a full minute.

"She has labored all night, my lady." Nesta's worried features turned back to her daughter. "You must push to bring this child forth."

Bronwyn did not like hearing that Cordelia had labored that long without relief. "She is very close to bringing her child into the world," she said to alleviate Nesta's worry.

Cordelia's grip clamped onto her arm. "Something is wrong, my lady. We would not have sent for you otherwise."

Bronwyn nodded. "Save your strength."

Nesta's eyes were filled with worry as she patted her daughter's shoulder. "Do as the lady bids you. All will be well."

But all was not well. Bronwyn examined Cordelia and suspected the baby was turned the wrong way. She mixed a strong potion and had Cordelia drink it to ease her pain. There was nothing she could do until the delivery started. The day passed slowly. As the contractions grew stronger, Cordelia grew weaker. Drenched in sweat and exhausted, she could not bear down.

Bronwyn feared her suspicions were correct. If the baby was breech she would have to turn the child, or both mother and baby might well perish. But the procedure itself was dangerous. She decided she had to try.

Bronwyn washed and scrubbed until her hands were nearly raw. Then keeping as sterile a field as she could, she knelt between Cordelia's legs and saw what she feared most: a little foot. "Oh, Lord," Nesta wailed, looking over her shoulder.

"Take hold of your daughter's legs and make sure you hold her still," Bronwyn ordered.

When Nesta had a secure hold on Cordelia, Bronwyn leaned forward. Dear God, help me, she prayed, then she grabbed the tiny little foot and pushed it back up into the birth canal. Cordelia screamed with the pain. Though not immune to the suffering, and feeling faint, Bronwyn focused on getting the baby back up into the womb and turned around. She pulled her hand free, and suddenly with the next contraction the baby's head appeared. Before she had time to think, the child was out and she had cut the cord and laid the infant on her mother's chest. With tears of relief rimming her eyes, she turned to deliver the afterbirth. When her job was done, she was trembling. She had brought a tiny life into the world. Exhilaration bubbled up inside of her at the miracle she had witnessed. She wiped her eyes and looked at mother and child. "A fine girl, Cordelia. What will you call this lovely daughter?"

Cordelia's smile was aged with the stress and strain of bringing forth the child. She reached out and touched her baby's soft cheek. "I shall call her Regan."

Bronwyn stilled, completely stunned. "What made you think of that?" she asked, unsure how common her name was in this time.

"I do not know. It suddenly came to me when you entered the room. I like the sound of it."

Nesta bustled around her daughter. " 'Tis a strange name, to be sure."

"Mother, the child's name will be Regan." Cordelia, though weak, looked every inch the determined mother.

Nesta patted her daughter's shoulder. "After what you went through, you can name the little darling whatever you wish. Although I think you should consider naming the child after the woman who saved your life."

Cordelia's face flushed. "My lady, forgive me."

"Nay, Cordelia," she assured. "You have every right to name your child. And," she encouraged, turning to Nesta, "I rather like the name Regan."

"If you would not mind," Cordelia said, "I should like to name my baby Regan Bronwyn."

Overcome by Cordelia's kindness, Bronwyn simply nodded.

Nesta beamed. "What a good child I have."

"Aye," Bronwyn chuckled. "And what a lovely grandchild."

"How can we ever thank you?" Nesta asked.

"I have my thanks," she said, gazing down at the beautiful baby. For just a moment a deep longing overcame her as she imagined how lovely it would be to hold her own child. Then she looked at Nesta. "I want to be called immediately if Cordelia develops a fever. She is to rest. I do not want her out of bed for a week."

"I will make sure she does nothing." Nesta held her grandchild and smiled. "She is lovely, is she not, my lady?"

Bronwyn touched the soft little cheek. "She is a miracle."

"Thank you, my lady," Cordelia whispered from the bed as Nesta called Wilford and Edwin in.

"Rest," Bronwyn ordered Cordelia and turned to see the men's awed faces as they stared at the baby in Nesta's arms.

"She is so tiny," Edwin said.

"Cordelia was just as small," Wilford reassured his son-in-law.

Bronwyn threw her mantle on, ready to slip out into the night.

"Wilford, Edwin," Nesta said, seeing Bronwyn edge toward the door. "See the lady safely home."

"Nay," Bronwyn said, not wishing to disturb the family.

"My lady, permit me," Wilford said.

Bronwyn nodded. Exhausted but exhilarated, she made her way home with Wilford seeing her all the way down the path, then through the dim-lit halls and up the stairs to her chamber, before he bade her good night.

She quietly opened the door and tiptoed in, so as not to disturb her husband. The golden glow of the fire warmed her chilled flesh.

"How is Cordelia?" Christophe asked, rolling over to see her.

"I am sorry that I woke you." She removed her clothes and felt a wave of tears. Her hands trembled and she tried to stop the emotions careening out of control, but when she looked at Christophe's understanding expression, a dam broke. "I thought she would die. The baby was turned the wrong way. Oh, God, I could have lost them both." Suddenly he was beside her, picking her up in his strong arms and carrying her to bed.

She shivered and felt his calloused hands rubbing the warmth back into her. She babbled on, needing to let out all her fears, and he listened silently. Then her words turned to tears and she sobbed.

He softly stroked her hair. "All is well, Wife. Mother and child are healthy."

He continued to offer reassuring words as his hands roamed over her. With infinite patience he soothed her fears.

When her sobs stopped, she laid her hand on his chest, felt his steady heartbeat, and stared into his dark eyes. "But, Christophe, I was so scared I would lose them both. And Nesta looked at me as though I was the only one who could save her daughter."

He kissed the top of her head, then his lips grazed the tender line of her jaw. "But, Wife, you are."

" 'Tis too much responsibility. I am not that strong."

"Oui, you are." He brushed a strand of hair from her cheek. "Even if there was another healer in the village, you would still tend the sick."

"How do you know?"

"I know you." He cradled her face in his hands. "Bronwyn Montgomery is a loving, caring woman."

She felt another wave of tears and turned her face so Christophe would be spared. She took a deep breath and said the first thing that came to her mind. "I pray when our child comes, the labor is not so long and complicated."

He rose up on one elbow and turned her chin toward him. "Are you trying to tell me something, Wife?"

"Nay," she said, blushing. "I am not with child." A sudden warmth flowed through her at the thought. "A child," she whispered in wonder. "I do not know if I am ready to be a mother."

"You would make a good mother." His husky voice sent a tingle through her.

She looked at him, and her throat tightened. Did she dare hope? Was that love shining in his eyes? "Then you think I am a good wife?"

"Oui, I do." He hugged her tight, and whispered, "I never expected you to fall in love with me, nor did I require it. But I must say I am pleased you have."

"And you?" she probed, suddenly desperate to hear the words.

When he hesitated, she quickly placed her finger to his lips. "Never mind. I should not have asked."

He kissed her then, and she knew a bittersweet joy. He could express his feelings, but not say them. They were starting over and she clung to the hope that in time he would be able to speak his heart. To think otherwise hurt too much.

Chapter Fourteen

In the dim tavern Lucien drank his ale in silence, and considered his future. A fortnight had passed since his meeting with the Welsh rebel, Rhett, but he had been in no hurry to return to Montgomery's castle. With over a month and a half's duty left in his current bloody assignment, he had plenty of time to waste. Yet the added leisure gave him time to think, and the more he considered Rhett's offer, the more it appealed to him. He took a hearty swig and mulled over the possibilities. When he lowered his cup he noticed a familiar face coming through the tavern door. "Miles," he called. "What brings you to this godforsaken town?"

Miles's face brightened. "Lucien, *mon ami.*" He made his way through the crowd and took a seat next to his friend. "I looked for you two weeks ago when I stopped at Castle Montgomery to deliver a message from Lord Odo."

"Lord Odo?"

"*Oui*, William is in Normandy." Miles shook his head. "Where have you been?"

Lucien picked up his head at that news. "I have been on a mission." The truth soured his thoughts and he changed the subject. "What business are you about?" Lucien asked as he motioned to the tavern owner to bring another round of ale.

Miles took a large drink, then wiped his sleeve across his mouth. "Lord Odo bade me to take his messages to all the Norman lords in Wales. I must say I was impressed with Castle Montgomery."

"I am on my way back there," Lucien said, keeping his animosity hidden.

Miles nudged his friend in the side. "Then you might be returning to London soon, my friend, possibly by the end of the month."

"I will?"

"Oui, Lord Odo has ordered all his lords, including Montgomery, to send their regiments back to London, allowing them only their personal guards to remain for protection. He fears a Scottish uprising."

Lucien smiled. With Castle Montgomery stripped of almost all of its Norman contingent, a small force could easily storm the castle and claim it. The news had just decided him. He would join the stupid rebels and use them for his own ends. "Well, then, my friend, let us drink to our king and commander, a leader we most willingly serve."

Miles raised his cup. "To William and to Normandy."

"Oui," Lucien said, enjoying the irony. He drank many more toasts with his friend, asking about comrades they had both known, and quaffing several more horns of ale to those who had given their life for the cause. When Miles retired, Lucien staggered out of the tavern and mounted his horse.

"By His wounds," he cursed as he rode off into the night.

He had a powerful thirst to satisfy, and not for drink, but for power. Instead of taking the turn to Castle Montgomery, he headed north to the caves, and quietly rode to meet a certain Welshman.

Dawn was breaking when Rhett was summoned from his pallet. He crossed the compound to greet the Norman soldier, who had obviously considered his offer and decided to throw his lot in with the victor.

"Do you have news to report?" Rhett asked, escorting him to a side tent, away from the cave where Caradoc and Ariana slept. Once they were inside he poured two healthy goblets of wine.

Lucien puffed out his chest and grinned. "All the soldiers but Christophe's personal guard have been ordered back to London by the end of the month."

Rhett grunted as the puckered skin of his face stretched painfully into a smile. "Ah! Now victory will be mine."

"*Oui,* and mine," Lucien reminded him, then took a big gulp of the strong wine.

"Do not worry, Norman. I always remember who has helped and who has hindered my cause. You will be properly rewarded."

"I look forward to it—and to seeing that bitch, Bronwyn, humbled. She is evil, a sorceress," Lucien said morosely.

"Nay," Rhett instantly denied, unwilling to let a rumor start that could ruin his plans. "She is of royal blood, a direct descendant of Arthur."

"I do not put stock in old wives' tales," he scoffed, and lifted his drink.

"Then you should," Rhett said, clenching his fists to restrain his anger. "A woman with that lineage could rule all of Wales."

"Rule!" Lucien spewed out his ale and coughed. "That woman has one use, Welshman. She has made an enemy of me and I want my turn on her." Lucien glared at him to make his point.

"Very well," Rhett agreed, though it was a promise he would never keep. He raised his drink to seal the vow. "You will get everything you deserve."

Lucien swallowed his drink and promptly poured another. "I will have the Welsh bitch at my beck and call," he boasted. He continued to drink, barely pausing between tankards to offer a toast. "Damn fine wine," he mumbled, raising his tankard and spilling half of his drink over his sleeve.

Shaking his head in disgust, Rhett watched the dark red stain seep into the Norman's tunic as Lucien swiped at the spill, making it worse.

Lucien drank several more tankards before finally growing quiet. His eyes closed; he slumped forward; his head hit the table with a thump.

Once the Norman's drunken snores rent the air, Rhett let his contempt show as he spit on the Norman's face. This sot was unreliable. 'Twas well that Rhett had already planned for another informant. He crossed the compound to the tent that held his prisoners, and motioned for the guard to lift the flap. "Get out here," he ordered.

A young girl of ten summers, with stringy brown hair and huge blue eyes, clung to her younger brother as they stumbled forward. Ill-clothed, both youngsters shivered as they huddled together for warmth.

"You." He pointed his finger at the girl. "I have a job for you."

She quickly nodded, her wide gaze wary.

Rhett grabbed the poor frightened girl by her tunic, ripping her from her brother's arms and shaking her. Exceedingly thin, her flesh was stretched tight over her small bones, and she wavered like a sheet in the wind. "You will go to the castle and report back to me the messages my man, Lucien, sends. If you fail, I will kill your brother."

He released her and she tumbled to the ground, then he turned to the boy, and viciously struck him across the face. The child fell to his knees, his eyes brimming with tears. Rhett smiled and turned to the girl. "You will do as I bid."

The girl scrambled on all fours to her brother and helped him up. The boy wailed in his sister's arms, but she uttered not a word, staring back at Rhett with vacant eyes.

Rhett knew the boy was terrified of him, but he could not abide the girl's silent defiance. Taking hold of her arm, he drew his hand back and slapped her hard across the face. Her head wobbled like an unsteady top, but she remained mute. She looked at him, her eyes cold, devoid of emotion, as if she had seen too much pain and heartache to care.

Her stoic strength diminished his power, and rage flowed

through him at her quiet contempt. He drew his hand back again, but his fingers curled into a fist and landed a mighty blow that rendered her near senseless.

His lips thinned into a wicked half-smile as he saw her bruised cheek discolor and swell. He yanked her to him. "Now you will have a reason to see the lady, and she you."

He threw her to the ground and watched both children cower away from him. God, but how he enjoyed the power that fear evoked. She still did not cry, but she cradled her cheek and protectively hugged her brother to her chest. He straightened his tunic, and leveled the child with an even stare. "Girl, you will tell the good mistress, Lady Bronwyn, that you are alone. She will befriend you." Then he pointed to the boy. "And remember, if you wish to see your brother alive you will do as I command. I will send a guard to escort you to the castle."

When the two frightened youngsters nodded and scrambled away, he grinned, feeling his shaft grow hard with mounting desire. Physical force always inflamed his need for a woman.

Rhett made his way to the back of the camp in search of a wench. Bronwyn's beautiful image was making his blood pound. He grabbed a camp follower and threw her to the ground, mounting her without care. She cried out and he smothered her scream in a harsh kiss that tasted of blood as he ground his teeth against her protesting lips .

He pictured Bronwyn's body beneath him as he savagely squeezed the woman's breast. He would build a dynasty with Bronwyn. Power was within his grasp, he thought, as he sweated and pumped, trying to spill his seed. With Bronwyn by his side, he could unite Wales and drive the hated Normans back to their shores. The idea was more exciting than the bitch he had just mounted. His breathing was labored as he continued to ram into the whore's body. Unfortunately, the wench was poor sport. Unskilled, she could not entice or excite him, and he rolled off her, unsatisfied. Before she could scurry away, he yanked her by the hair and pushed her head to ward his manhood. "Suck the seed out, wench."

He lay back, closed his eyes, and wondered why lately this was the only way he could find release. But he knew he would no longer suffer these bouts of frustration when he had a woman worthy of him—a woman like Bronwyn.

Gray daylight slipped through the high slotted windows, barely chasing the shadows away as Michau entered the great room to bow before Christophe and Bronwyn as they ate their morning meal. "My lady," he said, interrupting. "There is a peasant child who needs your attention."

Concern instantly pulled her from the conversation. "A child? Who?"

Michau shook his head. "I do not recognize her, my lady, but she has been poorly used."

Christophe's chin lifted at the guard's cautious tone. Without a word passing between the men, Christophe rose from his meal and offered Bronwyn his arm. He would accompany her.

Thick billowing clouds loomed overhead and a chilly wind swept the ground with a frosty breath. Bronwyn huddled closer to her husband as they crossed the courtyard and entered the gatehouse.

A frail, filthy girl of nine or ten summers stood shivering in the corner, her tattered clothes inadequate for the harsh weather. Bronwyn's heart went out to the little one as she knelt down beside her.

"What has happened to your face?" Bronwyn asked, recognizing the signs of abuse.

"I was wandering in the dark, and fell." The child lowered her gaze.

"Where are your parents?"

"Dead," the child said flatly, then raised her head. Not even a hint of moisture clouded her eyes as she stared off into the courtyard.

Bronwyn recognized that blank look, and placed her hand tenderly on the girl's shoulder, leading her into the castle. "Let me treat your face."

The girl offered no resistance, moving like a little puppet without a will.

"What is your name?" Bronwyn asked.

"Matrona," she softly responded.

"You are all alone?" Bronwyn asked as they climbed the wide castle steps.

"Aye, my lady."

Bronwyn gently squeezed the girl's thin shoulder, knowing only love could heal the emotional scars. "If you wish, you are welcome to stay, Matrona."

The girl's eyes flickered with a spark of interest. "Thank you, my lady. I will work very hard," she said, her voice grave.

"Right now I want you to mend. There will be time enough for work." Bronwyn looked at Christophe, silently pleading for his support.

"My lady is right. First you must get well before you can work." He reached down to ruffle Matrona's hair, and she cringed away. His expression solemn, he knelt down before her. "I am the master here, Matrona. Thus I want you to know that you have nothing to fear." He gently touched her bruised face. "If ever a heavy fist is laid to you, I will punish the knave myself."

Bronwyn's heart melted at the tenderness he showed the child.

Matrona looked at Christophe, trepidation swimming in her eyes. "Thank you, my lord."

Bronwyn understood the girl's hesitancy. A battered soul erected walls for protection. Matrona's injuries were more than physical.

Once inside the castle Bronwyn directed Nesta to fetch her healing tray, then led Matrona over to the hearth. The castle occupants turned to stare at the girl. Their curiosity overwhelmed her and she turned into Bronwyn's tunic to hide her face. Bronwyn glared at the Welshmen, motioning for them to go about their own affairs.

Nesta bustled in and handed Bronwyn a bowl of water and her herb tray. "There, there, child, Lady Bronwyn has a tender touch," she cooed.

When Matrona's face remained buried in Bronwyn's tunic, Nesta's eyes filled with compassion. "My lady," she whispered, so the child would not overhear. "with your permission,

Wilford and I would be most happy to take the child and raise her. Our house is empty now.''

Bless Nesta's caring nature. Bronwyn smiled and nodded her approval.

Nesta reached out and gently squeezed the child's hand. ''Matrona, if you would like, you can make your home with my Wilford and me.''

The child's head snapped up. Her huge blue eyes filled with confusion as she turned to Bronwyn, silently seeking the truth.

Bronwyn smiled reassuringly as she wrung out a linen cloth that had been soaking in warm water and herbs. Ever so gently she pressed the soothing compress to Matrona's cheek. ''You are a very lucky little girl, Matrona. Nesta is the cook here, and highly respected.''

Nesta beamed at the compliment, while Matrona lowered her eyes. ''I am not worthy of you,'' she murmured to Nesta, her voice soft and choked with emotion.

An equal mix of compassion and anger filled Bronwyn as she lifted the child's chin. ''You are as worthy as any member of the clan.''

Matrona looked from Bronwyn to Nesta, trying to read their expressions, before her gaze traveled to Christophe, seeking his approval, as well.

He smiled. ''My lady has the right of it.'' To distract Matrona, he sat down to hold her hand as Bronwyn began to treat the child's other bruises and cuts. Not one tear appeared, nor did Matrona cry out, even though the cuts had to sting when the astringent was applied. However, she gripped Christophe's hand, leaving tiny little imprints of her fingers as she silently endured the treatment. Bronwyn marveled that he stayed to comfort the child, offering soothing words with startling warmth and understanding. What an enigma he was.

With a head that felt two sizes too small, and a stomach that roiled with every hoofbeat, Lucien rode his horse very slowly, despite Rhett's orders to make haste. After emptying his belly several times on the way, he felt a measure of relief, and returned to the Montgomery castle late at night. He found many changes. A village had taken shape, containing more then three hundred huts. The castle and stone walls were completed. Everywhere he looked the progress was tremendous. It was as though a spell had been cast and the work done by sorcery. At the changing of the night watch, Welshmen replaced Normans. Rage flooded his soul and he ground his teeth. Black magic he could abide, but not this! It turned his stomach sour again to see them treated as equals.

He shook his head and entered the castle, going directly to the farthest table to pour himself a hefty drink. Though military protocol demanded he make his report immediately, Lucien rebelled. Nicolas Montgomery would have to wait until tomorrow. Lucien raised his horn and consumed half the contents, then wiped his mouth with his sleeve. When that heathen rebel defeated Montgomery's men, Lucien would rule this castle.

Suddenly the image of the Welshmen training to be castle guards flashed through his mind. "By His wounds," Lucien cursed. Christophe Montgomery used every opportunity to his advantage. With these heathens trained to fight, an attack would be much more difficult.

"I will still see Montgomery in hell," he snarled, quenching his thirst with another tankard of ale.

Michau's eyebrows met as he stood nearby, and heard the disparaging remark. Curious over the cause, he hailed Lucien. "What ho! You drink alone?" Feigning a fondness he was far from feeling, Michau slapped Lucien on the shoulder and took a seat beside him. "You are a man returned from a long journey and you seek out only ale?"

"My brethren seem to have developed strange tastes in my absence," he spat nastily as he stared at several Welshmen stringing their bows.

Michau's gaze followed his direction, and though he hated himself for the lies he was about to tell, 'twas the only way he knew to gain the drunk's confidence. "*Oui,* the Welsh. 'Tis not to my liking, either, but the lord has ordered it."

Lucien leaned back in his chair and studied Michau. "I never thought you would disagree with him."

"Circumstances have altered my opinion of Christophe Montgomery." His gaze narrowed. "I never expected him to turn on his own. But since he has taken that heathen to wife, his manner has greatly changed. I think she has bewitched him."

Lucien studied him long and hard. "I should have ruled," he abruptly snapped, then quaffed more ale. Slowly he lowered his tankard, a smirk covering his lips. "And soon I will rule."

A shiver of apprehension coursed though Michau, but he nodded his head. *"Oui,* and many would now follow you." He raised his drink. "Tell me of your travels."

"I have heard William has returned to Normandy."

"What? Are you sure? *Non!"* Michau shook his head in disbelief. "You must be mistaken," he insisted. "I would have known."

Lucien snorted and jabbed his finger into Michau's chest. "Montgomery does not tell you because he is afraid you and many loyal Normans would revolt. I have spoken to some Welsh who are discontent. Under my command, we could seize the moment. All of this would be ours."

Michau hid his disgust behind a forced smile. Leaning forward, he refilled their cups. "What if William returns?"

"What if he does?" Again Lucien wiped his mouth with his sleeve. "We will control Wales, and he will have to deal with us. The king does not have the men, nor the time, to put down a revolt."

"Ah!" Michau said. "Unrest at home can only work to our advantage."

All night the two drank, and when Lucien passed out and fell facedown on the table from the excess, Michau staggered upstairs to awake the lord. His steps were uncoordinated, but he managed to find the master's suite and pound on the door.

"What the devil?" Christophe swore. Climbing out of bed, he flung the door wide.

"Your pardon, my lord," Michau slurred, "but I have a report."

Christophe's nostrils flared as he smelled the strong spirits. "Michau, are you foxed?"

"*Oui,* my lord, but 'twas in the line of duty."

Christophe raised a dark eyebrow as Bronwyn crowded into his side, peeking around his arm to see.

"I must tell you this news," Michau bellowed as he tried to focus.

"Shhh," Christophe admonished, looking up and down the hallway for disturbed sleepers.

"But . . ."

Christophe grabbed Michau by the scruff of the neck and dragged him into the bedchamber. "Be quiet."

Michau placed his finger to his lips and nodded, but when he spoke his voice still boomed.

Bronwyn laid her hand on Christophe's chest. "I will fix Michau some medicine for tomorrow. When he wakes he will have need of something for his aching head."

Christophe nodded, then turned his attention back to Michau. Never had he known this trusted soldier to overindulge.

After Michau related the night's events, he leaned against the wall and chuckled. "Poor fool could not hold his liquor."

Christophe clasped the man's arm in fellowship. "Seek your rest. You have served me well tonight. I will not forget your loyalty."

Michau grinned and promptly passed out. Catching and hoisting him over his shoulder, Christophe carried Michau to his quarters below. He then looked in on his traitor, Lucien, before rousing his brother.

Nicolas grumbled as he yawned and pulled his tunic on while following his brother to the armory. Once inside, Christophe closed the door, lit a candle, then pointed to a seat at the table and began to pace.

Nicolas's eyes narrowed as he listened to the report. "I will arrest him at once."

"*Non.*" Christophe reached out and clamped his hand onto Nicolas's shoulder, pressing him back down in his chair.

"But he has seen our defenses," Nicolas argued.

"I want Lucien free. If he is unaware of our suspicions, he will grow overconfident and make mistakes. Until he contacts the rebels, let the ale flow freely and have Nesta lace his food with spirits." Christophe continued to pace. "I want him watched. And be careful whom you assign. Lucien might still have friends among the regiment."

"I will see to it."

Though no one's life was perfect, for once Christophe felt ahead of the game. Pleased, he walked the battlements in the early-dawn hours and surveyed all that had been accomplished. But that was not his only joy. For the first time in his life, he found himself in love. Never had he experienced such incredible bliss, he mused as he watched the dawn rise over his domain, brilliant, beautiful, and filled with promise. He would hold this land for his family. His wife would know security, and his sons would inherit a fine legacy. The men were proficient with the new bows he had made, and the double moat system, combined with the new fighting techniques, would see them victorious in a conflict. He wondered how far he could take his innovations. Already his army was far superior to any of this time. He thought on the matter. It did not take him long to decide that he would do whatever was necessary to keep his land and his family safe.

Bronwyn read the letter again in disbelief and felt her insides roil:

Demon spirit, Regan Carmichael, you have taken possession of Bronwyn Montgomery's body. I have PROOF, and can and will expose you as a charlatan if you do not meet me at the river. All those who protect you will die.

Her first impulse was to tell Christophe. But what would she say? *I am a time traveler.*

Her heart skipped a beat. The wicca knew her name. But what proof could she have? Terror traveled through her as the poorly scrawled words swam in front of her eyes. All who protected her would die. She couldn't allow Christophe or her family to suffer.

She knew an accusation of this magnitude could see her burned at the stake. She shuddered at the thought of the flames. This age was barbaric.

She recalled the flames engulfing her as the plane burned. "Oh, my God," she moaned. Just the thought of the fire and horrible pain made her break out in a sweat.

She could hear the hysterical calls from the superstitious crowd: demon, witch, changeling. The names echoed in her mind, each one causing her more dread than the last. With the great changes that had occurred this year, her people would easily believe her responsible for the earthquake and any other disaster.

Her knees felt weak as she sank to the floor, and dragged her fingers through Fang's thick, silky coat. She was more frightened than she had ever been in her life. She had to protect those around her. The missive burned her hands and she threw it in the fire.

Someone had slipped it under her door, shortly after Christophe had left. She watched it curl into ash and knew she would keep the appointment; she had to. Her heart pounded in her ears as she rose and walked to the door. Shivering, she drew her mantle over her shoulders and looked at the rich fabric. She would be too easily identified in the village if she wore it. Though the weather was cold, she put her mantle back and ran down the steps toward the kitchen. At the bottom of the stairs she saw Nicolas crossing the great room toward the armory.

"Nicolas, a word if you can spare me the time."

He turned and waited for her, but his features showed his impatience. "Please tell Michau I will be a little late today, but he can carry out the renovations we talked about. I must see how Cordelia and the baby are doing."

"I will give him your message," Nicolas said, turning before she could engage him in further conversation. She smiled as he quickly disappeared behind the armory door. Little did her brother-in-law realize that she was also in a great hurry. She entered the kitchen and found Nesta busy at the table making bread while Matrona watched, utterly captivated. The little girl glanced at Bronwyn, showing flour-streaked cheeks, before her attention returned to the thick glossy dough.

"I am going into the village," Bronwyn announced.

"My lady, where is your cloak?" Nesta asked as she pushed the dough toward Matrona to knead, then wiped her hands on a linen cloth.

"Upstairs," Bronwyn nonchalantly said, hating herself for her impending deceit. She grabbed the door latch and pulled it open, knowing Nesta would never allow her to go outside without a mantle in this weather.

"Have you lost what little wits the Lord gave you?" Nesta marched over and slammed the door shut. "Here, take my mantle." She wrapped the warm woolen cloak around her mistress and fastened the closures at the neck. "You would catch your death if I was not around to take care of you."

"Aye, I suppose I would," Bronwyn agreed, keeping her features solemn.

"Now, mind you are not late," Nesta admonished. Her hand on the latch, she paused before opening the door. "Where in the name of all that is holy is that hellbeast? He goes everywhere with you."

"I thought to leave Fang here," she hedged.

"Nay, you take that beast."

Bronwyn was about to refuse when Nesta placed her hands on her hips. Knowing the stance all too well, Bronwyn nodded. "Fang," she called. The wolf immediately appeared from around the corner.

"I never feel safe with that silver haired devil lurking in the corners," Nesta muttered as she ushered Bronwyn out.

Bronwyn walked down the steps and looked down at Fang. With Nesta's coarsely woven mantle, she would blend in with the villagers who traveled the path, but not with the wolf at her side. Although she remembered Fang's effect on the witch, she could not risk discovery. Peeking around the corner of the building, she sighed. Every guard had his back to her. With her hair covered by the hood, she walked around to the front of the castle and opened the door. "In," she ordered Fang.

The wolf looked at her once, then reentered the castle. She peered back over her shoulder. Thankfully, no one had noticed. Keeping her head down, she walked across the courtyard and out the gate with no one the wiser. Her identity safe, she made her way through the village, then left the main path and walked farther, past the old castle's ruins to the river's edge. There, camped by the water, was the old crone who had read her fortune. Strange as it seemed, the moment the wicca had touched Bronwyn's palm, she must have known Regan's identity.

When Bronwyn stepped into the camp, the old woman glanced up. "My lady," she cackled gleefully, then pointed to the campfire. "Rest your bones."

Bronwyn refused to share the woman's fire. "I told you to be gone. What is it you want?"

The smile thinned as the old woman pinned her with an icy stare. "I want a few things to make my life easier. You can do that for me."

"Why would I?"

A sly smirk appeared in the weathered face. "Because, my lady, if you do not I will expose you."

Bronwyn thought to bluff her way through the deal. "I do not fear you."

"If you do not, then you should." The wicca's voice was cold as she continued to stir the fire with a stick. "I have the power to destroy you. One word from me and you would be tied to a stake and burned alive. Have you ever seen a burning, my lady?" The wicca's eyes glowed with an avid light as she turned her gaze on Bronwyn. "The victim screams as the smoke fills his lungs, then the flames eat up his flesh. You can hear the skin crackle and sizzle. 'Tis most gruesome."

Bronwyn shivered at the horrible image that rose once again in her mind. But she would not be intimidated. "You had your chance to expose me and did not."

"Your wolf would have torn me apart. But I know the truth. You are not of this time."

Though every nerve in her body was stretched taut, Bronwyn was not about to be pulled into the woman's scheme. "No one will believe you. I am Bronwyn Llangandfan Montgomery."

The wicca's eyes narrowed to tiny little slits as she threw her stick into the fire and stood up. "You are not her! I have the proof! Not only will you pay for your deception, but your husband and family, as well."

Christophe, Bronwyn silently cried as a wave of icy fear swept through her. She drew a deep breath. "What proof?"

"Come closer, my lady," the wicca ordered, pointing to a small pan of water. "Stare into the waters of life and you will see my proof."

"I see nothing," Bronwyn scoffed.

"Look, my lady, you will."

"There is nothing there!"

"Keep looking at the gentle water as it ripples softly," she said as she touched the pan, causing little waves to ebb and flow. "See the waves, my lady. Look beyond them to the face that is hidden just below the surface, while I pray. You will see the face of the demon."

As Bronwyn stared, her eyelids grew strangely heavy, and just as she was about to look away, an image appeared in the water. Brown hair and features that exactly resembled Regan. Bronwyn stepped back, her heart racing as she stared at the old woman. "What sorcery is this?"

The crone's hand latched onto Bronwyn's arm. Her grip tightened as her nails bit into Bronwyn's flesh.

" 'Tis no sorcery, but the proof. I will use this, my lady, if you do not do as I say."

Bronwyn swallowed. She had seen the proof with her own eyes, and a horrible dread traveled to her heart.

She stared into the crone's eyes and knew this woman would make good her threat. She pulled her arm free and resisted the urge to soothe her bruised skin. "What is it you want?" She would not gamble with her loved ones' lives.

"Just a few luxuries to make this humble woman's life easier."

She pointed to the surroundings. "I could use a roof over my head, some food, some clothes." She reached out and felt the material of Bronwyn's mantle.

"I will see what can be done," Bronwyn said.

The old crone grinned, revealing several missing teeth. "As a show of your good faith, I would have you leave those pretty stones around your neck, and the matching ring."

Bronwyn sucked in her breath. " 'Tis my wedding gift."

"Aye, I know. And of great value. If you give them to me I will know you mean to keep your promise."

Bronwyn touched the necklace and balked, taking a step backward.

"I will return the baubles, my lady, when I see that you have fulfilled your bargain," the crone cooed.

"Nay, I say."

The old woman advanced, and jabbed a dirty finger into Bronwyn's chest. "If you do not leave them as a pledge that you will keep your word, our bargain is off. I will denounce you now."

Bronwyn stared into the pitiless black eyes and knew the woman would indeed follow through on her threat. Though it went against every fiber in her being to accede to blackmail, she knew there was only one course. But she would set the tone.

"I will give you a place to live, clothes and food, but that is all."

"Agreed, my lady. I am a simple woman with simple needs." The wicca held out her hand for the jewels. "I will keep my word, and remain silent."

Bronwyn held back the tears when she removed the amber necklace Christophe had given her. But two tears slipped down her face when she handed over her wedding ring.

Bronwyn walked sadly back to the castle and went unseen to the kitchen. After she had returned Nesta's mantle, she entered the great room and ran into Michau.

"My lady, I was looking for you this morning when Nicolas relayed your message."

"What is it you need?"

"I must see to some military matters, but after they are attended I will have the men start on the storage rooms."

"Michau, I wonder if you could have the men start on a crofter's hut first. The storage rooms can wait."

"Aye, my lady. Whose croft are we building?"

"An old woman who is in great need." An image of the wicca came to mind, and she buried her anger. "She is alone and has no lodging."

Michau nodded. *"Oui,* my lady, I will see to it first chance I have. Until then, would you like me to fetch her and bring her to the castle? There is room here."

"Nay," she said too forcefully. At Michau's look of surprise she rushed to add, "She is a wicca and would not feel comfortable with others about. She needs privacy. I will tell her when the croft is done."

"As you wish, my lady." Michau bowed and left.

Alone, she paced the great room and prayed she had not made a mistake. Her hand covered the bare spot on her finger. Pray God, Christophe did not notice her ring missing.

Chapter Fifteen

Caradoc approached the valley he had known all his life and felt a stab of pain. God's teeth, how had he wound up in this mess? Although he had lost his heart to the dearest, sweetest woman on God's green earth, love was not the culprit. 'Twas his arrogance. His mistakes crowded in on him, pressing down with a crushing weight that threatened to bury him beneath his stupidity.

As Rhett's words came back to him, he ground his teeth in frustration: "We will attack when you poison the food, and Lucien opens the gates. If you fail me, I swear by all I hold holy I will marry your beloved Ariana to a northern chieftain."

He had spent a sleepless night filled with regrets. Now, he knew what had to be done.

He stopped and let his gaze take in the view before him. The old wood castle lay in ruins, but the new stone castle awed him. In the afternoon sunlight its majesty reminded him of heaven.

After Nicolas leaned over the battlements and gave his permission, Caradoc entered the castle by the main gate.

As he waited for Nicolas, he turned full circle and could not believe the amount of construction the Normans had managed to complete. It did not escape his eye that the villagers looked well cared for and happy.

Nicolas approached Caradoc and removed his sword. "Remain here while I send for Christophe," he said, motioning for two soldiers, who quickly advanced and stood guard on either side of Caradoc.

After Nicolas turned and walked back up the stairs, Caradoc reviewed his plans again. He had considered so many schemes last night and today, his head pounded. But no matter how many times he deliberated the problem, he saw only one solution. A shaft of fear sliced to his heart. Dear God, he could not fail. Just the thought made his blood run cold. His beloved waited, and her trust and faith in him would be justified. When he saw Lucien leave the castle, Caradoc turned his back, showing no recognition for another of Rhett's traitors.

Several minutes passed, and Bronwyn, Fiona, and their father entered the courtyard. Caradoc shaded his face and watched his family, hoping they would not see him as they walked toward the stable. His sister Fiona walked with a slower gait than the others, and a twinge of guilt stabbed his conscience.

Bronwyn looked over just as they were abreast. Recognition darkened her eyes. "What are you doing here?"

Fiona and Hayden immediately followed Bronwyn's gaze. Fiona gasped, but Hayden's face crinkled into a mask of unbridled joy.

Caradoc reached out and took hold of Bronwyn's shoulders. "I have returned to face up to my responsibilities."

She shook her head. "You have not proven your trustworthiness."

Her doubt was well deserved, but he had to convince her otherwise. When she tried to pull free he held her tighter. "Bronwyn, I swear to you, I mean every word I say."

"Do you, Caradoc? Are you sure you do not want me to plead your case?"

"Nay. There was a time when I would have let you shoulder my burdens. But I must handle this on my own."

"My prayers have been answered," Hayden cried.

Disbelief, then hope, flitted across Bronwyn's features. "If you speak the truth, then I would be very proud of you,'' she whispered.

He kissed her cheek. ''I never realized how important family was to me. I have missed you all very much.'' He pulled Fiona over and gave her a warm kiss. ''I love you.''

Tears brimmed Fiona's eyes as Hayden happily hugged his son.

They were all talking at once when Michau appeared and escorted Caradoc inside.

Bronwyn watched him walk off to meet Christophe, and her throat constricted. Her father draped one arm around her, and the other around Fiona. ''My son has come home,'' he sighed.

Tears misted Bronwyn's eyes. She hoped Hayden was right and Caradoc had learned his lesson. If not, he would break all their hearts.

Christophe kept Caradoc waiting three hours before going to meet with him in the private room off the great room. Ignoring Caradoc's ire, he briskly took a seat.

Caradoc placed his hands firmly on the table and leaned forward. His face, only inches away, revealed lines of fatigue and worry. ''I was sent to betray you.''

Christophe raised an eyebrow at the blunt announcement. ''Why are you telling me this?''

Caradoc lowered his eyes. ''I've been a fool. But I need your help.''

Christophe studied the young man. He was neither surly nor disrespectful. Something had happened to him.

''What is it you need?''

''My woman is with child.'' Caradoc began to pace. ''I need to get her safely away from her family. To do this, I need you.''

Christophe steepled his fingers, and his eyes narrowed as he considered his brother-in-law. ''What makes you think I would help you?''

Beads of sweat formed on Caradoc's brow, and he held out his hands in a gesture meant to encompass the room. ''It would be to your advantage to have peace within the family and throughout the land."

Christophe contemplated the words, saying nothing.

Uneasy with the silence, Caradoc resumed pacing.

"A dowry can be arranged," Christophe finally said, thinking the man only needed to present money in lieu of land.

Caradoc whirled around, his face tightly strained. "Lord Rhett is my beloved's father."

The pieces suddenly fell into place. "How can I be of help?" Christophe asked, seeing a chance to destroy his enemy. Once the rebellion was crushed, and Caradoc, now allied with the Normans, married Rhett's daughter, the two houses would be joined, deterring any more warfare. He pointed to a chair, directing Caradoc to sit down.

Caradoc visibly swallowed, his eyes suspiciously moist. He accepted an ale, and took a long drink, then slowly lowered his tankard and leaned back in his chair. "Rhett plans to attack, when you are at your weakest."

"How?" Christophe asked, pouring his own drink. "Surely, he has no men left."

"Rhett has sold everything of value, he tries to barter his daughter. A northern chieftain has sent men and arms after Rhett promised him my Ariana in marriage." He slammed his tankard against the table. "I cannot allow this. She is mine."

Christophe understood. Love of a woman could change a man. But the question remained, was he still a traitor? "How many men does he have?"

"Two hundred and fifty, with another five hundred promised."

Christophe ran a hand through his hair. The numbers far exceeded what he thought the rebel could possibly raise. "What is his plan?"

"He has a Norman spy, Lucien, planted among your men, and also an informer . . ."

"Who is the informer?"

Caradoc shrugged. "Unfortunately, I do not know who carries Lucien's messages to Rhett."

Disappointed, Christophe waved his hand. "Continue."

''I am to win your confidence, then poison the food the night before the regiment leaves for London.''

''Rhett knows about that?'' Christophe asked, his stomach knotted. He had underrated his enemy.

''Aye.''

''Why the poison, if he plans to attack us?'' Christophe asked, fearing his enemy planned to kill them in their sleep.

''Rhett underestimated you once. The poison will make the castle inhabitants too sick to fight. He wants you at his mercy. When the attack starts, Lucien will lower the drawbridge and open the gates for the rest of his forces.''

Christophe considered Caradoc's words, testing them in his mind for any weakness, then he leaned close. ''What do you want?''

''When you fight Rhett's men, Ariana will be left at the rebel's camp. If you allow me to lead the Norman regiment that has been called back to London, I can redirect those soldiers to cover your flank when the attack is launched. While Rhett's men are busy fighting on two fronts, I can rescue my beloved.''

Christophe pursed his lips. ''Why should I believe you?''

''I cannot give you a single reason,'' Caradoc admitted. ''If you do not help me, I will leave here and try to rescue her by myself, and you will still be left with the problem of an informer, Lucien, and Rhett.''

Christophe contemplated Caradoc, looking deep into the man's eyes in an attempt to ferret out the truth. Everything Caradoc said about Lucien corroborated what Christophe had already found out. Though the information was impressive, it could also be a ruse. Finally he extended his hand. ''I will trust you.''

At first Caradoc looked dumbfounded, then he quickly grasped Christophe's hand and pumped it. ''I despised you once, Montgomery, but now I give my solemn vow: For the service you do me, I will gladly forfeit any sum you ask, or any service you require. If necessary, I would even give my life for you.''

Christophe smiled as he pulled his hand free of the man's enthusiastic grip. ''What you must do is play a part. The informer will no doubt be watching you. We will go ahead with your plan . . ." Christophe held up his hand when Caradoc started to protest. "Except we will not poison the food. Only two people will think the food is really poisoned. On the eve of the regiment's departure, Lucien will no doubt have a loss of appetite, as will the informer—and we will know his identity. Until then, no one, not even your family, can know of our plan. Nicolas and I will only inform our personal guard." He walked to the door and ordered the servant to fetch Nicolas.

When Nicolas arrived, the three men put their heads together, working out the details for the unmasking of their traitor and the coming battle. Christophe decided on the story Caradoc would tell his family, and Caradoc assured the brothers that he could fool everyone, including his own relatives.

"You had better," Christophe warned. "Our lives may depend on it."

Bronwyn twisted the seam of her tunic as she tread across the floor. The darkness of the hour crowded around her as she stared out the castle window. Christophe, Nicolas and Caradoc had been in the armory for hours.

"Cease, Daughter, before you worry a hole in the fabric of your garment."

She looked down at her crumpled tunic and sighed. "Do you think Christophe will order Caradoc flogged?" she asked her father, but Fiona answered.

"Nicolas would never allow it," she insisted, her expression outraged.

Before Hayden could respond, the door burst open and Caradoc stepped into the hall, followed by Christophe and Nicolas. Her brother's face was drawn and his eyes downcast. Bronwyn's heart sank.

"I am exiled to Normandy until I learn the ways of a Norman." Caradoc's listless voice was hardly above a whisper, but his deafening disappointment rent the air.

"You are not going to be punished?" Bronwyn asked, her spirits rising a little.

"Nay, I have agreed to the warlord's terms. I have been pardoned."

"Oh, Caradoc, that is wonderful." She started to rush toward him, but he held her at bay.

"I do not want to leave Wales," he said, bleakly.

Under the circumstances Christophe had been more than generous. Why could he not see that? Why did he remain so stubborn?

Caradoc slanted a gaze at Christophe's dark frown. "Although I do not relish the idea of Normandy, I admit I am glad to be spared the tails."

Fiona rushed over and kissed her brother. "Father is so happy," she whispered as Hayden approached. "Just look at him."

"Son, go with the purpose of learning, then return to us wiser," Hayden said as he grasped his son's hand, then turned toward Christophe. "You are indeed wise and merciful."

"When does he leave?" Bronwyn asked her husband.

"A fortnight."

Bronwyn reached up and gave her brother a kiss on the cheek. He stood stiff and detached. Although she could understand his disappointment, she believed his surliness was to cover his fear. She had a moment's pause when she looked into her brother's eyes and he could not hold her gaze. "God bless, Brother."

After the meeting, Christophe checked the armory, making sure the weapons were in order, then the larder to insure there was enough food to withstand a siege if need be. He personally inspected the water reservoir, putting a guard on duty at each station he found vulnerable. When he was satisfied that every precaution had been taken, the night was nearly over. He finally relaxed, walking across the battlements as he sorted out his thoughts. With the cloud cover blocking out the stars, the pitch-black night held a sort of comfort.

In the torchlight he noticed Nicolas leaving the castle. His brother quickly scanned the walls as he rushed across the courtyard. "Christophe, I have bad news." Nicolas waved at him as he ran up the battlements. "You said to report anything out of the ordinary. Sumner was on patrol when he saw your wife early this morning."

"So?"

"She was far from the village, and he followed her because she was alone and without Fang. She met an old woman by the river."

"I fail to see the problem. She is the healer of this village," Christophe said.

Nicolas sighed. "Christophe, she told me to tell Michau she would be late this morning because she was going to check on Cordelia and her baby."

Even though Christophe felt an all-too-familiar tightening in his gut, he smiled. "She probably went to check on the old woman after she saw Cordelia and the baby."

"Christophe," Nicolas persisted, "I checked with Wilford. Lady Bronwyn never saw Cordelia or the baby."

The words hung in the air.

Christophe looked down from the battlements toward the village. "If my wife went to see the old woman and not Cordelia, I am sure there is a good explanation for it."

"You are not upset?"

He had promised to trust his wife. His word and his faith would be put to the test. *"Non,* Bronwyn will not betray me." He turned back to his brother. "She is not the informer. I would stake my life on it."

Nicolas nodded, then grinned. "It seems to me, Brother, you already have."

Alone in their chamber, Christophe leaned toward his wife, unable to stand her silence. She had been distracted the whole evening, barely saying two words.

"Bronwyn, do you have something you wish to tell me?"

"What," she looked up, puzzled.

"Did you hear what I said?"

Her face flushed bright red. "I am sorry, my lord. What did you ask?"

"I said is there something you wished to tell me?"

Bronwyn blinked. "Tell you? Is there something I forgot to do?" Her beautiful amber eyes were clear, her gaze unwavering.

"*Non,* there is nothing you forgot to do," he said, growing frustrated.

"Good."

He watched her absently combing her hair, and a niggling of doubt wormed its way through him. He would know the truth.

"Bronwyn, what did you do today?"

"Today, my lord?"

"*Oui,* today," he repeated, growing tired of her distracted air.

She waved her hands in the air. "Just the same chores I do everyday, my lord. Nothing special."

"Tell me," he said, his voice harsh.

For just a moment he saw a hint of fear in her eyes before it disappeared. It happened so fast, he could have imagined it, but suddenly he knew she was hiding something.

"Of course, my lord, I will be glad to tell you."

He folded his arms across his chest and listened to every word she said, including how she had missed Cordelia and saw to the needs of the old wicca by the river. He shook his head. Though she had been truthful about her whereabouts, he knew something was amiss. She was too distracted and he had glimpsed remorse several times in her expressive eyes. Doubt entered his heart and he dearly wished it hadn't. He would know for sure if she could be trusted on the eve of the regiment's departure. He welcomed the coming date. And dreaded it.

"Who do you have watching our people as they eat?" Christophe asked his brother as they entered the great room.

"Our personal guard. No one will escape their surveillance. I have placed them at all the tables. Since this is their last night, that action will not be questioned."

Christophe nodded. He had not told anyone of his doubts, but he would watch his wife tonight. Over the past two weeks

her behavior had seemed normal. Pray God, she would prove
her loyalty tonight.

A feast was laid out on the tables, for every member of the
village was invited to the send-off for the men. Wine and ale
were poured. Nesta worked hard to see that the tables each had
a platter of roasted meat. In fact, she had lost her temper
with Caradoc when he had twice interrupted her routine in the
kitchen. Everyone had heard of the row.

Christophe smiled. Caradoc had played his part well. He
watched as Nesta and Bronwyn came into the room. He passion-
ately hoped that his plan ferreted out the spy, and prayed it
was not his beloved.

"Where is Matrona?" Bronwyn asked as she helped Nesta
carry out a platter.

"She is ill, my lady, so I sent her to bed."

"Do you wish me to look in on her?"

"Nay, she ate too many biscuits today when I was baking.
Her tummy is just a little upset." Nesta grinned knowingly.

Bronwyn smiled. "I remember doing the same thing when
I was her age and helped you."

"Aye, my lady, that you did," she chuckled.

Bronwyn looked around as they placed the platter before
Christophe. "You have outdone yourself, Nesta."

" 'Tis a wonder with your brother underfoot all day."

Bronwyn frowned. "I cannot understand him."

"He is no doubt apprehensive about his departure," Nesta
offered, then looked down at the meat. "I hope the meat is not
overseasoned. I was so busy today, I pray I did not use a heavy
hand with the spices."

" 'Twill be fine," Bronwyn assured.

Christophe stood up and raised his hands for everyone's
attention. He raised his goblet. "To good and valiant men. We
shall miss our comrades in arms. Safe journey."

Everyone raised their cup to the toast, then the feasting began.
He motioned for Bronwyn, and she took her place by her
husband and sat down.

He watched as she raised her fork, but before it reached her lips, she was called into the kitchen. She smiled at him, laid her untouched fork on her plate, and excused herself.

It seemed every time his wife sat down, someone called her away. Finally, when the meal was almost over, she returned.

Nicolas leaned toward his brother. "The men have reported back. Everyone has eaten but Lucien and—" He hesitated, then whispered, "Bronwyn."

Christophe fiercely wanted to deny his brother's words. He turned to watch his wife. She picked up her fork, but instead of eating she made a show of moving her food around the plate. His throat grew thick as he covertly studied every pass of her fork across her plate. The result of her efforts was that it looked as though she had indeed eaten, but she had not.

He waited until she put her fork down. If he had not been watching her so closely, she would have gotten away with her subterfuge.

"Are you feeling ill?" he asked solicitously.

Her face paled, but she managed to smile. "I am well, my lord, why do you ask?"

He looked to her plate, and would know the truth. "How was your dinner, Wife?" he asked.

Just then, Nesta reached for Bronwyn's plate to clear the table. Bronwyn smiled at Nesta. "Delicious," she said, patting her lips delicately with the linen cloth.

"Did you enjoy the meat?"

"Aye, 'twas most tasty."

Each word she uttered damned her. He saw his brother's anxious features and silently signaled him to remain quiet.

"Then you are satisfied, my lady?"

"Aye, my lord, my hunger no longer bites."

His eyes narrowed. "Are you sure you would not care for some dessert?"

She shook her head. "Nay, my lord. I could not force another morsel down. Delicious as it is," she added.

Liar, his mind screamed. He stared at her perfect mouth, stunned that those soft, pink lips had kissed his, and now uttered such deceit. Her amber eyes sparkled, yet the glow he had mistaken for love was nothing more than trickery and female cunning. Pain sliced through him, but he buried it and returned her insincere smile. He wanted to reach out and strangle her, but he clenched his fist and made a silent vow. She would pay ten-fold for her betrayal of his love. From the top of her golden mane to the tip of her tiny feet, she would feel his vengeance. No one played with his heart.

He stood and turned to his brother. "Nicolas, I crave a word with you before you retire."

When they had moved from the table to the stairway, Christophe spoke to his brother, but all the while he stared at his wife. His rage boiled to the surface and he had to exercise every ounce of his control to keep his voice level. "I know I have found our spy. Tell the others to act sick tomorrow. No one is to inform my wife of our plan."

Nicolas shook his head and touched Christophe's arm. "Christophe, are you sure?"

Christophe shook off his brother's hand. "She is the only one who has not tasted her meal."

His jaw clenched as he watched his deceitful wife laugh. He had trusted her. Never would he make that mistake again.

Chapter Sixteen

The next day the Norman regiment gathered in the courtyard. A cold wind blew and snowflakes swirled as Bronwyn wrapped her mantle tighter around her, but the chill permeated her thick woolen wrap.

Everyone but Bronwyn, Caradoc, and Matrona complained of a stomachache that morning. Christophe could barely stand with the pain that doubled him over, but had refused her help. She had tried to wrap her arm around his waist, but he had given her a disdainful glare that warned her away. Though she ached to help him, she knew he would never allow a show of weakness in front of his men.

His ailment aside, for the last two weeks he had seemed preoccupied and withdrawn. If she didn't know better she would think he had noticed her missing jewels. But he had never confronted her. No doubt it was her guilty conscience that colored her judgement, she thought, shaking her head at her own foolishness. He had a lot on his mind with his regiment being ordered back to London. In a way his absorption in military matters was a blessing, for he was too sharp not to have noticed her behavior. But soon she would retrieve her jewels and no one would be the wiser about the wicca's threats. She had managed to save her loved ones.

"You must go to bed," she whispered sternly to Christophe, who leaned against the door frame as her family stood on the porch above the courtyard.

"Leave be, woman." He pushed off the support and stumbled down the steps to see his men safely on their journey. She sighed at his stubbornness. Then she looked about and sadly contemplated the others who were ailing. Not just the immediate family, but the whole regiment of Normans who were traveling back to London, and the Welshmen who now guarded the walls. "What is wrong with everyone?" she murmured.

Fiona looked pale and could barely make it down the steps without the help of her husband. Upon seeing Bronwyn, she moaned and turned her head into her husband's shoulder.

"Nicolas, what ails the two of you?" Bronwyn asked as he reached her.

Though Fiona's head remained buried, a sad compassion colored Nicolas's eyes as he met her gaze. "I think we must have eaten some tainted meat."

Bronwyn doubted that the meat was tainted, and suspected it was the flu. Her own stomach was queasy of late and she had abstained from eating last night. She patted her sister's back. "I will see if I can make a purgative to help ease everyone's ills." She walked down the steps to say goodbye to her brother.

"Good fortune, Caradoc."

He kissed her cheek. "All will be well soon, Sister."

"You are not ill, that is reason to rejoice," she said cheerfully.

"Nay," he said curtly.

His voice seemed strained, yet when she looked at him, his boyish smile convinced her otherwise.

When the regiment had left, the castle seemed deserted. There were only ten Normans; the rest were Welsh farmers.

A shiver of apprehension ran up her spine as she looked into her countrymen's faces, and turned to Christophe. "What is it, Christophe? Is something wrong?"

He barely looked at her as he stared at the battlements. "Why not take Matrona to our room and teach her some songs," he suggested instead of answering her question.

She stared at him, willing him to meet her gaze, but he continued to study the defenses. After several minutes of his preoccupation, she reached for Matrona's hand.

"Very well." She marched off, wondering why everyone was behaving so oddly. Even Nesta had lost her jovial air. For a terrifying moment, Bronwyn began to fear that the old crone had turned the people against her. Nonsense, she admonished herself. They were ill, and worried about the loss of the Norman regiment. The blackmail had taken its toll on her nerves. She was as jumpy as a spooked cat.

Bronwyn had no sooner shut the door to her private apartment, when she spied a missive on her bed. Her heart fluttered, knowing it was from the wicca. She opened the note and scanned the lines. The final meeting had been set. Even though this would conclude their business, she closed her eyes and shuddered. "Dear God," she whispered.

"What is it, my lady?" Matrona asked.

Her eyes flew open at the sweet child's concern. "Nothing, dear," she soothed, but she was unnerved and even embarrassed by the little waif's interest.

Matrona continued to scrutinize her for several more seconds, until Fang yawned loudly, capturing her attention. He stretched, then turned in a circle and lay back down on the floor.

"Can I pet him?" Matrona asked.

Bronwyn remembered how Christophe had placed her palm on Fang's fur and introduced them. She did the same with Matrona's hand, and said "Friend." The little girl squealed with delight. "I never had a pet."

"Fang is not a pet. He is more a protector."

The girl's eyes sparkled. "The warlord's animal," she said reverently.

Even though the child still acted wary sometimes, it was amazing what a fortnight in Nesta's and Wilford's loving care had done to bring the girl out of her shell. She had arrived at Castle Montgomery a quiet, introverted victim; now the poor little dear had a big case of puppy love. She had chosen her "knight in shining armor"—Christophe. Everything Matrona did or said echoed her infatuation. Bronwyn understood the child's hero worship. In truth, he had a way with people.

The day passed slowly, but Bronwyn played games with Matrona, trying to take her own mind off the assignation with the wicca. By late afternoon dark clouds blocked the sun, and the room grew darker. Bronwyn lit more candles and stoked the fire. "Matrona," she said, "I have to gather some herbs for the illness everyone has. Can you run down to the kitchen and join Nesta?"

"Aye, my lady." Matrona sped for the door. Once in the doorway she stopped and turned back. "Thank you, my lady."

"You are welcome," Bronwyn said, then the girl raced down the hallway. She chuckled at the child's exuberance, then sobered, remembering her appointment with the wicca. "Come, Fang," she ordered. She would not go again without the wolf.

In the great room she noticed a surprising number of women in the castle. "What brings all of you here?"

Cordelia, her baby in her arms, stepped forward. "My lady, we all decided to give eight-hour duty today, so we may have some time off to prepare for the coming Yule. Lord Christophe agreed."

"Is the whole village here?" Bronwyn asked wonderingly, gazing at the familiar faces of the women as their children huddled by them.

"Aye, my lady."

"Very well," she said, wondering why Cordelia could not look her in the eye. "I have some herbs to collect. I will be back shortly."

"My lady, would you take Matrona with you?" Nesta asked, her features drawn, her expression strained. "I have an errand for her to do."

"Nay, Nesta, I cannot take her with me. I have to dig up some roots for a purgative."

"Very well, my lady," Nesta said, but her eyes held disapproval. "I will send Matrona alone."

"Sister," Fiona cried out. "You cannot leave." Her features were pinched with fear as she made her way through the crowd.

"Fiona, what has you so upset?"

"Please, I beg you do not venture out of the castle today. We are much better."

Bronwyn patted her sister's arm. "Calm yourself." She noticed all the women had stopped their work and now paid avid attention to the conversation.

"The weather looks foul. You must not go!" Fiona pleaded, uncommonly distressed.

Bronwyn could not explain why she had to go, and felt the bite of her deception when she looked into her sister's troubled eyes. "I must."

Bronwyn hugged her sister and left the room. When she stepped out into the courtyard, she noticed all the men of the village were on the battlements. She found it strange, but perhaps they too wanted to give extra duty to earn some time off. She put the problem from her mind. She had other worries far more immediate.

She huddled into her mantle as an icy blast of damp air hit her. With her head downcast she walked toward the gate.

"Where are you going?" Christophe demanded.

She jumped at the sound of his voice and whirled about to see Christophe standing with the duty guard. His lips were thinned, and his expression dark and foreboding.

Her heart skipped a beat. She had not expected to confront her husband. "I am going to get some healing herbs."

He stared at her so long she thought he was going to deny her. "It will be dark in another hour. It cannot wait?"

"Nay, though the women seem better, you do not, nor does this guard," she said, looking at their strained expressions. "I need this remedy to treat those who are still sick, and to have on hand in case the sickness returns."

"Very well," he acceded, pointing to the gate. "Wait for me. I will accompany you." He turned to the guard, giving him several instructions.

Panic seized her as she moved to the gate. One excuse after another flashed through her mind. All of them sounded weak, but she had to convince him to let her leave alone. When he joined her she laid her hand on his chest. "Christophe, you are still ill, and do not have all your strength. It is not wise."

"Wife, I am better."

She placed her finger to his lips. "The root does not grow far from here. You have duties and are busy."

He started to protest and she kissed him, throwing every ounce of passion into her kiss. 'Twas not a chore to love him, but she knew if he ever found out that she had used his attraction to her in order to sway him, he would never forgive her. Then her thoughts scattered as her strategy turned on her, and desire flared. When he pulled away she was breathless. "Please, Christophe, I have Fang. I promise to be back before dark." He did not seem as affected by their kiss as she was. His eyes were clear of passion, almost cold. Then she remembered the guard who was standing duty behind them.

"As you wish, my lady," he said quietly, and stepped back to allow her to proceed.

Surprised but relieved he had allowed her to leave without an escort, she scooted through the gates.

"You will return directly?" Christophe called after her.

She winced at his question and spun to face him. "Aye, my lord, I will be back directly."

He nodded. She lowered her eyes, unable to meet her husband's gaze. She was becoming quite an adept liar. Shame filled her, but she turned and started walking toward the village.

The sharp evening wind stung her cheeks as she made her way to the wicca's croft. When the sun set, she walked down toward the old ruins and heard a distant night owl. The forlorn sound sent a shiver through her. A half-moon shone bright, peeking in and out of the clouds, the intermittent light throwing ghostly shadows over the ground. She reached down to pet Fang for reassurance, but he was as disconcerted as she, for his fur was standing straight up. She had the eerie sensation that she was being watched, and kept looking over her shoulder. But no one was there. Her heart raced as she hurried along. Not until she spied the wicca's croft did she feel a measure of relief. Even though it was her nemesis's home, it was at least a harbor from what lurked in the night.

The old woman opened the door on the first knock. Bronwyn rushed in with Fang.

Though the wicca gasped and fell back at the sight of the wolf, Bronwyn ignored her to close and bar the door. She took several deep breaths to calm her nerves, then looked around approvingly at all that had been provided. Though it was only rough-hewn furniture, it was far better than what the other villagers had. "Our bargain is done. I have kept our agreement, and have come for my jewels. I will not see you again."

A sly smile crossed the wicca's face as she held up Bronwyn's ring and amber necklace. "You do want these back?" Sarcasm laced each word as she swung the amber stones.

Bronwyn's bluster immediately dissolved into trepidation as she reached for her wedding ring and betrothal gift, but the old woman meanly snatched them away.

Fear coursed through her as she realized that the old woman wasn't about to keep their bargain.

"All in good time," the wicca rasped. "I require one or two more things before you can have your baubles back."

Bronwyn ground her teeth. She was being toyed with, and she hated it.

Christophe had his men in place and his strategy firmly laid out. The only problem that troubled his mind was Bronwyn. Last night he had known she was the informer, but a part of him had hoped he was mistaken. Today, as much as it destroyed him, he admitted the truth. The clues had been there all along. Rhett's presence at the wedding and her failure to tell him who he was. And, fool that he was, the greatest proof of all—his counterpart's death. Her supposed loyalty when she led them to the weapons was just a ruse. He had believed her . . . because he loved her. Now he could not ignore the truth. "Bitch," he breathed.

Nicolas approached him. "There is the signal," he said, pointing to the night sky and the flaming arrow. "Caradoc has kept his word and sent us a warning that Rhett is on his way." He smiled. "As soon as Caradoc rescues his lady he will bring his men around and outflank Rhett's army so they cannot retreat."

Christophe stared at the bright streak, forcibly burying his anger to concentrate on the battle to come.

"We may not even need the returning Norman men," Nicolas said, eyeing the men on the wall. "Look at the Welshmen. They are ready."

"They had better be," said Christophe, somberly. "Their mettle will be sorely tested this night. From this contest we will know the loyalty of each man." Christophe slowly surveyed his Welsh soldiers, crouched low on the wall. God help them if these men failed.

Lucien entered the courtyard to take his shift, and Christophe nudged Michau. "Who is guarding him?"

"My lord, I assigned Sumner," Michau said.

Christophe nodded, knowing a good soldier guarded Lucien and he would never get an opportunity to open the gate.

Nicolas just shook his head in agreement, then peered over the castle wall. "Look," he whispered.

Christophe turned and watched the rebels slowly advance on their position. The moon broke through the clouds and he saw the bodies crawling through the fields toward them.

"Good Lord, they outnumber us twenty to one," Nicolas whispered as he watched the horde advance.

Christophe placed his hand on Nicolas's shoulder. "They will hit the first moat anytime. Have the archers stand ready."

The first wave of rebels crossed the outer moat filled with leaves and wood, and headed toward the inner water moat. When the men were caught between the two, Christophe raised his arm, giving the archers the signal to shoot their flaming arrows. Their aim was true and the arrows set the far moat ablaze, trapping the men between fire and water. A billowing cloud of smoke rose from the outer circle.

Screams and war cries rose from the field below as the men charged forward, swimming toward the castle walls. Soot and ear-splitting shrieks hung in the air as wave after wave of men swelled over the ground in an enormous tide that advanced without end. Christophe nodded to Michau, who gave the archers the next signal. A rain of arrows descended onto the rebels, and thanks to the hours of practice, greatly reduced the numbers in the field. Screams of pain echoed from below as men tried to find shelter in the melee.

When the rebels who had managed to breach the second moat stormed the gates, Nicolas raised his hand and they were met with boiling oil. Christophe glanced down to see Sumner holding Lucien at sword point. Apparently, Lucien had tried to open the gates. A measure of relief flowed through Christophe. His traitor was apprehended and the gates were still locked. But even though Lucien had proved his guilt, Christophe could not forget the informer. Bronwyn was still not here.

When Rhett's soldiers found the gate barred, they began to scale the wall. Christophe's men fought valiantly, but the vast number of rebels overwhelmed the castle guard. Steel clashed against steel as men met their enemy face-to-face. Christophe would never have reason to doubt the loyalty of his fine Welshmen again. Nicolas and Christophe fought back-to-back, ruthlessly and meticulously dispatching their enemies.

Christophe saw Hayden heavily outmatched and fought his way toward his father-in-law.

Beneath the superior strength of his opponent, Hayden stumbled and fell. The rebel drew back his sword to stab the fallen Welshman, but his blow was deflected by Christophe. This man was a mercenary, he knew, a soldier who made his living by the sword. Red-hot lightning creased Christophe's side as the enemy's blade sliced his ribs. Through a red haze of pain Christophe managed to block the next blow and slip his sword under his opponent's, running him through. Holding his side to stem the blood, he moved forward, fighting the men who dared attack his fortress. The castle soldiers fought on, showing their training and skill in hour after hour of hard fighting. Near dawn the tide began to change and Christophe's men gained the advantage. With Caradoc squeezing off the rebels' retreat, they realized their cause was hopeless, and surrendered.

Christophe held his side and moved among his men, giving them praise and receiving reports. A shout went up as the gates opened and the Norman regiment rode in.

"Did you see any sign of Rhett?" Christophe asked Caradoc.

"Nay," he replied, helping a lovely young woman off her horse.

Christophe extended his hand. "Even though your father is my enemy, you are welcome in Castle Montgomery, Lady Ariana."

"Thank you, Lord Montgomery." She curtsied, then raised her chin and looked straight into his eyes. "Do not worry about my feelings on the matter. Rhett is not my father, but my stepfather. I was just one of his prisoners until Caradoc rescued me."

Christophe nodded, then turned back to Caradoc. "Did you see Bronwyn?"

Caradoc's eyes narrowed as he took a challenging stance. "Why would I see my sister on the battlefield?"

"She left after you did, and has not returned," Christophe spat and turned away.

Caradoc grabbed Christophe's arm and spun him back. "You let her go, knowing Rhett was out there?"

Christophe removed Caradoc's hand, and leveled him with a piercing stare. "She is the traitor in our midst."

Caradoc's face paled. "Wherever she is, rest assured she is not with Rhett. She hates him."

"How can you be so sure?" Christophe thought it a bitter irony that Bronwyn had once defended her brother, and now he was forced to do the same.

"I know my sister." He took Ariana's arm. "You will rue the day you ever suspected her. Her heart is true."

Christophe watched his brother-in-law storm up the castle steps and wished he could believe him. But too much evidence weighed against her.

With a grunt Christophe hailed Nicolas and said, "Have a burial detail formed." He looked around the courtyard, and drew a ragged breath. "How many are injured? What are our losses?"

"Under the circumstances we fared well. Only fourteen men died, but many are injured," Nicolas replied. "I have asked Fiona to supervise the women in the treatment of the injured."

Christophe nodded. But what was left unsaid hung heavily in the air. Bronwyn, who was the healer of the village, and greatly needed, was missing. "Form a patrol," he barked. "I want Rhett and my wife found at once."

Nicolas moved to his horse. "See to your wound, Brother. I will handle the patrol."

"*Non,* I need you here. Send Michau. And tell him I want Rhett alive." Christophe's hand was soaked with blood as he gripped his side, but he shrugged off Hayden's hand, not allowing anyone to help him into the castle. Nesta brought a bowl of water and soap to him. "I will clean the wound, my lord."

He reached for the ale and downed a whole tankard. "Proceed."

Nesta's face paled at his gruff command, but she wrung out the linen and removed his tunic.

The moment the water hit his wound he sucked in his breath, swallowing a bellow. Pain sliced his gut like a hot poker. "Will you stitch it?" he gasped.

"Aye, my lord, the wound will not heal unless closed."

He held up his hand for her to wait and reached for another tankard of ale. Christophe downed the brew without taking a breath. Then he filled and drank two more. His mind became somewhat foggy as he motioned for Nesta to continue, and soon he saw Bronwyn's lovely eyes before him. Like a ghost, she haunted his very thoughts. She was a rebel and had used him, mocking his love. He felt a terrible pain, not from his wound, but in his chest, and his breathing became labored. "Bronwyn," he whispered as he stared at the image before him. "Bronwyn, damn you to hell for deceiving me."

Bronwyn heard her husband's curse as she entered the castle, escorted between two burly Normans. When she saw Christophe seated at the table with his side bloodied, she broke free of their hold and ran to her husband. Her heart clenched at the ugly wound in his side, and she felt dizzy. The carnage she had passed through had left her weak. But the knowledge that Christophe believed her a traitor had devastated her. She moved Nesta aside, and watched as Christophe swayed in his chair from the strong drink. Nicolas tried to intervene and she stopped him. "I am the healer. Let me treat him."

Nicolas looked at Christophe's wound, then nodded.

"I have already cleaned it, my lady," Nesta offered.

Tears blurred her vision as she reached for some wine to cleanse the wound. After pouring the harsh spirits into the wound, she swayed and had to sit down for a moment. The room spun and it took several deep breaths to steady herself.

"Are you well, my lady?" Nesta asked.

"Aye," Bronwyn said, ignoring her own weakness to stand. Her hands trembled as she reached for the needle and thread. With iron determination she concentrated on the task at hand, blotting out every other thought. Her composure returned and the tremors ceased. Carefully she stitched his side. His groans pierced her heart, but not as much as the condemnation she heard in his voice. She swallowed her pain. She couldn't explain her whereabouts, and without proof of her loyalty, Christophe would never forgive her.

She sighed as she finished the stitches. He had passed out and she swiftly bandaged his side, then stood ready for Nicolas to escort her to the tower.

"Husband," Fiona pleaded, laying her hand on his arm. "We need her."

He looked at his brother. He would be asleep for hours. Nicolas sighed and waved Bronwyn away to treat the soldiers.

She bandaged Caradoc's arm, then stitched Sumner's neck wound. Everywhere she turned someone needed medical care. But whoever she treated remained quiet and withdrawn. She read the condemnation in their eyes and couldn't blame them. Thankfully, their wounds were minor.

When she finished with her last patient, she walked slowly with Caradoc over to Nicolas. A charge of treason was a serious matter. With her husband ill, she knew Nicolas was in command. He would decide her fate. "I am ready."

Nicolas looked around the room as if counting the good she had done. His gaze settled on her. "Tell me where you were."

"She is innocent," Caradoc interjected before she could speak. "Can you not see with your own eyes her loyalty?"

She patted her brother's arm. "Nicolas is doing his duty." With a sigh she faced him. "I swear I did not aid the rebels," she said. "But I cannot tell you where I was."

He ran a hand through his hair, then glanced at his brother. "Christophe will decide your fate. In the meantime, will you give me your promise you will stay in your room?"

"Aye."

"Then I will allow you to go to your apartment rather than lock you in the tower."

Before she left the great room she turned back and glimpsed the beloved features of her husband. How she longed to explain, and clear her name. But, he needed his rest and she needed a miracle.

Hopefully, by morning both would occur. She did not ask for the men to carry Christophe to their room. He could remain in the great room where all the wounded slept. After all the ale he drank, he might not awaken till morning. And confrontation—now—was the last thing either of them needed.

She awoke when Christophe entered the room hours later. He removed his clothes and slipped into bed without a word, then lay on his back, staring up at the ceiling.

"Christophe, I swear to you, I had nothing to do with the rebels' plot. I give you my word."

Silence met her plea.

She leaned on her elbow to get his attention. "Please, Christophe, you must believe me. I am telling you the truth."

He continued to stare at the ceiling.

She touched his arm. "I love you."

He shrugged off her hand and glared at her before turning away to sleep on his uninjured side.

She closed her eyes and swallowed the pain of his rejection. Later, after he had calmed down, they would talk.

He would listen, and this misunderstanding would be behind them.

Chapter Seventeen

She awoke late in the morning, still hopeful that they could put their marriage right. While Christophe slept she dressed quickly, thinking to bring back a tray of food so they could talk when he awoke. "Come, Fang," she whispered as she held the door open for the wolf, then softly closed it behind them.

In the kitchen Nesta allowed her to prepare a light repast, but watched her closely.

"What is it?" Bronwyn asked, feeling the weight of Nesta's displeasure.

Nesta looked carefully around the kitchen, then covered Matrona's ears to confide. "My lady, do you not know how many people wonder where you were?"

Matrona's eyes grew round with avid curiosity. Bronwyn reached out and removed Nesta's hands, knowing that everyone in the demesne now condemned her. "All I can say is my errand was important." It hurt her to the bone to think Nesta doubted her. She looked at her friend and whispered, "I vow I did not betray anyone."

"My lady, I know you would not. But it is hard to have faith when you will not explain your actions."

"Thank you," Bronwyn's voice quivered. Refusing to be drawn into an explanation, she left the kitchen and ran straight into her family, who were gathered around the hearth in the great room. Her heart sank when they motioned for her to join them. She looked longingly at the staircase as she walked over to where they sat.

Caradoc rose and introduced the lady sitting beside him. "Bronwyn, this is Ariana." A grin playing upon his lips. "She is to be my wife."

"Wife?" Stunned by the unexpected announcement, Bronwyn's gaze traveled back to the beautiful young lady. Light-brown hair framed a soft, delicate face as a dimpled smile showed briefly before a demure composure returned. Though not breathtakingly beautiful, she possessed pleasing features indeed.

"Aye," he said firmly. "Ariana and I are in love. Her father, Lord Rhett, has used that love to manipulate both of us."

Bronwyn's heart skipped a beat when she heard the rebel's name. Then slowly the meaning of Caradoc's words sunk in. Bronwyn, balanced the tray on her hip, then extended her hand to Ariana. "I am pleased to welcome you to our family." Then she turned to her brother. "And I am glad you have returned to the fold."

He smiled, albeit sheepishly. "I have returned older, but I hope wiser."

There was a subtle change in his manner, one Bronwyn approved of wholeheartedly.

"Lady Bronwyn, is your husband awake?" Ariana asked, her voice as pleasing as her features.

"Not yet," she replied, almost dreading the confrontation. "I have fixed a little food for him." Her eyes strayed to the stairs as she raised the food-laden tray.

Nicolas stepped forth, clearly reading her anxiety. "All will be well when you tell him where you were."

"I cannot," she breathed, feeling that familiar tightening in her throat as she absorbed her family's censure.

Caradoc eyed her strangely, as did Ariana, while Hayden shook a finger at her. "Daughter, I forbid this secrecy."

Before she could reply, Fiona rushed over to her. "You must tell him. You love him, do you not?"

No one understood her silence. "Aye, Fiona, I do, but I fear my husband will not believe me."

"You are right, Wife," Christophe's voice lashed out from behind her. "I do not."

She whirled around. "Christophe," she gasped, shocked to find her husband standing at the top of the stairs. The harsh look on his face made her ill. *Dear God, however will I explain?*

"*Oui,* Christophe. Your husband. The man you betrayed," he growled, gingerly descending the steps, favoring his wounded side.

"Listen to me." she began. "Please, you must try and understand. I—"

"*Non.*" He brushed her aside. Standing beside his brother, he turned to look at her, his face a dark mask of vengeance. "I will not listen to any more of your pretty lies."

His words cut her as sharply as any blade.

"Hear her explanation," Caradoc snapped. He turned to his sister, his gaze pleading with her. "Tell him."

She swallowed her pain. "I cannot."

Caradoc lowered his gaze, but not before she saw his defeat. He stepped back as Christophe reeled around and grabbed her. Her tray fell to the ground, spilling the food over the rushes as his grip bit harshly into her arm. "Where are your necklace and wedding ring, Wife?"

She closed her eyes, feeling hopeless. He had noticed.

"Where are they?"

She could neither lie nor tell him the truth. She opened her eyes and stared into his, silently pleading for his understanding.

At her silence he smiled, but his expression held no warmth. "Caradoc, did you not say that Lord Rhett needed money to raise an army? That he had to sell his land and everything of value in order to purchase men and arms?" Christophe continued to stare at her, his anger a palpable thing.

"Aye," her brother responded somberly.

"Daughter, tell your husband what he wishes to know," Hayden urged, his voice exasperated.

An image of her family tied to stakes engulfed by fire rushed into her mind. Taking a deep breath, she slowly shook her head. "I am sorry, Father. I cannot."

"Are you aware of the penalty for treason?" Christophe asked.

Fiona sobbed. "Do something, Nicolas."

Bronwyn's face paled as she heard the pleas on her behalf.

"You cannot condemn your wife," Caradoc argued hotly.

Christophe's expression turned to loathing. "I can, and I will. But do not worry; she will not be my wife when I carry out the sentence. I will have the bishop annul this farce."

A tight band of pain constricted Bronwyn's chest. Her throat burned from the sorrow lodged within, and her eyes stung as his scornful words shattered her.

"My lord, spare her," Hayden implored.

Christophe's eyes narrowed as he turned to Hayden. "I am merciful," he said. "But not stupid."

Blinded by tears, Bronwyn shuddered as he pulled her up the stairs toward what she hoped would be their bedroom, and not the tower. She thought this some nightmare she would awaken from, but knew it was not. Every sense within her recoiled from his rage. "Is there nothing that would change your mind?" she asked desperately.

"Why?" He stopped so suddenly and released her that she stumbled. His gaze raked over her dispassionately as though she were merely an object. "Would you try to convince me?" he asked suggestively.

She edged farther away, until she backed against the wall. "What mean you?"

"You are a beautiful woman, Bronwyn." He advanced, placing a hand on either side of her face, then slowly traced a finger down her cheek. "Would you like to entice me again with your charms?"

She felt sick, knowing he remembered how she had kissed him at the gate when she left the castle. Shame filled her and she drew a ragged breath. "Christophe," she cried, "I love you. If you believe nothing else, believe that."

His heartless laughter filled the air as his expression turned harsher. "Your lies are good, my dear, but not that good." He leaned forward and brushed a cold kiss across her lips. "However, if you care to convince me, I am willing to listen."

"Nay, never!" Tears of humiliation stung her eyes. "I will not play the whore."

"Then, Wife, your fate is sealed."

She closed her eyes and swayed, unable to bear his hatred. "Then, Husband, so is yours."

Fang growled at him as he turned to lead her away. Christophe silenced him with a sharp rap to the nose. She cringed. Never had she seen Christophe strike an animal.

"Do not take your mean spirit out on Fang," she cried.

He said nothing as he dragged her to the tower, but once there he ordered the wolf inside her cell. "Stay with her, you ungrateful, mangy beast."

"Help me!" Fiona cried, running into the main room after eventide. Tears streamed down her cheeks as she halted before Nicolas and Christophe.

Caradoc jumped up from his chair by the fire and Ariana followed.

Nicolas grabbed his wife. "Fiona, what is it? What is wrong?"

She gripped his tunic. "My father has collapsed. Please, he will not awaken."

Christophe, Nicolas, Caradoc, and Ariana hurried after Fiona, following her up the stairs and toward the tower.

Hayden lay senseless on a landing just below the tower. His right arm was across his chest, his hand clutching at his left shoulder. A gray tinge colored his skin and his shallow breaths barely moved his chest.

"What is he doing out here?" Christophe demanded.

"What do you think he is doing here?" Caradoc snapped impatiently.

Fiona burst into tears, sobbing so hard her stuttered reply was impossible to understand.

"Christophe, help me get him to his room," Nicolas said as Caradoc knelt beside his father.

Christophe lifted the old man's shoulders and cried out. Grimacing in pain, he gripped his side. Blood stained his bandage. "Move aside," Caradoc ordered, edging in to pick up Hayden's shoulders as Nicolas picked up his legs.

"Come, we will turn back his bedcovers." Fiona grabbed Ariana's hand and pulled her down the staircase in front of the men.

Still clasping his side, Christophe followed behind the men as they carried Hayden into his bedchamber.

As soon as they had placed him in bed, Fiona covered her father with a fur robe, then turned and looked at Christophe. "We must get Bronwyn."

Christophe straightened in the doorway, his face a mask of indifference. *"Non.* Attend to your father yourself."

Fiona's hands trembled and she turned to Nicolas. "We need Bronwyn. Please, do something. Make him release her. He must see reason."

Christophe's eyes hardened. They made him seem the ogre when it was she who was the traitor. "She remains in the tower. Do not ask again."

Fiona cried out and grasped Nicolas's arm.

"Enough, Christophe, you are upsetting my wife," Nicolas said, then turned back to Fiona. "I will help you tend your father. If you feel you need to ask your sister for advice we will go to the tower." Then he looked at his brother. "Because you are angry at your wife, do not take your ire out on mine."

Christophe stared at his brother with jaw clenched, unwilling to offer an apology or admit an error that simply was not so. Bronwyn was guilty; why could no one see that?

"You are as blind as I was," Caradoc's voice cut into his thoughts as the angry young man brushed by him.

Torchlight from the hall shone through the small square window in the door, spilling across the floor and part of the far wall.

Bronwyn looked around at the rough chiseled stones. "At least I am not manacled to the wall or alone," she muttered to Fang.

He nuzzled his nose into her hand, and she looked down into the animal's big soulful eyes. "It's all right, fellow, I'm not about to break down," she said, needing to hear the reassurance in her voice. She patted Fang as all manner of thought traveled through her mind at an alarming speed. She remembered her prior life, recalling the highs and lows, then compared them to this life. She couldn't go back to her previous life, and if she didn't come up with a reasonable explanation, she wouldn't have a future. "How do I extricate myself from this mess without endangering myself or the ones I love?" She sighed. "The truth will set you free," she repeated the axiom she had once believed. The truth would indeed set her free, but at what cost? The mood her husband was in, she doubted he would believe her. In fact, it was highly likely he wanted to believe the very worst about her. There was only one course of action. She would remain silent.

Suddenly Fang's hair raised and his teeth appeared. She tensed, squinting into the dark corners of the cell, wondering what had alarmed the wolf. Standing, he padded to the door and growled. She held her breath, waiting, then heard approaching footsteps.

"Bronwyn, Father has taken ill," Fiona's anxious voice sounded from the hallway outside.

She rushed forward and gently pushed Fang aside. The window opening was just above her head, so she could not see her sister's face. "What happened?"

"He collapsed. What should I do for him?"

Bronwyn grabbed the handle and shook it. "For God's sake, open the door. Tell Christophe to let me out so I can treat him."

There was a pause. "Bronwyn," Nicolas said, his face appearing in the small opening, "he has refused to release you."

Bronwyn's heart sank. Never had her husband behaved so callously toward one of her family members. She swallowed her pain and put her problems aside. "Fiona," she called out. Nicolas moved and the light poured back inside. "Listen to me carefully. You must mix a pinch of a dark powder from the red pouch in my medicine bag with a glass of warm cider. Make him drink it. Make sure he rests and does not move around."

"How will I know the powder?" Fiona asked.

"You cannot mistake it for any other. There is only one red pouch and the odor is strong. If you smell it, it will bring tears to your eyes."

"Thank you, Bronwyn."

"Fiona, let me know how he is."

But no answer returned. Her sister and Nicolas had already left. Bronwyn sighed and moved away from the door. She rubbed Fang's fur, comforted by his undemanding company. The wolf licked her hand and snuggled into her leg.

The minutes merged as time passed, and after a short while she could barely stand the waiting. Fang became anxious, sensing her restlessness, and followed her every move. Pacing her cell, Bronwyn turned over every alternative, but the same problem existed. If she told her incredible story, who would believe her? And if they did, what harm would befall her, or them for their belief?

Nighttime fell and she consoled herself with the thought that Hayden must be better, or her sister would have returned. She sank to her knees and curled up with Fang. The cold floor sent a chill through her, and she huddled next to the wolf, trying to gain some warmth. Though the wolf's soft fur offered comfort, she felt bereft and alone. She had truly ruined her life. Christophe would never believe her, nor could she blame him. She knew her actions were suspect. But if he loves you, her mind argued, he should trust you. That was the problem. Perhaps he did not love her, perhaps he never had. Or perhaps, her conscience warned, he had fallen in love only to be devastated by her defection. "Nay," she breathed, the truth too painful to accept.

Chapter Eighteen

Bronwyn's cell door opened at dawn. A small sliver of light poured across the floor and engulfed her. She squinted against the bright light as Fang growled a low warning. "Be quiet, Fang," Nicolas ordered, entering the cell.

She heard her brother-in-law's voice, and her spirits plunged. "Is Father worse?"

Non. Hayden has recovered and Nesta is at his side."

A wave of relief washed over her, then receded. Nicolas's appearance meant one thing. The time for her punishment was at hand. That Christophe didn't even bother to fetch her himself signified there would be no reprieve.

"Bronwyn, are you coming?"

"Aye," she sighed, rising to face Nicolas.

As her eyes adjusted to the light, she noticed Nicolas's features were strained. Before she could leave the cell, he took hold of her arm. "Christophe is ill."

"Ill?" Her heart pounded as she stared into Nicolas's dark eyes and saw the shadows of concern.

Oui, he has a fever and does not know anyone."

She gasped. Dear Lord, he had developed an infection.

"Will you help him?" Nicolas asked.

Without a word she pulled free of his hold and rushed by him, Fang following in her wake. Taking the steps two at a time, she barged into her chamber to find Ariana and Fiona hovering over Christophe. Eyes closed and skin flushed, he looked so vulnerable with the white bandage covering his side and the linen strips wrapped across his massive chest.

Despite everything, his features were still so dear to her. She tore her gaze from Christophe and faced Fiona. "How does he fare?"

Before Fiona could answer, Christophe moaned and called out her name. Bronwyn turned, thinking he had awakened, but his eyes were closed. Again he called her name. He was delirious. She moved to the bed just as he started to thrash, his hands flayed the air, then swatted at the bandage, trying to rip the confining strips off his side. "Nicolas, help me," she ordered, unable to restrain her husband.

Nicolas held his brother still as Bronwyn tried to contain Christophe's hands. She softly crooned his name. As if her voice reached him, he began to relax. His skin was hot to the touch as the fever raged through him.

She turned to her sister. "I need more bowls of cool water to bathe him, and my tray of herbs."

Fiona swiftly fetched the herbs, then went to help Ariana carry the water.

Bronwyn checked Christophe's wound. The white puffy color told her that her supposition was right, an infection had set in. Dear God, she thought. Of all the herbs she possessed, only one contained an ingredient that she suspected might be a mild antibiotic. She quickly mixed the precious powder with water, and with Nicolas's help lifted her husband up into a sitting position. Because he was not conscious, she had to pour little sips into his mouth. "Drink this," she ordered, frustrated with his inability to swallow. Again, as though he heard her, he slowly swallowed three quarters of the cup, and relief rushed through her. But now she would have to open the stitches, clean out the wound, then restitch it. Her stomach lurched at the idea. She squared her shoulders. It had to be done.

"Nicolas, would you light some candles? I need as much

light as possible,'' she said as she placed a dagger into the flames to sterilize it and started some water to boil to cleanse the needle and thread.

She looked up and caught Nicolas watching her. His intense scrutiny made her uneasy. But he said nothing, and she continued with her chore.

When the women had returned with the desired bowls of water, she poured wine into one of them. With everything ready, she took a deep breath and removed the dagger from the fire. The blade glowed red-hot as she plunged it into the wine. Steam rose as the metal cooled, then she placed the blade to his injured side and reopened the wound. Once lanced, the infection poured out. Gritting her teeth, she pulled the skin back and started to wash out the infected area. Time after time she bathed the injury, repeating the slow process of flushing the area with water, then wiping it dry with a clean linen. An hour passed and her arms ached, but she ignored the pain and fatigue, knowing that this had to be done, and done right. Suddenly she saw a black thread on her linen swab. A piece of his tunic had been forced into the wound. She did several more rinsings, but she was sure she had found the foreign body responsible for the infection. Finally satisfied that nothing else remained inside the wound that might cause another infection, she poured wine into the area and quickly stitched it up again. Tears rolled freely down her face when she finished.

Nicolas covered her hand. "You do love him, don't you?"

She drew a shaky breath. "Aye, I do. But as you have seen, my love is not returned."

"He only wants the truth," Nicolas said.

She looked into his eyes and shook her head. "If I clear my name, others will be harmed."

He raised an eyebrow, but did not pursue it. "I am sorry, Bronwyn. Truly, truly sorry." He patted her hand before moving to usher his wife and Ariana out of the room.

"Nicolas, wait. You are leaving me with him?" she asked, stunned by his compassion and trust.

He nodded. "In my brother's illness I am in charge. I want you to stay with him until he is well."

She glanced at Christophe and pictured his reaction. "He will not thank you," she sighed.

"Saving his life is more important than his stubborn pride."

She nodded as he shut the door behind him. Her thoughts turned to her husband. While he slept, she feasted her eyes on his handsome features, memorizing every detail, for the time when she would need to recall his face. He would hate her abusing his privacy but she didn't care. She loved him. She covered his chest with the fur and touched her hand to his forehead. The fever was still there, but his flesh did not burn. She mixed more medicine and forced him to drink, then she rested above the covers next to him. With one arm thrown protectively over his chest, she went to sleep.

The moment her eyes opened she felt the heat of his skin. Dear God, the fever raged anew. She stripped the covers from him and began to bathe his feverish flesh. She checked his wound. Though the skin was pink, it was not an angry red. She mixed more potion and held his head up, forcing the liquid past his cracked lips and into his mouth. He spit some out, but she persisted, making sure he swallowed at least a third of the cup before letting him rest. Through it all, he remained unaware of her. He thrashed about in delirium and she bathed him again, trying to lower the fever. The process continued all day and through the night.

Nicolas offered to spell her, but she refused. She would not allow anyone else to treat him. "I cannot leave him," she said when Michau delivered her a tray of food and bid her eat.

The moon had risen when Christophe began speaking disjointed phrases. His incoherent ramblings terrified her. She felt his head, but his fever seemed the same—no better, no worse. She leaned close, thinking he was trying to tell her something.

"I won't leave you." The raspy words sounded eerily in her mind, but she could not place where she had heard them. She only knew they held some kind of significance. If only she could think through the fog of exhaustion, but her tired senses refused to work.

Once again he began to thrash about, and even in his weakened state, it took all her strength to hold him down. After he had depleted his strength and hers, she began to bathe him again. She changed the bed linen and put dry covers over him, then forced more medicine down his throat. At dawn she slipped off to an exhausted sleep, her hand on his so she would awaken if his fever increased.

The next day his fever lessened, but he remained fast asleep, too exhausted to even awaken. Around noon, sweat formed on his brow and drenched his entire body, and she prayed he would not worsen as the fever broke. She continually wiped his skin dry and kept his covers fresh. She groaned when she stretched. Her arms ached from carrying clean linens and changing the damp sheets.

"My lady, you must rest," Nesta begged, when she brought up fresh water.

"I will, after his fever has broken," she assured the well-meaning woman, then bid her to leave them alone.

"Easy, my love," she soothed as she laid a cool compress on his forehead. But he slept through her efforts, too fatigued by the infection and fever to rouse.

When Nicolas again tried to relieve her, she ordered him out. "Please, Nicolas, I will call you when I am in need of rest, and not a moment before."

Though surprised at her outburst, he retreated without a word.

All evening she continued to bathe his fevered flesh. When Cordelia carried her food tray up, her interruption was the last straw.

"Be gone!" Bronwyn snapped.

"But, my lady, you must eat," Cordelia insisted.

"Take it away, and bring some more broth," she said, turning back to the bed.

Suddenly the fever broke. As his temperature dropped, she hurried to pile on the furs to keep him from developing a chill. She had just sunk into a chair when the door burst open. It was Nicolas, and his expression was darker than she had ever seen before.

"Bronwyn, enough! You will at least let Fiona stay with him while you get cleaned up and eat a meal."

"Thank you, Nicolas," she said demurely, ashamed of her earlier outburst. "I am sorry I have been so curt . . ."

His gaze slanted to Christophe and his features relaxed. "You do not have to apologize for being concerned about my brother."

Tears formed in her eyes. "His fever has broken, but he is so weak," she choked out.

Nicolas smiled, then pulled her into his arms for a hug. "Do not worry, he will be fine. Now, I will have the servants bring a tub up so you can see to your needs."

He released Bronwyn and motioned Fiona in before he left to have her bath delivered.

"Christophe looks better, but you do not," Fiona said, her tone blunt as she entered the room.

Bronwyn's gaze traveled to her husband. He did look a little better. She leaned close and kissed his forehead, relieved that his skin was cooler to the touch. "Nicolas is right. He will recover."

Fiona put her hands on her hips. "And then what, Sister?"

Bronwyn shrugged. "I don't know. Once he is well I will worry about my fate."

Fiona's features showed her displeasure, but thankfully, she did not pursue the argument and remained silent. When Bronwyn sat down to the first substantial meal in days, she found her appetite lacking and could barely finish the broth. While Fiona watched Christophe, Bronwyn discreetly covered her tray and handed it to a servant.

After a long soak in the tub, Bronwyn let Fiona wash her hair. The luxury was pure heaven, and Bronwyn enjoyed every minute of the small pampering. After she dried her hair and changed into fresh clothes, Fiona bid her good night.

The warm water had made her exceedingly sleepy, and she crawled into bed beside her husband. When her hand slipped over his chest, she closed her eyes and fell into a deep sleep.

Dreams haunted her rest. The plane crashed and then strong arms surrounded her as the fire engulfed them. She heard a promise and it echoed through her unconscious mind: "I won't leave you.'' The fire burned their flesh and she relived the horrible pain of the flames.

When she awoke, all she remembered was the horror of the fire. She could not let anyone suffer that death. She glanced over at her beloved. No matter how angry he was, or what punishment he imposed, she could not expose him to such danger.

Unaware of her thoughts, Christophe slept. She reached up and felt his head. His skin was still cool to the touch and she closed her eyes. ''Thank you,'' she silently whispered.

Not until late afternoon, when she was checking his bandage, did Christophe awake.

His eyes blinked as he tried to focus on her. The instant that recognition lit his eyes, they narrowed into tiny slits. ''Get away from me,'' he rasped. He tried to rise, but fell back on the bed, glaring at her. After taking several deep breaths he pointed to the door. ''Get my brother.''

If he hadn't been so weak she would have argued with him, but instead she whirled around and left.

Several minutes later Nicolas accompanied her back to the bedchamber. ''Christophe! Thank God you are awake.''

Christophe stabbed his finger in Bronwyn's direction, his distaste obvious. ''What is she doing here?''

The question stopped Nicolas in his tracks. His gaze slanted to Bronwyn, and his relief faded into a serious mien.

''I sent her to the tower.'' Christophe went on. Though softly uttered, his words held the tone of a battle charge.

Nicolas ignored his brother's rage and calmly put his hand on her shoulder. ''If not for your wife, you would have died.''

At the announcement that he owed her anything, Christophe went into a rage as thunderous as any she had ever seen. ''Get the bitch out of here,'' he yelled hoarsely. ''Now!''

She winced at her husband's open hatred, but feeling Nicolas's hand squeezing her shoulder in support, she tried to be strong.

''Christophe, until you are recovered you will have to abide by my judgement. Which means, she stays until you are well enough to enforce your rule.''

Christophe threw his arm over his eyes as though he could not bear the sight of her. His loathing ate at her, but he said nothing as she returned to his bedside with Nicolas. Unnerved by Christophe's animosity, her hands trembled when she removed his dressing. She dropped several bandages, prompting Nicolas to hand her the clean linen strips, and she managed to rewrap the injury. At least his wound was free of infection, she thought as she rinsed her hands and discarded the soiled linen.

After Nicolas took the refuse from her and left, she gazed at her husband lying so still and silent on the bed. Though he looked relaxed, she had felt his tightly contracted muscles beneath her fingertips. Hostility radiated from his body. Weak and helpless now, he needed her. But once his strength returned that would no longer be the case.

Nesta knocked on the door, then entered with a tray. She pointed to the plate of food beside Christophe's bowl of soup. Her meaning clear, she left.

Bronwyn looked at the food Nesta had meant for her and bit her lip. Just the sight of the hearty meal made her stomach lurch and knot. Though she should be hungry, lately she could barely keep anything down. She would try it later, she thought. Right now, she had a patient to care for, and a very cranky one at that. She held the broth before him. "You need to eat this."

Christophe lowered his arm, and his gaze sliced into her, then traveled to the bowl and spoon. "You're enjoying this," he rasped.

Bitterness rang in his every word. He despised being at her mercy. "Nay, I do not. But you are sick, and until you are well I am the healer." She helped him sit up, the effort sapping her strength. Once he was settled and comfortable, with pillows propped behind him, she began spooning the broth into his mouth. Every mouthful he swallowed he clearly resented. When he balked at the last spoonful, she held it in front of him and raised an eyebrow. "The sooner you recover, the quicker you will be free of me."

Immediately he gulped down the last drop. His eagerness to

be rid of her hurt, but she buried the pain. When he was through eating, she brought a bowl of water, a bar of soap, and two towels over to the bed.

"What exactly do you think you are going to do?" he asked, eyeing her suspiciously.

"I do not think, my lord, I know," she replied. "I am going to wash you."

A muscle jumped in his jaw as he glared at her, but he made no response.

"Christophe, I will need to wash you all over." She held up the washcloth for his attention. The sweat had poured off him when his fever broke. She also intended to change the bed linen.

He stared at her, his gaze flat and unresponsive. *It's to be the hard way, is it?* she thought, then pulled down the covers. He hissed as the warm wet cloth glided over his lower abdomen, and turned his eyes determinedly to the ceiling.

The reason was clear. Though he professed she meant nothing to him, his body reacted to her in an entirely different way. His manhood was strong and firm, and damn his stubbornness, he could not deny she affected him.

But it was a punishment in reverse, for touching him without being able to love him was an agony she had never anticipated. How she longed to run her hands over his muscles and receive the response she hungered for. But Christophe literally cringed from her touch, and she bathed and dried him as quickly as she could.

Under his silent treatment the day passed agonizingly slowly, but she managed to find little projects to do as she sat by his bedside. When she mended his tunic he turned and glared at her as though she had defiled the garment with her touch. With a cheeriness she did not feel, she smiled at his every frown, reminding herself that even the best patient became irritable. Not until she left the room to fetch his meal did she realize the toll his hostility had taken on her.

She brought up the tray with his dinner and noticed his scowl. "Christophe, could we at least call a truce until after you are well?" She placed his meal beside the bed.

"Non."

"Very well, I can stand it if you can." She fed him his meal and ignored his ire. Once his meal was finished, she changed his dressing and measured out his medicine.

He sniffed it carefully.

"It is not poisoned," she said, thoroughly exasperated.

"It would not be the first time you tried to rid yourself of an unwanted husband."

"Oh," she snapped, then swallowed half his medicine before offering him the rest.

"As I recall, you also took the poison."

She closed her eyes. "Very well, if you do not want the medicine, then you can go without." She started to pull the spoon away, but he surprised her by staying her hand and swallowing the liquid.

She dearly wanted to comment on his childish behavior, but refrained. After placing the spoon down, she blew out the candles and again crawled up onto the bed, lying down upon the top of the covers.

"What do you think you are doing?" he asked, peering through the shadows at her as though she had committed a crime.

She covered herself with a shawl. "In case your fever returns, I need to be near."

"That is the only way you will ever get into my bed," he sneered.

Mentally counting to ten, she reminded herself that he was ill and cross. She closed her eyes, blocking out his glare. While praying for his recovery, she could not help but think that the moment his health was restored, hers would be in jeopardy.

The next day Christophe's foul mood worsened. Bronwyn had to clench her teeth under his pointed barbs. Though it was a small consolation, she took comfort in the fact that if he felt strong enough to be miserable, then it was a good sign his wound was healing and his infection gone.

A knock on the door heralded his breakfast. "Enter," she called out, hoping food would improve his sour disposition.

Nesta brought the morning tray, but he insisted on solid

food. When Nesta made the mistake of looking at Bronwyn for approval, he took the poor cook to task and soon had her in tears.

"Christophe!" Bronwyn chastised as she put her hand on Nesta's shoulder and walked her to the door. "Bring him hale and hearty food," she said for Christophe's benefit, then leaned forward and whispered: "And if he retches, he deserves it."

Nesta's sniffles subsided and she offered Bronwyn a wan smile before leaving. The moment the door closed, Bronwyn rounded on Christophe. "That was uncalled for."

"Never reprimand me in front of a servant again," he shouted.

Nicolas chose that moment to enter. "Christophe, the whole castle can hear you. Apparently, you are better." Nicolas ignored his brother's frown and turned to Bronwyn. "You have done an exceptional job, and from the braying I hear, it could not have been easy. Rest assured, everyone in the castle knows that he owes you his very life."

"That will not save her," Christophe snapped, struggling to sit up.

Nicolas helped him. "Brother, even I know it is not wise to tell the healer who treats you that when you get well you will have her punished." Nicolas straightened and winked at Bronwyn. "There is simply no incentive to see you on your feet."

Bronwyn couldn't smother her chuckle and she knew her amusement irked Christophe, but it was too bad. She saw the humor in the situation, even if he could not.

Nesta returned and Nicolas eyed the tray warily, looking at the half-cooked meat and scorched vegetables. "Brother, do you think that is a good idea?"

"Get out," Christophe growled.

Nicolas chuckled and held the door for Nesta, then followed her out.

Bronwyn watched her husband struggle with his knife and fork. She walked over and took the utensils from him, cutting his food into bite-size pieces, then handing the utensils back.

"Do you not want me to choke on the delicious food?" he muttered.

The idea suddenly had merit and she smiled as she considered it.

His ire only increased, and though he tried, he could hardly finish two bites. "Take this slop away."

She carried the food back to the kitchen and returned with a bowl of soup.

He looked at it with distaste but drank the thick broth.

She managed to keep her spirits up, but as the day wore on, it became harder to pretend his glares or barbs did not hurt. It was worse when he had visitors.

"Do you see how she flaunts her power over me, Michau?"

Before Michau lowered his eyes, he shot her a commiserating look. "My lord, you will be on your feet soon enough. Why not enjoy the rest."

"How are the men?"

"Everything is well. The defenses are well manned. Lucien is in the dungeon, and the patrols search the land, but still they fail to turn up any clue as to Rhett's hiding place."

Christophe held up his hand to silence Michau, then shot her a glare. "If you would be so kind as to leave us."

Of course. She was a traitor.

"Very well, my lord. But if you decide to die, please have someone send for me."

He scowled at her but she couldn't help the barb. Putting up with his nastiness had worn her thin. He was well out of danger now and she did not want to return.

She slammed the door, then ran blindly down the hall. Unable to stem her riotous emotions, she turned a corner and collided with Nicolas.

He grabbed her shoulders and held her steady. "Here, now. What is all this?"

She pulled free of his hold. "Christophe will live, Nicolas. Believe me, he is in no danger of dying, except if I kill him." She turned away, unable to bear his censure. "I suppose you must now decide what to do with me until he carries out his threat."

Nicolas cleared his throat, then took her chin in his grasp and turned her face toward him. His eyes held the light of compassion, not condemnation. ''Are you sure he will not have a setback?'' he asked, a hopeful note in his voice.

She almost laughed at his attempt at humor. ''Nay, he is too ornery to have a relapse.''

Nicolas ran his hand over his beard. Clearly, he did not want to be involved in what he saw as their quarrel. ''Why not return to his room, give him a sleeping potion, and get a good night's sleep,'' he said, patting her on the shoulder.

''Please, I cannot.'' She looked away.

''Try, Bronwyn. If all is not right by the morrow, I will see you have other quarters, I promise.''

She nodded, but did not return to Christophe. Instead she walked down the hall, intending to check on her father. She needed time to compose herself, and Hayden was easy company. He had a way of softening her woes.

Lightly she knocked on his bedchamber before entering. Her father rested in his bed with a collection of writings on his lap. ''I am sorry, Father. Should I come back?''

''Never fear, Daughter,'' he said. Setting his writing aside, he patted the bed. ''I cherish your visits.''

She sat on the bed next to him and he grasped her hand. ''How are you?''

''I am well.'' He peered at her with a parent's scrutiny and she looked away. ''He is still furious, is he?''

''Aye,'' she said, knowing that there were no secrets in a small community.

''Then I urge you, Bronwyn, disarm his anger. You have saved his life. It is time to make peace. You cannot allow this rift to continue.''

''Father, I cannot tell him where I was. If he truly loved me, he would have faith in me.''

''Faith, child, has many faces. He has given much trust to you. Trust that other men would never have given. Perhaps he is somewhat justified in demanding to know where you were.'' When she tried to object, he held up his hand. ''If he cannot make the first move, then you must.''

"I will try," she said.

Before her father could respond, Caradoc entered with Ariana. "Bronwyn," he said, smiling with surprise and pleasure. "I am glad to see you." He escorted Ariana over to the bed, where she took a seat.

"I only have a few moments," Bronwyn lied. She could not explain it but being around her brother and his betrothed made her melancholy. She was truly happy for them, but their joy seemed to magnify her sorrow, and she did not want to diminish their happiness. She leaned over and kissed her father on the cheek. "I will visit later."

"Bronwyn, is there anything I can do?"

Caradoc's offer surprised her. Apparently, she had not hidden her unease as well as she thought. "Nay, all will be right soon."

She kissed her brother and hugged Ariana, then left. It was time to face her husband. She entered the room without knocking; after all, it was her bedroom also, or at least it was until he said otherwise. She marched in and stood before the warlord. His harsh regard nearly crippled her resolve.

Immediately he turned to Michau, coldly dismissing her. "Michau, would you fetch my tunic?"

While Michau rose to retrieve the lord's clothes, she went to the hearth.

"Good day, my lady." Michau bowed as he passed her.

She smiled, for he had shown her far more respect than she had believed possible after her questionable actions and Christophe's attitude. "Good day," she responded as he tried to help the lord up.

She glanced back and found Christophe's gaze boring through her as he struggled into his tunic. Taking a deep breath, she said, "What price would you ask of me for forgiveness, my lord?"

" 'Tis a weighty question," Christophe replied. Michau tried to help him with his tunic but he pushed the man's hands away and stared at her, his insolent regard stripping her of any dignity. "Would you agree to whatever I asked?"

"Aye, as long as you do not ask where I was."

He signaled Michau to leave. The moment the door closed, he placed his hands on his hips. "Come here."

Fear streaked through her for the first time. He was too controlled, too calm. "What is your pleasure?"

"I said come here." His voice was quiet and his expression didn't change. "It is either fulfill my will, or you will return to the tower to await your fate."

She stepped closer. He would not, could not, hurt her. Trusting in him completely, she stood toe-to-toe with him as she lifted her chin and held his regard. A shiver climbed up her spine at the intensity of his gaze. Danger and desire flashed in his eyes, and excitement and alarm raced through her.

He brushed her hair away from her cheek and cradled her face in his hands. "Convince me you did not betray me," he whispered as his lips descended on hers.

His mouth moved over hers, the passionate kiss creating havoc with her senses. Slowly, softly, his tongue stroked her lips as though tasting them for the first time.

She tried to move her lips from his, needing to know if he had forgiven her, if he believed in her, but his fingers held her chin, refusing to let her end his kiss. His warm mouth worked magic on her. Was this his first step, his reconciliation? It must be. Distantly, she remembered there was something to ask him, something to get straight. But all thought disappeared beneath the seductive mastery of his touch. She wanted, needed to melt into his embrace, to believe in him as deeply as she wanted him to believe in her.

She moaned and leaned into him. Her hands slipped over his shoulders, her nails grazing his muscles ever so lightly. "Christophe, you must be careful," she whispered against his lips .

"Thanks to you, I am well." He pulled her back toward the bed.

When he stumbled she wrapped her arm around his waist. "You are too weak for this."

He drew a ragged breath. "The day I am too weak for this, is the day they plant me in yon field."

"Really, Christophe," she pleaded.

He placed a finger to her lips. "I like you much better when you do not argue with me."

She sighed. She wanted to put the past behind them. "Then let me," she said, pushing him down onto the bed.

He smiled, but she thought she caught something dark in his expression, then it disappeared as his arms pulled her close and she dismissed the impression as her active imagination.

She slipped her hands beneath his tunic and slid the clothes up and over his head. Since she could never explain why she had left the castle, she resolved to love him as she had never done before. Fully, without any reservation, or hesitation. Her hands swept his massive chest, being careful of his stitches. Though he had been ill, his body reacted to hers with a vibrancy that belied his recent injury. She rained tiny kisses on his chest. Boldly her lips traced a trail to his navel, and his muscles flexed and contracted. When she moved lower, he sucked in, his muscles taut. She grew bolder, taking little nips of the tender skin of his lower abdomen, then blowing to ease the pain of her soft bites. The groan she elicited from him thrilled her. She needed to drive him over the edge, and her hands caressed his body with a soft reverence, while her kisses both teased and tantalized. When his body was tense with desire, her teeth grazed the side of his shaft, and he moaned. His breathing became labored as her mouth moved over the tip, and his hands slipped through her hair, urging her on. Her tongue flicked across the warm peak as her lips closed firmly on the head, exerting a drawing pressure. Her fingers traced up and down the firm rod, moving forcefully as her mouth worked a rhythm over his throbbing member. His body trembled, then grew rigid as he cried out. A salty essence lined her mouth as his body relaxed and his moan of pleasure filled the air. She reveled that she had brought him to fulfillment. Suddenly his hands fastened on her shoulders, pulling her up. His breathing was ragged, his eyes bright.

He held her away for a moment and just looked at her. "Remove your kirtle," he whispered.

She smiled as she slowly pulled the tunic up over her head and watched his nostrils flare and his eyes glow with desire.

For just an instant another wave of apprehension washed over her, but again she put the uneasy feeling aside. This was Christophe; she gave him her entire heart, trust, and hope. There could be no room for fear if they were to make this union work. He had already put aside his apprehension, and mistrust.

Still, a niggling of doubt wormed its way into her thoughts. Revenge, retribution, retaliation, a voice whispered in her mind . . . until his lips covered hers and his passionate kiss drove every thought from her head. His arms held her against him in an embrace that melded their bodies into one.

Liquid fire coursed through her as his lips, mouth, and tongue loved her. Flames of passion engulfed her as his teeth grazed her breast. She gasped when his mouth covered the tip. Shivers of desire coursed through her when his tongue stroked across her nipple. Her nails raked his back when his lips closed over her nub and gently tugged. She could scarcely breathe as his mouth tenderly, titillatingly, kissed her other breast. She moaned, lost in the heat of his seduction. "Christophe," she whispered, trying to gather her thoughts. Although she had decided to seduce him, he was taking the lead. His hands roamed her body like a collector caressing his prize, then his lips followed. He didn't give her time to think. His hands teased and his lips tantalized her flesh. Streaks of excitement traveled to her very core as his mouth moved slowly down her chest. His tongue circled her belly button as his fingers slipped between her legs. Lights streaked in her mind as he teased and tantalized her womanhood, rubbing the tender nub until she thought she would fly off the bed. Then his fingers dipped inside of her, and a roar of excitement washed over her. "Christophe," she gasped, her hands greedily kneading his shoulders and arms.

"Shhh," he whispered, then his mouth followed his hands and she lost every thought. When he touched her, a million sizzling currents flashed through her. Fire burst in her soul as passion burned out of control.

Oh, God! She was coming. His tongue flicked in and out, pushing her over the edge, and a million stars burst as she called out his name.

She was still in her climax when his hands slid over her,

increasing her ecstasy. His body beckoned. He wanted her. He lifted her up and onto his shaft. His manhood slipped into her. The heat poured through her, again, but in a tidal wave of desire. Liquid music flowed, ebbing over her as she rode the wave to its end. Nothing equaled this as she floated higher, reaching the stars and touching the sun. Her second climax shattered her. One moment she soared through the air, then the next she crashed, diving deep through the water, only to rise and break the surface. She gasped, trying desperately to breathe. ''Christophe.''

His body, so in tune to hers, wrapped around her, holding her, answering her need of security. Together they held each other and slowly floated down from the reaches of paradise. Joy filled her, he was heaven-sent, and oh, so perfect for her. With a sigh she caressed the springy hairs of his chest, wanting, needing to touch him as she envisioned their future. Laying her cheek to his chest, she heard his heartbeat, the sound a soothing balm that drummed through her. Suddenly she sensed his withdrawal. Frightened, she reached out for him, but the warmth of his embrace had vanished. Trying to deny what he was doing, she lifted her head to kiss his lips, but the look of loathing on his face caused her to gasp.

''Christophe?'' she breathed, her heart confused and frightened.

''You certainly have a body a man would lose his mind for,'' he rasped. ''I have never known anyone who could best you in bed. My dear, you are the perfect whore.''

It took a moment for his cold, cruel words to register. She shook her head, pushing away the reality, but his dark expression could not be ignored. Tears formed in her eyes as she watched the satisfaction steal into his gaze. ''You will have our marriage annulled,'' she choked out, suddenly knowing his intent.

''Oui.''

She could not face him. She tried to move away, but he held her still, forcing her to meet the rage in his eyes.

Bronwyn swallowed her pain. ''So this is your revenge. You

want to humble me because you feel betrayed. You are the one without honor.''

His face turned red and he made no effort to hide his anger. "You are right, *mademoiselle*. Tonight I paid you in full for your deceit.''

"Someday, you will learn that I am innocent. Then it will be too late. You have killed our love.''

"Love! For love I was a fool, but no more," he said, thrusting her away.

Her spirit wounded beyond words, she rose from the bed and wrapped a pelt around her as she went to the window. Tears, fresh and hot, fell onto her cheeks as she watched without emotion the day's death.

She heard Christophe rise, but did not turn around.

He called to the guard.

When Michau entered, he pointed to her. "Take her from my sight, and do with her as you will. She is no longer my wife or Lady Bronwyn. I cast her out.''

Stunned, she spun around. The pain in her chest felt unbearable, but she forced the words out. "You are putting me from you?''

"Oui.''

She closed her eyes as a wave of pain washed over her, but as soon as she could, she opened them again and lifted her chin. She would not give him the satisfaction of breaking her.

Michau handed her her tunic and turned as she dressed. Fang instantly came to her side. "Stay," she ordered, softening her command with a gentle pat. The wolf did not belong to her, nothing did.

Still clutching the pelt, she silently followed the guard. Her heart had broken and she was without hope. Her sacrifice to save her loved ones had been for naught.

Tears fell unbidden and she could not stem the tide. She hated the man, she hated him so, and what hurt so much is that he felt exactly the same about her.

Chapter Nineteen

Numb to winter's cold bite, Bronwyn crossed the courtyard and left the castle behind as Michau held a small torch to light their way.

"My lady, this way." He pointed to the village, where warm light shone from the windows, and smoke curled from the chimneys.

But she shook her head and continued walking away from both the castle and the new village. Her tunic whipped in the wind as she stumbled along the rough track leading to the abandoned old village. Bronwyn entered the only hut left standing. The walls leaned from the quake, but thankfully, the roof still covered the structure. Fang stubbornly trailed behind, his head low and his ears back as the structure groaned with every breeze.

"Please, my lady, I wish you would reconsider." Holding the torch aloft, Michau looked around at the surroundings. "'Tis not safe here."

"Neither is the castle. If I remain, I will be without the lord's protection and prey for any soldier who wishes my company." Tears stung her eyes and she quickly lowered her gaze. The truth was, she could not stand to see if Christophe would take another woman to their bed.

Michau solemnly shook his head, his silver and black hair shining in the torchlight. "I have not seen the warlord behave this callously since before your wedding, my lady."

She touched his arm. "Do not worry about me. I am thankful for your escort, but I will be fine. You may return to your duties."

"*Non,* I will remain."

Her heart lurched and it occurred to her that despite his offer to see her safely from the castle she might be in danger from Michau, too. "Michau, please." She held up her hand and backed away. "Do not dishonor our friendship."

"My lady, I would never do anything to harm you. I will stay and make some repairs on the hut while you rest."

Relief surged through her. "I am sorry I misjudged you, Michau. It is just the . . ."

"*Non,* my lady. You are right to be leery. Most of the men could be trusted to respect you, but there are some, like Lucien, who could not."

Hugging herself for warmth, she nodded and watched him light the fire in the hearth from his torch. "I am fortunate that you were on duty."

"I believe in you, my lady, and I hope the warlord will see his folly soon. Until then, if you will accept my protection, I would be honored to give it."

"You do not doubt me, then?"

"I know you must have a good reason to remain silent. The truth will be out soon enough. For now, I only wish to repay your kindness."

Tears welled in her eyes. "It is I who should repay your kindness. You are a true friend. I shall never forget this boon."

When he left her to look for tools, she let the tears fall. Though in her own time she had been crippled, at least her heart had been left whole.

* * *

Christophe sat wearily at the trestle table in the great room. He had paced half the night and this morning he still felt uneasy. In his past life he had made hard business decisions every day, and his childhood had been a horror of poverty. But never in all that time had he ever lost sleep over anything. Now, however, he could not close his eyes, for every time he did, he saw her image. He could not forget the look on Bronwyn's face, but by God he could not absolve her, either.

The room slowly filled up as the castle occupants drifted in to break the fast. As the servants carried out the morning fare, the aroma of baked bread, hot porridge, and cider hung in the air. Chairs scraped across the floor and soldiers took their places, but Christophe sat unmoving.

"Brother, a moment of your time." Nicolas's voice intruded on his thoughts. Glancing up, Christophe saw his brother in the doorway with an old crone at his side. If memory served him right, the woman was the wicca who had visited the castle on Samhain.

Christophe waved them in. "Come forward."

Nicolas pushed the wicca into the room, his actions uncommonly harsh. "Tell him," he ordered the moment they stopped before Christophe's table.

Eyes downcast, the wicca's fingers twisted the ties of her waist-girdle. "My lord, your wife is a heretic who practices the black arts. You must punish her."

Silence fell as every occupant stopped eating to listen.

Preening at the attention paid her, the old woman's voice grew louder. " 'Tis the truth. She paid me to keep silent. See these." She thrust out her hand, showing him the amber necklace and ring as proof.

Bronwyn's jewels hung before him, and a sudden dread took hold. He had thought her gems had bought Rhett's army.

Christophe leaned forward and grabbed them from her. He crushed the jewelry in his hand as he remembered his accusations. He had to know the truth. "Why would she pay you?"

The old wicca cackled. "Because I threatened to expose her. She is in league with the Devil. A demon she is, and must be purified."

A collective gasp filled the silence as the villagers, soldiers, and servants leaned forward, their eyes wide with curiosity.

A knot formed in the pit of his stomach, making him sick with regret, but he had no time for that now. He had to gain the wicca's confidence.

The wicca's eyes glowed as she looked around the room, her greed evident.

"When did Lady Bronwyn see you?"

The wicca scratched her head. "Several times, my lord. The last time was the night of the attack. I made her stay with me. I did not want to be alone."

He raised an eyebrow, all the while damning himself for accusing Bronwyn of being the informer. "You knew of the attack?"

She raised her chin. "I sensed it," she said belligerently.

"What evidence do you have against the lady?" he suddenly asked, his tone deceptively mild.

The old crone pointed a finger at him. "If you do not purify her, then you are as guilty as she." She straightened and looked at Nicolas. "I warned the lady, as I now warn you." She turned full circle, looking at each member of the castle. "I could have everyone in this town put to death."

The villagers paled as fear descended on the room from the cloud of their ignorance, and Christophe suddenly understood Bronwyn's silence.

Caradoc rose from his chair. "The ancient ways are no longer our ways."

A low murmur filled the air as villagers whispered among themselves.

Christophe motioned for silence. "If she paid you what you asked, why have you come?"

The wicca shrugged. "She had the croft built and supplied some of my needs. But she has reneged on our bargain. She has not been to see me for over a week. Because I can no longer trust her, I have come to deal with you."

"Have you?" Christophe murmured, realizing with a pang that his wife had acted to save them all.

"I trust you will uphold the faith and have her burned."

Christophe rose and walked around the old crone. "What makes you think I will not have you burned for false witness?"

She blanched. "My lord," she pleaded, her voice turning reedy, "I am but the messenger."

"You are a fool to come here and accuse the mistress! My wife gave you a home and food. And in return you slander her name."

"I am telling the truth. I will seek out the king and have every one of you burned!"

Rumbles of misgiving and anger met her declaration.

But Christophe calmly crossed his arms. "With my blessings. William is a staunch supporter of the church—the true church. Your religion is superstitious nonsense. William will have you hanged, then burned as a witch for practicing the Devil's work."

His eyes narrowed as he leaned close to the wicca. "Do you think there is one person here who would defend you?"

She quickly glanced around the room, only to see condemnation directed her way. She took a step backward. "My lord, I can see I was mistaken. I will leave."

"*Non.* You will make a public apology to the lady. I will have no intrigue surrounding my wife. Is that clear?"

Though the wicca curtsied, her eyes flashed with anger. "Aye, my lord. Perfectly clear."

Christophe caught the light of rebellion in the old woman's eyes. Although he had no proof, he was sure she was the informer. "In the meantime, you will remain in the dungeon."

Nicolas grabbed hold of the woman, and handed her over to a guard. After the wicca was dragged away kicking and screaming, Nicolas turned to his wife. "Fetch Lady Bronwyn from her room."

Christophe shook his head and motioned for Fiona to sit. "She is not in our room."

"You sent her back to the tower?" Nicolas asked, confused. "*Non.*"

"What did you do, Brother?"

Though his insides twisted, Christophe faced his brother,

bracing himself as he admitted his folly. "Last night I passed judgement on my wife."

"Nay," Fiona cried.

"Pardon her," Nicolas said without hesitation. "She is not guilty of treason. Her only crime is foolhardiness."

Other voices echoed the sentiment as heads bobbed in united agreement.

Christophe ran his hand through his hair and looked at his brother. "It is too late for a pardon."

At his brother's frown Christophe poured a large chalice of ale. " 'Tis too late, I tell you. Last night I set the Lady Bronwyn from me and sent her away."

"Oh, no," Fiona moaned and turned into Nicolas's arms.

"God's teeth, Brother! I thought you had changed."

With a roar of frustration, Christophe ordered the guards to search the castle, but two hours later Bronwyn was still missing. Even worse, was the discovery that his captain of the guards had taken a furlough. "Do with her what you will," he had said to Michau. How the words tormented him now. His gut twisted as he imagined Bronwyn in another man's arms— Michau's arms.

"Find Michau and bring him to me," Christophe snapped, and paced the room, unable to find peace.

At daybreak Bronwyn fixed a light breakfast for herself and Michau. She had cried all night and felt weak this morning, but she had to see the wicca. It had been a week since her last visit; by now the woman would have grown impatient. "Michau, I must see the old woman for whom you built the croft."

A frown settled on his brow, though thankfully, he did not argue. "I will accompany you, my lady. The weather looks as though a storm is brewing."

"Do you not have duties at the castle?"

"While you slept this morning, I returned to the castle for our supplies and made sure I would have a fortnight's leave." He took a big bite of his meal and chewed thoughtfully. "As

I gathered my belongings, and slipped out of my room, the castle was in an uproar over your disappearance.''

She shook her head. ''I do not want to talk about the castle, or anything to do with Christophe.'' She felt more tears well up into her eyes. ''I am sorry, Michau, but I cannot think of it. The pain is too fresh.''

''Very well, my lady.'' He sipped his hot cider. ''Why must you see the old crone?''

''She is alone and afraid. I promised to take her some supplies.''

Michau looked around at the meager things he had brought back from the castle last night. ''You have precious little to share.''

''Aye, but she has even less.''

He shook his head, mumbling his misgivings. Clearly, he didn't share her ideas of charity, but to her relief, he did not challenge them.

When she opened the rickety door, the wind bit through her clothes and she shivered. Michau wrapped his mantle around her and pulled another from his belongings. ''My lady, we must seek your things from Lord Christophe.''

''Nay, I want nothing from him. I will ask my sister for some clothing.''

Michau merely nodded. But a slight smile appeared as he helped her along the trek. Snow began to fall, coating the ground with a brilliant white cover. Her arms laden with food, Bronwyn slipped on the slick ground several times, and would have fallen if not for Michau's strong arm.

The storm steadily increased, and by the time they reached the old woman's croft, it was difficult to see. She glanced through the white flurries and noticed there was no smoke coming from the chimney. A niggling of fear curled in her stomach. ''Michau, something is amiss.''

When they entered the croft, they found it empty, but the coals in the fireplace were warm. ''Where could she be?'' Bronwyn asked as she dropped her supplies on the table.

''My lady, do not upset yourself. Perhaps she is visiting one of the villagers.''

"Nay, she has no friends save me." Though she saw the curiosity in his eyes, her thoughts strayed to the old woman's whereabouts. She prayed the wicca had not gone to Christophe and spread her foul accusations. "I must find her."

She ran toward the door, but Michau stopped her by taking hold of her shoulders. "My lady, you cannot leave now. Look outside." He pointed to the window. The snowfall had turned into an icy blanket of blinding white. "Nay," she cried, dispirited beyond reason. All their lives depended on keeping the wicca satisfied. She closed her eyes and groaned. "I have to search for her."

"We will stay here," Michau said gruffly. "No doubt, the old woman has taken shelter elsewhere. If not, she is bound to return. Where else would she go?"

Feeling a sense of doom, Bronwyn sank to a chair. "Where else indeed?"

The storm continued all day and well into the night. Each hour the wicca did not return increased her fear. Images of flames and the memory of searing pain traveled through her mind. A sense of helpless frustration shadowed her every thought. Repeatedly she walked to the window and stared out at the blinding storm. In between her silent vigils she kept busy by preparing the evening meal and straightening the cottage.

As they sat down for their dinner, Michau lit the candle on the table. Bronwyn only stared at her plate. "Michau, we must find her," she blurted out.

With the food halfway to his mouth he paused. "What frightens you so?"

Michau's accurate assessment disconcerted her. She moved the food around on her plate and then met his piercing scrutiny. "I wish I could tell you."

He laid his fork down and stared at her for several more moments as he considered her admission.

Her heart raced as she silently pleaded with him to understand.

His calloused palm covered her hand. "In the morning I will search for her."

Relief filled her and she beamed.

"But," he cautioned, "only if I have your word of honor that you will remain here."

She nodded, knowing he was right. Although she also wished to search, the old wicca might return home. She reached down to pat Fang's head, thankful that they had allowed him to accompany them. Her thoughts turned to Christophe. Though she was loath to admit it, she missed him terribly. Even as much as he had hurt her, she could never wish him harm: *Please let the old crone be with some villager, or better yet, on her way back to wherever she came from.* Her husband and family did not deserve to suffer because of her. She fed her bread to Fang, and sat quietly until Michau had finished eating, then rose to clean up the table. He touched her wrist. "My lady, you must eat something."

Surprised he had noticed her lack of appetite, she tried to move her plate out of sight. "Tomorrow I will do more justice to the meal."

He looked directly at her dish and shook his head. "I am sorry, my lady. I must insist you sit down and eat."

She sighed. "Michau, truly I cannot. My stomach has been easily upset as of late."

He studied her for a minute, seeming to search for an answer other than the one she had given. What could she say? *I have a touch of the flu?* He would not understand. She quickly cleaned their dishes, then started the bread for the morning meal. When she fell into bed, Fang jumped up and nestled beside her. On a pallet across the room before the fire, Michau began to snore. With the door barred, and both Michau and Fang for protection, she felt safe, but the loneliness of her heart was hard to bear. The moment she closed her eyes, Christophe's handsome face appeared. How she wished he could forgive her.

If he only knew. If only she could tell him.

"You see love has conquered what the sword could not," Hayden said to Fiona, pointing to Caradoc and Ariana, then to Nicolas beside her, and at last to Christophe.

Christophe felt the bite of the overheard remark. What in God's name would he do about Bronwyn?

He watched the snow fall and wondered where his wife could be. The thought of her hungry and shivering ate at his conscience, but just as readily as that image appeared, another followed. One of her in bed, her arms around him, loving him with carefree abandon. The image nearly drove him insane—especially when it was followed by one of her doing the same with Michau. *Non!* He would not entertain such thoughts. Dear God, if only he could find her. If anything happened to her, he was to blame. Frustrated and afraid, he slammed his fist against the table and stood without a word.

He stormed from the room no longer able to bear the family's company. As he left, Hayden's voice drifted to his ears. "I told you. He loves her."

Hayden had no idea how much. But she would never forgive him. The look of agony on her face when he had extracted his revenge haunted him. Fool, his mind screamed.

Though the weather was miserable, he walked the battlements, staring out into the storm-filled night with remorse. "God keep her safe, for I have failed to do so."

As he turned he glimpsed the silhouette of a soldier leaving the guard tower.

However, it was not any soldier who placed his hand on Christophe's shoulder, but Nicolas. "Come inside. You will be ill again."

Christophe shrugged out of his brother's grasp. "I have made the worst error of my life. She will never forgive me."

"*Oui,* you are right. You made a grave mistake. But she loves you, Christophe, and I am sure she will forgive you."

Christophe stared at his brother. "You believe she still loves me?"

Nicolas nodded solemnly. "She was so worried when you took ill. She would not allow anyone else to care for you."

Hope flickered in Christophe's heart, then died. "I have hurt her so badly," he whispered. "If only I had known her reasons. If only she had trusted me."

"You both have memories to put to rest. It will take time and patience."

Christophe sighed. "You are right. We do indeed have an unfortunate history," he agreed, wondering if he could last the night worrying about her.

"Then set it right, Brother." Nicolas clasped Christophe's shoulder with a comforting squeeze, before heading toward the door.

As Christophe watched his brother disappear, he considered his words. How would he do that? He pulled her ring and necklace out of his tunic and moved beneath a torch. The inscription caught his eye, and he closed his eyes and leaned against the cold stone wall. The snow stung his face and mingled with the wet tracks on his cheeks. "Believe in Love." The words filled him with self-contempt. She believed in love, but would she ever believe in him again? He crushed the ring in his fist. He would not rest until he had placed the ring back upon her finger, never to be removed.

But he could not envision any reason why she would ever agree to return to him. Even if she loved him, he had broken her heart. And he had reaped the reward of his foolish anger. Utter loneliness surrounded him, crushing his heart and will beneath an avalanche of remorse.

God, he had to find a way to win her back. He vowed to win her forgiveness, even if it meant trampling his pride. He only prayed that she would listen, and believe.

The storm raged through the night, and it was late when he fell into his bed, overcome by emotional exhaustion. Though he had ordered everyone to search for her, there had been no news of his love.

When at last he dozed off, his sleep was troubled by nightmares. He tossed and turned, hearing familiar voices that did not match the speaker's face. All night long an unsettling sense of *déjà vu* pervaded his dreams. When he awoke to a bright day he was still exhausted.

"Christophe," Nicolas called from the hallway. "She is found."

Christophe flew out of bed. The weary cobwebs dissolved as he dressed and flung open the door. "Where is she?"

Nicolas beamed as he reached out and pulled his brother's tunic shut. "A villager spotted Fang outside the old crone's cottage."

"Did he see Bronwyn?"

"Non. But she must be inside."

Christophe grabbed his brother. "Let's go."

They hurried down to the great room, where her family was gathered. Christophe could hardly bring himself to meet their gaze, but he spoke to Hayden. "I will bring her home today."

Hayden smiled. "I never doubted it."

"I will take care never to hurt her again," he choked out, then hurriedly left.

At the croft, he waited outside as Nicolas knocked on the door and talked to Michau.

After Michau closed the door and walked a few steps with Nicolas, Christophe stepped out of his hiding place at the side of the building and stopped the soldier.

"My wife, she is well?" Christophe asked, his gut twisting with jealousy.

"You have forgiven her, then?" Michau asked.

"Oui, I was mistaken. She told me the truth."

" 'Tis good I kept her safe." He bowed before Christophe. "Rest easy, my lord. I dishonored no one."

Christophe's heart pounded in relief. "You don't know how close you came to wearing my sword."

"I do, my lord. But fear of you did not prompt my actions, 'twas respect for your lady wife."

Christophe shook Michau's hand. "You will not need to return to this croft tonight."

"I am glad the lady will be returning to her home," Michau said, then without being asked he left with Nicolas.

The minute the men were out of sight, Christophe walked over to the hut and opened the door, his heart pounding harder than it did in combat. At his entrance Bronwyn whirled around, her expressive features revealing several turbulent emotions. First terror, then relief, and finally withdrawal. "Where is Michau?" she asked, taking a nervous step backward.

His heart twisted at her retreat. "Michau will not be back to this hut, and neither will you."

She closed her eyes. "I am to leave here?"

The pain on her face sliced his heart. "Bronwyn, I have come to apologize." At that, her eyes flew open, and he held up his hand when she tried to interrupt. "I could not bear the pain of what I thought was your betrayal. I lashed out, hurting you as I had been hurt." He drew a deep breath. "You told me I was mistaken, that someday I would find out the truth. I have."

She stood stock-still, staring at him as though she was almost afraid of him.

"I am so sorry." He reached out to touch her cheek, but she jerked her face away. Undeterred, he stepped closer and wiped her tears away with his fingertips. "Please come home with me. I promise I won't ask any more than that. I want you safe."

When she did not answer, he turned her face to the light, and brushing the hair away from her cheek, looked into her glistening amber eyes.

Finally she said, "I cannot live by your whims, Christophe. One day you care for me and promise you trust me, then the next you give me to your man."

He blanched at her accusation.

"Forgive me," he said softly.

"Why? You lied to me when you said we would start fresh, when you said you would trust me."

"Did you trust me?" he asked, holding her still when she tried to turn away. "You could have told me about the wicca. Did you really believe I would have condemned you to death?"

She drew a ragged breath and shook her head. "Christophe, you don't understand. I had to protect you."

"*Non.* You say that, but deep in your heart you know you doubted me."

Her lips quivered. "Christophe, if you only knew." She lowered her eyes, and he pulled her close, needing to feel her within his arms. "We have only two options, Bronwyn; either we start over, or we end it."

Her body trembled as she cried. "I . . ."

His throat thickened. "I am sorry." His hands gathered her close, then softly stroked her back. Her sobs shook her tiny frame and he tried to absorb her pain. Every tear she shed caused him an agony of regret.

She cried until there were no more tears, then slowly pulled back. "I cannot bear any more pain," she stammered haltingly.

"Bronwyn," he soothed as he pulled her back against his chest. She trembled so violently in his arms, he feared for her. "Bronwyn, please give our marriage a chance. I promise you, I will never hurt you again."

"I do not know if I can trust you," she whispered, wiping at her tears with the back of her hand.

"Whether you trust me or not, you must return to the castle. The wicca must make a public apology to clear you and those close to you."

She drew a tortured breath. "She can make that confession here."

His jaw tightened. "You cannot stay here. It is not safe."

She turned tear-bright eyes to his. "Then in what capacity shall I return? What strikes your fancy today?"

"Enough, Bronwyn," he said, his patience thinning. "I have apologized and can do no more. Whether you trust me or not is up to you. But I give you my solemn vow that whatever you decide, I will honor it. Our relationship is up to you."

"You would do this?" she asked, gazing up at him, her lashes spiked, her amber eyes large.

He softly kissed her forehead, and rested his brow against hers. "Do not worry, Bronwyn, I will not touch you. Not until you can forgive me. I ask only one thing of you: that you sleep in our room, where I know you will be safe."

"You swear to honor this vow?"

"*Oui,* I do." He paused a moment, giving her time to accept his words. "Then you will come?"

Several minutes passed, then she sighed. "I have little choice."

His heart soared, but holding her in his arms was a purgatory he had not anticipated. Every fiber in his being wanted to love her, yet he had given his word he would not.

Chapter Twenty

"Ariana, do you love my brother?" Bronwyn asked, shaking out and fluffing the lovely wedding tunic.

Ariana's fair cheeks blushed a becoming pink as she let Bronwyn slip the tunic over her head. "What kind of question is that?"

"Verily, a simple one. You are marrying the man today. Do you, or do you not, love him?" Bronwyn persisted as Fiona began to fuss with Ariana's skirt.

Ariana sighed. "Oh, aye. In truth, I fell in love with him the moment our eyes met. And when we had spoken, I knew I had met the man who lived in my dreams. Caradoc is so strong, yet so kind. So generous, and handsome."

Fiona stared at Bronwyn, then they both laughed.

"Caradoc?" Bronwyn could not help but ask.

"Aye." Ariana nodded. "You are his sisters, therefore blind to his virtues."

"Someone is blind, but it is not us," Fiona giggled, playfully nudging Bronwyn.

Smiling, Ariana tilted her head. "Tell me, do you not see your husbands as the most wonderful men in all of Christendom?"

"Aye," Fiona laughed.

Bronwyn, however, had to force herself to smile. After all, it was no secret that her relationship with Christophe was strained. But she did not want to spoil the couple's wedding day with needless questions and doubts.

"Come," Bronwyn said in an effort to dispel her own despair. "Let me help you with your hair."

Once her soft brown tresses were combed and curled, Ariana stood ready for the wedding ceremony. "Much good fortune, Sister," Bronwyn said, kissing her cheek, then moved back so Fiona could do the same.

Bronwyn signaled to Fang. The animal had not left her side since her departure from the castle two weeks ago. He followed close at her heels as she and Fiona led the bride down the hall to the staircase beyond.

"I hate to see you so sad, Sister," Fiona whispered discreetly. "Are things the same between you and Christophe?"

Bronwyn took a deep breath, wishing Fiona had not broached the subject. Though in public, she and Christophe were civil to each other, they lived liked total strangers in private. "We will work it out."

"But it makes no sense. In your absence Christophe behaved like an injured animal. No one could say anything around him without feeling his ire." She shook her head. "Why, then, is he so cold to you?"

As perturbed as she was at Christophe, she could not let her sister think he was treating her badly. "It is not Christophe who has kept us apart, but me."

"You?" Fiona said. "But why?"

"I have my pride," she said, remembering the pain.

"Ah!" Fiona said, with total understanding. "You are teaching him a lesson."

"Aye."

"Sister, if he is the one who is supposed to be suffering for his sins, then why is it that you are so miserable?"

Bronwyn was brought up short by her sister's pronouncement. She was about to argue the matter, but they had reached the bottom of the stairs.

"I am sure he has learned his lesson by now," Fiona whispered as she reached out to smooth Ariana's hair. When the bride stepped forward toward Caradoc, Fiona touched Bronwyn's arm. ''Why not put both of you out of your torment by accepting his apology?''

Fiona's words pricked her conscience. She did miss her husband, and in truth, could not stand the gulf between them. But his cruel rejection had devastated her. Her gaze traveled across the room, passing over every face until she found her husband. Lord, but he took her breath away.

As though feeling her gaze, he looked back and their eyes met. A warm glow of longing entered his dark gaze as he stared at her. Her heart beat faster and heat curled within her belly at his blatant desire. The time had come to either forgive him, or forsake their marriage vows, she thought as she joined Christophe in the great room, and Fiona went to stand beside Nicolas.

Silence descended on the room as the friar began the ceremony. Married couples held hands, clearly reliving and reaffirming their own marriage vows. A lump formed in Bronwyn's throat as she watched those around her share in the wedding. Wilford looked at Nesta with love and tenderness. Nicolas slowly raised Fiona's hand to his lips. She had to close her eyes to block out the happiness that threatened to break her composure. When she heard the bride and groom repeat their vows in strong and clear voices, tears filled her eyes, spilling over and trailing down her cheeks.

Christophe inquired several times as to what troubled her, but Bronwyn refused to answer him. When the kiss of peace was given, Christophe took her hand and tucked it around his arm. Her body tingled from the soft contact, longing for more. Being this close to him, but unable to reach out and caress him, was both heaven and hell.

''I am pleased you are happy,'' he whispered in her ear. She shivered as more tears gathered in her eyes.

''You did say women cry at weddings from happiness, didn't you?'' he asked, handing her a fresh linen cloth.

She tried to smile, but her heart remained too heavy. Oh, how she missed him. How she wanted . . .

''Let us hope that this wedding has brought peace,'' he went on. ''That is all that matters.''

She nodded, still unable to answer. Aye, she wanted her husband. She needed him to believe in her, too. She wanted desperately to believe he would not hurt her again. Even if it meant believing in a dream, she was willing to have faith. What else could she do? *I love you, Christophe. Please love me,* she silently wished.

At that moment the friar blessed the couple, and Nicolas leaned toward them. ''Caradoc has made the right decision.''

''Aye, Father is pleased,'' added Fiona.

Bronwyn turned to her father, and her heart melted. Hayden's face was wreathed in joy. True, his features were still lined and craggy, but this time it was from age, not worry. He looked better than he had in a month. This wedding was the best medicine for him, and seemed to have restored his strength. She prayed his health remained as good.

The music played, signaling the end of the ceremony, and a loud cheer filled the air. Laughter and conversation swirled around her and she knew the bride and groom had started to circulate among the guests, receiving congratulations and good cheer.

Before long, the happy couple stood before them. Caradoc pumped Christophe's hand, then stepped up to her.

She smiled and gave him a kiss. ''Be happy, Brother.''

''And you,'' he replied, cutting a glance at her husband.

''She is,'' Christophe said curtly, ending any speculation.

As Caradoc and Ariana moved off, music filled the air. She wanted to dance, but her husband did not ask. So instead she watched the dancers, and let her thoughts drift.

As though reading her mind, Hayden bowed before her. ''Daughter, would you do me the honor of a dance?''

She turned to Christophe, who nodded his assent. ''Thank you, I would love to.'' She glided off, happy to be on the floor and doing what she had been denied in her previous life. There was something therapeutic about dancing, something heartening and magical. Her soul listened and absorbed the melody.

'' 'Tis wonderful,'' she breathed.

Hayden chuckled. "You should ask your husband to dance. I vow, if you did, he would not be able to resist such a charming lady."

"Father, please."

"Do not reprimand me for being worried. But I will pry no further."

She sighed, relieved she would not have to explain her marital situation to yet another family member. "I am so happy for Caradoc."

"Aye. But I wish he had told us about Ariana."

"He had to find his own way, Father, as all of us do. And as much as you would like to make our road less rocky, you cannot always protect us," she said, realizing that no one but she could decide what to do.

He pulled back and looked at her intently. "I am guilty of a father's sin," he said, shaking his head. "I have looked at you so often as my little girl that I am afraid I did not see the woman you have become."

"I will always be your daughter."

He smiled. "Indeed, I have three fine children and I am very proud of each of them. But a part of me misses the time they ran to me to make the world right."

Hayden's nostalgic words touched a chord within Bronwyn, making her think of her carefree happy childhood. Of days long before the war.

"Ah. Do not worry, I will have grandchildren to spoil soon enough," he said, looking at his son.

She couldn't help but smile. Over her father's shoulder she had been covertly watching her husband. He was dressed in somber colors, and his dark handsome visage made her heart swell. Her father's words echoed in her mind. "A baby," she murmured reverently, suddenly wondering if she was pregnant.

The song finished and Christophe turned to her. The happiness of the couples crowded in on her. If they were to find peace, she would have to make the first move, and forgive him. 'Twould be awkward after their rift. Mayhap she should show him with actions instead of words. Flashing him a coy smile hat made him raise his brows, she began to move among the guests, playing the perfect hostess. However, in the back of her mind she plotted and planned a private seduction that would make her husband beg for mercy, and more.

Before she could make her escape, Christophe held his hands up for attention. "There is still one matter that has to be resolved. Now that everyone is present, we will see it done."

Wondering what he was about to say, Bronwyn edged closer to where he stood.

Christophe nodded and the doors leading to the dungeon opened. A guard dragged the wicca into the room.

At the sight of the old woman, Bronwyn's eyes widened. The wedding was not the right place for this. She looked around, appalled at Christophe's timing, but no one else seemed to have a problem with the arrival of the ugly old crone.

Silence fell over the proceedings as Christophe motioned for the old woman to come forward. "You have slandered the good name of my lady wife. You will here and now recant your accusation."

The wicca spared Christophe a nervous glance before she knelt before Bronwyn. "My lady, I humbly beg your pardon. I am sorry for the false witness I bore and the threats I made against you and your loved ones."

Hayden, Caradoc, and Nicolas crowded in on Bronwyn as Christophe approached and pointed to the old crone. "Bronwyn, only you can forgive her. If you do not, she returns to the dungeon."

It was obvious by her forlorn expression that two weeks in the dungeon had tempered the old woman's bluster. She looked frail and repentant. "You are forgiven," Bronwyn said, wishing the matter done at last.

The old woman rose and kissed Bronwyn's hand. The wicca's eyes gleamed the moment she touched the mistress's fingers. "There is joy in your heart and life in your body." Then her eyes softened. "Cherish them, my lady, for nothing ever lasts."

Though Bronwyn held no animosity toward this woman, she pulled her hand free.

" 'Tis done," Christophe pronounced. The old woman smiled and backed away, leaving the assembly.

Christophe pulled Bronwyn close. "She cannot hurt you now. But you should have told me."

He was right, he had handled the old woman far better than she. She wondered how he would react if she told him the whole truth. Then she dismissed the thought.

Rhett paced before the children huddled by the campfire, his scarred face capturing the firelight in red flashes as he passed back and forth.

Matrona gripped her brother's hand, trying to calm his fear. Dewi was terrified of the monster. Dried, dirty tear tracks smudged his pale face as he stared unseeing into the fire.

"When the regiment and the wedding party leave for London, you will open the jail cell and tell Lucien to meet me here."

Matrona nodded.

"How did my daughter look tonight?" he asked, his sardonic tone unmistakable.

Matrona's eyes grew wide. "She was very lovely." She looked regretfully at her brother, then stood. "I will be missed if I do not return now."

"Go then," he said, waving his hand. "I have a little surprise for my daughter and son-in-law." Then he turned and stared at her with such hatred, she shrank back. "Do not fail me," Rhett warned.

Terror surged through her. She bowed before him, then hugged her little brother. "Soon," she whispered. "Be brave."

"Do not leave me," he softly pleaded. Grasping her tight, he sniffled back a cry.

Her heart broke as she wrenched out of her brother's clinging arms. She could not stand his tears. Though the memory of the lord and lady's kindness flickered through her mind, she had promised her mama to always care for him. She knew where her duty lay, but even so, guilt plagued her young soul.

* * *

Bronwyn nervously paced the floor of their chamber. Her decision to expose her feelings to Christophe would again leave her vulnerable, and utterly helpless. So be it.

Trying to stay calm, she brushed her hair until it shone, and slipped into the thinnest smock she possessed. On the hearth sat a tray of meat and cheese, and a chalice of wine.

She lay back upon the pillows and fluffed her hair so it fell about her in wild disarray. Bold and sexy were two words never associated with her in her past life. Well, the little brown mouse had come into her own and she would fight for her happiness. She knew she loved him. His male pride and her wounded dignity were their obstacles. As much as she hated to admit it, she could not blame him for some of the assumptions he had formed about her, any more than she could change the ones she had made of him.

Her thoughts eased her mood. If they did not bury the past, they would never have a future.

Approaching footsteps sounded outside her chamber and she held her breath in anticipation. The door swung open and Christophe's dark eyes widened. For an endless moment he looked at her, then abruptly turned and shut the door.

Bronwyn swallowed, her heart fluttering in her chest. His reaction was not what she expected, and her confidence began to ebb.

"You are abed early this evening." He sat down stiffly in the chair.

"There is food and wine for you by the hearth. Can I tempt you?" Languidly she rose to wait on him, and was discouraged when he only nodded curtly.

She went to the hearth and picked up the platter knowing he had an excellent view of her silhouette.

She leaned over and offered the tray. "What is your desire, my lord?"

Her bold gaze met his, leaving no doubt what she meant.

His dark eyes glowed, full of fire and need. "You forgive me then?"

"I . . ."

"Either you forgive or you do not," he said, touching her cheek ever so gently.

"I forgive you," she said, setting down the tray, "but I do not know if I can forget."

"Fair enough. There are things that live in my memory as well. Can you live with that?"

"I suppose we must."

"No relationship is perfect, Wife. It is what we make it. Shall we agree to let time be our answer?"

Although she had wanted more and sensed he did, too, perhaps this was the best start they could make. "All right, my lord." She held out her hand, but he seized her waist and pulled her down onto his lap.

"Seal our bargain with a kiss."

The taste of wine on his lips, the texture of his tongue against hers, made her forget everything, and she savored every sweet minute.

I missed you, she silently cried as she wrapped her arms around his neck and held him tight. He felt all muscle and brawn, his skin smooth and hot.

His lips nuzzled her neck, causing little shivers to travel through her body, down to the very tips of her toes.

"Christophe," she whispered, "did you miss me?" She needed to hear the words, to feel them glide over her, soothe her, fill her heart.

When he raised his head to look at her, she covered his lips with her finger, suddenly afraid of what he would say. "Never mind. I do not want to know."

He kissed her finger and ever so softly, drew it into his mouth. "I missed you. If you must know the truth, when I thought of you with Michau, I nearly went mad, such was my jealousy."

His husky words filled her with incredible joy. But she pulled away and said soberly, "He but protected me, Husband. Alone I would have been fair game for any soldier."

Christophe drew a deep breath. "I know. He told me. I owe him my gratitude."

She saw in his eyes that he was as vulnerable as she. It was time to ease his doubt. Besides, they had to start somewhere. "I would never let any man love me but you."

Christophe squeezed his eyes shut. "Thank you." He rested his forehead against hers.

Her eyes misted over, his words stealing her soul. "You really do care," she said in some surprise, cradling his face with her palm.

His muscles tensed beneath her fingers. "I swear to you, I will never lose my temper with you again." He pulled her closer, so that his whisper warmed her skin. "I beg your forgiveness, Wife. I am afraid where you are concerned my judgement is sorely lacking."

In response she kissed him longingly, and said, "Oh, my lord, I love you."

He pulled her ring from his tunic, slipped it on her finger, and kissed her palm. "Then never take my ring off again." He smothered her lips in a searing kiss and she accepted it with equal passion.

The moment she returned his ardor, she sensed a great release in him. Holding nothing back, he began to love her with an abandonment that took her breath away.

Her hands caressed his shoulders and slipped beneath his tunic to brush the material away. She ran her hands over his chest and the coarse hairs tickled her fingers, then her lips as she teased his flat nipples. The moan deep in his throat made her stomach tighten with excitement and she kissed his chest, teasing him as she moved lower, then back up to tantalize his nipples once again. She could feel his muscles bunch beneath her fingers, and he pulled her against him, showing her proof of his need.

With a jerk he pulled her gown down over her shoulders, and she stood to let it slide off her body to the floor. Wearing nothing but his topaz ring, she held her arms out to him. He stood and clasped her to him, burying his face in her neck. Then he lifted her in his arms and carried her to the bed, placing her upon the fur. His gaze never leaving her, he quickly divested himself of his tights, and lay down beside her.

His body was magnificent, bronzed, warm, and strong. She would never grow tired of caressing, exploring, and needing him. She heard his breathing become labored as her hands slowly slipped down his torso toward his manhood.

He gasped when she took hold of him and began to stroke.

"God, how you excite me," he rasped as he took her lips in a torturous kiss of heat and sensation.

She could barely breathe when he lifted his head to feast on her neck, nipping and licking the line of her jaw as he made a delicious trail to her ear.

"Christophe."

"Shhh," he murmured, his lips moving from her neck to her breast.

"Please, Christophe!" She sucked in air as she frantically scored his back with her nails.

"I am only returning the favor, my love." His lips moved farther over her nipple, his teeth lightly grazing the edge. She gasped, unable to speak as a warmth pooled between her thighs.

Her hands clasped his shoulders. "You are driving me out of my mind."

" 'Tis nothing compared to what you do to me." His lips descended on hers. Red-hot flames streaked through her. He pushed her past her endurance, and back. "Christophe," she moaned.

His hands and lips caressed every inch of her body and waves of desire washed over her. When his finger slipped inside her, the need he created was unbearable. A current of fire raced through her, and she climaxed, crying out his name. He held her in his arms until the storm of emotions began to slow and pass. The pounding of her heart had barely lessened when he finally entered her. The rhythm he created revived the sensuous ecstasy, and within minutes she was crying out again, his arms a crushing cushion, before he too found his release.

She felt weightless, bodiless, euphoric. She could barely lift her hand to caress his shoulder.

"I missed you, Wife," he whispered. His husky voice felt like a rough caress.

Satisfied, she smiled. "If this is what your loneliness does, mayhap I should leave more often."

"Never," he said, and pulled her into his arms.

"Never," she echoed, too happy to speak.

Chapter Twenty-one

Caradoc and his bride, Ariana, walked out of the castle and down the steps in the cold morning air. Dark clouds, heavy with snow, blocked the sunlight, promising a dreary day's journey. The soldiers slouched deep into the warmth of their mantles as they waited on horseback in the courtyard.

"Have a safe journey." Bronwyn gripped Caradoc's hand as she tried not to cry.

He kissed her cheeks. "Thank God you two are no longer at odds."

Her cheeks blushed at his observation. Was it really so evident? "Aye, we have come to an understanding," she whispered.

Caradoc's eyes sparkled. "I am glad."

A glance at Fiona showed she, too, had tears in her eyes as she and Nicolas made their farewells.

If Caradoc had any reservations about London, they didn't show as he helped his wife onto her mount.

The Norman troops straightened when Christophe left Bronwyn and marched toward his brother-in-law. "When you arrive, send me a detailed report," Christophe said, then handed Caradoc a packet. "I have written to Lord Odo explaining the regiment's delay."

By making Caradoc his emissary, Christophe had singled the man out as a valued soldier, both trusted and important. Her brother stood straight and tall when he held out his hand to Christophe. "I will not let you down." Caradoc quickly mounted, then raised his hand, signaling the convoy to leave.

Bronwyn's eyes stung with fresh tears. Christophe's gesture would aid her brother's acceptance.

Before the troop could leave, a horseman rode in through the gates. He dismounted and quickly bowed before Lord Christophe. "My lord, Lord Rhett sent me with the lady's dowry." He turned and handed the pouch to Caradoc. "Lord Rhett approves of this match and wanted all to know that he is pleased."

Ariana's relief was visible. "Oh, Caradoc," she cried. "My stepfather has approved of our match." Her smile lit her face.

"As well he should," Hayden said. "The name Llangandfan is respected in every hamlet."

Relief flowed throughout the courtyard as villagers cheered, knowing they no longer had to fear an attack from Rhett's rebels.

Though Bronwyn smiled, she had her misgivings about Rhett's sincerity, and judging by Christophe's reserved expression, he apparently was of the same mind.

But Hayden knew more about Welsh politics, and he seemed satisfied. Still, Bronwyn did not relish the thought of being related to Rhett.

Christophe raised an eyebrow at the messenger's avid curiosity in the sentries. When he was dismissed, instead of taking a rest, the strange Welshman mounted his horse and rode out as fast as he had entered.

"Thank God," Caradoc said, holding up the pouch for all to see. Then he turned to Christophe. " 'Tis proof my father-in-law has accepted this marriage. We will have peace."

Caradoc flashed a smile that matched his bride's, then again raised his hand and motioned the soldiers forward.

As soon as the troops disappeared through the gates, the

crowd quickly dispersed. Christophe watched until the Norman troops were out of sight, then glanced to the battlements, now manned almost wholly by Welshmen. He turned, and a frown aged his handsome features, showing lines of worry about his eyes and mouth.

Bronwyn's heart ached at his distress and she moved to join him. With a gentle caress, she smoothed the lines of his brow. "The people are behind you, my lord."

He captured her hand and kissed her palm. "I know, they have already proven their loyalty."

She gazed out toward her people and experienced a swelling of great pride. What he said was true. They had indeed proven themselves. When she glanced back at Christophe she caught another frown, before he hid it with a smile.

Wondering if it was a question of loyalty, she reached up on tiptoes and kissed his lips. "I will stand by you always, and if I do, my people will."

He chuckled, wrapping his arm around her waist. "I know, Wife. Rest your fears, my mind was simply on other matters."

All the same, she knew he was uneasy.

Matrona waited until Nesta was busy in the kitchen and Wilford was in the stable before she made her move. While the troops were waiting for Caradoc and his bride to leave, she saw the dungeon master leave his post for the garderobe. Knowing the dungeon master would be at least five minutes while he answered the call of nature, she stole down the dungeon stairs. Her heart pounded with every step, but she knew if she failed, her brother would die.

As she descended the torchlit stone steps, the temperature dropped. The cool, clammy air raised chill bumps on her arms and legs, but she hugged her shawl tighter and continued. Her shadow spilled out across the stones, the flickering silhouette her only companion as she dashed across the stone floor toward Lucien's cell. Every second that went by, her fear magnified. The dungeon master could return before she had even opened the cell. She swallowed her fear as she reached the door. On a hook above her head hung the long iron keys. Her hands shook as she placed the big key into the lock. With a quick turn the door opened and the putrid smell hit her nostrils. She almost gagged as Lucien, dirty and unkempt, staggered out. " 'Tis about time," he snarled, his eyes bloodshot and his beard shaggy.

She cringed away from him. "Lord Rhett wants you to meet him at the caves."

Lucien sneered and tried to grab her, but she easily ran from his reach, not stopping until she was up the steps and into the welcome heat of the great room. Her eyes misted over when she skittered to a stop and looked at the lord and lady, then at her adopted parents. She did not know how she was going to live with herself.

The excitement of the regiment's departure made it simple for Lucien to slip out of the castle undetected.

As Christophe received the news from the dungeon master, his mind turned over every possibility.

"No doubt Lucien has a friend among the departing soldiers, who did not want to see him rot in jail," Nicolas suggested as he poured himself a cup of wine.

"Who?" Christophe asked.

"Does it matter? The man is gone. Perhaps there was one man who did not want to see a Norman in a Welsh jail."

"You are probably right," Christophe said, knowing such loyalty existed among soldiers. But unable to quell his unease he added, "Even so, I want security tightened."

A fortnight passed without Lucien's capture, and the weather turned bitter. Winter's cloak descended on the land. A carpet of white spread out across the valley, and the game grew scarce as animals hibernated and took refuge from the elements. Thanks to Christophe's measures the larder was full. Though the land slept in the throes of winter, the people did not. Wood had to be chopped or the heat ran out. The animals needed special care to survive the harsh elements.

Bronwyn was more and more convinced she was indeed pregnant. Though excited about the prospect, she was also terrified. In the Middle Ages women often died in childbirth, and she shuddered at the imagined sound of her own cries. However, she could not dwell on that. She would think only of the good, of the love and joy a baby would bring. The sheer wonder soon dissolved her fear. "A baby," she would whisper to herself, hoping it was so.

If nothing else, it would explain her strange emotional outbursts. She wondered how Christophe would take the news of being a father and decided to wait until she was absolutely certain before broaching the subject.

"What are you up to my lady?" Nesta asked one morning as she entered the kitchen with the rest of the servants to start the day's work. Little Matrona, her face solemn, shuffled in and climbed up on a stool to watch the proceedings.

"I am preparing something special for the men," Bronwyn replied. "They have no time for a decent meal while they ride patrol."

Nesta leaned forward and took an experimental sniff. "My, that smells wonderful."

"You don't have to look so surprised, Nesta," Bronwyn said, a little miffed.

"My lady, you will pardon me, but you have never been known for your culinary skills. In truth, I thought your casserole a mistake because it was edible."

Cordelia chuckled and Matrona's eyes grew large as the other women in the kitchen turned to hide their grins, their shoulders shaking.

"Very amusing." Bronwyn noticed Matrona's awed features and leaned forward to stage-whisper, "Your adopted mother has a strange sense of humor. In truth, the poor woman is happy all the time. Hopefully, you will be spared such a tiresome affliction."

Chuckling, Nesta wrapped her arms around Matrona. "If she has to suffer through goodwill and joy, my lady, she will."

Then giving the child a kiss, she looked up at Bronwyn. "Pray thee, tell me the name of the dish. It is unseemly for the castle's cook not to know the name of the food prepared and served. Especially if it is good and I wish to take credit for it."

"You may have all the credit." Bronwyn grinned, knowing that Nesta would never act so foolish. However, her gibe, as was intended, produced a smile, albeit a small one, from Matrona.

"What is it called, my lady?" Matrona added her voice to her mother's question.

"I call it a pasty. You see, first you make a pie dough, then chop up the meat and vegetables, add butter and pepper and seal it up to bake. For dessert you do likewise, but instead of a meat and vegetable filling, you place sugared fruit inside a smaller dough and fold it over. They are meat and fruit pies that fit in the palm of your hand." She held one up for the women's inspection. "The men can carry them easily, ending the problem of meals while on patrol."

" 'Tis a marvel, my lady," Nesta said excitedly, passing the meat pie among the women. "However did you think of it?"

"Necessity is the mother of invention."

"Necessity is the mother of invention. Hmmm ... I like that."

"My lady," Cordelia said, between mouthfuls. " 'Tis a wonder. The men need food they can eat without stopping to prepare. This will vary their diet in a pleasant way."

"Aye, it will. But will they accept this strange preparation?" Gwen asked. When silence descended in the kitchen, she quickly added, " 'Tis simply not what they are used to."

Bronwyn knew change was difficult, so she merely smiled. "They have no choice—either they eat what we prepare, or go hungry."

At that, everyone chuckled.

"Also, I have a few things here that I will use to make a special drink. Mind you, I want no one peeking while I am busy preparing it. You ladies can finish the pasties."

She glanced over her shoulder to find Nesta repeatedly trying to glimpse what she was doing. Shaking her head, she chuckled, but kept her back presented to the curious cook.

She ground up the dried fruit and poured the fermented wine over it, then she added sugar and covered the bowl. "No one is to touch this. Nor can you look, as it will ruin the surprise."

"A surprise, my lady?"

"Aye, for the celebration."

"What celebration, my lady?" Nesta asked, her neck straining to see around Bronwyn's shoulder.

"My husband's birthday. I wish to celebrate it."

Cook's bobbing movements froze. "My lady?"

" 'Tis to honor him."

"I know the Normans have strange ways, but think you he will be pleased?"

"I am sure he will. He has never had a special day and I intend to give him one."

"My lady, 'tis most unusual," Cordelia said, lifting her crying baby up from the basket and cooing soft little words to hush the tears.

Bronwyn's heart melted when she saw the baby. She longed to hold the child but turned her attention back to the women.

"Perhaps, but 'tis a practice I think will catch on." She looked pointedly around the room. "Do you not think your husbands would be pleased if you were to honor them in such a fashion?"

" 'Tis foolishness," Gwen called out.

" 'Tis never foolish to find time for joy," Bronwyn argued.

"My Wilford would be surprised." Nesta's eyes sparkled. "Aye, I think it a fine idea."

Bronwyn nodded. "We will see how this celebration is received and then we will decide if it is foolish or not. I would wager that the men will be in a fine mood. They have been so busy lately a little lighthearted diversion might relieve their hardships."

"But, my lady, it will not make their burdens go away," Gwen said.

"Aye, but if we celebrate the little joys in life, it makes our difficulties all the more bearable."

The serving maid finally conceded as the other women milled closer to ask questions about the forthcoming celebration.

"I want to bake a huge cake with sticky icing and a candle in the middle," Bronwyn announced.

"A candle in the middle?" Nesta asked, her bafflement mirrored in every woman's face in the room.

"Never mind the oddity. The important thing is that the men will relax and we will all have great fun. Oh, I will also need help with the decorations."

"Decorations?" everyone asked in unison.

"Aye, I want the hall decorated for the festivities."

The faces brightened. This was something they understood. "I can gather some fresh evergreens," Gwen offered.

"I can sweep the rushes and add extra spice to them," Anne volunteered.

"Good, now we need to make a banner," Bronwyn said.

"Oh, yes, that would be lovely. How about dried flowers, too?" Cordelia suggested.

"I can ask old Thomas if he would play his lute," Fiona piped in joining their enthusiasm.

Surprised, Bronwyn turned and smiled. "I didn't see you come in, Sister."

"You were too busy making plans, but I have been here," Fiona said. "I agree, we need to celebrate. And I love the idea of doing so on a birthday. I can't wait to have one for Nicolas."

Soon everyone was caught up in the spirit of the upcoming festivities. The news spread through the castle like wildfire, and by the noon meal everyone was helping.

Fiona brought down some old ribbons. "What do you want to do with these?"

Bronwyn accepted the ribbons and moved to the wall, where she had hung a poorly drawn picture of a horse. "I am going to teach everyone a new game."

"What is the game?"

"You will see," she said.

"Oh, this will be so much fun," Nesta said, clapping her hands together like a little child.

"I hope Christophe thinks so," she whispered under her

breath, doubts suddenly assailing her. But it was too late to stop now. The whole castle had a purpose, and everyone was looking forward to the birthday party.

Nicolas had hailed his brother as the warlord mounted his horse for the dawn patrol. "I will leave Hayden in charge of the training today. I will ride with you."

Christophe nodded. Nicolas evidently had something of importance to discuss.

Dawn was lighting the sky when they moved out of the valley. Paused on a ridge that overlooked the countryside, Nicolas surveyed the landscape before saying quietly, "The soldiers have heard rumors that Rhett has sworn vengeance on the Llangandfans."

"*Oui,* as have I. Remember they are only rumors, but rest assured, I am not ignoring them," Christophe said, wondering what was really troubling his brother.

"Do you think Rhett will gain any more support among the chieftains?"

"I do not know."

Nicolas sighed. "Do you think we should send the women to London?"

"You can if you want, but Bronwyn will remain here."

"Why?"

"Because I cannot accompany her, and I will not leave her safety to a small escort on open roads. And if I send her away it will send a clear message to the people that I do not intend to hold the castle."

"You are right, but remember Rhett once boasted to have your wife."

Although Christophe's stomach twisted in sudden anger, his reply was calm. "If Rhett covets my wife, my land, and my life," Christophe looked at his brother, "there is only one way to safeguard all three. I must kill him."

Nicolas nodded in understanding, then straightened as something suddenly caught his attention. Turning, he pointed to the east. "What do you see?"

Christophe reined his horse around and watched as a rider sped through the valley below. It wasn't until the soldier drew near that he was recognized. "He carries Lord Odo's colors."

"I wonder what has happened now," Nicolas said.

Lord Odo's messenger galloped up to them, pulling back on the reins as he handed a missive to Christophe. "My lord, I was on my way to Castle Montgomery when I spotted your patrol."

Travel-stained and covered in mud, both the rider and horse showed evidence of a hard ride. With a curt nod Christophe directed the messenger to take his rest with the column of soldiers behind them.

As the tired soldier moved away, Christophe opened the document and read. His stomach tightened at the words, and he crunched the missive in his fist. "We are called to London."

"What!" Nicolas grabbed the paper from his hand. As he read, his face also hardened. "We cannot go."

"We must," Christophe said, taking the summons back and shoving it inside his tunic. "We have little choice."

Nicolas inhaled deeply, then slowly exhaled. "When do we leave?"

"Tomorrow." Christophe leaned over his saddle, glanced about, then lowered his voice. "Send for Michau. I will leave him in charge of the castle while we ride out with our personal guard."

"That will make Michau the only Norman here," Nicolas cautioned.

"He is more than capable, and has shown his prowess in battle. He is a born leader. The Welsh respect him."

"As they should. But only because he is your man. With you as their lord, they have found another life. One with endless possibilities."

"They have shown me another life, as well," Christophe said, suddenly remembering his existence as Drew. Regan had always shown an unusual compassion toward those that corporate society normally overlooked. He knew now that governments and monarchs rose and fell. But the society remembered by history as great is the one that survived by seeing to the needs of its poorest members.

"You took a huge gamble by trusting the Welsh. But it has paid off greatly."

"I knew that given a choice, the Welsh would choose prosperity over deprivation."

When Nicolas had left, Christophe thought about how quickly he could make this trip. If he could, he wanted to stay in London only one night. He hated the thought of leaving his castle. However, in midwinter with Rhett's forces destroyed, it could not have come at a better time. Even if Rhett managed to gather another force, it would be near impossible to storm the castle now. Though his rationalization somewhat mollified his fears, he was bothered by the sudden image of Bronwyn in danger briefly flickering through his mind. He could not envision leaving her behind, yet he knew he would have to. The journey would be too hard on her. Never would he endanger his wife, especially now, when he suspected she was with child. A grin stole across his lips. He had the best reason to return home with haste.

"My lord," Michau said as he approached, "Nicolas told me you had a matter to discuss."

Christophe motioned him over to the bluff and offered him a drink of wine from his wineskin. He explained the situation, and warned him of his concern about Rhett. "What do you think your chances are of holding this fortress?"

"They are reasonably good, my lord. The Welsh have already seen the advantage of working with us, and for the most part they are ready to start a new life. They have left the old ways and loyalties behind."

"I plan on being gone only a short time. But I would rest easier knowing you are in command."

"I will hold the castle for however long you are gone. And I will protect Lady Bronwyn and her family with my very life."

"You read my mind."

" 'Tis not hard, my lord. Anyone can see how besotted you are where the Lady Bronwyn is concerned. And with good reason. She is the breath of this land and her people. You have chosen well, my lord.''

Christophe nodded and shook his man's hand in fellowship, then they shared a drink before the soldier returned to his duties. Michau did not have to worry. Christophe already had learned the value of his lovely bride. Now, he faced a far harder task. He had to tell Bronwyn he was leaving without her.

Chapter Twenty-two

The surprise birthday party for Christophe was not difficult to plan, for he was away all day. A suspicious man by nature, he would have driven her mad had he been under foot. With the history they shared, she could not blame his cautiousness. She hoped this celebration would reenforce their growing trust.

By eventide they were ready, and Bronwyn could barely contain her excitement. The cake was baked. And what a cake! A huge double-layered, white-iced confection, which could have easily served as a wedding cake, sat on the table with one tall tapered candle in the middle.

Earlier in the afternoon she had taught the women and children pin the tail on the donkey, changing the name to pin the tail on the warhorse. All had laughed and enjoyed it immensely. "Wait until my Wilford plays this," Nesta had said, holding up the ribbons. "I only hope he can find the wall after a few cups of mead."

Everyone had caught the excitement and ran about giggling, doing last-minute preparations. After sunset word came that the men were approaching. Bronwyn ran out to wait on the steps for Christophe, with Fiona on her heels.

Christophe and Nicolas rode into the courtyard and dismounted as the soldiers led the horses to the stable. His clothes were travel stained and his movements stiff. When he climbed the steps slowly, the torchlight sliced across his face, revealing his taut expression.

"What is wrong, my lord?"

Fatigue lines ringed his eyes and mouth. His eyes were red rimmed from the cold, his gaze listless. "Before I discuss the day's events, let me sup first."

"Certainly, Christophe," she whispered. How she hated to see him this tired, this upset.

Nicolas joined them, wrapping his arms firmly around Fiona. "You have no idea how good you look, standing here waiting for me. I have missed you, Wife."

The soldiers had returned from the stable and milled about the courtyard, waiting for the warlord to enter the castle.

"Come, the men are hungry." Christophe opened the doors, letting his lady and Fiona precede him as he spoke to Nicolas. Deep in conversation, neither brother noticed the decorations as they entered the hall, but the men who followed them did. Silence immediately fell over the soldiers as they gaped at the lavishly decorated hall draped with lovely, dark evergreen boughs that filled the room with sweet pine scent. Then their gazes lifted upward and their eyes widened at the sight of the bright banner hanging from the ceiling proclaiming, "Happy Birthday."

Suddenly, only Nicolas's and Christophe's words echoed through the silence. Then ever so slowly their voices trailed away, aware that something was amiss.

Nicolas stood stock-still as Christophe stared about the room, a look of perplexity marring his handsome visage.

Breathless, Bronwyn waited for some sign of elation, but her husband just stood there staring up at the banner.

"My lord?" she finally ventured, touching his arm. "What do you think?"

He lowered his gaze to hers. "Is this for me?"

"Aye," she said, wishing she could see a glimmer of appreciation in his dark eyes. "My lord, is it not to your liking?" Her pulse raced as he looked back at the banner, then slowly took in the decorations.

At last, a broad smile spread across his face, softening his stern features. "I am surprised and pleased," he murmured, putting his arm about her shoulders. "Very pleased, Lady Wife."

Bronwyn's heart almost burst with joy.

Christophe walked over to the table and looked at the huge cake. "For me?" he asked again, eyes twinkling merrily.

Bronwyn nodded.

"But, Wife, what will the rest of you eat?"

"Nay, my lord," she laughed, "you will make a wish, blow out the candle, then we will *all* eat the cake."

His smile faded. " 'Tis not for me?"

At his expression, she truly began to worry. "My lord, it is your cake. You may do what you will with it. 'Tis a gift."

"Then," he said solemnly, "I will share it."

The minute she saw the glimmer of humor lurking in his eyes, she sighed. "I should have known you jested. I will not be so easily fooled the next time," she vowed.

He chuckled. "The thought of teasing you delights me."

Nicolas strolled over to them, his gaze taking everything in as Fiona followed. "What is this banner for?"

"We are celebrating the day of his birth," Fiona explained as she looped her arm through his.

Nicolas stared at his wife, then Bronwyn. "But why are we celebrating my brother's birthday in December?"

"Oh, no!" Bronwyn smiled, wagging her finger at Nicolas. "I will not be so easily fooled again. Today is Christophe's birthday."

Nicolas shook his head, with not a shred of humor in his eyes.

"You must be mistaken," she said, feeling a moment of doubt. "I am sure I heard Christophe say this was his birth date. Mayhap when he was sick . . ." she ventured hopefully, then turned to Christophe.

He glared at his brother, then smiled at her. "Then mayhap in my fever I confused my birth date."

"I am sorry, Christophe." Disappointment edged her words as she lowered her gaze. "For some reason, I was so sure." She sighed, looking around at the gaily decorated hall and the banner.

"We can still honor my birthday," he said softly, lifting her chin with his thumb to brush a whisper-light kiss across her lips. "And if I like this party I may tell you my real birth date so I can have two within a year."

Her heart filled to near bursting as she chuckled. "You may have as many parties as you like, my lord. I truly wanted to surprise you."

He kissed her forehead. "That you did, Wife. I never expected a party on my birthday, and certainly not one on the wrong day."

They all laughed as the men went to inspect the games she had laid out, while the women began serving the birthday feast.

Nicolas led his wife to the table as Christophe offered Bronwyn his arm. The wonderfully prepared dinner quickly disappeared before the starving men. Bronwyn could barely eat, waiting for Christophe to finish so she could light the candle on his cake. As soon as he consumed his meal, she jumped up. Fiona helped her carry over the luscious cake, which she placed before Christophe. When he reached for a knife, she placed her hand on his. "Wait."

"How can I share this cake unless you let me cut it?" Christophe asked, his eyes sparkling with amusement as the men eyed the cake with longing.

"I am going to light the candle and you must make a wish, then blow out the candle."

The men groaned at the delay. Turning, she gave them a stern look. "You want the lord to have good fortune, do you not?"

Wilford leaned forward. "Of course we do, my lady. But we also want a piece of that cake."

"And you will have one. After Christophe makes his wish." She turned around to catch Christophe licking his finger and knew he had tasted the frosting when her back was turned. Michau called out to her but as she started to turn she saw

Christophe's finger inch toward the frosting. She whirled around. "Nay, my lord, you must wait until your candle is lit and your wish made."

"Verily, I will be another year older by the time you light the cake," he teased as his brother chuckled.

She shook her head; men were really boys, plain and simple. She rushed to the hearth to light the piece of straw, then carefully carried it back and placed it to the candlewick.

"Make a wish," she whispered.

A roguish light twinkled in Christophe's jet-black eyes as he looked right at her, then blew out the candle.

"My lord, what did you wish for?" Michau called out.

"I cannot tell, or my wish will not come true." Before Bronwyn could wonder how he knew that, he took her hand and placed a kiss in her palm. "I can take no chances."

A shiver of pure desire coursed through her.

"Will I get my wish?" he asked, his voice a husky murmur.

"It depends," she hedged, suddenly noticing the interest the others had taken in their conversation. She withdrew her hand from his hold. "My lord, cut your cake."

"Tonight," Christophe promised, before his men lined up to receive their piece. Each man commented on how pleased he was with the idea of a birthday and the gift of a cake. While the soldiers moved through the line, several men teased the lord, asking about his wish. At each inquiry Christophe would stop cutting the cake and stare at her. His dark suggestive gaze would travel slowly up from the tip of her toes, touching every curve of her body, to softly caress her face. Under his slow perusal, heat stole up her cheeks and her heart fluttered. Though she tried to brazen out his flirtations, her face flushed, bringing a wink from her husband and knowing grins from his men.

The sounds of conversation flowed around her and she reveled in the joy that shone in Christophe's face as she bantered with his men.

After the birthday cake was eaten, Bronwyn pulled Christophe to the center of the hall. "I have a game for you to play." She turned to her husband. "Bend down so I can blindfold you."

He smiled as his men burst into laughter. One man called out, "My lord, this game sounds like it has possibilities."

Her face flushed bright red again and she glanced at the offending soldier. "This is not what you think."

"And exactly what is it my man thinks?" Christophe asked his wife, bringing guffaws of laughter from the men.

"You have bested me, my lord." She saw the sparkle in his eyes and leaned forward to whisper, "But I swear those games will come later when we are alone."

A captivating smile curved his lips as he leaned down and took her mouth in a deeply sensuous kiss. His tongue stroked her lips like velvet over silk and she melted in his arms. Her hands slid up his arms to caress the back of his neck, and the room receded, as did all thought of their audience.

When his mouth left hers and he released her from his embrace, she stood flustered and confused. She cleared her throat, trying to ignore both his and the crowd's smug look. Flustered, she held up the blindfold. "Now, the object of this game is to put this tail on the picture of the horse on yon wall, while you are blindfolded. The winner will be whoever comes closest to the horse's rump."

She covered his eyes, turned him around three times, and pointed him at the wall. "Very well, my lord. Go ahead."

He reached out and grabbed her, laughing at her shriek.

"Behave," she admonished and evaded his hands.

"I like my game better," he said, and heard the approval of his men.

"Christophe, please," she implored, pointing him once again toward the wall.

He walked unerringly toward the horse, then reached out and stuck the tail on the horse's nose.

Everyone burst into laughter as he pulled the blindfold off.

As the men guffawed and threw out disparaging remarks about Christophe's ability, she went to the center of the room. "I am glad you find this so amusing, but remember each one of you will have a turn to prove your skill."

The soldiers looked at one another, then suddenly charged to the middle of the room, jostling for a better position in line.

The women smiled, then followed suit. In a few short minutes all the people lined up to test their skill, anxious to have a chance to prove their bragging.

One after another, they proceeded to pin the horse's tail to the wall, a servant passing by, and the banner. By the end of the game, the only one close enough for the prize was Christophe.

"What is my reward?" he asked, suggestively.

Bronwyn returned to the center of the room and handed him a gift wrapped in a linen cloth.

He opened the cloth and found a lovely pie.

"Do I have to share this, too, my lady?"

"Nay, any prize won at the game is yours to keep. But since you have already won, my lord, it is only fair that you remain out of the rest of the games to give the others a chance."

"Agreed," he said, crooking his finger at Matrona.

When she ran up he pointed to the game. "You may also win a pie if you play."

She stared at the floor. "I am too small," she squeaked. He looked over the child's head to his wife.

"I tried to show her earlier, but she refused to try," Bronwyn explained, then leaned forward and whispered, "The truth is, she is afraid of the blindfold."

Nodding, he took Matrona's hand as he handed the pie to Bronwyn. He walked back to the new game as his men were again lining up to improve their showing, and interrupted the tall Norman soldier. "Mind you, Sumner, I have a little girl who would try her luck."

The soldier stepped back and Christophe reached for the blindfold. Matrona jumped back, fear etched on her small face as she stared at the strip of cloth in his hand. Christophe smiled. "You can shut your eyes"—he raised the blindfold—"instead of wearing this. Of course you must promise not to peek."

Elation lit her features as she bobbed her head vigorously. Scrunching her eyes shut, she let Christophe lead her over to the horse drawing. When he saw her stretching to reach the bottom of the picture, he lifted her in his arms and whispered clues in her ear. Once he steadied her arm, she reached out.

"Too high," he coached.

She lowered her arm.

"Getting closer," he said.

Her arm dropped another inch.

"Very close indeed. In fact, you are exactly on the mark," he said.

A huge grin slipped across her lips and she pinned the tail to the right place. Applause went up and she opened her eyes.

"You are the winner." He twirled her around before setting her on her feet and motioned for Bronwyn to bring over his pie. "Look what you have won!"

Matrona squealed with delight.

Bronwyn's heart melted when the child threw her tiny arms around the lord and gave him a soft kiss on the cheek. "Happy birthday, my lord." Then she grabbed the pie and disappeared through the smiling crowd.

The men continued the game as the women moved around to play twelve men out. In the background the musicians began to play soft music. Christophe chuckled as he pulled Bronwyn close. "Come, dance with me."

She glided onto the floor within his embrace. "I am so glad you were surprised," she whispered, feeling his heart beating next to hers.

"Every day I spend with you is a revelation."

He glided her around the floor as other couples followed their lead. She felt the music and matched his steps, loving the feel of being in his arms while whirling to the soft, lilting strains of the lute and mandolin. She had discovered that dancing was a sensuous experience, two bodies maneuvering as one, the rhythm of the music and their mood carrying them away. Her body swayed, alive to the sound of her heart.

When the last note faded, she noticed his eyes shone with pride and possession. "As long as I live I will remember how you feel in my arms and the seductive expression in your eyes when you dance."

She beamed, and reached up to touch his face. "I have never felt this way before."

He smiled before turning to the curious eyes that studied

them. "I think this celebration is of such exception that we will honor all our birthdays from now on. Especially," he bent quickly to kiss his wife, "Lady Bronwyn's."

The crowd cheered, but he held up his hand and waited until everyone stilled. "Since I have been given this gift of respect, I think it only fitting that I return the favor in kind. Because every man here has proved his loyalty, I have been giving much thought as to what this shire needs most." He looked around the room, his gaze touching every member of the assembly. "Next year I will bring in a teacher. I want every child who lives on my land to receive an education."

Every pair of eyes stared at him as though he had just announced the end of the world. Wilford stepped forth, and removed his hat. "My lord, did you just say you wanted every child on your demesne educated?" he asked.

"Oui, you heard right. You have my word that every child will have an education."

"My lord, do you mean to educate the girls?" Braden asked, voicing the men's concern.

Christophe's features sobered. "I know it is an unfamiliar concept to educate our women."

The men nodded their heads, while the women stood still, their features a curious mix of anxiety and hope.

"But," Christophe said, pointing to his wife, "Lady Bronwyn is educated. Has she not worked for the betterment of our demesne?"

The men murmured agreement, but one ventured, "Aye, my lord, no one can deny the lady's heart, but she is so willful."

Christophe hid a smile as Bronwyn glared at the man. "Indeed she is, but I would wager Lady Bronwyn has always been so. Her education has not changed her."

"True," Wilford agreed. "As a child she was the stubbornest girl in the shire."

Christophe chuckled, enjoying the jest, then he slowly walked around the room. "You fathers have an opportunity to change your children's lives for the better. Education is knowledge. Knowledge is power. Look to your rulers—are they not all educated?'' He paused to let them digest his words, then added, ''You will reap the benefit of their success. What say you?''

Bronwyn held her breath as his brilliant argument washed over the crowd.

Wilford suddenly let out a loud whoop of approval. His voice startled the others into action and the crowd raised their voice in a deafening ovation. The men rushed forward to pump their lord's hand, or thump him on the back in gratitude as the women curtsied. The wounds of the occupation had healed. Tonight they were truly the people of Castle Montgomery. Tears welled up in Bronwyn's eyes as she gazed at her husband, modestly accepting the assembly's appreciation. Her throat tightened and she knew she would cry. She ran from the room before she disgraced herself in front of everyone. Once in the kitchen she wiped her eyes, humbled by his generosity. The cheers of approval carried into her hiding place.

''What are you doing in here?'' Christophe asked her a few minutes later.

She turned away, unwilling to let him see her eyes.

He walked over and turned her toward him. ''Are you happy again?'' he asked, teasing her about her tears.

''Nay, my lord, I am ecstatic. I love you. Not because you are a powerful warlord, and not because you are the most handsome man in all Christendom, but because of your generous heart. You have given my people, along with yours, new hope.''

He smiled and took her into his arms. When his lips touched hers, the steamy warmth in the kitchen paled in comparison to the heat that they generated. She clung to him, giving a sensuous response that left nothing to the imagination. Her tongue darted in and out of his mouth as she pressed up against him. He groaned as he deepened the kiss. Her hands slipped over his shoulders and down his back to clasp his buttocks, pulling him even tighter against her. Waves of need and wanting washed over her. Her lips moved over his, tasting, touching, tantalizing.

Christophe pulled away from her and rested his head against hers. ''Someone is coming,'' he gasped.

She blushed as Cordelia walked into the kitchen and caught

them in an embrace. "Your pardon," she said, clearly flustered. "I . . . I came to fetch the wine."

"I will bring it." She barely recognized her husky voice as she dismissed the servant, then reached for the bowl she had prepared.

Christophe touched her arm as he drew a deep breath. "Give me a minute."

A warmth grew within her; he was affected by their kiss.

A few moments later she carried out her wine mixture. To her pleasure, not only the women, but the men tried it.

"My, what a wonderful taste, Daughter," Hayden said. Several soldiers nodded their heads in agreement.

She smiled at the praise. "Be warned, it is a potent drink."

" 'Tis wonderful," Nesta said, pouring herself and Wilford another chalice.

Bronwyn shook her head. "They will be sotted before too long. I must caution them."

"You already have. Leave be. Let them enjoy," Christophe advised. "They have earned a night of relaxing."

"Aye, they have. And you, my lord?"

"Indeed I have." He carefully surveyed the room, then winked at her. "I think no one would miss our departure."

She blushed, remembering their kiss in the kitchen, "Aye, I am ready."

Clasping hands, they turned to leave at the same time that Nicolas and Fiona joined them.

"By your leave, my wife is extremely tired," Christophe said. "You will see to the festivities in my absence."

Nicolas grinned at the sight of Bronwyn's flushed face. "I think you must stay since the party is in your honor."

Christophe glared at Nicolas, but Bronwyn touched her husband's arm. "He is right, we must now stay to the end."

The merriment and drinking did indeed continue well into the late hours. It was after the witching hour when they made their escape. "I am glad you enjoyed the party." He had never seemed so relaxed and happy.

"Where did you ever come up with the idea for this celebration?" he asked, speculation and wonder shining in his eyes.

She could not tell him that where she came from it was common to observe birthdays, so she smiled and said, "I needed a way to show you how much I appreciate you."

"But the cake, the games—I am curious, how did you decide on them?"

A coy smile curved her mouth as she stepped closer to disarm his suspicions. "You are not the only innovative one in this castle, my lord. I also have ideas. And I think this one happens to be exceptional."

His puzzled expression changed to chagrin as he pulled her into his embrace. "I know you are indeed a rare and special woman. Never doubt that I think otherwise. Together we are unbeatable."

She loved the feel of his arms wrapped around her, and leaned into his body. "I am truly glad you came to our land, although I will admit that was not always the case."

He cradled her tighter, holding her closer to his heart. "We have put the past to rest. Although we did not start off on the right path, I believe we are traveling it together now."

"Are we?" she asked, daring to hope.

"*Oui.*" He brushed her lips with his. "The sweetest victory, my lady, is the one hard won."

The kiss he bent to give her was both sweet and hot, pure and sensual. When he pulled away, her legs were trembling. "I have something for you. Close your eyes," he breathed. He left her for a few minutes, admonishing her not to peek. When he returned he placed a long, slender package in her hands.

"What is this?" she asked.

"Open it and find out."

"But it is not my birthday."

"Neither is it mine," he chuckled, then pointed to the gift. "A man does not need a reason to give his wife a present."

Tears formed in her eyes. "I also have another present for you."

He covered her hands with his. "Open your gift first, then you can give me mine."

She opened the long narrow package to find a fine small

sword with jewels gracing its hilt. Her brow furrowed. "A sword? Do you expect me to do battle?"

"Hardly, Wife." He grinned at the image of her in battle dress. "Since you are a descendant of King Arthur, I thought it only appropriate you have a miniature version of Arthur's sword to hand down to our son when you tell him the legend. From all accounts your loyal subjects have given me, this is a close match to the Excalibur."

"You know I am with child?" she gasped.

He nodded. "When were you going to tell me?"

"I was waiting for the right moment." She raised her eyes to his, and fresh tears filled her vision. "That was my surprise. I wanted it to be special."

"It is."

"Nay, I had it all planned."

Several large teardrops fell down her cheeks. He wiped them away. "I am overjoyed, my love. Do not cry, you can surprise me the next pregnancy."

She wiped at her tears, but they continued to fall. "I was going to tell you tonight. However did you guess?"

He took hold of her shoulders. "I would have to be blind not to. Your loss of appetite, followed by your dizzy spells."

"But I was not even sure until this month. Are you happy about becoming a father?" she asked cautiously.

He wiped her tears away and pulled her into his arms. "I am glad." He kissed her long and tenderly. "So very glad."

His joy filled her with the greatest happiness she had ever known. When the kiss ended she placed a finger to his lips. "It could be a girl. Will you still be happy?"

"Oui, boy or girl, I will love *our* child."

He tipped her chin up. "You are the only woman I know who looks radiant when she cries," he teased.

Her heart overflowed with love and joy. She wasn't about to argue with him over her appearance. For once she agreed that he was absolutely right. Tears and all, she felt beautiful, and she wrapped her arms around his neck and pulled him to her.

She belonged in his arms. Home, she realized, meant Christophe, not a place. She wished for nothing else. Even thoughts of her own time troubled her no longer. She had found her happiness.

Chapter Twenty-three

Only red embers glowed in the hearth when Christophe awoke. Dawn's light glimmered just below the horizon as he quickly left his bed and built up the fire to chase off the chill. Shivering, he slipped back into bed and wrapped his arms around Bronwyn, cherishing her closeness. In a little while he would have to leave her.

Her soft, sweet scent filled his senses. As he drew her closer, her silken blond hair covered his embrace, flowing down her back and over her shoulders like a wild river of molten gold. He didn't want to leave her. The memories of all their heartaches and happiness fluttered through his thoughts, yet only the loving images lingered in his mind. It had only taken two lifetimes to reach heaven. He loved her, wholly, completely, body and soul.

She stirred in his arms and he kissed her forehead softly, relishing and savoring his contented bliss. He dreaded the daybreak, when he would have to tell her of his departure.

Soft, muted colors of pink and gray sliced through the dawn sky, chasing the night away. Ever so slowly, sunlight lit the heavens above as it warmed the earth below.

A soft moan escaped Bronwyn as she turned in her sleep.

The moment she nestled her bottom into his thighs his body hungered for her as strongly as his lungs craved air. An ache grew in his loins, but there wasn't time to love her as he needed to, or as she deserved.

"Bronwyn," he whispered, trying to gently awaken her.

"Hmmm," she murmured.

"I have something to tell you."

"Can it wait?" she yawned. "I am so tired."

"If you fall back asleep, the next time you awake I will be gone," he told her, nibbling on the tender skin of her neck.

With her eyes closed she stretched, sliding her legs down against his. "I will see you tonight," she reasoned, before snuggling back to him for warmth.

He cleared his throat, fighting the temptation to take her into his arms. *"Non, tonight I will be in London."*

Her whole body tensed as if suddenly coming awake. "London?" She turned slowly. "I must be more tired than I thought. I could have sworn I heard you say London?"

He took hold of her shoulders. "I have been summoned by Lord Odo."

She stared at him, as though she didn't understand. "London?"

"Oui."

Suddenly excitement lit her features. "Oh, my, I have so much to do for a trip like this." She started to laugh, then looking at his serious expression, she sobered. "You are planning on traveling there without me?"

"Oui."

Her eyes widened, then she swiftly looked away. "I see."

Her disappointment wounded him. Court was the pinnacle of anyone's dream. All the Norman lords and ladies gathered there. "Bronwyn."

When she refused to meet his gaze, he clasped her shoulder and firmly turned her back. "Bronwyn, why do you think I am leaving you behind?"

Her eyes narrowed as she lifted her chin. "I would imagine you do not want all your friends to see your Welsh-born wife."

His lips thinned. "I am not taking you because the journey will be too harsh for you and our child."

An instant blush covered her soft cheeks. "Oh," she said, her gaze searching his. "It really is for my safety that you are leaving me behind?"

He had to smile at her uncertainty. *"Oui,* you are too precious to endanger on such a long march."

She sighed. "Forgive my foolishness, Christophe. I feared you wanted to keep me hidden from your friends at court."

"You are partly right, my dear. Your condition aside, I do want you to stay in Wales." When she started to interrupt he placed a finger to her lips. "But not because I am ashamed of you. I want to keep you safely tucked away from the debauchery at court. You are my own private treasure."

Her eyes glistened with unshed tears.

"Let me guess, you are happy," he teased, his smile loving.

"Extremely," she breathed, pulling him into her embrace and soft, waiting lips.

He kissed her back, tasting the sweetest nectar this side of heaven. Then reluctantly he peeled her arms from around his neck.

At her pout he kissed her forehead. "If I linger in your lovely arms I will find it impossible to leave."

A smile of pure delight creased her love-kissed lips. "I am glad you find it difficult to leave me, but someday, warrior, I vow you will find it impossible."

He chuckled at her words, but when he looked into her eyes he swallowed, his throat suddenly dry. A siren's sultry expression glowed from within her bright amber eyes. Did she doubt her allure? God, all he wanted to do was pull her into his embrace and make love to her all over again. Last night they had exhausted each other in a most rewarding way.

Forcing the tempting thoughts aside, he rose from bed and dressed. He heard her rise, her soft little steps that swept the floor as she approached from behind. "Guess who?" she murmured, wrapping her arms around his waist.

"I cannot dress with you hanging onto me," he grumbled.

"I know," she whispered, her voice a throaty purr as she nuzzled and kissed his back.

God, how he cherished her. Pulling her to face him, he stared at the love shining clearly in her eyes. He had come full circle. A man who had found the meaning of life in the love of a woman.

Though blue painted the sky overhead, and the sun shone bright, the day was bitter cold. Bronwyn stood on the steps, huddled in her mantle, watching Christophe and his Norman and Welsh regiment march through the gates. "Godspeed," she whispered.

"I wish they would take us with them," Fiona said, her gaze forlorn as it lingered on her husband's retreating back.

Feeling guilty because she knew it was her pregnancy that stopped Christophe, she turned to her sister. "I think they want to, but the journey is too dangerous."

"You are both lucky women," Hayden said.

Bronwyn turned to her father, and noticed his frown. "What concerns you, Father?"

"A castle is always vulnerable when the lord is away."

Fiona shook her head. "Nicolas assured me, all is well."

Bronwyn agreed. "Father, we are safe. Look around you." She pointed to the high battlements and the guards manning the stations.

"Even though we are behind stone walls, I would be more assured if Lord Christophe was in attendance."

Knowing her father's stubborn nature, she did not argue the point, but instead she tried another tack. Her face brightened. "Then we will have to be prepared. All of us will have to do our part."

Hayden nodded. "I will see the captain of the guard and offer my services."

Bronwyn nudged Fiona, urging her to speak. Suddenly understanding shone in Fiona's eyes, and she looked toward the wall. "The women can help. We can carry more vats of oil and water to the wall. Being shorthanded, the men will need help."

Hayden smiled. "I will see to organizing a night watch so the men can take their rest." He started to march off toward the battlements, until he realized he was alone. "Come, we have work to do," he said, waving his daughters forward. "We must find Michau."

Bronwyn linked her arm through Fiona's. "Father is determined," she whispered.

Her sister nodded as they followed Hayden up the stairs, across the battlements, toward Christophe's captain of the guards.

Michau listened as he stood with his hands on his hips, his legs braced. A big bear of a man, he shook his head when he heard all their plans. "Do you not think you should consult with the man left in charge before you decide to take matters into your own hands?"

Hayden and Fiona looked at the Norman with great hesitancy, but Bronwyn had seen Michau's half-smile and she chuckled. " 'Twould not matter, Michau. We have made up our mind to help you. If you do not give us your blessing, why, we will just do it anyway."

He grinned. "Then I suppose I best give you my blessing."

"Indeed, that was my very thought. I have always told Christophe you were an intelligent man."

"Did you, my lady? Did you also speak to him about your plan?"

Her face blushed. "Nay, but I am sure he would see the wisdom of it, were he here."

Michau raised a brow, his expression skeptical. "Are you?"

She saw the humor and again laughed. "I am so glad he left you in charge."

"My lady, because I do not scream at you does not mean I agree." His voice was low, but carried authority in each softly spoken word. "You, along with everyone here, will follow my orders. Is that understood?"

She nodded, knowing she had just been given a lesson in deportment. "Thank you, Michau." She curtsied, so those Welshmen looking would see her respect.

Michau smiled when she rose and extended his arm. "And now, my lady, if I may escort you inside."

Rhett surveyed the castle defenses. Though he had barely enough men to storm the castle, he had a better plan. The person he needed was safely inside. He would lure her out. Once in his grasp, those within would do anything to keep her safe.

He laughed at the simplicity of his scheme. Nothing would deter him now from his dream. He looked with distaste at Dewi and Matrona. Unlike his sister, who was now groomed well, the ragged boy's threadbare, dirty clothes hung loosely on his gaunt body, and his eyes held a haunted expression.

He grabbed the boy. "Dewi, you will go to the gates and tell the mistress that you need a healer. Your mother is in a bad way birthing her child and has sent you for help."

Dewi looked to the great castle, then back again. "Do you think she will come?"

"Aye, she will come."

Matrona stepped forward. "My lord, she will not come alone."

Rhett's eyes narrowed at the girl. "Hold your tongue, or I will make you wish you had." Then he turned toward the boy. "Bring Lady Bronwyn to the place where we made camp last night. Dewi, you do know that your sister will die if you fail to convince the lady to come."

Dewi's face paled as he glanced at his sister, then quickly bobbed his head.

"Good. See to your job, boy. I will be waiting for you. Do not disappoint me."

When the lad scurried off, Rhett mounted his horse, and motioned for his men to follow.

They had an appointment with destiny.

"What brings you here, boy?" Michau asked, leaning over the castle wall.

''Please, you must let me in. I must see the healer. I b-b-beg of thee, my ma is ailing. I fear she will die if I fail to b-b-bring the healer.''

''Send for Lady Bronwyn,'' Michau ordered his aide, then turned to the gatekeeper. ''Let the boy in.'' Michau ran down the fortress stairs to greet the boy.

The moment the gates opened he pulled the youngster in by the scruff of his tunic. ''Now, what is the matter with your mother?''

''She is b-b-birthing a b-b-babe,'' he stuttered. ''B-b-but something is wrong. She sent me to find a healer, and if ma needed anyone, then there's trouble for sure.''

Michau looked up to discover Lady Bronwyn had joined them, determination in her eyes. ''I cannot let you go.''

''I must if his mother is ailing. She could die in childbirth.''

''But it could be a trap. I do not recognize the boy nor does any Welshman on the wall.''

'' 'Tis b-b-because I am not from around here. We were traveling to the north to join my father. B-b-but mother started b-b-birthing. Please, if you are not going to help me, then let me return. My mother is alone and in a b-b-bad way.'' He pulled against the Norman's hold and Bronwyn nodded to release the lad.

''I will go with you.'' She laid her hand on the boy's shoulder.

''*Non,* Lady Bronwyn. I will not permit it.''

She lifted her chin. ''You had best decide what soldier you wish to send with me, for I am going.''

Michau shook his head at her determination.

She stood toe-to-toe with Michau. ''I do not dispute your authority, but if it were not for me, you would lie in yon grave.''

He sighed. ''Very well, but you will take two Welshmen. I wish I could send more, but I dare not leave the fortress unprotected.''

''Thank you,'' she whispered, relieved. Then she turned to the boy. ''I will be just a minute. Wait here while I fetch my healing tray.''

Bronwyn's mind worked as she looked for her medicines. How could anyone have a child without proper care? For a

moment, her thoughts strayed to her condition, then she blocked
them out of her mind. The poor woman needed her. She prayed
as she grabbed what she needed and rushed down the stairs
that she would be in time.

Michau met her. "I have left orders that under no circum-
stance is anyone allowed to leave the castle. Should this be a
trap we are on our own."

"You are coming with me?"

"*Oui,* I do not want to be here to face the warlord when he
returns and finds out you are not where you should be."

She chuckled. "And here I thought you were seeking my
company."

"I am afraid the answer is simple," Michau said. "I prefer
your ire to the warlord's wrath."

"I am flattered, I think."

" 'Tis a compliment," Michau insisted.

She chuckled. "Then shall we go?"

"May God be with us," Michau muttered.

Oblivious to her three-man escort, Bronwyn ran along the
path with the boy. Michau kept pulling back on her arm. "My
lady, please exercise caution, if not for yourself, then for me."

She sighed, but slowed down to a fast walk. She feared for
the pregnant woman. Even though she knew Michau was right
to be suspicious, anyone could see that the boy was truly afraid.
They walked through the fields and beyond the village.

"How far is it, boy?" Michau demanded, stopping to survey
the countryside.

"We should have found her b-b-by now," he said, fearfully
looking around. "I did not think I had traveled this far."

She heard his concern and put her arm around the boy. "We
will find her."

Michau approached and handed her a bag of water. "Refresh
yourself, my lady." He looked back down the trail. "I do not
like the looks of this. Stay here. I will return presently." He
turned and ordered one of the Welshmen to follow him. The
other guard took his stance by her.

While she took a drink and caught her breath, Michau wandered off. The boy fidgeted as she handed him the water bag.

She covered his hands. "Do not fret, we will be there shortly." She walked over to the edge of the clearing, wondering where in heaven's name Michau had disappeared. Suddenly she felt a tinge of apprehension, and wished she had not left Fang behind.

Tempted to call Michau back, she stopped and reconsidered as a sixth sense came over her. The hairs on her arm raised and she turned to warn the boy, but his face was white.

"Forgive me, my lady," he beseeched her.

Terror gripped Bronwyn as she turned to see what had captured the boy's attention. The leafless bushes rustled and parted, and she mentally cringed as Rhett's ugly scowl appeared through the dark branches.

"My lady, how good of you to join us." His sarcastic taunt mocked her.

She turned to flee, but Welsh rebels surrounded the small clearing. More ragged peasants than true soldiers, they looked scruffy and unkempt, hollow and emaciated. When her guard drew his sword, an enemy soldier shot an arrow through his chest.

Her heart lodged in her throat as she saw her soldier slump to his knees and fall backward. She ran toward the man, but his already lifeless eyes stared back at her. She jumped back, horrified, and looked around at the men who encircled the area. Every avenue was cut off. Her gaze centered on the boy and she moved toward him.

"Be quiet about our escort," she whispered, then drew her hand back for show and feigned slapping the lad across the face.

She turned and faced Rhett. Tilting her chin in defiance, she looked at him, her gaze filled with loathing.

Rhett clapped his hands. "You are a very good performer."

Her eyes widened at his remark and her courage faltered when Lucien appeared through the bushes, wiping his bloody knife clean on his tights.

Her heart drummed louder within her ears as she looked from Lucien's drunken grin, to Rhett's twisted smile.

"Alas, my lady," Rhett mocked as he bowed low, "your escort is already dead, not pursuing help."

Grief filled her. No! Not Michau, and, oh, God, her poor countryman. Her chest constricted and she glared at the hateful man. "May God have mercy on your demented soul. I shall never forgive you, nor will my husband when he avenges these deaths."

Rhett approached her and drew back his arm. His harsh blow sent stars spinning in her head. She heard the boy cry out and then another child's voice, higher, stronger, protested as darkness engulfed her. Her last thought was of Christophe and of the baby they had made.

Chapter Twenty-four

After a hard ride Christophe and Nicolas arrived in London late that night, and sought an audience with Lord Odo at first light. Unfortunately, there were other Normans scheduled ahead of them. While they waited they sent a message to Caradoc.

An hour later Caradoc joined them in the anteroom, where they were still waiting. "What brings you here?"

Christophe rose to grip Caradoc's hand. "The liege lord's emissary, Lord Odo, sent for us."

Caradoc's face puckered in concern. "Odd, but I heard nothing of your coming, and I have met with Lord Odo every day this week."

An eerie premonition settled over Christophe, but he shrugged it away. Though his instincts were honed, he was not going to borrow trouble.

He directed Caradoc to have a seat, then turned to his brother. "Nicolas, tell our brother-in-law the news from home."

While they talked, Christophe paced the floor, his mind turning over several disturbing thoughts. As the wait drew into early afternoon, his patience grew short. Again, an unsettling sense of foreboding descended on him, this time stronger than ever. He was about to voice his misgivings when a servant summoned them. They entered the court room to meet with William's man, who had his head buried in an official-looking document.

Christophe bowed, tamping down his irritation over the long wait and the man's preoccupation with the papers before him. "Lord Odo, we came immediately."

When Lord Odo finally looked up from his documents, he had a puzzled look on his face. "Christophe Montgomery, what are you and your brother doing in London?"

Shock and dread painfully prickled Christophe's nerves as he stepped forward and handed over the missive.

"I did not send for you." Lord Odo looked over the missive. "This is not my seal," he said, handing it back to Christophe. " 'Tis a fake."

An ominous air descended on the room as Christophe absorbed the news, and mentally turned over the possibilities. Nicolas grimaced, taking the missive from Christophe to study. When Caradoc looked at the script, his eyes widened. "I recognize the writing."

"Who?" Christophe demanded, dreading the answer.

"Rhett," Caradoc replied. His features hardened. "God's teeth, the dowry was a ploy."

Fear twisted through Christophe's insides and he slammed his fist into his palm. His lands could be under attack, his people in peril. He started to leave, but was halted by the emissary's voice.

With elbows perched on the table, Lord Odo rested his chin on his folded hands. His eyes narrowed as he leaned slightly forward. "Since it is obvious that a trap has been laid, I will send a force of two regiments with you."

The offer stunned Christophe. The man had virtually stripped him of men.

Lord Odo looked at Christophe over his steepled fingers. "I cannot allow this insurrection to go unpunished."

"Thank you." Christophe nodded, then rushed out with his brother and Caradoc.

"Rhett must be storming the castle as we speak," Caradoc said as they marched down the halls.

"Non," Christophe replied. "He did not have the men."

"Do not underestimate him," Caradoc warned. "He will breach your defenses. He is very good at subterfuge."

Christophe's fist clenched as he thought of how he had been duped. "Nicolas, we leave at once. If we ride all night we will be home by early morning."

When Nicolas left to muster the men, Caradoc grabbed Christophe's arm. "I am coming with you. Ariana can be ready in an hour."

Christophe pulled free. *"Non,* your wife could never stand the journey at the pace we will set."

Caradoc blocked Christophe's way, his stance rigid. "She will not complain. She is Welsh and will keep up."

"I warn you, Caradoc. I can make no allowances for her." Christophe leveled him with an icy glare. "If you must travel with your wife, then follow later." He turned, but again Caradoc seized his arm. Christophe rounded on the man ready to take him to task for wasting time, but upon seeing Caradoc's tortured expression he stopped himself.

"Christophe, have a care. 'Tis my family that is in danger."

He clasped Caradoc's shoulders, understanding the man's pain. "I will keep them safe."

Caradoc nodded. "I will join you soon."

Christophe heard Caradoc's determination and knew he meant every word.

All the way through the castle, he wondered about his kingdom. Preoccupied with his thoughts, he ignored lords and ladies who hailed him, not allowing anyone to impede his progress. Christophe marched out the door, heading down the steps to the courtyard. Abruptly an image of his wife entered his thoughts. He could not get her from his mind. An icy fear stole over him. Bronwyn needed him.

"We must hurry," he said to his brother as he took the reins of his horse.

"We will be home by dawn," Nicolas vowed.

Christophe's men and Lord Odo's regiment had been called to arms. Fresh horses were provided and they set off at an alarming rate. No one spoke of what awaited them.

* * *

Christophe couldn't believe he had failed to recognize Rhett's agenda. The thought that others would suffer for his mistake ate at him. The English countryside fell away beneath the pounding hooves of their horses as they galloped toward Wales. As a full moon rose overhead, he prayed his castle was not under attack. In the wee hours of the morning he wished Caradoc had accompanied them, for he wanted his counsel where Rhett was concerned.

Light was just streaking across the sky when Castle Montgomery came into view. He carefully scanned the area, searching every detail for discrepancies, from the castle battlements to the smallest knoll in the terrain. All was as it should be, and he relaxed. Breathing easily for the first time in hours, he headed his men home.

Christophe rode through the gates and saluted the morning sentries who walked the battlements. After stabling his horse, he quickly entered the fortress keep. The castle occupants were still sleeping when Christophe sent for the duty officer and wondered were Michau was.

Smothering a yawn, Hayden walked down the stairs and joined them.

Wilford, the duty guard, entered the great room and bowed before the lord.

"Has there been any sign of Lucien or Rhett?" Christophe asked.

"Nay, my lord, all has been quiet."

Nicolas grinned as he clasped Christophe's shoulder in mock anger. "Our hard ride was for naught."

Christophe softly chuckled and poured two chalices of ale, handing one to Nicolas. " 'Tis good to be home," he said, glancing toward the bedchamber with anticipation. He downed half his chalice, then turned back to Wilford. "If there is nothing else to report, I am going to retire."

"My lord," Wilford said hesitantly, "Lady Bronwyn and Michau have not yet returned."

Hayden frowned. "They are still not back?"

The hairs on the back of Christophe's neck rose. "Where are they?"

"The lady Bronwyn was summoned yesterday to treat a woman who needed a midwife."

"Yesterday?" Christophe slammed his chalice down. "Who was this woman?"

Wilford shrugged his shoulders. "I do not know, my lord. Her son came to the castle begging for a healer. Michau thought they were travelers passing through the shire and forbid Lady Bronwyn to go."

Christophe's jaw clenched. "Then, why is my wife not here?"

Wilford looked sheepish, his gaze slanted to the floor.

"God's teeth," Christophe swore, knowing his wife's stubbornness.

"Why did you let her go?" he asked Hayden.

Deep furrows appeared over Hayden's brows. "I do not understand your concern. Bronwyn has tended pregnant women before."

Before Christophe could explain, Nicolas stepped forward. "Rhett forged our summons to London."

"Dear God," Hayden said, his face ashen as he gripped a chair. "Are you sure?"

Nicolas nodded and helped ease Hayden into the chair.

Christophe paced back and forth as he tried to work out in his mind what had happened. "How long have they been gone?" he asked Wilford.

"Since last eventide."

Hayden leaned forward. "She could still be with the pregnant woman," he ventured hopefully.

"I hope and pray she is," Christophe replied, then turned to Wilford. "Send out the castle guards to search for Bronwyn."

"Aye, my lord."

But before Wilford could leave, Christophe called out, "See you assign a man to watch the wicca."

Several castle occupants began to stir, and would soon be filing into the great room for the morning meal. Christophe looked around for the wicca, and when he did not spy her, he ordered a meeting for later. He had to decide what information to leak to Rhett.

After the exhausted regiments had their breakfast, they retired. Christophe made several battle plans, before he also retired to his room. He snatched only a few hours' sleep before he awoke with a start. His dreams were filled with troubling images. He stared up at the ceiling, unable to relax. Every moment that passed reminded him of his beloved. He had so much to tell her. So damn much.

The morning patrol found no trace of the lady. The news hung like a death knell over the castle. At the midday meal a missive arrived, confirming Christophe's suspicions.

"Dear God, is Rhett out of his mind?" Nicolas asked.

Fiona's mouth dropped open as she stared at the note over her father's shoulder. "Where does he think we will raise that sum?"

Gaining everyone's attention, Christophe turned to face his father-in-law. "One thing is lucky: Rhett specifically instructs that Caradoc deliver the money."

"How will that aid us?" Hayden asked.

Christophe looked around the room, studying every face until he spotted the wicca, who had come to the castle for her allotment of food. He cleared his throat. "Because Rhett will have to keep Bronwyn alive at least a week," he said, knowing Caradoc was already on his way.

Light dawned in the old man's eyes. "Aye, it will take several days for Caradoc to receive a message and at least that many to journey home," he said loudly.

Christophe smiled at the old man's astuteness. *"Oui,"* he said, thinking they had some time to prepare. Christophe looked around the room again and seeing the wicca had moved to huddle by the fire, he leaned forward. "Let us adjourn to my chamber."

Once out of earshot of the wicca, he slammed his door shut and dropped the bar. "Once she moves, we can." Christophe paced across the room, chafing at the wait. "Now, we have to raise the ransom," he said to Nicolas and Hayden.

"If we are going to rescue her, why are you paying the ransom?" Nicolas asked.

"When Caradoc arrives in the rebels' camp he must have something to hand over to Rhett in order to allay any suspicion that a rescue attempt is at hand," Christophe said as he stripped off his heavy gold signet ring, then touched his wedding band. Remembering how he had admonished Bronwyn not to remove hers, he hesitated briefly, before pulling it off. He would get it back, he told himself. Besides, it was necessary to save Bronwyn's life. He walked over to his chest and pulled out several gold chains. He hefted the pile of gold, testing their weight. He reached in and lifted the topaz wedding necklace from his chest, mentally calculating its worth. Its value alone would be half the amount demanded. He turned to his brother. Without a word Nicolas removed his family ring and handed it to Christophe. Hayden surprised Christophe by undoing his gold chain and removing his rings to add to the pile.

"That should be enough." Christophe wrapped the jewelry up in a leather bag.

The fact that Caradoc was on his way boded well. Christophe outlined his strategy. Once they learned Rhett's whereabouts from the wicca, Christophe planned to surround the rebels' camp. When his brother-in-law walked into the camp with the ransom, Christophe would have his men hidden and ready to attack. The fear that they might be too late entered his thoughts, but he refused to consider it. Timing was crucial. Once Caradoc entered the camp, the need for a hostage would be nonexistent.

A sudden knock on the door interrupted their discussion. Christophe lifted the bar and moved aside to allow Wilford to enter.

His face wore a grave expression. "My lord, Michau has returned. The men carried him into the great room."

Christophe ran out of the room, followed by the others. His heart raced. Michau would have news of Bronwyn. He took the steps two at a time, but in the great room his elation turned to despair. The sight that greeted him almost made him retch.

Michau lay blood soaked on a pallet in the middle of the room. Fiona knelt beside him, trying to stem the crimson flow, as soldiers hovered around their fallen comrade. Michau's face was ashen in color and his breathing shallow. He raised his arm, and rasped, "My lord."

Christophe rushed to his side, taking the blood-soaked hand in his. Up close he could see that Michau's side had been pierced with a lance. "They left me for dead."

"Hayden," Christophe bellowed. "Find a healer to help Fiona." He turned back to the injured soldier. "Rest," he urged.

"Non," Michau sputtered, gripping Christophe's hand harder. "I learned much before they captured Lady Bronwyn, and Lucien found me." He gasped for air, almost losing consciousness as the color drained from his face.

Nicolas poured him a large tankard of ale, and Christophe helped support the soldier so he could take a drink.

"They want Caradoc, they need him."

"I know. Michau, how many rebels are there?"

He choked again and reached for the ale, swallowing another mouthful. " 'Twas a small party, my lord, numbering only about twenty. They are a rough bunch. From the cut of their clothes and the look of them, they are desperate men." He grasped Christophe's hand. "But I heard more are on the way."

"What about my wife?" The question Christophe most feared asking, yet needed answered.

Michau's eyelids drifted shut. "My lady was brave," he whispered. "She stood up to him. She even tried to protect me." His eyes opened and he stared at Christophe with fire in his gaze. "As I lay bleeding in the bushes, that knave smote her a mighty blow that rendered her unconscious."

Christophe's stomach churned. "Where are they?" he asked as Nesta edged her way in between them.

Michau sucked in a deep breath as his tunic was gently pulled back. "I believe they are taking her to the caves, but I do not know which one."

"Thank you." Christophe rested his hand on Michau's shoulder, then felt the muscles tense beneath his fingers.

Suddenly Michau's eyes widened and he pointed straight at Matrona. "Tell the lord, girl. Tell him who betrayed us."

Christophe's heart sank as he tried to hush Michau. His plan depended on secrecy. His heart racing, he quickly scanned the room. Thankfully, the wicca had already left.

He turned back to Michau to question him, but his eyes were closed. He had slipped into unconsciousness. Nesta and Fiona shooed him away as they tended to Michau.

Christophe began to leave the room when he noticed that Matrona was crying. When she saw his gaze on her she backed away from him fearfully.

"Matrona, what is wrong?"

She shifted from foot to foot as she stared at the floor. Christophe softened his voice. "Matrona, I need your help."

She only sobbed louder, and heaven help him he wanted to throttle the child, but instead drew her into his arms. "Did I not promise you that I would never let anyone harm you?"

She hiccuped and nodded.

"Then, why do you cry?"

"I am afraid." She sniffled several times, holding her apron to her face.

"Of whom?"

"The invader."

"What invader?" he asked, wondering why she still feared the Normans.

Tears filled her eyes, again. "Not ye, my lord."

"Who?" he demanded, tempering his voice.

"My lord, forgive me," she cried. "I had no choice, and neither did my brother, Dewi. He is the boy who came to the castle, begging help from the lady Bronwyn." Tears streamed down her face. "I did not want to harm Lady Bronwyn. She was so good to me."

His gut twisted as he berated himself for his foolish assumption, and accepted his error. 'Twas Matrona, not the wicca, who was Rhett's informant.

"By His wounds," Hayden cursed.

The child cringed and turned her face into Christophe's chest. He felt her little body tremble and shot Hayden a meaningful glance. "I will not harm you," he whispered as he looked down on the poor little girl, a helpless victim in a deadly game.

Matrona's shoulders shook as she clutched his tunic.

What monster would use an innocent? He took a deep breath. "Did Rhett beat you?"

She nodded, burying her face deeper in her apron. "He says if I do not do as he bids, he will kill my brother."

"Have you told Rhett that we have returned?"

"Nay." She shook her head.

"Good."

Her sobs subsided. Slowly she lifted her face and lowered the linen from her eyes. "I have not had time."

His hopes soared, and he smiled at her. "Do you know where Rhett is?"

"Nay, my lord. When I fetch firewood for the cook and need to send a message, I leave a knife stuck in a tree in yon field. Then the next day someone is there."

"Listen to me very carefully. I will protect you and rescue your brother if you do me a service."

Her eyes shone with hope as she hung on his every word.

"Do you believe me?" he asked.

She nodded her head vigorously.

"Do you want to help your brother and Lady Bronwyn?"

Again, she nodded.

"I wish you to take a message to Rhett. Can you do that?"

"Aye, my lord."

"Good, in two days time you will inform the man that we have sent for Caradoc but it will take several days for him to journey home."

"Is that all, my lord?"

"*Non.* Tell him that I am not going to raise the ransom. That I do not care if he executes the lady."

Hayden's gasp filled the air, but Christophe held up his hand to silence his protest. "But I owe it to her family to give them a chance to free her."

Her eyes were red and puffy, and she nodded in understanding.

"I have given you my word to protect you, and I will, and I will protect your brother, as well. But you must be very brave so we can rid this land of Lord Rhett's evil. Lady Bronwyn and myself both love you, and will always take care of you."

Her little arms wound around his neck before he set her on the ground and motioned for Wilford to accompany her. "Watch over Matrona."

"Are you sure you want to do this?" Nicolas asked when Matrona was out of sight.

"*Oui,* he must be convinced that I will not risk anything for the lady. Then he will not expect us to attack."

"But, Brother, he might kill her."

"*Non,* he has gone too far not to see this plan out. He needs her to draw out Caradoc."

"I hope you are right, Christophe. For you gamble with your beloved's life."

"Do not worry, Nicolas. I will either save her, or die trying."

Hayden patted his son-in-law's shoulder. "I know you love her. I ask one boon: that I may accompany you."

Christophe hated to deny the old man. Though a proven warrior, in his condition this campaign was too dangerous for him. Then he noticed the moisture in Hayden's eyes. "Of course," he said.

Hayden's head snapped up, his eyes wide with surprise. "Thank you," he whispered, simply.

"Ride out and meet Caradoc. While Caradoc returns here, I want you to take his men to the ridge and wait for my orders."

Hayden nodded.

Nicolas's frown spoke of his disapproval, but he voiced no objection.

When the men left, Christophe sat in his chair in the great room. He could not retire. Bronwyn's image crowded his thoughts, and the agony of what she must be suffering at the man's hands kept him awake. The night passed slowly, and every minute of it was torture.

* * *

Bronwyn awoke with a headache and the metallic taste of blood coating her mouth. She reached for her lips, but found her hands bound. Rhett was there staring at her with his piggish eyes. Inwardly she cringed, but she lifted her chin. "My lord, does it make you feel more powerful to tie up a woman?"

Rhett's scars darkened with anger. "If you wish to remain alive, do not test my temper."

She held up her hands and forced a sweet smile to her lips. "Is this an example of your hospitality?"

A wicked blade suddenly appeared in his hand. He moved forward, the sun glinting off the steel.

She held her breath. She should cower and apologize, but she could not bring herself to beg. Instinctively she knew that to plead with him would bring her more pain.

He laid the cold blade against her face. "Perhaps I should scar you, then you would not be so haughty."

Her stomach lurched as the icy metal pressed into her cheek. Too terrified to speak, she met his gaze.

He studied her for a seeming eternity. How she managed not to quiver beneath his cold scrutiny, she did not know. His black pitiless eyes looked directly into hers, then a hideous grin appeared, revealing discolored teeth. "I admire your courage." He removed the knife and she drew a silent sigh of relief.

"It is a good thing I appreciate beauty." He stroked the side of her face.

She closed her eyes, blocking out the lecherous gaze that devoured her curves. She swallowed down her rising bile as she felt his fingers trail down her face, passing her neck to fasten on her breast. Suddenly he pressed a kiss to her lips and squeezed her breast hard. The pain he inflicted brought tears to her eyes.

"I eagerly await our bedding, Bronwyn. That was just a taste for you to ponder in anticipation of our wedding night."

As he walked away, Bronwyn shuddered. She drew deep lungfuls of air to keep from retching.

Thoughts of escape crowded her mind. She must succeed. It was not just for herself, but her child.

No one at the castle knew she was in trouble, and there would be no rescue attempt. She had to come up with a plan. Several ideas swirled in her mind. No doubt she would get only one chance, and when it came she vowed she would be ready.

She thought longingly of Christophe and hoped he could forgive her foolishness. Michau had been right, it was a trap. Now because of her stubbornness, he and the guards were dead.

Time had played her false. She regretted so many things. Now, there might never be another moment to tell Christophe that she loved him and trusted him completely. She had been given a second chance and had wasted it. She closed her eyes and pictured his face: the smile that lit his eyes, the handsome features that thrilled her, the strong physique that never ceased to awe her. The memory gave her comfort. Christophe would not be afraid; thus, neither would she.

Chapter Twenty-five

Lucien dragged Matrona into camp by the scruff of her neck, then threw her to the ground. The girl quickly crawled away and immediately sought out Dewi, hugging him to her chest. As the children huddled together, their similar coloring and features were evident. "Brother and sister," Bronwyn whispered, recognizing the family resemblance.

A memory from her abduction surfaced of another child's voice crying out just as she passed out. Matrona had been there. Bronwyn's eyes widened. Oh, my God, Matrona was the informant.

"By His wounds," Rhett swore, advancing on Lucien. "You were supposed to receive the message, not bring the messenger here."

Lucien belched and pointed to the child. "I thought you should hear her report," he said belligerently, then staggered off.

Rhett shook his head in disgust and followed after the drunken soldier. His loud, angry reprimand echoed throughout the camp.

Matrona's little face turned back and forth, scanning the camp, until her gaze fastened upon Bronwyn. The child's soulful eyes reminded Bronwyn of a whipped puppy, filled with shame and sadness and silently begging for forgiveness. Matrona's pain reached out to Bronwyn before the child turned to Rhett's approach.

"What have you found out?"

Matrona's arm tightened on her brother, drawing him protectively closer to her side. Bronwyn's heart sank at Rhett's exploitation of these children.

"The warlord does not care what you do to the lady."

Bronwyn gasped and looked away, unable to stand Rhett's gloating. But deep in her heart she refused to believe it. Christophe was not a man to give up, not on life, not on her. He was planning something. She had to believe in him.

Matrona's voice floated to her through a sea of pain. "Caradoc Llangandfan has been summoned, and is expected tomorrow evening. Christophe Montgomery will allow her family to ransom her if they choose, but he does not desire her return."

Rhett roared with laughter. He marched across the compound and pulled Bronwyn to her feet. Slipping the knife through her bounds, he freed her hands and held her to his chest. "You will marry me, or die."

She strained away from him, trying to wedge a space between them. "How can I marry you, I am not free."

"You will be." A snarl appeared on his twisted face as he drew her closer, smashing her lips against his.

His beard scratched her face as his teeth ground into her tender flesh, demanding an entry she refused. Bile rose in her throat and she gagged.

He released her with a curse. " 'Tis the image of your husband that stands in our way. I will not only kill him in the flesh but also in your memory."

She wiped her mouth and turned away from his foul breath.

He spun her around and backhanded her so hard she fell into the pile of weapons. Pain knifed into her upper arm where a lance grazed her. Immediately her hand pressed the injured area. Blood seeped from the cut and she gripped the wound harder trying to stem the flow. She rolled over and struggled from the pile, her arm aching and her face aflame.

He drew his hand back. When she flinched, he laughed. "I will not mar that face. You will learn in time who is your master."

"I will never honor you."

"You are a fool. When I dispose of your husband and force your brother to join with me, all of Wales will unite under our banner."

She looked away. Caradoc would never meet with this villain, and Christophe would kill the bastard.

The blood slipped through the creases of her fingers, staining her hands red, and Matrona rushed over, her brother in tow. "Dewi, help me bind Lady Bronwyn's injury."

Bronwyn sat down to allow Matrona to attend her. Dewi's eyes grew huge and he began to tremble. "It is all right," she soothed to ease the child's fright.

Her sleeve rolled back, she felt a burning in the wound and looked down to see Matrona pouring wine over her cut and reaching for some bandages.

" 'Tis not that bad." Rhett shook his head, shooting a scornful look at both her and the child. He waited until the wound was bound, then withdrew a missive from his tunic and handed it to Matrona. "You will take the ransom instructions to Christophe Montgomery and say someone handed it to you," he said before he went to the campfire and took his meal. He offered Bronwyn none, and neither did his men.

She was cold, tired, hungry, and wounded. And oh so lonely. How she wished Christophe was here. Even when they were at odds, she knew he would keep her from harm.

"I wish I could do more to help you." Matrona's huge blue eyes were filled with sadness. "You need a protector, my lady." Matrona made a sling out of some rags, then leaned close and whispered, "Courage, my lady, all is not lost." She straightened and looked frightened for relaying her confidence as she glanced about. But when no one paid her any notice, she offered a weak smile, then hugged her brother goodbye before leaving the camp.

Tears misted Bronwyn's eyes and she blinked them away. She couldn't afford to feel sorry for herself. If she was to get out of this mess, then she would need to keep her wits about her.

All day she watched her enemy. Their routine was committed to memory. She knew when they took their turns at sentry and how long they stood duty. Every detail was noted and filed away. She would not be a victim.

Her thoughts flitted to her beloved and she buried them. She had to focus on the reality at hand. She folded a strip of her undergarment and made another crude binding. Keeping the cloth pressed tight against her arm, she wound another layer over the soaked dressing. Pain knifed through her as she knotted the bandage.

She had never realized how she had taken her modern conveniences for granted. But a hospital and a SWAT team would be welcomed now.

Laughter suddenly bubbled up inside her. What would this bully think faced with twentieth-century technology? She was a modern woman trapped in time. She had the knowledge, she just had to use her advantage to affect her own rescue.

Mentally she ran down a survival list.

No weapon.

No telephone.

No help.

No hope.

No, there was always hope. She would wait. When the right moment presented itself, she would make her move.

Christophe's heart soared at learning the location of Rhett's camp. He turned to Nicolas. "Send out twenty patrols of four and five men each." He pointed to the map. "Have them surround this area."

"Thank God," Fiona whispered as she sank into a chair.

Nicolas nodded.

"I will take the last patrol out," Christophe said, knowing he could not wait until tomorrow to see his wife. He drew a deep breath, ignoring his brother's frown.

"Christophe, we have always fought side by side. 'Tis a rash decision."

"I must be there. You would do the same."

Nicolas reluctantly agreed.

"Hopefully, Caradoc will arrive before I leave. If not, you know the plan. Do not fail me."

Rhett was unaware that Caradoc was already on his way home. Instead of tomorrow night he should arrive this evening. Rhett was in for a surprise.

When Nicolas returned from carrying out Christophe's orders, he tucked Fiona's hand in his to escort her upstairs. At the stairs Nicolas turned back to his brother. "Go to bed, Christophe. You must get some sleep before you leave. I have left word to be awakened when Caradoc arrives."

Christophe nodded, but had no intention of going to his room. "I will sleep down here," he said, bidding his brother and Fiona good night.

Exhausted, he sat in a chair and leaned his head back. When he finally closed his eyes he could see her image and hear her voice. He drew a ragged breath. If he did not rest he would be unable to rescue her, and rescue her he would.

An hour later he finally dozed off. His dreams were filled with strange images of a plane crash and a crippled girl. He could not stop the flashes of his past life, they intruded now with a vengeance. The memory of the fire engulfing them, the girl, Regan's screams, the voice of the angel, all came back, as vivid now as when they had first happened. He awoke bathed in sweat.

He took a deep breath, losing Bronwyn was worse than losing his life. The truth hit him straight in the heart. When someone means more to you than your own well-being, you can not deny your true feelings. The depth and strength of his emotions nearly paralyzed him. He had found his reason for living. God, let him keep her.

A guard was dispatched to wake the Montgomery brothers as Caradoc and Ariana rode through the gate. Caradoc dismounted before his horse had even stopped and helped his wife dismount, then hurriedly escorted her up the main steps.

Christophe rose stiffly from his chair, stretching the sleep away.

"Christophe," Caradoc hailed from the doorway as Fiona and Nicolas ran down the staircase. "Father met me on the ridge and briefed me. He has taken the men. Has anything else happened?"

Christophe waved him in. "We have learned where Rhett's camp is."

"Where?" Caradoc asked, ushering his wife into the great room as Nicolas and Fiona joined them.

"Come, I will show you on the map," Christophe said.

"Oh! Husband, you must be careful," Ariana cried.

Caradoc peeled off his wife's hands and gently pushed her toward his sister. "See to her, Fiona, and take comfort from one another."

When the ladies retired, the men sat at the table and discussed the role each would play. Caradoc raised a mug of ale to his lips, his blond brows knit together in thought.

"You will deliver the ransom at dawn," Christophe said. "Rhett is not expecting you until tomorrow night. We have our men in place. I intend to join them tonight." He drew his hand through his hair. "I cannot bear the thought of her in his clutches."

Caradoc nodded. "Aye, but Rhett will not kill her."

"Because of your name?" Nicolas asked.

"There is another reason." Caradoc looked apprehensive, but he met Christophe's gaze. "Rhett wants her as his bride. A month before you came to Wales, I promised the man he could wed her if he would join forces with me to overthrow the Normans."

Though Christophe felt sick, he forced his mind to work. "Will Rhett consider the bargain met with the payment of the ransom?"

Caradoc shook his head. "Not until you are dead."

"Then she is safe for now," Christophe said.

"Nay, she is safe as long as you live. You should stay behind."

"*Non!* I will be there. She will not wonder about my love or loyalty ever again." Christophe turned to his brother. "Remember, Nicolas, her safety first."

Nicolas threw his arm over Christophe's shoulders and escorted him to the door. "Brother, she will be fine."

Christophe nodded. He could not allow his men to see his worry. He clasped Nicolas's arm. "Take care tomorrow."

"And you," Nicolas said as he pulled away.

Christophe turned back to Caradoc. "Ride slow. Give our men time to get in place."

Caradoc nodded.

"I am relying on you to reach her once you are in Rhett's camp," Christophe said. "You must succeed."

Caradoc marched over and extended his hand. "I will not fail my sister, nor your trust in me."

Christophe tightly gripped his brother-in-law's hand. The young man's gaze never wavered. He meant business.

Rhett ate his evening meal, this time allowing Bronwyn a small portion. Afterward, Rhett handed the rope to Dewi. "Tie the bitch up."

Regret filled the child's eyes as he loosely wrapped Bronwyn's hands.

Rhett growled as he tested her binds and turned to smash the child with his fist. Not content, he drew back his fist again.

"Nay," she screamed, grabbing at Rhett's arm to stop the beating. He turned, and grabbed her by the hair, yanking her to her feet. "Do not interfere."

"Leave the child alone." She saw the blood on Dewi's nose, and knew an overwhelming rage. "I tell you now that if you harm this child again, I swear I will see you punished."

He roared with laughter. "You threaten me?"

"You have great plans," she said, mustering all her courage to present a bravado she was far from feeling. "I believe you wish to marry me."

"Not wish—will," he snapped.

Forcing a smile, she stared him directly in the eye. "Then, sir, how will you sleep? Will you need a sword in bed?"

As he stared at her, a muscle in his disfigured jaw twitched. "Give me your hands." He retied her bonds and left.

"Thank you, my lady," Dewi said as he crawled toward her.

"Just stay out of his way," she soothed.

"I will try, my lady." He had tears in his eyes as he bobbed his head, then quickly scurried off into the night.

Hours passed as she lay on her side, shivering at the outer fringe of the camp. How she ached for the warmth of the fire. Then a soft rustling sounded in the bushes behind her. She glanced over and froze. There in the shrubs an animal's eyes glowed. She imagined long vicious fangs and knew she would be ripped to shreds. Just as she was about to scream out, the animal moved. His dark silver fur came into view, and relief surged through her. Her rescue was at hand.

"Fang," she whispered as her pet crawled closer to her. She craned her neck to see who was with him. But the bushes remained still. No one was out there. Her hope of rescue died as Matrona's words echoed in her mind: "You need a protector." In her own way, Matrona had done what she could to help.

Bronwyn's heart ached as she lifted her mantle, and Fang slipped beneath the material to lie down beside her. Her throat constricted as the stark reality of her situation hit her and she huddled close to the wolf. Tears formed in Bronwyn's eyes, but she would not shed them. How could she protect her unborn child and little Dewi from Rhett's brutality? Sobs filled her soul with silent cries that wailed her anger and frustration. On the heels of her sadness a deep burning hatred followed. She would see Rhett punished.

Fang's low growl alerted her to Lucien's drunken presence as he staggered by, on his way into the bushes.

"Shhh," she soothed, "our time will come." Then she curled up close to the animal and closed her eyes, blocking out the nightmare of Rhett's abuse, while planning revenge and praying fervently for help.

Exhausted and drained, she dozed off into a fitful sleep. The sound of screeching metal and burning fumes filled her dream. She was in the plane crash, frightened and dying, but she felt Drew's arms around her. She relived every horrid moment, including the angel's eerie voice, before she finally awoke. Odd, but the lingering terror from the crash and her subsequent death did not fill her with the amount of despair she felt at being separated from Christophe.

She touched the ring he had given her. Remembering the inscription she had the farrier inscribe in order to help Regan, she repeated the words aloud. "Believe in love." She closed her eyes, remembering her past life. Regan had been alone, Bronwyn was not. "Believe in love," she whispered. Christophe will come.

Chapter Twenty-six

Christophe's party rode out of the castle when the moon was high. "God's teeth," Christophe swore, seeing the full moon. In this bright, silvery light, they would be easily spotted when they left the cover of the ridge and forest.

He prayed the earlier groups of men had found cover. If not, his men would not be in place when Caradoc arrived at Rhett's camp at dawn. At least the moonlight helped them safely navigate the terrain, which was difficult to traverse at night.

He led the small band of Normans through the fields and forest. It felt strange to have Julien, a Norman soldier, at his side instead of Nicolas.

Slowly the horses picked their way up the steep, rocky incline. Christophe joined Hayden on the ridge and was dismayed to see so many of the soldiers from the small patrols still there.

"They could not move down the open hill toward the safety of the forest, because of this blasted full moon," Hayden said.

Again Christophe looked upward and silently cursed. The moon shone like a bright beacon, mocking him with its brilliant cyclops glare. The men could only move when intermittent clouds swept across the sky. Each time, several would slip away.

The delay wore on Christophe's nerves, until, at last, only his party was left to traverse the ridge. He shook hands with Hayden.

"I will cover the flank with Nicolas. Rhett will not escape this time."

When Christophe finally reached the forest, he had to wait another twenty minutes in order to give the last patrol time to get into position. The moments dragged, endlessly testing his patience.

He knew Hayden was in place, and by morning Nicolas would join him to outflank the enemy.

Squinting, Christophe watched the shadowy figures of the Normans slipping over the night-darkened land, eventually they disappeared into the landscape. He chafed at the delay, but kept his expression schooled. This clandestine operation was worse than being in combat. It gave one too much time to think. So many thoughts rushed through his mind. He pictured Bronwyn reaching out her arms imploring him to save her. Fear shone in her eyes as she begged for her life. He could see every detail, and the image tore at his heart. He could not fail her. Nothing else mattered! He would rescue her. Yet, in the darkest corners of his intellect, fear hovered. If he failed, how could he live with himself? For the first time he knew the meaning of terror. He was vulnerable now. He understood why men had sacrificed their empires, their self-respect, their very lives, for love. He wanted nothing else than to live with her forever.

The moments passed achingly slowly, until a patch of thick heavy clouds rolled in, blanketing the moon and stars like a thick woolen coverlet. "At last," he murmured to himself, then left the cover of the forest with his small band of men. They rode across the field, heading in the opposite direction of the others. Soon he was far enough away from his men's position to change direction and circle around the valley, then head for the far side of the cliffs. Every nerve in his body screamed for action, but he forced himself to remain calm. A cool attitude was the only one that would see the day won.

Slowly they approached their cover at the far edge of the forest. Every inch of the way he had thought of his beloved. "God, give me a second chance to make things right," he entreated as he stared up at heaven. But only stormy clouds met his anxious gaze. He prayed they were not an indication of things to come.

Julien's somber features appeared more sober than usual as he approached.

"I hope all goes well today. I would not want anything to happen to Lady Bronwyn. I have no use for men who make war on women," Julien said.

Christophe nodded. "If we want to surprise the rebels, we will have to leave the horses in the valley and proceed on foot."

He left his steed tied with the other horses and gathered up his weapons. They still had several miles to cover. They needed to be on the far side of the rebels' camp when Caradoc arrived.

His breath billowed out like a cloud in the cold night air as he straightened, every muscle tense and alert. "Tell the men not another word until they see my signal."

Julien nodded, then quietly passed the word. Only six men were in his party. Rhett could have from ten to a hundred men. The soldier who had gone ahead could not be sure of the numbers.

Still, whether he faced five or fifty warriors made little difference to Christophe. He would fight his way through hell to reach Bronwyn.

At that moment he knew, as surely as if he had been struck by lightning, that he would die for her. A soft voice sounded in his head: *You already have.* In a heartbeat his thoughts raced back to the plane crash. *Regan?* He remembered her determination, her spunk, her optimistic nature, and her passion to help others. *My God! Regan was Bronwyn. Of course!* How could he have been so blind?

It all fit. He and Regan had died together and entered the bodies of their counterparts. Lord, give him a chance to tell her. He had to tell her. The ground slipped away as he rushed toward the enemy's camp, his men in hot pursuit.

The sight of the clearing up ahead crystallized his thoughts. He crouched low, crawling forward, and his men slowly inched into place. At his hand signal they lowered themselves onto the cold ground, hidden in the winter grass.

He carefully scanned the area, his stomach tightening as he measured the soldiers they would battle. They did not look like seasoned warriors; their carriage and manner were those of farmers or tradesmen. But even untrained, desperate men were dangerous.

His gaze found Bronwyn just as the cloud cover broke. In the bright moonlight a silvery glow showered down upon her. His blood ran cold at the sight of her shivering upon the ground with only her mantle for warmth. Rhett had much to answer for, and would this day be held accountable.

All night he rested on his belly and watched her. His first instinct was to rush in and rescue her, but patience was needed. At dawn's light he tensed knowing he would be in battle soon. Adrenaline surged through his body; every muscle, every fiber trained to unleash the power of revenge.

Suddenly her mantle wavered and he gasped as Fang crawled from beneath the meager cover toward the bushes where he lay hidden.

The distant sound of a horseman captured his attention. He looked up to watch a rider approach the band of rebels. Relief stole over him when Caradoc's features came into view. He noticed Rhett's guards were lax and did not muster out to meet the intruder. His spirits lifted. They had to take the men before they had a chance to draw their weapons.

Caradoc rode right through their path and calmly dismounted in the center of camp. "Take this horse," he demanded.

One slovenly man stepped forward and grasped the reins. As men crowded around him, their leader pushed his way through the throng. Rhett grabbed Caradoc's arm and spun him around. "You are early."

Caradoc slapped the travel dust from his tunic, meeting the man's glare with nonchalance. "I left London before the Normans wanted me to."

Rhett raised an eyebrow. "I had heard you decided to become a Norman?"

Caradoc roared in laughter. "Nay, but you would have done the same as I."

Christophe marveled at Caradoc's convincing manner. If he did not know better, he would think he had misjudged him.

"Mayhap, I would have if it served a purpose," Rhett said. "Still, we are family now." Without warning he slammed his fist into Caradoc's face and the younger man faltered, then fell. "There is my forgiveness for not receiving my blessing before the marriage."

Christophe held his breath, his hand covering the hilt of his sword. If his brother-in-law should need assistance, he was ready to give the command.

"What is all this nonsense about kidnapping? It was hardly necessary," Caradoc said as he rose. Wiping the blood from his mouth, he marched toward the fire.

"It provided me with what I needed."

"And that is?"

"You." He folded his arms and stared at Caradoc. "Your name will rally many loyal Welsh. I was not sure you would remember the cause after you married my daughter. Once again join my house to yours by marrying your sister, we will be invincible." Rhett's twisted smile slipped across his gruesome features. "Hand over the ransom."

Caradoc handed him the jewels, waiting patiently until Rhett had looked at the booty, then handed half the jewels to his man. "Ride to the coast and deliver these to the chieftain in payment for his men." Then he turned to Lucien. "You have met with Normans who would overthrow their lords?"

"*Oui,*" Lucien said. "I have drunk with them many times. Do not worry. They are as sick of this country as I."

Rhett's eyes narrowed. "Remember how I reward those who cross me," he said pointedly as he handed the amber necklace to Lucien. "Get your supporters and meet me at the arranged place."

Lucien's eyes narrowed to tiny little slits. "Remember," he sneered, "Christophe Montgomery is mine." Then he turned

d ran to his horse. Jumping astride, he galloped away from
e camp.

After both messengers left, Rhett turned back to Caradoc.
'Tis well you came.''

"How many men have you managed to muster?''

Rhett looked away. "I have sent out the summons. With this
nsom, others will come. And . . .'' he added, looking directly
Bronwyn and smiling evilly. "If that doesn't work, a martyr
r two will aid the cause.''

Christophe's heart skipped a beat. The sick bastard would
deed murder her to further his cause. The warrior in him
merged. He would kill the knave, and take great pleasure in

Caradoc looked around the camp. " 'Tis a pitiful showing
f power. This is not an army.''

"When we are united, our ranks will swell. Already I have
everal pledges,'' Rhett blustered.

Caradoc snorted. "Are these the same pledges that you
oasted of when you raided my land?''

"We had little choice,'' Rhett defended.

Suddenly hooves pounded as reinforcements approached the
amp, and Rhett grinned.

Caradoc glanced at the arriving soldiers, then folded his
rms. "What of my sister?''

"She is there.'' He pointed several yards away, then cuffed
young lad walking by. "Dewi, you lazy cur, take the lady
er meal.''

The child scrambled toward the fire and grabbed a hunk of
read and meat. With one cautious glance at Rhett, the boy
tumbled toward Bronwyn and deposited the food on the ground
eside her.

Caradoc's face tightened as they walked toward her.

Bronwyn's eyes filled with tears as she looked up at her
rother. "Caradoc, how could you join forces with this man?''

"Bronwyn. Are you hurt?''

"Aye.'' She pulled her hands from beneath her mantle, her
ace tightening in pain as she extended her bandaged arm. She

raised her head and glared at Rhett. "It takes a fearless ma[n] indeed to injure a defenseless woman."

"Dear God," Christophe swore. His eyes narrowed as rag[e] consumed him. Only his warrior's discipline held him back.

The wolf lifted his head, baring his teeth, and Christoph[e] stroked him soothingly.

Fang quieted, but his fur stood straight up as his eyes watche[d] Rhett.

"Your associate is very brave with a woman, but I have ye[t] to see him fight a man," Bronwyn taunted.

"Silence." Rhett raised his fist.

Caradoc stepped forward. Though his face was tight wit[h] tension, his voice was smooth. "This is hardly the way to sho[w] your authority."

Rhett looked around at the men who stared at him wit[h] disdain.

"My sister has a point," Caradoc continued. "Why hav[e] you tied her hands?"

"To stop any attempt at escape."

Caradoc looked around. "You need to bind a helples[s] woman, for fear she will overpower or outsmart you?" H[e] clicked his tongue as Rhett's face burned with embarrassment[.]

"Here, Sister, let me undo your binds."

The men turned away as Caradoc untied his sister. "Yo[u] are sorely used. I would not have made this alliance had [I] known the man was so bent."

The moment Bronwyn's hands were free, Christophe raise[d] his arm and the soldiers swarmed into the clearing, screamin[g] a bloodcurdling war cry and slashing at their unsuspectin[g] victims.

Christophe hacked his way to his beloved. He shove[d] stabbed, and parried anyone who dared to stand between hi[m] and Bronwyn.

Caradoc tried to guard her and the child, but Rhett ran hi[m] through with his sword.

"Caradoc!" she cried, bending to see how bad his woun[d] was.

Rhett tried to pull her away from tending Caradoc, but Dew[i] dove at Rhett, his tiny fists pummeling his rage and anger into the man. Rhett leveled the child with a mighty blow that sent the boy tumbling backward, then reached for her. But she fought him, kicking, scratching, and screaming to be free. He raised his fist to render a nasty blow, but Fang lunged through the air, teeth bared as he attacked. The snarling beast toppled Rhett to the ground as Bronwyn crawled away to help her brother.

A blur of fur, Fang attacked with natural instinct. Growling, he bit and shook whatever flesh his teeth latched onto. Rhett screamed in agony as he tried to wrestle the wolf off of him. Suddenly Fang uttered a high whine. Rhett had shoved his dagger into the wolf's rib cage, then pushed the animal off. Fang's eyes closed as he whimpered, trying to get up.

Covered in blood, Rhett crept over to where Bronwyn knelt tending her brother. He yanked her to her feet and held the bloodred dagger to her throat as Christophe dispatched his last soldier. "Yield, Montgomery, or I swear I will run her through!"

Christophe stopped dead. "Nothing you do or say will save your life. All you can do now is choose your manner of death."

"You think I will not kill her?" He pulled her hair back, exposing her throat to his blade. "Watch, Norman, watch your bitch die!"

"Non," Christophe yelled and laid his weapon down.

"Nay, Christophe," she gasped, her eyes wide with fright. "He will kill you."

The moment Rhett released her, he raised his weapon to thrust it into Christophe. Before anyone could stop her, Bronwyn threw herself in between Christophe and the sword, taking the blow he would have suffered.

"God's teeth," Rhett swore, pulling his blade out as Christophe caught her in his arms. Though her weight was slight, he felt the wind knocked from his lungs as he gathered her in his arms. The growing red stain covered her tunic. *"Non,"* he screamed, trying to cradle her within his arms.

Caradoc roared like an injured bull, and holding his wounded side, he hurled his sword through the air and into Rhett's throat. The man fell backward, dead before he hit the ground.

Caradoc crawled over to his sister.

"Bronwyn," he whispered hoarsely. His eyes glistened with unshed tears as he gaped at the bloody wound, then raised his gaze to Christophe's. "Will she . . . ?"

"I do not know," Christophe said, but he feared the worst. The wound was in the chest, bleeding profusely. He tore off his tunic and folded it into a bandage, then he wound his belt around the dressing to keep it in place. The stain grew larger and he could only stare at his beloved, feeling helpless and frustrated.

"You little fool," he admonished her gently, choking back his tears.

A forced smile covered her lips. "I had to. He would have killed you." She caressed the side of his face. "I could not have lived without you."

So weak was she, her fingers barely grazed his cheek. Tears stung his eyes. "But, my love, how am I to live?"

He could not finish his thought. It was too painful. He tenderly picked her up, cradling her in his arms.

The fight was over, the ground littered with dead Welshmen. Christophe looked dispassionately at the carnage. "Let them rot in their own blood." Then he saw little Dewi, cringing away from the adults, and remembered his promise. "Bring the child so he can be reunited with his sister."

Carrying Bronwyn to his horse, they mounted, and holding her close to his heart, he rode as fast as he dared toward the castle.

"I love you," he whispered into her hair.

"I love you, too."

She shivered and he gathered her closer.

"I am so cold, Christophe."

He wrapped his mantle around her and softly rubbed her back. "We will be home soon."

"I think I have been searching for you all my life," she murmured. "What time we have wasted, when we could have been sharing each other's love."

"Bronwyn—"

"Let me say what I must. I know in the past you have

distrusted me. I also know you have had good reason. But I swear to you, I am not the woman you married. I am the woman who loves you.''

"What fool would doubt that? You have saved my life at the cost of your own. I shall never doubt you again, Regan," he whispered.

"Regan?"

"Oui, you are Regan, and I am . . .''

"Drew," she breathed. "I should have known.''

He rode through the castle gates and dismounted with her, then he ran across the courtyard, bellowing for help while taking the castle steps two at a time.

His footsteps echoed on the hard stone steps, sounding hollow and forlorn. The torchlight flickered wildly as he rushed through the narrow hallways. A coldness permeated the castle and his heart. The icy bite traveled to his bones, and he knew the chill was not from the weather, but his fear. He pulled her closer, glancing at her pale face.

"You must stay with me, Wife. Destiny and fate have conspired to bring us together.''

She clung to his tunic. "I will try," she gasped.

Her thready voice frightened him.

He placed her gently on the bed, lowering her head tenderly to the pillow.

"Nesta," he bellowed. Servants scurried about as he leaned closer and brushed her golden hair back from her face, placing a whisper-soft kiss upon her brow. "Help is coming. Be strong. I love you." He stared at her, needing to drink in every nuance of her face.

She captured his hand and held it to her heart. "We have been gifted a miracle," she whispered. "We were given new lives in which we were still enemies, but this time we fell in love." She drew a deep breath, struggling to finish. "Though our lot was extremely difficult, I would never change it, because we found each other." Her eyelids slipped down as her voice faded.

He gripped her tight, denying with everything he had that

her life was draining from her body. "Bronwyn, speak to me. Do you hear me?"

Her eyes remained closed, her breathing shallow. Silence answered his plea. She had slipped into unconsciousness. Still and lifeless, a serene expression on her pale face, she looked a perfect angel—beautiful, ethereal, and unattainable.

"Bronwyn, don't leave me." He buried his head into her shoulder. "I need you."

Chapter Twenty-seven

Christophe's sobs were a tortured sound he refused to acknowledge as his own. "I cannot live without you! Come back," he begged. This can't be happening, he thought. But it was. She hung in his embrace like a lifeless doll. He rocked her limp body in his arms, and the grief tightened in his chest. His world had shattered.

"Christophe," Nicolas said, laying a hand on his shoulder.

His brother's voice seemed to come from far away. He turned and met the worried gaze. "She has left me. I cannot wake her."

"Let the ladies tend her." Nicolas motioned to Nesta.

Christophe knew he was right, but he could not let go of her. He allowed his brother to help him lower Bronwyn back on the pillow, but he would not release her hand. She had never looked so small and vulnerable. Her dark blond eyelashes fanned across her pale, soft skin. Her lush lips were pink and closed. He strained to see her chest move. It barely rose, then fell. If only she were asleep, and he could wake her with a kiss. But this was not a fairy tale and he was far from Prince Charming. As ridiculous as it was, he leaned forward and brushed his lips across hers. Her mouth remained still beneath his.

He pulled away and studied her cool features. How he wanted to feel her warm response, just for one moment. He stared at her so long that he thought he saw her eyelashes flicker. But they had not. When Nicolas tried to pull him from her, he flung his brother's hand away.

"Non," he cried, hanging onto her lifeless hand. "I will stay."

Nicolas sighed. "I will see to your duties."

Christophe nodded, too choked to speak. Reverently he traced the soft arch of her brow. He wished more than anything to take back all the hurt he had caused her. Fool that he was, he had wasted the precious time allotted them. One minute, he craved just one minute to look into her eyes and see the sparkle and shine return.

In a daze he watched the flurry of activity around her bed. Nesta placed a cool cloth on Bronwyn's head, then cleaned and bandaged the wound. She tisked when she turned to Christophe. "You must have a meal, my lord. Please, go and eat, I will call you if there is any change."

He adamantly shook his head, and she left.

Several minutes later Matrona returned to hand Christophe a tray with food. She slipped her little hand in his and kissed his cheek. "Thank you for saving my brother," she whispered. Then she leaned forward and kissed Bronwyn's pale cheek.

After Matrona departed, he stared at the tray. Tears formed in his eyes at the sight of the tableware Bronwyn had ordered made. He picked up a fork, remembering how she had brought about their introduction, then put it down and angrily pushed the plate aside. Though his stomach rumbled from hunger, he could not stand the thought of food.

She had touched so many lives. Everywhere he looked he saw her hand.

Fiona came to pray by the bedside, as did Hayden and Caradoc. The cook and servants all tried their known remedies, but nothing helped. The villagers were thrown into despair by their lady's state. Nicolas sent out word that any healers who could help were to come to the castle at once.

Night fell on the castle, and the candles and fires lit the gloomy darkness, but the light did not chase away Christophe's sadness, nor the fear. Like two enemies they hung close to him, a constant reminder that his dreams of happiness were fleeting.

All day Fang had howled for Bronwyn, whimpering and whining, snapping at those who tried to treat his wound, allowing only Nicolas near. At last, he carried the animal to the master bedchamber. The wolf quieted the moment he was taken to her room. A pallet was placed beside her bed, and Fang stayed there by Christophe's side. 'Twas a strange sight, the man and the wolf holding a silent vigil by her bed.

Fiona's drawn and pale face said more eloquently than any words how Lady Bronwyn fared.

"Take heart, Wife."

Fiona burst into tears. "She must not die."

Nicolas wrapped his arms around her. He agreed, but she had not awakened, and none expected her to live—save one.

While the castle slept, Christophe prayed to God, asking for a miracle. He knew they existed. He had been part of one.

"Please," he begged. "Send us back to our time if you must. I will give up this body, the youth, just let us be together." Over and over, he repeated his plea. He could not imagine a life without her.

"My love," he said, leaning close to her, "I believe in my heart you can hear me. I have made so many mistakes in my life, but the biggest was mistrusting you. I ask your forgiveness and humbly beg you to come back to me. We will have a wonderful life. I promise to dance with you every day of our lives. Children"—he choked back his fear—"will play at your feet and I, my love, will adore you forever."

Through the long night, he talked to her of his dreams. "We have so much to look forward to. This country and land are in their infancy, together we will see them grow. Someday, when we are very old, we will look at our children and their children, and know we left a better world for them than we found." He continued to hold her hand and slept fitfully through the night.

Whenever he awoke, he anxiously checked her, but each time she lay as still as she had before.

By early morning a fever had started. He knew the wound was infected, and that she probably needed surgery. But he was unskilled in medicine and knew that if he tried to repair the damage, he would only make her worse.

A blind rage overtook him. She was suffering from the fever and the pain and had begun to thrash about, but there was nothing he could do to help. He wanted to smash something. The anger and frustration built to such a point that at midday he stormed from the room and rode away from the castle. He was running from the pain, but he found he could not escape it.

For hours he rode until his exhausted horse stopped and he was forced to walk back to the castle. Bronwyn had taught him that healing began with forgiveness, he had to forgive himself before he could others. So he would accept his actions and forgive himself for her wound. For her sake, he had to go on. She would not want him to wallow in this state. He said one last prayer, promising to accept what God had in mind for them both. Once inside, he expected to hear the worst. He climbed the stairs with listless steps. He hated to see his beloved in pain. Nor did he think he could watch her slip quietly away.

But she was just lingering, neither totally gone nor completely here. The violent thrashing had stopped, but the stillness frightened him more. She seemed closer to death. He sat by her side, unable to hold back his tears.

"My lord, might I try?"

A vaguely familiar voice intruded on his thoughts, and he looked up to see a nondescript friar.

"What is it you want?"

The heavily robed man stepped into the light. "Might I pray over her?" The friar held out his folded hands, a Bible in their clasp.

"*Oui.*" Christophe stepped aside, allowing the tiny little man room by his wife's bed. "Friar, have we met?" he asked, sure there was something he should remember.

"It is possible. I meet many of God's children."

Christophe nodded, but he thought that this was no casual meeting. As he listened to the friar's prayers, the intonation struck a chord deep within his memory.

"The angel," he whispered.

He knelt down and bowed his head to the friar. "Send us back to our time. I cannot bear to live without her. If she is to die, then let us die together."

"Your time has not arrived, my son."

"And neither has hers," Christophe declared.

"She made the ultimate sacrifice. She put her love above her very life. Have no fear, she will be rewarded."

Relief swept through Christophe, then anxiety as a thought suddenly occurred to him. Was her reward life—or heaven?

He tried to ask, but the angel did not allow another disturbance to distract him from his prayers.

Silently Christophe added his voice to the friar's, and his hand slipped across the covers to take his wife's.

Lucien held a dagger to the wicca's back as they entered the castle. Disguised as a druid monk, with his head bent in a pious pose, he shoved the wicca before him and climbed the stairs leading to the master's chambers.

His anger and hatred were beyond consolation. He was pleased the lady was dying. Every step of the way he planned his revenge. He had one last thing to do to make sure his task was completed. He would kill Christophe Montgomery.

She felt a burning pain. It was unpleasant and she wanted to go back to the cool, restful sleep, but something was pulling her away from the comforting slumber. Noise intruded and she was angry. There had been no sound, no movement, no color, just peace and the gentle current of the air she floated on. She tried to protest, wanting to return, but more intrusions occurred. Light filled her mind, painful and intense. Voices drifted in and out of her thoughts. She heard so many prayers, it was as if she were in church. Her eyelashes fluttered open and she saw Christophe kneeling beside her bed, his hands folded and head bowed. He was praying. Suddenly she remembered. Poor Christophe, he must be racked with worry. There were others, Nicolas, Fiona, a friar she did not recognize. She could hear and see them all, but no one mattered but her beloved. She reached out her hand to touch him, grazing her fingers through his hair.

He looked up and for an instant just stared at her. Then he gently gathered her in his arms. He was trembling.

Caressing the side of his face, she soothed, "It's all right, Christophe. Please tell me what is wrong."

When he pulled away, tears glistened in his eyes, but he quickly brushed them away. "I thought I had lost you." He cradled her face. "I love you. I always have, and I always will."

His mouth moved over hers tenderly, as though he were afraid to bruise her. Her arms wrapped around him, and she kissed him with a hunger he soon met. She had just realized that they had been given another chance. Thank you, she whispered silently. His arms crushed her to him. The kiss deepened and she responded, needing to give as well as receive. Every sense came alive in his arms. She reveled in the musky aroma that was his alone and the husky voice that whispered her name.

The sound of the others moving from the room drifted to her ears. Voices receded and she knew they were alone.

She nestled closer to him, enjoying the warmth of his body, needing to feel the closeness. "I will never leave you."

He chuckled softly in her ear. "You could never get away from me even if you tried." He touched her face reverently. "We have many more dances to dance."

She chuckled, remembering the joy in his arms.

He kissed her again.

The taste of his lips was pure nectar. She tingled, and wrapped her arms around him as her lips opened and their tongues mated. It was heaven. His mouth slanted over hers, increasing the pressure, and a heat grew within her. She wanted more, needed more. Then his lips moved to her neck, nuzzling her tender skin and sending shivers up her spine. "I should let you rest," he said, kissing her jaw.

"I don't need to rest," she breathed, wanting to draw him back, but he was already pulling away.

Fang whined and she turned to see what disturbed him. The wicca stood in the shadows along with a robed monk. "My lady, I have come to humbly beg your forgiveness." The wicca's face was drawn, and she kept slanting her eyes to the side.

Christophe had bent over to hush Fang.

"I have forgiven you," Bronwyn said and started to turn away when a shiny flicker caught her attention.

"Look out, Christophe." She pushed him away and the blade aimed for his back pierced her heart instead. The room receded and she tried to speak, but a blackness engulfed her.

With an unearthly cry Christophe turned to face Lucien. The agony in his heart could not be contained. She had been taken away from him just when she had returned. His bellow of rage was heard throughout the castle.

Though Lucien tried to escape him, Christophe tackled him and pulled him to his feet to strike blow after blow at his face and body.

Drawn by the noise, Nicolas and Fiona rushed into the room, followed immediately by several soldiers.

"Dear God!" Fiona ran to her sister. She turned toward her husband with tears streaming down her cheeks. Her mouth moved several times before the words surged out. "She is dead."

"Non," Nicolas denied, rushing to her side. Then, pushing his wife behind him, he grabbed his sword ready to help.

"Stay out of this," Christophe ordered. "Lucien will answer to me."

Nicolas resheathed his sword and gestured to the soldiers to do the same. He remembered this man. He was the man who had come to Wales, a man without a heart. Christophe beat Lucien mercilessly. When the assassin sank to his knees, Christophe bent down, seized him by the robe, and pulled back his fist to deliver a deathblow. But from within the folds of the robe Lucien produced another dagger. Christophe's eyes widened as the blade struck him in the stomach. With the strength of his rage he wrapped his hands around the assassin's neck and squeezed the life from him, then staggered toward his love.

Nicolas reached out to help him, but Christophe shook his head. He fell on the bed and reached for Bronwyn's cold lifeless hand.

"My beloved," he gasped, "I will join you soon."

The wolf began to howl, long mournful notes that filled the air with sadness.

Christophe felt a bone-chilling cold. His eyesight faded in and out and he knew his time was short. With numb fingers he raised her hand to his lips. "Once upon a time there was a love so great, the lovers traveled through time to be together," he whispered, then kissed her and knew no more.

Chapter Twenty-eight

Bronwyn awoke to find herself lying at the bottom of a cliff. Her clothes were tattered and stained. Branches and twigs clung to her long red hair. She immediately felt her abdomen as a quickening occurred. She sighed in relief, recognizing the tiny ripples of life in her early pregnancy. Her child was safe. Tears of gratitude stung her eyes as she looked heavenward. "Thank you," she whispered.

Next to her lay a man, his Nordic ancestry slashing every sharp angle and hollowed plane of his face. The bold features looked harsh, unyielding, cold, as if chiseled out of ice. Though he looked every inch the Viking, his rugged clan attire declared him a Scot. His plaid kilt covered very little of his muscular legs, the tartan sash and open shirt displayed his muscular chest. A brawny Highland rogue, she thought, as her gaze explored his impressive physique. He was golden all over, from his long hair, the color of hay, to his bronzed skin, to the shiny medallion nestled in his thick, crisp chest hair. She reached curiously for the medallion, then glanced to his face. His long fringed lashes lay closed as if dreaming, but he was lying too still to be asleep. Her heart skipped a beat as she leaned over him and pressed her ear to his chest. "Dear God." He wasn't breathing.

Without hesitating she started CPR. Damn you, don't die, she silently screamed as she worked over him. After only a few moments he responded. Sluggish and disoriented, he came to.

His eyelids opened and blinked several times, revealing vivid blue eyes, brighter than a June sky. For a few moments he stared at her, drawing deep breaths to fill his air-starved lungs.

"Are you all right?" she asked.

He seized her hand, his grip digging into her fingers as he looked at her topaz ring. "Bronwyn?" he whispered.

"Oh, Christophe," she cried and threw herself into his arms.

He held her tight. "Where are we?"

"I don't know."

"What time is this?"

She looked down at her dress, noticing the strangeness of the lines. "I don't know. The twelfth century perhaps?"

Then she looked at his attire and hers. "I appear to be a lady and you a formidable Highlander. And we both seem to have been thrown off a cliff," she said, with a mixture of amusement and trepidation.

"It doesn't matter. We are together. And our prayers have been answered."

She smiled. "Once upon a time a lady wished for a heaven-sent love. She found him, only to discover that he had been at her side always—and would remain there forever."

AUTHOR'S NOTE

There was a Castle Montgomery built in 1070 that inspired this story. However, the Castle Montgomery, as well as most of the characters portrayed in this book, are purely fictional.

AUTHOR'S NOTE

Dear Reader:

Bronwyn and Christophe have just begun their journey. Here's an excerpt from the sequel, *Heaven's Return*.

Sincerely,
Marian Edwards

"Wife," a gravelly voice rasped out from behind Bronwyn.

Her breath caught in her throat as she lay stretched out upon Christophe's chest. He stiffened at the imperious demand, and wrapped his arms protectively around her.

"Wife." The summons came again and a lump of apprehension thickened within her as Bronwyn turned in Christophe's embrace to look over her shoulder. A burly old man with white hair and wizened features had just climbed down the cliff. Letting go of the rope, he came to stand over her, his light-green eyes clear, his gaze penetrating.

"Come." The old man extended his hand to help her up.

Her heart raced. Unlike in the last time travel, she had no memories of the life that she had apparently inherited.

She got to her feet uncertainly, followed by Christophe. Her husband gripped Christophe's hand. "Thank ye. Ye have saved my wife from a bad fall. I willna forget that ye put aside yer animosity toward her and offered aid." Then to Bronwyn he said, "Before I take ye home, show yer stepson yer appreciation."

Bronwyn closed her eyes. *Dear God, Christophe was her stepson.*

"Ach, canna ye at least put aside yer dislike and give my son the kiss of peace for saving yer life?"

She leaned forward and stood on tiptoes to kiss Christophe. "What will we do?" she whispered.

"Believe in love," he murmured in reply. Then he stepped back, bowed, and lifted her hand adorned with the ring that carried the hopeful inscription. He placed a soft kiss in her palm. "I will see to yer welfare always."

She smiled and stepped back from him. Immediately the old man grabbed her hand. "Tell me what happened."

Suddenly a vivid memory flashed through her mind. She pulled against her husband's hold. " 'Twas no accident—we were pushed."

"By who?" her husband asked.

Bronwyn shook her head. "I didna see him." She turned to Christophe. "Did ye?"

"Nay." His features had hardened to stone, and his regard was now devoid of emotion. But his gaze slanted to her ring as her husband dragged her away, and his lips formed the word, "Remember."

Visit Marian Edwards's web site for up-to-date information about her upcoming books, book-signing events, workshops, seminars, and television, radio, and personal appearances. Marian loves to hear from her readers. She has received fan mail from as far away as Japan, and she answers readers' questions about her future releases. Both her home page and e-mail address are listed below.

http://home.att.net/~MARIANEDWARDS
MARIANEDWARDS@WORLDNET.ATT.NET

ROMANCE FROM JO BEVERLY

DANGEROUS JOY   (0-8217-5129-8, $5.99)

FORBIDDEN   (0-8217-4488-7, $4.99)

THE SHATTERED ROSE   (0-8217-5310-X, $5.99)

TEMPTING FORTUNE   (0-8217-4858-0, $4.99)

ROMANCE FROM FERN MICHAELS